NO MERCY

Houston ripped the pistol away from the gunman's grip, then withdrew his K-Bar and knocked the guy onto his back.

The guy gasped. So did Houston.

This is it. I'm going to end your life. And I'm not God.

Houston still held the guy's pistol, but hc had learned that, if possible, it's better to kill an enemy with your own weapon, the one you've cleaned and double-checked, the one you trust not to misfire. More than that, Houston needed a quiet gutting instead of a loud capping.

He needed his knife.

"Don't kill," the guy pleaded. "Don't kill."

Houston didn't.

McAllister did. Slashed the guy's throat right in front of Houston's bulging eyes. "Okay, kid," the old sergeant rasped. "You were right. Mercy sucks."

FORCE 5 RECON

DEPLOYMENT: PAKISTAN

P. W. STORM

AVON BOOKS
An Imprint of HarperCollinsPublishers

This is a work of fiction. Names, characters, places, and incidents are products of the author's imagination or are used fictitiously and are not to be construed as real. Any resemblance to actual events, locales, organizations, or persons, living or dead, is entirely coincidental.

AVON BOOKS
An Imprint of HarperCollins*Publishers*
10 East 53rd Street
New York, New York 10022-5299

Copyright © 2003 by Peter Telep
ISBN: 0-06-052349-2
www.avonbooks.com

First Avon Books paperback printing: October 2003

"Some people spend an entire lifetime wondering if they've made a difference in the world. The Marines don't have that problem."

Attributed to President Ronald Reagan, 1985

Acknowledgments

I'm indebted to Jennifer Fisher for the motivation and inspiration to create this series.

My editor, Mike Shohl, listened patiently to my ramblings and provided the guidance and support every writer needs. His detailed notes and suggestions were much more than welcome; they were invaluable.

John Talbot, agent extraordinaire, knows how to lift my spirits when the writing days are long and lonely.

Bryce Zabel, friend, fellow scribe, and creator of popular television series for networks such as NBC, taught me how to write a well-organized and engaging proposal.

Jim Newberger, dear friend, writer, paramedic, and military enthusiast, slaved over every word of my story outline and provided compelling suggestions. He then went on to read and critique every page of this sizable manuscript. I am honored and blessed to know this man.

Retired Force Recon Marines Karl Chambless, Nick Bano, and Dallas Foyte helped me with the logistics of creating a reconnaissance team. While any technical conceits remain mine, these Marines kept me honest, inspired, and most of all in awe of their accomplishments. They reminded me that Force Recon Marines are first class operators without exception.

Author's Note

While this is a work of fiction, I have endeavored to faithfully portray the Marine Corp's Force Reconnaissance community, relying upon information made public via the internet, the many texts on the subject, and email exchanges with the Marines themselves.

That said, there remain weapons and tactics employed by Force Recon Teams that are not described here in deference to national security. Some of what you read is the product of my imagination, but every word is meant as a tribute to those brave men who serve as the eyes and ears of their commanders.

P.W. Storm
Orlando, Florida
Force5recon@aol.com

FORCE 5
RECON

OI

TEAM DOGMA

POINT MONGOOSE

QUADRANT D9H

NORTHWEST FRONTIER PROVINCE

PAKISTAN

0130 HOURS LOCAL TIME

A single round of small-weapons fire boomed from somewhere behind the hillock, and E-5 Sgt. Mac Rainey, who had been peering through the night-vision scope of his M4A1 carbine, bolted upright, his ears pricked in anticipation of another shot. That first round had come from a .45-caliber MEU pistol modified by the Precision Weapons Shop at Quantico— meaning that unless the enemy had been doing some black-market shopping on eBay, that gunfire had come from one of Rainey's own men. But that was impossible. The other four members of his Force Recon Team knew the stakes, knew their warning order inside and out. And moments before they had fast-roped into the DLZ, Rainey had issued his grave reminder:

"If we fire a single shot, we have failed our mission."

Tugging down his bush cover, Rainey spoke tersely into the voice-activated boom mike at his lips. "Dogma Three, this is Dogma One, report your post, over."

Sounds of a struggle came through Rainey's tiny earpiece, and even as they did, he gazed hard at the three adobe huts lying in the moonlit valley below, the spicy scent of something cooking, maybe chicken yakhni soup, wafting up on the breeze. The front door on one hut swung open, and five men whose wee-hour meal had obviously been interrupted darted out, bringing their AK-47 rifles to bear. While they might have been Pakistani citizens, they had sworn their loyalty to the Warriors of Mohammed, a terrorist organization led by the charismatic twenty-five-year-old Mohammed al-Zumar. The group was based in Pakistan, but new cells had reared their ugly heads in India, Kashmir, Iraq, Canada, and the United States. These bastards were responsible for a rocket-grenade attack on a congressman from Florida, fourteen separate car bombings in California—including two on day cares that resulted in the deaths of fifty-nine children—and the attempted bombing of the Palo Verde Unit #1 nuclear power plant near Phoenix. There were no four-letter words strong enough to describe al-Zumar and his ultrafundamentalists, though Rainey had tried a few combinations. Better to concentrate on making them dead.

For their part, Rainey and his team employed the AN/PSQ 13 Man Pack Secondary Imagery Dissemination System to take digital pictures of the training camp and transmit them, along with labels and grid coordinates, to their HQ, Camp Liberty Bell, located approximately one hundred kilometers north of Islamabad. With that data, the Top Guns getting antsy in the cockpits of their A-10 Warthog fighter-bombers could catapult off, ID their target, then leave behind a crater that even Apollo astronauts would appreciate. During the briefing, it had all sounded like a straightforward deep reconnaissance mission. Get in, take some photos, note enemy capabilities and equipment, maybe do a little "painting" with their laser target designators, then get the hell out.

But now something had gone terribly wrong.

Rainey took off running across the dark hillock, the magazine pouches of his amphibious assault vest banging hard on his belly, his big field ruck tugging hard on his shoulders. "Dogma Four, cap those five—now!"

"Dogma Four, capping five, roger, out," replied E-4 Cpl. Jimmy Vance, the team's recon scout and sharpshooter.

A heartbeat later, shots exploded from Vance's M40A3 sniper rifle, and Rainey imagined terrorists flailing like rag dolls as titanium-alloy slugs bored holes in their heads. While every member of his team was a crack shot, Vance had patience and precision in spades. You'd think he would hunt in his free time; rather, the twenty-two-year-old was an avid fisherman. Rumor had it that he had once used his rifle as a fishing rod in an attempt to catch some peacock bass during a deep recon in South America. Fishing wasn't a matter of life and death to Vance—it was more important than that.

"Dogma One, this is Dogma Three, over," called an

anxious-sounding E-3 Lance Cpl. Bradley Houston, recon scout and radio operator.

"Dogma Three, this is Dogma One," Rainey replied. "I'm rallying on you. Report your post, over."

"Uh, Sergeant, my weapon discharged, over."

The words ignited in Rainey's ears. "Wait there, roger, out."

It had to be Houston, the rich-kid new guy and heir to a real-estate empire. He said he had joined the Corps to piss off daddy, but that was the lie he used to irritate you. No one made it through the training pipeline without sweating, bleeding, and wishing he were dead, but Houston said he had yawned his way through it. He had once told a reporter in his hometown of San Diego that "yeah, some people think we're all hell-bent psychos who love to kill people and blow up shit. That's wrong. We also enjoy sushi, hot tubbing, and the occasional pedicure." That was Houston, all right. A snob, a know-it-all sea-lawyer-type who thought he was funny.

But Rainey wasn't laughing as he shuffled past a large outcropping on the mountainside, shifting between talus and scree until he reached Houston. The broad-shouldered brunet with heavy face paint and glassy eyes was hunkered down before a local guy, a Pashtun of about twenty whose bearded face shown eerily gaunt in the half light. Houston still held the bloody Ka-Bar he had used to gut the man. He wiped the blade on the Pashtun's sleeve, removed the MEU pistol from the man's hand, then pursed his lips and straightened his crooked bush cover. "Sarge, this guy slipped up behind me while I was working the camera, got hold of my sidearm. I mean he was incredibly silent. I didn't hear a thing."

Rainey scowled at the lance corporal as a breathless voice sounded in his earpiece: "Dogma One, this is Dogma Four. Capped five, over," called Vance.

"Roger that."

"Count six or seven more taking up positions within the compound. Got more movement on the southeast perimeter."

"All right. Dogma Team? Rally on the trees near that slope we marked earlier. Roger, out." Rainey leveled his index finger on Houston and switched off his tactical radio. "Maybe they pronounced you dead twice when you went to dive school, but you'll make the hat trick right here, right now, do you read me, Marine?"

"Yes, Sergeant. But maybe you can tell me where this guy came from and why he's here? He was no soldier. Maybe a farmer. Remember those wheatfields we saw?"

"So he's a farmer. So what? You let him compromise our mission! Jesus, we're Force Recon, man. *Force Five!*"

"I know that, Sarge. Shit happens, y'know?"

Rainey did not know. His team represented the sharpest operators in his platoon and had been nicknamed "Force Five," as in the five best. But when Cpl. Matt Thomas had broken his back during a training exercise a month prior, Houston had stepped in to replace him. Despite that, Rainey had assumed his people weren't just the best in the platoon but the most organized, most professional Marines walking the planet.

"Did this guy have any other weapons—besides yours?"

Houston hesitated, shook his head.

Rainey snorted, took a deep breath against the drumming of his pulse, then shifted off. "Come on."

A few seconds later, after they had covered but a dozen or so meters, the rich boy stage-whispered, "Hold a minute, Sergeant! Look at this!"

Rainey turned back, and there it was: a small burrow containing a few bags of grain and some Red Cross medical supplies. That farmer might have been coming up the mountainside to retrieve something from the stash when he had stumbled upon Houston. What a pair of balls the guy had had to take on a United States Marine. And what profoundly bad timing.

"You have to feel sorry for these people," said Houston, staring at the meager cache. "They got no Wal-Mart, no HBO."

The kid used glib remarks to temper his fear. Basic reaction. But Rainey wasn't in the mood. "Move out."

Keeping their heads low, they ran hard along the mountainside, darting between rocks and scrub, as gunfire from the compound below gnawed ceaselessly at their wake. Rainey swore inwardly over the fact that those fanatics had thirty-round magazines and were intent on emptying them, which meant they could afford to waste ammunition—not a comforting thought.

Point Zebra lay a quarter kilometer due south, and from there Rainey would call for the chopper to thump off toward Extraction Point Stingray, a six-hour hump from Zebra. Since the team's presence had been compromised, the rules had changed. Rainey could not count on artillery support, and that extraction bird might be a long time coming. He and his team needed to think, shoot, move, and communicate. Period. They lacked the firepower needed to engage in a direct assault—and that was intentional. Force Recon teams were the commander's eyes and ears, not his bayonet.

The whistle of incoming mortar fire turned Rainey's blood icy. He and Houston charged for the stand of trees near a lazily curving slope as a hellacious explosion tore a ragged hunk out of the mountainside and sent clumps of rock, earth, and shrapnel barreling toward them. They reached the trees and ducked behind the first pair as assistant team leader E-5 Sgt. Terry McAllister and special amphibious recon corpsman HM2 Glenroy "Doc" Leblanc hauled ass from the south ridgeline and met up with them.

"Damn, where are my stroke books when I need them?" cried Doc, clutching his M249 Para SAW. During an early mission with another recon team, the husky, bald black man had infiltrated a guerrilla camp in the Philippines and had left behind copies of *Hustler* magazine. While the bad guys were "preoccupied," Doc and his teammates had snatched a warlord. Now that was creative thinking, and Rainey couldn't be happier to serve with the hospital corpsman. Doc had his priorities straight. He understood that he was a shooter first, a caregiver second. And to that end, he carried the team's largest, most lethal automatic weapon, the Para SAW, because—as well-trained recon corpsmen know—fire superiority is the best combat medicine.

"Hey, Doc, I have a feeling that even your stroke mags wouldn't help us now," said McAllister, the thirty-nine-year-old's face creased heavily with concern, his lip twitching where he had lost a piece to an ex-wife with sharp teeth. *Semper Fi* means always faithful, but when it came to women, McAllister was a teenager with blue balls. He gazed warily at Rainey. "What the hell happened?"

"Farmer strayed near Houston's position," Rainey answered, then swept the zone with his nightscope.

"So you shot him?" McAllister asked Houston.

"Stabbed him, actually."

"Then why did your weapon—"

"Marines, we're out of here," Rainey said. "Go now!"

Although Rainey didn't like to play favorites, if he had to die alongside one man on the team, he'd pick his assistant team leader—not because they had both been born and raised in Denver, and not because they were nearly the same age (though Rainey had breached the big Four-0 by a couple of years already)—but because all his life McAllister had dealt with death and had come to accept the inevitably of it better than any Marine Rainey knew. McAllister's family had run a funeral home for three generations. All right, so McAllister was the most morbid person you'd ever meet, but he was also the most fearless. He made Schwarzenegger look like an old lady armed with a bag of marshmallows. And if you died with him, you would die the way hairy, barrel-chested men should die: with dignity, with honor, and with ferocity.

"I'm point man," said McAllister.

Rainey nodded, and his assistant was first out, followed by Houston in the number-two spot. Doc fell in next, then Vance, who had just arrived and whom Rainey patted on the shoulder. "You had eyes-on. How many?"

The fair-skinned fisherman narrowed his gaze, green eyes flashing as he struggled to catch his breath. "Maybe another twenty, thirty? Maybe more in the caves to the south."

"If that's right, they'll be moving around to cut us off."

"Not if we're faster," Vance said, then sprinted on.

Rainey followed as automatic-weapons fire sliced through his ghost.

They worked their way forward, brand-new boots trampling over ancient invasion paths that crisscrossed the mountainside. War was nothing new to the people of this land, and it was a damned shame there were still extremists who brought misery and suffering to their own people. That farmer might've been killed by Houston, but the fact remained that Houston wouldn't have been there had it not been for al-Zumar and his followers. Would the murder of innocents ever end? Rainey purged the question from his mind. He would keep his head low and focus on one battle at a time.

The trees thinned out, and Rainey ordered McAllister to descend a few hundred meters to a point where the ground grew more level. Getting there wouldn't be easy. Gravel, rocks, and fallen tree limbs obstacled their path, and Rainey tripped once, twice, a third time before swearing to himself and hoping Vance hadn't shot a quick look over his shoulder.

Within a minute they reached a dried-up creek channel and beat a serpentine path down it. Rainey flipped over a protective cover on his wrist-mounted GPS and activated the device. While he still preferred a good old-fashioned map and lensatic compass, the GPS worked well when you were on the run and being shot at by terrorists. According to the LCD display, they were a few hundred meters northeast of Point Zebra. "Dogma Five, this is Dogma One, over."

"Dogma One, this is Five," answered McAllister.

"Hang a right up near those two big rocks, over."

"Roger that. Hanging a right, out." McAllister ducked behind the boulders, with Houston, Doc, and Vance hard at his heels.

Rainey was but a handful of yards away from the boulders when gunfire paralleled his steps and stitched a mere meter from his boot. Combat rule #1: incoming fire has the right of way. Rainey dropped to his gut and brought his carbine to bear on the muzzle flashes twinkling on the mountainside above. If those terrorist soldiers had been smart, they would've fitted their AKs with Krinkov Flash Hiders, but Rainey wasn't arguing with that oversight. He cut loose a triplet of rounds, then spoke calmly into his mike: "This is Dogma One. They got me pinned."

"Roger," said McAllister. "Orders?"

"Split and flank 'em to draw fire but don't return."

"Roger that, One," McAllister confirmed. "On our way."

As Rainey unleashed a salvo at his shadowy attack-

ers, Vance and Houston left the boulder and raced
across the creek bed. While they drew fire, Rainey
broke off his attack, rolled, then came up running for
the boulders. He reached them, ducked behind, then
peered furtively around one side, spying McAllister
and Doc making their own advance as swirls of bullet-
licked dust lifted like tiny tornadoes near the tree line.
While those guys now played bait, Vance and Houston
returned, and once they were behind the boulders with
Rainey, all three ticked off a few seconds, then raised
their weapons and preached the good word of *you're
going to fucking die* to the terrorists perched on the
mountainside. McAllister and Doc exploited the ser-
mon, hightailed it back, and once they were safe,
Rainey ordered the cease-fire.

"Sergeant, would you mind not drawing enemy
fire?" asked Doc as he tanked down air.

Rainey nearly grinned. "Yeah, I know. It irritates
everyone around me."

Doc tapped the Para SAW slung over his shoulder.
"So why didn't you let me open up?"

"I'm sure you'll get your chance. But let's conserve
ammo while we can."

"Should we contact St. Andrew?" asked McAllister.

"Not yet. They call, we stall. Shit, we'll be lucky to
keep our jobs when this is over." Rainey flashed a dark
look in Houston's direction before gesturing the team
onward.

The temperature had dropped at least ten degrees in
the last ten minutes, and Rainey gritted his teeth against

the chill as they forged farther south, into a narrow, wind-swept ravine that marked Point Zebra. They squatted behind a string of low-lying stones as Houston switched to the extraction chopper's tactical frequency, then handed the mike to Rainey. Captain Tom Graham and his UH-1N Huey slick helicopter, stripped of weapons to fly light and fast, had better be waiting for them. "Delta Eagle Seven, this is Dogma One, over."

"Dogma One, this is Delta Eagle Seven, over," came Graham's voice.

"Delta Eagle Seven, we are designated driver. En route to Extraction Point Stingray. ETA approximately five hours, over."

"Roger. ETA five hours. Got some weather moving in. Could slow us down, over."

"All right. Will attempt to check in hourly or as needed. Dogma One, roger, out."

"What's up?" asked McAllister.

"Graham says we got weather." Rainey sighed in frustration, faced the others. "All right. We're going to reach the pickup point before daybreak."

Without warning, a dusky-skinned man with two large knives jutting from his fists leaped into the air, sailed over the string of rocks, and came down on the group like a rabid raven, all talons and phlegm and shrieking a bizarre battle cry.

Vance's hands flashed as he raised his rifle and jammed down the trigger, turning the man's chest to Swiss cheese before he hit the ground—and the other Marines sprang to their feet.

What happened next was like something torn from a history book of old battles, something unexpected in a world of high-powered rifles and electronic targeting systems. About ten of the terrorists charged the group—none of them armed with rifles. Some had knives, some pipes, and a tall man waved a large, curved sword, looking as though he'd just stepped off a flying carpet.

Vance and McAllister got off the first rounds, while Houston and Doc fell back, trying to lead a few away so they could get clean shots without hitting their fellow Marines. Rainey jabbed the business end of his rifle into the bony chest of an oncoming man who screamed something in Pashto, his broken teeth flashing, his beard matted and unkempt. Rainey steeled himself and pulled the trigger, blasting the guy onto his back as blood arced over him.

Doc emitted a grunt and laid down a heavy spray of suppressing fire with his Para SAW, dropping three bad guys with one fluid wave of his rifle.

And it was over.

Gunfire echoed off into the howling wind, into heavy breathing, into a groan from the guy with the big sword who now writhed spasmodically on the dirt, his chest a bloody pin cushion, a dark pool swelling at his shoulders.

"What's up with this?" Vance gasped, still sweeping the zone with his rifle.

"Suicide squad," Houston said, believing he'd figured it all out. "Armed with knives because AKs are too valuable when you're throwing yourself at the enemy. I bet one AK is worth more to our buddy al-Zumar than all these men."

"Who knows, Lance Corporal?" Rainey said, grinding out the words. "You might get to ask him yourself."

Someone shouted in the distance. Two more shouts. Rainey jolted as he recognized the Arabic words. "Incoming!" he shouted as he and McAllister dove for an embankment to their left, while Houston, Vance, and Doc slid on their asses down a long chute of rock that spilled onto a rocky ledge below.

The mortar round struck like God's hammer, sending shock waves through the ground and heaving the entire killing zone into the air. Flyboy Graham had been right. Weather was an issue. It was raining terrorist body parts.

While the dust rose and the debris continued to thump, Rainey and McAllister exchanged a nod that they were okay and began listening for the approach of soldiers who'd be eager to see if they had bull's-eyed the team. Nothing for a few moments . . . then . . . footsteps. The sliding of rock. A whisper. Rainey and McAllister exchanged a look, and McAllister knew. The sergeant reached for his vest, fished out an M-26A1 fragmentation grenade, your standard-issue firecracker that weighed about a pound and gave you the better part of four seconds in which to lose it. McAllister tugged free the pin, then raised his shoulders and carefully lobbed the little ball of death. Any fighter within thirty yards of the blast was about to receive a shrapnel enema compliments of American taxpayers.

Three . . . two . . . one. Dud?

McAllister grimaced at Rainey, but his disappointment cut short as the grenade finally went off and brought quick thunder and faster hell to the mountain above. Hidden by the smoke and din, Rainey and McAllister mounted the stone slide and dropped like grenades themselves to the ledge, where the others had crouched down to shadow-hug the rock, the whites of their eyes flashing against camouflaged faces.

In all the chaos, Rainey hadn't noticed the falling snow, and as he stole a few seconds to check the GPS, he lifted his gaze from the screen to the tableau of snow-capped mountains ahead, a tableau running like watercolors into a gray haze. You didn't need a degree in meteorology to read that picture. Damn it, he didn't like the math on this one: bad terrain plus big storm multiplied by long hump with terrorists in pursuit equals a shitty day at the office. But if anyone could meet the challenge, they could. They were hard men. Force Recon Marines.

02

"It's the middle of the night here, Steve. But when dawn comes, the devastating effectiveness of the American bombing missions becomes very clear. Elaborate cave networks lie in rubble, sealing forever the bodies and fates of those mindless enough to follow al-Zumar. According to a few of the locals we've spoken to, ground troops are closing in on al-Zumar's nest. I have to tell you, Steve, I'm burning with the desire to be there when it all goes down. There are a lot of people back home who would like to hack off al-Zumar's head and FedEx it to his mother. If I get the chance, I'll do it myself—because we're all looking for justice."

Former Marine Corps-sergeant-turned-bodyguard John Arden watched as Rick Navarro continued his satellite report, the stark white tarpaulin of the group's meager tents rising up from rocky ground behind the notorious correspondent. Arden wasn't sure what he hated more: getting up in the middle of a frigid night to stand watch—or actually listening to the bullshit spewing from Navarro's goatee-framed lips. The guy had donned his khakis and had come to Pakistan not because he was a dedicated reporter trying to uncover the truth but because he wanted to live out some macho, patriotic fantasy that would make him an active participant in historical events. Oh, Navarro would go down in history, all right, and Arden hoped *real* reporters would interview him for "the truth" about the asshole's work.

Engineer Kevin Matthews, a scruffy-faced geek in his thirties with glasses as thick as his gut, shifted over to Arden, breathed into his cold hands, and whispered, "If you hack off Navarro's head, I'll call FedEx, but I'm not sure they got a route number for no man's land."

Arden mustered a weak grin. "Deal. But first I get to shove that microphone up his ass."

"Take a number."

They listened a moment more as Navarro related with exaggerated detail how snipers had fired upon the group two days earlier. The snipers turned out to be Pakistani Marines test-firing their weapons, and not one of the rounds had strayed anywhere near the camp.

Matthews shook his head and sighed heavily. "This has been the longest two weeks of my life, but at least he ignores me. I feel sorry for them."

The engineer lifted his chin at producer Martina Vasquez and cameraman Paul Hopps, who stood opposite Navarro, their faces vacuum-packed with tension.

"If I was her, I'd quit," Arden said. "And if I was him,

I wouldn't have taken the job in the first place. You guys aren't just feeding the beast. You're living with him."

Navarro's shoulders slumped, indicating that the network had gone to commercial. He raked fingers through his bushy hair, then scowled at Vasquez, the cheeky Latina with more than enough ambition to get her killed. "This fucking sucks, you know that? You told me Steve would have the questions. But he obviously doesn't. I'm standing here and volunteering the goddamned information. And you've got him sitting there like a limp dick, Martina. A limp dick."

Vasquez crossed to Navarro, clutching her clipboard to her chest. "Look, there was probably another downlink problem. That's all. We'll work it out."

"I hope so, sweetheart, because with 'work' like this, you'll never make a name for yourself. I brought you out here as a favor to Carlson. Don't make me regret it."

"You won't. I'm going to be the best damned producer you've ever had."

Navarro rolled his eyes then turned his scowl on Paul Hopps, who had lowered his camera to stare bug-eyed at the correspondent. "What the fuck are you looking at?"

The clean-shaven kid with the long neck and double-piercing in his left lobe recoiled. "Sorry, I'm just wondering if, you know, if you're all right."

"Paul, remember what you said about your girlfriend? About how proud she was that you were coming out here with me? About how you were like a fucking celebrity to her, being Rick Navarro's cameraman and risking your life and traveling into a war zone?"

"Yeah, I remember."

"Well, I want you to think about that. I want you to think about how she's going to screw your brains out when you get back home because you're like an American hero to her. That's going to be great, right?"

"Yeah, it is."

"Then I want you to think about what it'll be like going home and telling her I fired you because you had your finger up your ass when you should've been capturing an important image, something that would've been replayed over and over on every network. Paul, do you understand what I'm telling you?"

"Uh, I'm not sure."

Navarro bared his teeth. "Lift the fucking camera and get ready."

"In five, four, three, two . . ." Vasquez pointed at Navarro.

"Hello again, Steve." Navarro hunkered down to scoop up a bit of earth. "You know on the way up here we passed a few small farms being plowed with ox teams, and we saw people digging crude irrigation ditches. We saw children working on the road with shovels and pickaxes, filling in potholes and smoothing out ruts. They held out their hands, looking for tips, and I realized that working on the road is all they do. There's nothing else for them here. And suddenly it's not surprising to find these same children putting down their shovels and picking up rifles. There's nothing else to do."

For the first time since coming to Pakistan, Navarro had conveyed something honest and telling. Even Arden found himself listening with great interest, since he had shelled out a couple of bills to the kids and had seen similar children during Operation Desert Storm. You could harden your heart to almost anything, but when it came to kids, Arden had seen even the most callous of Marines turn to mush. He glanced down at the M16A2 rifle in his grip, imagined one of those kids wielding it, and shuddered. He remembered stories his uncle had told him about the war in Vietnam, about women firing AKs and children being wired with explosives. But you didn't need history to consider that kind of shit. You needed only to turn your eyes to the Middle East, to the Israelis and the Palestinians, to find prepubescent suicide bombers and bloody little appendages strewn across the pavement. And you just knew there weren't six degrees of separation between acts like that and al-Zumar. The bastard was conducting it all.

The group's translator, Shaqib, crossed around the satellite dish and brought a cup of tea toward Arden. "This one is perfect. You'll see."

"Thanks," Arden said, then lifted the mug to his lips and inhaled the wonderfully warm fumes. He took a tentative sip. Not bad. "Is it local?"

"No, it is Lipton."

Arden winked. "No wonder why I like it."

Shaqib stroked his long beard and just smiled that missing-toothed smile. Arden wasn't sure how old the guy was, maybe in his twenties, but the wind and sand had turned his skin to leather. Pitying the man, Arden had given Shaqib a toothbrush and tube of name-brand ultrawhitening toothpaste, but the translator had used the brush to clean his nails and had squeezed a huge portion of the paste into his mouth, only to roll it around and swallow it. "This one is bitter snack," he had said. Arden could scarcely believe that Shaqib had never seen those items. In fact, he had, and he got a huge chuckle out of fooling Arden. "Shaqib plays with you good, huh, Mr. John?"

Arden took another pull on his tea, then cocked his brow at Shaqib. "So, did you find out anything?"

"Everything the same. But one man tells me that his brother fights with al-Zumar."

"Does he know where his brother is?"

"Yes, but maybe it's just rumor. I don't want to get Mr. Navarro mad at me for lying. I once had a mule with a temper like his . . ."

"Fuck him if he can't take a joke."

Shaqib just stared at Arden, then finally said, "Mr. John, you are a soldier. And you do not seem happy with your work. Why do you do this?"

Arden groaned at the question, his breath thick on the icy air. "Funny. Every night we get up to do this, I ask myself the same question. I want to say for the money, because the company's taking good care of me. But if I had it my way, I'd still be in the Corps."

"The American Marines?"

"Yup. But I hurt my back." Arden rubbed his spine, feeling the familiar stabs of pain from the fall five years prior. "I couldn't hack sitting behind a desk for the Corps. And they sure as hell weren't letting me in the field, so I got out and put myself on the market. A friend of a friend hooked me up with Wolf News, and here I am."

"But not happy."

"Happy's just being in denial. And oh, well, it could be worse. I could be sitting on my fat ass inside some gatehouse, watching fat old bitches in Cadillacs come and go from their Palm Beach condos. Yeah, it could be worse."

Shaqib frowned. "You would take care of dogs?"

Arden threw his arm over the wiry man's shoulder. "You know, I'm beginning to think you're a bit of a con artist. You keep telling me how good your English is and how you speak Arabic and all the other goddamned tribal languages here. But half the time, you don't know what the hell I'm talking about, do you?"

Shaqib brightened. "When I was young, I was an artist. But now I am a translator."

"Sure you are." Arden glanced up at Navarro. "Looks like he's wrapping up. Let's go tell him what you got. Maybe a lead will put him in a better mood."

"Okay. But some day we go to Palm Beach. I would like to raise dogs."

"I bet you would. Uh, hey, Rick?"

Navarro zipped up his parka as Arden and Shaqib approached. "Tell me you got something or don't waste my time, because I haven't showered in two weeks and I am freezing my ass off."

"We might have something. Shaqib talked to a guy whose brother might be working with al-Zumar."

Navarro pushed past Arden and grabbed Shaqib by the shoulders. "Did he know anything?"

"Mr. Navarro, it's just rumor, but maybe al-Zumar is in the mountains, about twenty kilometers north of here. But maybe it's just rumor."

"But maybe it's not," said Navarro. "Shaqib, what do you think? I mean, did the guy seem like someone you could trust?"

Shaqib shrugged. "When he spoke of his brother, it was with pain. Maybe it's true. Maybe."

Navarro swung around toward the north, where the mountains, once cutting a jagged silhouette across the stars, now hung in gloom. "How far will the road take us?" he called back to Shaqib.

"Maybe halfway. Maybe more. After that, we would need mules, but there is no way to get them. We will have to walk."

"Better we wait till morning," Arden said. "Have you checked the latest weather?"

"I know about it," said Navarro. "And if al-Zumar is up there, he'll wait out the storm. So we have to move now."

Arden threw up his hands. "This is nuts."

"Maybe it is," said Navarro. "But you're not getting paid to make the fucking decisions." He paraded off toward the campsite. "Martina? Paul? Kevin? Let's get the tents down! The world's most wanted man is up there in those mountains, and we're going to find him."

Shaqib glanced worriedly at Arden. "I like you, Mr. John. You shouldn't go. Maybe you quit now."

"I'd love to. Then again, if by some miracle this idiot actually does find al-Zumar, then I'd curse myself for not being there."

"I understand."

"Yeah, maybe. But don't worry. The storm will come in. We won't even make it up there. Navarro can't blame you for that."

Shaqib glanced away and started slowly for the camp. "I never asked you, Mr. John. But do have any children?"

"Both of my ex-wives wanted them, but they couldn't tolerate me long enough for that to happen."

"You have no family then?"

"No, I don't."

"That is good."

"Yeah, not many people will miss me when I'm gone."

"You want to be missed?"

"I don't know. It's too cold to think about it. But I know one thing. I did it to myself. Who knows? Maybe one day I really will quit this shit."

"And go to Palm Beach?"

"Exactly, my friend. Exactly."

AL-ZUMAR CAVE COMPLEX
NORTHWEST FRONTIER PROVINCE
PAKISTAN
0130 HOURS LOCAL TIME

Mohammad al-Zumar could not sleep. If any of his fighters asked, he would blame it on the lamb kebabs and rice they had eaten earlier. He shifted violently in his sleeping bag, then rolled over to stare absently across the cave at Shaykh Taha Khalil, his long-time friend and the trusted aide of al-Zumar's father. "Shaykh?"

The old man stirred, then finally awakened. He turned up the kerosene lantern, his long gray hair and beard taking on a powerful sheen. "There will be many more sleepless nights, Mohammed. Try to get some rest."

"I prayed to Allah to give me peace. But there is nothing but turmoil in my dreams."

"Allah is great. And he will help us bring down America and Israel. Remembering that will bring you peace."

"I don't forget, Shaykh. But sometimes I wonder if there will ever be justice for us. The infidels are many, and they keep coming day after day, year after year."

"Justice will come. Through the *jihad*."

Al-Zumar smiled thinly. "You are right." He leaned over and tapped his new Kalashnikov with grenade launcher. "Through the *jihad*."

But al-Zumar smiled only for Shaykh's benefit. A cold sensation—the turmoil—still clawed at him. Something was wrong. Something.

And as if on cue, footfalls erupted and echoed hollowly in the distance. Even as al-Zumar craned his head, one of his lieutenants, Fathi ul-Ansar, a young fighter of just twenty with short beard and blue eyes perpetually narrowed by ambition, dropped to his knees, breathless. "My Sheikh!"

"What is it, Fathi?"

"Malik called. His group intercepted a squad of soldiers near the decoy camp. They believe the soldiers are Americans. Malik has already lost as many as fifteen men. But the Americans are on the run."

Al-Zumar regarded Shaykh, who pulled off his sleeping bag and rose. "The Americans have taken the bait."

"Yes," al-Zumar agreed. "And the bombers will be on the way. But it's this squad I'm most worried about. They will be rendezvousing with their helicopter, and that location might be too close to us."

"Then we must cut them off," said Shaykh, pulling on his camouflage jacket.

Al-Zumar hurried into his own jacket, grabbed his rifle, and started with Shaykh and Fathi toward the cave's exit, some one hundred meters ahead.

Here I am, al-Zumar thought. *In the middle of these terrible mountains, fleeing from the infidels the same way my father did before they took his life. I will finish your work, Father. I will.*

A mere decade ago, al-Zumar had been vacationing with his father in Florida. Back then, the innocent fifteen-year-old had no idea that the man had been making contact with his cells in the United States. Young al-Zumar knew only that their trip had been cut short before they even had had a chance to visit Disney World. He had pouted during most of the plane ride home, but then his father had leaned over the seat and said, "Mohammed, some day you will understand everything. Some day you will continue my work. It is Allah's will."

Indeed, it was. During the next ten years, al-Zumar watched as the Americans and Israelis murdered and seized property in the name of God and Freedom. And then he had watched his father's people strike against them, on their own soil, often with their own weapons. But then, in Germany, they had chased his father, had cornered him, and al-Zumar had watched from a car window as bullets had riddled his father's chest. The man had reached out for al-Zumar a second before falling to his death. Even worse, the night before it had all happened, al-Zumar had had a dream in which he and his father were on a boat, sailing through a dense fog:

"Where are we going, Father?" he had asked.

"I'm going to Paradise."

"How long will it take to get there?"

"A lifetime."

"Father, I'm afraid."

The gray-eyed man had put a finger to al-Zumar's lips and had whispered, "Don't be afraid. Be strong. In your faith. And in your duty. Always."

With that, al-Zumar had found himself treading water. The boat carrying his father had vanished into the mist.

Since that night, al-Zumar had been haunted by feelings, by premonitions, by messages from Allah, perhaps. And he listened to them, obeyed them, but he wanted nothing more than to purge them from his thoughts forever, for every time they came, his heart grew a little colder—

Colder even than the howling wind that struck his cheeks as they left the cave, stepping gingerly along the cliff, now carpeted icy white. Al-Zumar turned his face up to the sky and felt the heavy snow dappling his cheeks and beard. He longed for Saudi Arabia, for home. He brushed off the snow and led the others toward a shallow depression in the cliff wall, not a cave entrance but an alcove where they had set up communications. He snatched the mike from his radio operator and relieved the young man, telling him to go into the cave and get warm for a few minutes. The radio man cried out his thanks and hustled off as al-Zumar keyed the mike and called for Malik.

They spoke rapidly in Arabic, using stolen American military-issue radios set up with the latest encryption technology. With American incompetence and Japanese technology on their side, al-Zumar and his bodyguards might very well escape into Tajikistan.

Once Malik acknowledged his call, al-Zumar told his lieutenant to send a suicide squad after the Americans, and while Malik's tone was less than enthusiastic about the order, he acknowledged it without protest. Al-Zumar emphasized the fact that every weapon was valuable, that every man should be prepared for martyrdom. Then he asked for Malik's GPS coordinates and the suspected position of the Americans. As he read them aloud, Shaykh jotted down the numbers in the journal he carried with him everywhere.

Al-Zumar shivered and waited impatiently for Shaykh to plug those numbers into his portable GPS. After studying the coordinates a moment, he looked up, his face grave. "They're headed here. And the valley will provide an excellent landing zone for their helicopter."

"They won't fly in this weather."

The old man hoisted his white brows. "You underestimate American foolishness."

"And they underestimate me." Al-Zumar immediately contacted his other four lieutenants and issued orders to establish an ambush.

Then Shaykh interrupted. "Mohammed, if those Americans were gathering intelligence on the decoy camp, then they may be Force Reconnaissance Marines."

"I don't care who they are. With Allah's help, they won't leave this valley."

"You might consider taking a prisoner or two. They have great value in trade."

"We shall see. Come now. We must prepare for another move." Al-Zumar rose and checked his watch.

On the other side of the globe, his sleepers were about to waken. . . .

BYRON G. ROGERS FEDERAL BUILDING
DENVER, COLORADO
1345 HOURS LOCAL TIME

As he neared the intersection, and the light turned green, the driver of the rental truck squirmed against his erection. The thought of what he was about to do and the rewards it would gain him made him feel more virile and powerful than he had in his entire life.

The driver had spent nearly twenty years assimilating into American society. He had even married an American citizen, and she had borne him two sons, both of whom now attended Harvard Law. And he had spent those twenty years owning various cash businesses, but knowing, always knowing, that one day a call would come in, and then it would be time to reveal his true occupation, his true destiny. He only wished now that his wife and sons would understand—because he had been ordered not to leave any notes, any explanations, any evidence.

Security was tight around the building, but he didn't have to get very close. The voice of his people would come from afar, but it would be heard and not soon forgotten. He need only flick back the toggle switch on the remote in his right hand, and Allah would speak to these infidels.

He stopped the truck in the middle of the road, thumbed on the emergency flashers. It took all of forty-five seconds for a security officer to bang on his window, just as the driver finished masturbating.

"Oh, you got to be kidding me," groaned the old security man as he spied the driver's penis and soiled shirt. "Oh, man. Jesus . . . Put yourself away and step out of the vehicle right now."

"Allah is great," said the driver in Arabic. "Allah is great." He held up the remote.

The security man's eyes widened.
The driver's thumb moved.

DODGER STADIUM
LOS ANGELES, CALIFORNIA
I245 HOURS LOCAL TIME

If you are a terrorist, you cannot strap yourself with explosives and expect to walk into Dodger Stadium, figuring that all the locals leave by the seventh inning, so you'll blow the place to smithereens by the sixth. You simply cannot do that. There are security measures in place. There are people. There are cameras. There are methods that the civilian population knows nothing of.

But it might be possible if you were the head of security, a job you had held for the past nine years. Your knowledge of the stadium's security measures, your ability to fool and misdirect those working for you, and your fierce and uncompromising loyalty to Mohammed al-Zumar and his family would enable and inspire you to commit such an act.

And so it was as the bottom of the sixth inning began that a man wearing the security chief's uniform, a man easily recognizable as the grand gatekeeper of the stadium, took a seat among the fans, bought himself a beer and Dodger dog, consumed them quickly, then leaned back, belched, and, with a trembling hand, found a small plastic button beneath his shirt.

CHICAGO JEWISH HIGH SCHOOL
CHICAGO, ILLINOIS
1445 HOURS LOCAL TIME

They were both nineteen and had come to America as young boys. Now their English was as good as their marksmanship. The brothers were fans of Ozzy Osbourne, of the Whopper with cheese, of NASCAR, and of the Spice Channel, which they received illegally in their small apartment. One had a pierced eyebrow, the other a pierced tongue. They each had the same tattoo on their left forearm, some kind of writing "written in that funny, hieroglyphic Egyptian shit," according to their American friends. The brothers would not translate the tattoos for anyone.

When the call had come in, they had discussed what they were going to do, knew that if they failed to accomplish their mission, they would be disgraced. Their families would be disgraced. And they might never see paradise.

But they had grown used to America and were entirely in tune with what it was about. They had joked about how they would miss the greed, the materialism, and most of all, the girls with their hard nipples poking through their shirts and their jeans yanked down to expose their navel rings. Yes, they would miss high school girls wiggling their asses, but there would be plenty of them in paradise.

As they marched through the school's main entrance, they set off the metal detector. Their automatic assault rifles probably had something to do with that. The big-nosed, curly-haired guards went down in unison, then it was off to the auditorium, where a student production about the Holocaust had just hit the stage. Was their sheikh fully aware of the irony here? Of course he was. He was all-knowing.

The brothers squeezed their rifles tighter and started running.

VERRAZANO NARROWS BRIDGE
EN ROUTE TO BROOKLYN
1545 HOURS LOCAL TIME

The man behind the wheel of the GMC Yukon had pissed his pants. Fuck it. He couldn't go through with it. He hated the American people, but the freedom and the super Wal-Mart were too damned good to give up. Moreover, at thirty, he had been laid only a few times. And therein lay the problem: time. He needed more of it. But al-Zumar had run out. Fuck him, the nut. The driver of the Yukon hoisted his middle finger as he took his vehicle past the detonation site and failed to trigger his remote.

A quarter mile behind him, in a ten-year-old Nissan Maxima, two men who had been monitoring the driver's progress exchanged a look, then the passenger opened a briefcase and withdrew a remote of his own.

Back in the Yukon, the driver began chuckling madly and swearing. But then he realized that he couldn't go out to some strip club to celebrate his independence as he wanted to. When "they" found out that he had failed his mission, they would come for him. Shit. He would have to go on the run. Probably leave the country. *Shit, shit, shit!*

The driver's fears quickly evaporated as a series of beeps erupted from the backseat.

They weren't letting him fail.

03

CAMP LIBERTY BELL
FIFTH FORCE RECONNAISSANCE COMPANY
THIRD PLATOON HEADQUARTERS
NORTHWEST FRONTIER PROVINCE
PAKISTAN
0205 HOURS LOCAL TIME

Inside the command tent, platoon radio operator Sgt. Kady Forrest did everything she could to keep her report to Lieutenant Colonel St. Andrew devoid of emotion. "Sir, the last transmission from them was to Delta Eagle Seven, advise Designated Driver, en route to Extraction Point Stingray, ETA five hours."

"And we've had no transmission from them since?" St. Andrew asked, scratching his snowy, high-and-tight crewcut, his voice burred by frustration.

"No, sir. No transmission since, sir."

"All right, Sergeant. Keep monitoring. Alert me immediately when they check in."

"I will, sir." Kady lifted her head a little, listening as

St. Andrew spoke with Maj. Michael Roxboro, the executive officer.

"Rainey knows better than this," said St. Andrew. "They've been compromised and are on the run. He owes me a report."

"Give the man some time, Scott. He'll check in when he can. Besides, you know how he is about radio silence. In fact, he's the same way you are—when it suits you."

St. Andrew snorted. "I've got five Americans out there whose mission has been compromised. This turns into another Somalia, I'll need a jackhammer to pry the commandant's boot out of my ass."

From the corner of her eye, Kady saw St. Andrew go to a laptop, where the images Rainey's team had transmitted glowed on the display.

"Something about this, Michael. It's just too small, and look where he set it up. Southwest perimeter's way too vulnerable."

"What are you saying?" asked Roxboro.

"I'm saying al-Zumar's smarter than this."

"You're giving him way too much credit."

"Come on, Michael. This lunatic's been playing a brilliant game of cat-and-mouse. Seems like we only find what he wants us to find."

"Well, sir, whether the camp is a decoy or not, I'd order the strike."

"And what about that little town down there, just south? No doubt, there'll be collateral damage."

"Negative, sir. Those boys will hit their mark."

"Just like they did with the food drops, huh?"

"A few accidents, sir. Nothing more."

"We try to save a village, so we accidentally drop food crates on their huts, destroying their shelters, not to mention all the camels and mules we've whacked with our humanitarian support." St. Andrew lifted his voice. "Yeah, we're killing them with kindness . . ."

"Sir, are you all right, sir?"

"Just having a bad night. Sergeant Forrest?"

Kady shivered and swung around in her chair. The rest went by in a blur. She patched St. Andrew into the A-10 Warthog pilots, who said the weather might cause problems for their laser designators and that if St. Andrew was striving for accuracy, he'd best wait until after the storm passed. St. Andrew thought a moment, threw up his hands, and ordered the strike anyway. Then he marched off, muttering something about another cup of coffee.

Major Roxboro smiled politely at Kady. "Sergeant, it's been getting pretty cold and pretty tense around here. I appreciate your confidence and your professionalism."

Translation: don't tell anyone that St. Andrew is about to drop like a heavyweight in the thirteenth round.

"Yes, sir."

The major crossed to the portable space heater to warm his hands. "You're new here, Sergeant, aren't you?"

"I've been in third platoon for about six months now, sir. I guess we've just been working opposite each other."

"I guess so, although I have seen you on occasion. I take it that you know Sergeant Rainey fairly well?"

"Sir?"

"Oh, I've just seen you dining with him on occasion."

Kady wasn't sure where the conversation was going, but there was at least one avenue she prayed it would avoid: the exact nature of her relationship with Rainey. And while she prayed, Roxboro must have noticed the radical shift in her expression.

"Sergeant, I don't mean to pry. Rainey's father served with my old man, so I've known him for a while. And he's not the kind of guy who will let either of us down." The major started for the tent's exit.

"We don't know the same Rainey," Kady whispered, recalling their most recent date.

"You're two hours late," Kady had said, standing in the doorway of her apartment, her dress wrinkled, the pumps digging into her heels. "This is ridiculous."

Rainey had fired up the blue light in his puppy dog's eyes. "Yeah, it's ridiculous. Sorry, I'll go." He pouted and turned away.

"Wait."

He had shifted back, raised a brow, and had just looked at her with all that heat emanating from his broad chest.

And like a fool, Kady had grabbed him by the wrist and had dragged him into her apartment. Sexual tension hadn't just crackled like electricity; it had sparked like lightning as she had torn off his clothes.

"Don't you want to know why I'm late?" he had asked.

"Nope," she had said, pressing her mouth against his.

And for a man who shot and ghosted himself through life, Rainey had been very much there, very much aware of her needs, of her desires. She had never been so sore. And so satisfied.

Feeling her cheeks warm, Kady flashed forward to just the day before, when Rainey had promised that they would steal a moment to make love before he went up into the mountains. Rainey had left early, and that moment had never come.

So it was with them, nothing planned, their relationship like a coin spinning across a sheet of ice, sliding every which way, wobbling, threatening to fall because there was no stable ground. Why stay? In fact, Rainey had asked her that very question.

"Why do I stay? I don't know," she had said. "I guess because there are only a few good men in the Marine Corps."

"And I'm one of them?" he had asked, wearing a sappy grin.

"No, I'm just the one good woman here."

"Ha, ha." He took her into his arms. "Look, things will settle down."

"You don't really believe that."

"I'll tell you what I believe: when I go out there now, I'm doing a better job."

"Why do you say that?"

"Because more than anything else, I want to make sure I get back to you."

"Right. You heard that line on my soap opera," she had said with an accusing stare.

"So what if I did?"

Kady shivered off the memory, then narrowed her gaze on the radio. "Check in, you son of a bitch."

Someone rushed into the tent, and even as Kady swung her head, Major Roxboro shouted, "They've hit us again back home. These bastards have hit us! In Denver, Chicago, Los Angeles, and New York."

It was all happening again, and Kady reacted the same way she had the first time. She simply froze. In disbelief. In horror. Then she shuddered as an epithet begged to escape her lips. Only Roxboro's gaze kept her silent.

But ironically, the major saw her pain and muttered, "Those motherfuckers."

"What happened? How'd they do it?"

The major massaged his temples and began to choke up. "Sleepers again. He's got people everywhere. They could be anybody. They say the death toll's already in the thousands . . ."

TEAM DOGMA
EN ROUTE TO EXTRACTION POINT STINGRAY
NORTHWEST FRONTIER PROVINCE
PAKISTAN
0210 HOURS LOCAL TIME

"If you can hack it, pack it," Sgt. Terry McAllister mumbled as he walked point, leading his teammates along one side of a rocky if not treacherous ravine already dressed in two inches of the white stuff. But it wasn't the trail or the snow or the pursuing terrorists that really irritated McAllister. A recon in mountainous terrain required extra gear, sure, but McAllister was one of those guys who religiously overpacked. Thus, his cache included thirteen thirty-round mags for his rifle and seven mags for his pistol, a first-aid pouch, two flashlights, canteen pouches with canteens, matches, condoms (one condom can hold one quart of water), a black trash bag used to collect water, a small mirror, his night-vision goggles, vitamins, money, a space blanket, rubber bands, a flexible saw blade, candles, a bag of trail mix, twenty AA batteries, two Ka-Bars, fishing tackle without pole, a small bible, a copy of Robert Heinlein's *Starship Troopers* (on the Marine Corps' Suggested Reading List), a copy of the last letter his ex-wife had sent him telling him what a miserable prick he was, toilet paper, two pens, a brochure from the family's funeral home, the Otis weapon-cleaning kit, a receipt from an oil change for his Ford pickup truck back home in Denver (he'd been meaning for six months to throw that out), a half-dozen Meals Ready to Eat, two packs of sugarless bubblegum (he was watching his weight), the Nightstar night-vision binoculars with laser ranging and laser pointer, and shit, his good luck magazine, the one he'd never had to use. Oh, yeah, and some translation book that he doubted would ever work since there were so many tribal dialects in Pakistan. Was that all of it? No. The ruck felt too damned heavy to be holding only that. He couldn't remember the rest, didn't want to. Didn't need any more reminders of his paranoia. Didn't want anyone to know about it. All of them, including Rainey, had him pegged for some guy who had grown up around death and knew how to dance around it without getting burned physically or emotionally.

They didn't know him at all.

McAllister was scared shitless of getting killed. Had dreams about it. Saw himself getting embalmed. Saw his brother and mother crying, saw his ex-wives laughing and spitting on him, saw his old golden retriever lifting a leg over his grave. Yes, he knew a lot about death. Yes, he had watched his father waving the magic wand to turn road pizza into recognizable people. But that hadn't made it easier; it had made it harder. He knew the intimacy of his own demise, knew it better than anyone else on the team. Knew the wax figures in coffins. Knew the tears and lies of relatives corroborated by more lies from the priests.

Better to pull a John Travolta and stay alive—

Which made the whole idea of joining the Marine Corps seem ludicrous. In fact, the idea was still ludicrous to McAllister's brother, Mark, who resented him for kiting off to see the world while Mark was stuck home like George Bailey in *It's a Wonderful Life*, tending to Dad's "embalming and loan," as he called it. Days before his enlistment, McAllister's mother had sat him down and had asked him if he was joining the Marines because, well, he didn't want to run a funeral home but still wanted to be around death. He had laughed, had told her not to psychoanalyze him, but later on, he had wondered if she was on to something. After the first time he had killed a man and had stared into those lifeless eyes, McAllister realized that he was not a Marine because he wanted to be around death. He was a Marine to prevent death.

And therein lay the answer to the big question: why the Marine Corps? As the director of a funeral home, he wouldn't be in the position to save lives; he could only make the living more comfortable. Those duties, though necessary, honorable, and appreciated, weren't enough for him. He had seen the helplessness in his father's eyes for too many years, and he wouldn't be that man. McAllister needed to affect a change. Marines did that.

But, God, it had been an awfully long haul. Five years of proving himself as an infantryman, with a GT score of 105. Then he had decided to test his mettle and go out for Force Reconnaissance. In one, hot California day he had passed the grueling physical-fitness test, had survived the near-drowning swim exercises, then had completed the ten-mile "boots and utes" hump over the hills of Las Flores and down along the beach. He had carried a fifty-pound pack and a heavy rubber rifle from start to finish.

Following that, he had undergone a psychological screening and then had tried to avoid wetting his drawers during an interview with the company sergeant major and several of the senior enlisted operators. McAllister remembered a few of the sergeant major's comments:

"Do you know what we're looking for? A special fire, son. Something in your DNA. A mean gene. Something that makes you just a little bit better than the other guy. Something that tells us you'll hang tough under the most difficult circumstances. What do you think?"

"Sir, I believe I'm prepared mentally and physically for Force Reconnaissance. I understand very well what will be required of me. And I'm committed to succeed."

"Well, that's the right answer, but there's still one problem. Your first sergeant has expressed some reluctance in letting you go. And when I say 'some reluctance,' you know I'm being generous."

McAllister had known that was coming, and he had also known that his first sergeant controlled his fate. "Sir, he knows how badly I want this, sir."

"Then you'll have to talk to him yourself."

And McAllister had. For nearly a solid hour he had presented logical arguments to the man, leaning heavily on the pride and tradition of the Corps, on the contributions he could make, and on the fact that the first sergeant himself had once dreamed of joining Force Recon.

"All right, McAllister, I'll cut you loose. And here I go again, losing another good man to Force."

"That just goes to show you the kind of job you're doing here, First Sergeant. You produce hard men. Force Recon Marines."

"Stow the brown-nosing bullshit. You have my blessing. And now I'm going to hate Force Recon a little more."

"Why's that?"

"Those boys suck up all the money and good men. And for what? They don't even have a career path. You understand that the tour for enlisted men is five years, right?"

"I do."

"And maybe, if you're lucky, you can extend that by a couple more years. But after that, after giving them seven long, hard years of your life, you're coming right back here to infantry. Kind of a letdown, after running all those special ops and playing with all those fancy toys, don't you think?"

McAllister hadn't given that much thought at the time. Seven years had been a long way off. Anything could happen in that time. You could get married twice, divorced twice, have part of your lip chewed off. Pretty much anything. And now he had only two months left on his two-year extension. He had given them the full seven. He would give them many more, but they wouldn't let him. Wouldn't explain it to him, tried to persuade him that reassimilating into the infantry was the best thing for the Corps. That might be true, but it certainly wasn't the best thing for him. He had found in the company a sense of mission and purpose stronger and more rewarding than he would find anywhere else within the entire Department of Defense. He didn't want to give that up. All right, he knew he was being selfish, but after giving so much of himself for so long—after putting the Corps first, even before his relationships—he didn't believe he was asking for much. He just wanted to keep his job.

A job that now took him across the frigid asshole of the planet, complete with turbaned hemorrhoids that kept you anywhere but on your seat. McAllister should be thankful the end was drawing near. But it seemed the shittier it got, the more he loved it. Loved it all.

The snowfall grew thicker as he led the men farther along the ravine, where, about a thousand yards ahead, thick stands of pines whose limbs were already beginning to sag marked the edge of a broad valley. The air seemed even more crisp, even more spanned by static electricity. And for a moment, McAllister projected himself back home in Denver, though his M4A1 carbine with attached 203QD grenade launcher hardly resembled his old walking stick.

In the shadows draped below the pine trees, something moved. Moved again. McAllister signaled a halt, stole a glance back. Vance had dropped to a knee, and behind him, Doc, Houston, and Rainey had tucked themselves tightly against the sixty-degree embankment to their left.

While Rainey spied the rear through his night-vision scope, McAllister held his breath, withdrew his Nightstar binoculars, and ranged out on the shadows. Laser ranging and pointing was good to two thousand meters, and if he wanted to, he could transfer data from his bino to GPS or SINGARS radio. At the moment, though, he would only transfer the info to his brain and decide what the hell lay ahead of them. He probed the ground below the trees, spotted a pair of small birds pecking at something in the snow. A flood of satisfaction and relief washed over him, satisfaction that his old eyes still worked well and relief that he had spotted birds instead of bad guys. He gave the signal to move out. But even as he rose, a burst of static came from his earpiece.

"Hold," Rainey ordered over the radio.

McAllister swung around and swept the ravine behind them, focusing in to detect two, no three, four, shit five AK-wielding fighters hustling into the ravine, about a thousand meters out.

"Dogma One to Five. How many you count, over?" Rainey asked.

"I count five, over."

"Confirm, five. Get us down to those trees."

The hairs on the back of McAllister's neck stood on end, and with good reason. He knew that once he made the break, the odds of being spotted were in the bad guys' favor. He stowed his binoculars, steeled himself. And, keeping his head low, he broke for the trees, his dull, black boots thumping hard, his breath coming fast through his nostrils. A shot rang out. No, he expected to hear a shot, expected it so much that he had imagined the sound. Just the thunder of their jog. Vance hard at his heels. The kid Houston coming on strong, with Doc and Rainey right there behind him.

After a half-dozen breaths, he reached the first tree, rough bark sliding over his fingerless gloves as he swung around it, one-handing his weapon, pine cones crunching beneath his feet a second before he kicked through them and hunkered down.

The rest of the team strung out along the tree line, as Rainey's cool voice broke over the radio. "This is Dogma One. I don't like stopping, but an opportunity is at hand. We're going to seize it."

"Dogma One, this is Dogma Four, over," Vance called to Rainey. "Be advised I have the leader in my sights, over."

When things got tight, Rainey sometimes threw radio protocol out the window, and McAllister appreciated that. The big guy simply replied, "All right you bad asses. We're going for five shots, five kills. Vance has the leader. I got the guy with the red scarf. Houston, you got the guy in the brown jacket. Doc, take that fat guy pulling up the rear. And Terry, you got the short one."

"Sergeant, I'm having trouble seeing my target through all this goddamned snow," moaned Houston.

"Lance Corporal, find your mark," Rainey growled.

"Trying, Sergeant."

The kid wasn't the only one having a hard time. Twice McAllister blinked against the snow collecting on his eyelashes and lost his target. His carbine no longer felt right. He usually ran with the rifle's collapsible stock in the first position, but he immediately closed it completely, tucking the rifle in closer to his chest and trying to keep his thick breath away from the night-vision sight's lens. He found that wobbling short guy, then lapsed into his breathing, the steady breathing that calmed him and always got him through rifle requalification, the breathing that made him adjust for the moving target fluidly, effortlessly, paying no heed to the falling snow. He estimated the wind coming in from the north at about ten miles per hour, but even mild wind above five could ruin a good shot. You took the good with the bad.

The five Warriors of Mohammed kept on, the leader hollering back to his comrades and obviously having no idea that the Marines he was pursuing might stop, turn around, and offer parting gifts of lead moving at high velocities. Al-Zumar's army—comprised of Pak-

istanis and Afghans and a few Arabs like al-Zumar—
had no Mission Training Plan like Force Recon had.
They had guns, misguided courage. But some of their
cousins and brothers and fathers had had the balls to
take on the Soviet Army. They weren't the most brilliant combatants, just the most stalwart.

"Steady now," Rainey said. "Let them get a little
closer."

The maximum effective range for the rifles Rainey,
McAllister, and Houston were carrying stood at about
250 meters, but Rainey wasn't concerned with that as
much as the storm, McAllister knew. No doubt Vance
would hit his mark, as would Rainey. Doc rested his
Para SAW on its bipod and leaned into the weapon, his
body unmoving. Even for a corpsman, Doc was still a
damned good shot. McAllister couldn't see Houston,
and he was worried about the kid. So worried, in fact,
that he shifted his sight onto the terrorist in the brown
jacket, taking mental note of the guy's position in the
event that Houston missed. McAllister would get off
his shot, then bail out the rookie.

When you thought about it, Rainey had asked for the
impossible: simultaneously taking out five targets at
long range, at night, during a driving snowstorm. And
worse, when the shots rang out, their location would be
compromised. Knowing Rainey, he had already
weighed the risk and, as usual, had something up his
sleeve to get them out. If he didn't, the other members
of the team would produce bricks the hard way.

The lead terrorist raised his hand, and the other four

crouched down, the snow falling so hard they were fast becoming snowmen. Their turbans only added to the effect.

"Aw, shit, they've marked us," said Houston.

"Radio silence," Rainey snapped.

McAllister once more held his breath, staring intently through the night-vision sight. He had the short guy squarely in his sights, yet the longer he held the target, the more he realized that he wasn't targeting a man at all, but a boy—a boy who finally lowered his scarf a moment to confirm peach fuzz instead of a long beard. McAllister allowed himself a second's guilt before remembering his training, his mean gene, and the fact that kid would have no qualms in killing him were the situation reversed.

"Vance?" Rainey called. "What do you got?"

"He's still holding. The snow's buried our tracks pretty well, but I think he spotted something, over."

"What's that? Do you hear that?" Houston asked.

McAllister concentrated on sounds coming from the distance, heard only the howl of the wind a moment before a distant bark. Another. Dogs.

"I hear it," said Doc. "And I don't believe it. These bastards got a K-9 unit. What are these guys, Nazis or what?"

"All right, stand by," ordered Rainey. "Find your mark. And fire in five, four, three, two—"

The boy terrorist in McAllister's sights suddenly rose, even as McAllister squeezed the trigger. The echoing thunder of five weapons discharging simultaneously in the icy, dark mountains startled even McAllister, a seasoned Marine. He shifted his weapon, peered through the scope, didn't know if had hit his target.

Two muzzles flashed ahead. Rounds scissored and hissed through the limbs above, whipping up a maelstrom of cones, twigs, and snow. There it was. Five shots, three kills. And they would never know who had missed. Maybe it was better that way—or maybe the not knowing would drive all of them insane.

"Doc?" Rainey called.

"On 'em," cried the corpsman, opening up with his Para SAW, tapping deeper into the first of his three, two-hundred-round magazines. Unadulterated Hell spewed from the 13.5" barrel of Doc's weapon, and in just a few heartbeats, the muzzle flashes out in the ravine went dark.

The bark of dogs echoed more closely, and a pair of shouts followed as the Para SAW's report died into the wind.

"Let's go!" Rainey ordered.

They rallied toward the next stand of pines, with McAllister falling back into the number two spot as the younger and more nimble Vance high-stepped through a drift rising up to his calves. It was all about breathing and running now, the familiar scent of gunpowder wafting up from McAllister's rifle, the trees like sentinels watching over and shielding their retreat.

Retreat. Now there was a word Marines had trouble with. The brass often preferred "orderly withdrawal" or simply "withdrawal." Apparently, there wasn't a lot of honor in getting the hell out of Dodge, but when you were Force Recon and became a trigger-puller, escape, retreat, withdrawing, falling back—whatever you wanted to call it—was foremost on your mind. Besides, Force Recon always fights the enemy on Force Recon's terms . . .

The valley appeared much smaller than McAllister had anticipated. Within five minutes he and the rest of the team found themselves hiking up a slope. McAllister didn't understand why Rainey wanted them to stay in the tree cover to their right and left. Their tracks through the valley beneath all those limbs would remain clearly marked for some time. If they shied more into the open, the falling snow would quickly hide their passage. Rainey was up to something. Something lifesaving, McAllister hoped.

"All I want to know is who missed," Houston muttered to no one in particular.

"We got all five," said Doc. "That's all that matters."

"More humping, less talking," Rainey said.

"I used to tell my girlfriends that," said Vance. "But they never listen."

That drew a few hushed laughs from the team. McAllister had fallen back to the rear, where he paused a moment to peer through his Nightstars. The place looked like a Christmas card, blanketed in white, glistening with silver, and eerily quiet. But Robert Frost wasn't out there, writing poetry and riding on his sleigh. Neither was Santa. There were other guys with beards, and they had toys, all right. Nasty toys.

The dogs barked again. How many? Sounded like

two, maybe three. McAllister zoomed in on the valley's perimeter, following the tree line until he came upon the first bad guy, his AK shouldered, his free hands gripping the leash of a German shepherd who charged after an invisible T-bone. Next came two more dog handlers, three in all, followed by a half-dozen more terrorists, only their eyes showing beneath their turbans and scarves.

While standing there, peering at those guys, McAllister got caught up in the surrealism of the moment. His life had become an old WWII movie, *The Great Escape* or something. The cold air, the snow, the mountains, the dogs, the hunters. A Hollywood director couldn't have orchestrated it better. Then again, that same director would probably get some big name heartthrob to play Rainey, while McAllister's role would go to an unknown putz with a crooked nose, torn-up lip, and big ears. Hey, maybe he could play himself.

Lowering the Nightstars, McAllister hustled back to catch up with the group. He called Rainey over the radio, issued a report, and even as he finished, he found the man waiting up for him and unzipping his fly.

McAllister stopped, dumbfounded. "What're you doing?"

"What's it look like I'm doing?" Rainey asked, shifting to his left and wincing a moment.

"They got dogs, Rainey."

"I know." And with that, McAllister's team leader groaned softly and released a steaming piss into the snow.

"Sergeant, what're you doing?" Doc asked, trudging back down the slope, bringing Houston and Vance with him.

"Laying down some suppressing fire," Rainey said. He gave himself the requisite two tugs, then zipped up, went to Houston, and grabbed the radio operator's mike. "Delta Eagle Seven, this is Dogma One, over?"

Static.

Rainey frowned. "Delta Eagle Seven, this is Dogma One, over?" While he waited once more for the reply, he added, "If any of you have to pee, do so now."

Vance shrugged and swung away from the group. "Okay . . ."

"Dogma One, this is Delta Eagle Seven, over," acknowledged Graham.

"Seven, we're still en route to Point Stingray. Our ETA approximately four hours, thirty minutes, over."

"Dogma One, we might be a few minutes late, over."

"Just don't leave us hanging," Rainey said.

"Or peeing in the wind," Houston added, then became the only team member smiling.

"Roger, out," said Graham.

"All right, move out," Rainey boomed, smirking at Houston.

McAllister fell in beside Rainey. "You going to tell me or leave *me* hanging?"

"Tell you what?"

"Why you want those dogs to find us."

Rainey winked. "All part of the master plan."

McAllister snickered, broke away from the team

leader. McAllister knew that tone. No way in hell was Rainey talking.

And shit, all that talk of peeing had taken its toll. He grabbed his crotch and gazed longingly at the nearest tree.

04

John Arden sat in the backseat of the old Land Rover as the scruffy Kevin Matthews took them over a road so full of potholes that Arden didn't know what hurt worse: his head from hitting the truck's roof or his ass and spine from slamming back into his seat. He sat between Paul Hopps and Shaqib, while Vasquez rode up front with Navarro. Yes, Navarro liked keeping the pretty, young thing close to his hip, and Arden suspected that before they left Pakistan, the reporter would be banging her, wife and kids notwithstanding. To him, it'd just be a little dick-diving justified by the urgency of war. And Vasquez wouldn't take it personally, either. She'd see it as career advancement, whoring herself to Navarro and her own ambition. Still, she was one hell of a hard body, and Arden had to guard himself from staring too obviously. She had once caught him gawking and had said, "You're picturing me naked already, aren't you . . ."

"No, ma'am," he had said, blinking away the image. "Actually, you remind me a lot of my sister."

"And she's a nun, right?"

Arden had grinned. "Uh, yes, ma'am."

Hopps, who'd been listening to the BBC via the portable radio jammed to his pierced ear, suddenly cried, "Stop the truck!"

"What?" Matthews shouted.

"Stop the fucking truck!"

Navarro swung his gaze on the cameraman. "What's your problem?"

"Just pull over."

"Give me that thing," Arden said, swiping the radio from Hopps's grasp. He jammed it to his own ear, heard the announcer's British accent, heard the words *multiple terrorist attacks against the United States*, as Matthews hit a final pothole and brought the Land Rover to a brake-squealing halt, falling snow flickering in the headlights, a vast sheet of darkness beyond.

"Well, we've run out of road, anyway," said Matthews.

Navarro cocked his brow. "Hopps, you'd better start talking."

The facts poured disjointedly from the young man's lips, and twice Navarro interrupted him for qualifiers and corrections.

Finally, Arden broke in. "If I were you, I'd get Liberty Bell on the phone, find out what's going on before we stray into some bombing zone."

As Navarro fished around in his jacket pockets for

his cell phone, he said, "All right, people. We're setting up right here."

Arden shook his head vigorously. "No reports until we let them know where we are."

"If it makes you happy, you can keep pretending you're in charge," Navarro said, producing the phone.

"Between the headlights and the camera lights, we might as well get out and wave to the bad guys," said Arden. "You really want to make a report? Let's head back to the old camp."

"We're not waiting," Navarro said incredulously. "And if you have a problem with security, then deal with it. That's your job. My job is to let the American public know what's being done here to punish the motherfuckers who just attacked us. Get with the program, Mr. Arden, or get out."

"But Rick, unless you get in touch with Liberty Bell, we have no idea what's being done here—if anything," Vasquez said. "You need something more concrete before we go on the air."

"You want concrete?" Navarro screamed, then thrust the phone into her hands. "You get me concrete." He opened the door and burst from the Rover, the icy wind rushing in and blasting over them. "Everybody out! Let's go!"

Arden grabbed the rifle from between his legs and gave Hopps a look.

"Welcome to my nightmare," the cameraman said. "We're on the side of a mountain, in the middle of a snowstorm, in the middle of Pakistan, in the middle of the night."

"Which is the long way of saying we're in deep shit," Matthews mumbled.

Hopps nodded. "When we get back—if we get back—I'm going to write a formal letter of complaint."

"What are you complaining about, hero boy?" Arden asked, tugging up his collar against the wind. "This is what you signed on for—to meet people who want AK-47s more than diplomas."

Hopps crossed to the tailgate, opened the rear hatch, then paused. "He'll get us all killed."

"Not all of us," Arden said, looking to Navarro, who stood near the Rover's hood, arms crossed as Vasquez frantically worked the cell phone. "Just keep one eye through your lens, the other on me, okay?"

Hopps huffed. "Yeah, whatever."

Arden stepped away from the Rover, realizing with a start that the rocky ground beneath the snow had iced up. He measured his steps while digging out a pair of night-vision binoculars that had cost him half a grand. Sighing through a curse, he scanned the snow-covered trees and rocks, hoping they were the only people stupid enough to be out on a night as miserable as this. He directed his attention back to the road, noting with a chill at how quickly their tire tracks were being covered. If the storm didn't let up soon, on the way back their Rover would toboggan down the mountainside.

While Navarro and Vasquez quibbled over something, engineer Matthews and cameraman Hopps rushed around, swearing, grunting, and setting up their equipment. Arden expected they would ask for his assistance, but if they did, he would decline. His old Marine Corps instincts told him stay alert, stay moving, stay warm.

A hand came down on his shoulder, and he jolted. "Mr. John," Shaqib began. "Only me."

"Sorry, man. Being out here's got me wired." Arden laughed aloud at that, then raised his chin at Navarro. "But being with him is making me lose my mind. That, and what just happened back home."

"I'm sorry. It's a terrible thing. It seems your people know war like we do now."

Arden nodded gravely. "Everybody said it was coming. It was just a matter of when. But no one wanted to think about it. Now, back home, that's all people will be thinking and talking about. You can't get away from it when it's on every TV and radio station, and people who can't even say the pledge of allegiance are putting American-flag bumper stickers all over their cars."

"What they did, does it give you anger?"

"I don't know if anger is the right word, Shaqib. You think about all the people who were just, you know, innocent. Just working in their offices or going to school or driving in their cars or even just watching a baseball game, for God's sake. What a waste. What a fucking waste."

"Do you think the American army will ever catch al-Zumar?"

"I don't know. But if you thought the bombing was bad in the beginning, you ain't seen nothing yet. And the sad thing is, a lot of civilians here are going to die. Al-Zumar's just making more enemies—and so are we. Nobody wins."

Shaqib proffered his hand.

Frowning, Arden took it, and they shook. "What's this for?"

But Shaqib just smiled, then trudged back toward the Rover.

"Weird little man," Arden whispered, then resumed his watch, panning the horizon with his binoculars.

Within ten minutes, Matthews established the satellite link, and Hopps shouldered his camera, ready to shoot. Vasquez huddled next to them as Navarro stood beside the Rover, brushing snow from his eyes and beard before he turned up the Hollywood bravado and hit his cue:

"Steve, I'm still here in the Northwest Frontier Province. We were following a lead on al-Zumar's location when we heard the BBC report of new acts of terrorism against the United States. I have to tell you that the rage I'm feeling is difficult to contain. It's a feeling that's going to carry me up this mountain, in search of al-Zumar. He's still up there somewhere, orchestrating his cowardly acts, hiding in his cave, waiting to taste American justice. I know that when we finally get close to him, it's going to be visceral combat, eyeball to eyeball, breath to breath, bayonets and bullets. The final chapter is just waiting to be written, and our fingers are poised over the keyboard."

Arden winced over that. The guy thought he was a fucking poet.

"Yes, that's right, Steve," Navarro continued. "Our contacts at Camp Liberty Bell have indicated that the bombing missions here will resume in earnest once this front passes through. And let me tell you, every time I hear a boom, I'll be saying, 'There you go, Mr. al-Zumar. A gift from the sons and daughters and mothers and fathers who lost someone because of your sick and brutal acts. There you go, Mr. al-Zumar. You're going to pay for what you did.' And even if the B-52s dropping their precision-guided munitions and cluster bombs don't get the job done, our boys on the ground will. They're going to come down from the mountains like Moses, only they'll be carrying terrorist heads instead of tablets."

Arden couldn't help but gag. He had grown up watching the impartial reporters, the distinguished and well-educated anchors who just read the damned news without commenting on it. Journalistic impartiality was an oxymoron to Navarro, and, ironically, the man began to address that very issue.

"Yes, Steve, I'm well aware of the criticism. But I'm feeling more like an American than ever before, and I'm not going to hide my outrage or attempt to present their side of the story. You can tell me all you want that al-Zumar was a misunderstood child who was sexually abused by his uncle, and I'm going to tell you that I don't care. I'm going to tell you that the man is evil. Pure evil. And we're going to terminate more than his command. We're going to terminate his life."

Wishing he could flush his ears out with snow, Arden concentrated on the images in his binoculars. "Oh, shit. What have we got here?"

Two figures emerged at the top of the nearest slope,

about a hundred meters away. They wore heavy jackets, turbans, and had AKs slung over their shoulders. Then, four more equally clad and armed men joined them. Then another four. Pakistani Marines clad in tribal clothing? Maybe. Arden had seen them working out of uniform before. How many in all? Ten. The lead guys brought their rifles around and started tentatively down the slope, one of them waving.

Arden called Shaqib, who came jogging over, slipped, fell on his ass. "Easy there," Arden said, helping the man up. "We need you to talk to them."

Shaqib brushed himself off, squinted up the slope. "We have the company?"

Arden repressed his grin and handed Shaqib the binoculars. "We got somebody. Marines?"

The translator inspected the group for a moment. "I don't think so. Afghans, maybe. Refugees. Or smugglers. Let me go talk."

"No, *we'll* go talk. Believe it or not, my friend, you might be our most valuable commodity—and you're not going anywhere without me."

Shaqib flashed his Halloween grin. "Thanks, Mr. John."

For all of two seconds Arden thought of warning Navarro and the rest, but they were so dialed into their broadcast that he doubted even Matthews, the mostly bored engineer, would notice their exit.

So they trudged off, their boots dropping into snow just over their ankles, the wind knifing across their cheeks. As they neared the first two figures, Shaqib shouted in a rapid-fire of words, the reply from the waving man coming equally as quick and clipped, followed by another pair of exchanges.

"Are they going to shoot us?" Arden asked, frustrated over his ignorance of their language.

"I don't think so. And I was right. Most of them are Afghan refugees who fought for the Northern Alliance. They left when the food ran out. I told them we're looking for al-Zumar," Shaqib said.

"And?"

"And they know where he is."

"Well, this is our lucky day," Arden groaned. "Everybody we run into knows where al-Zumar is—except our military."

As they came within fifty meters of the lead man, Arden lifted his rifle a little higher. Seeing this, all ten fighters brought their weapons to bear as Shaqib hollered once more, probably telling them they were wary but friendly newspeople—or some such shit.

Without hesitation but feeling his Adam's apple beginning to work overtime, Arden stepped right up to the leader, who lowered his scarf to reveal a sun-darkened and heavily wrinkled face plagued by moles and a sparse gray beard. "My name is John Arden. I'm with the American news crew down there. And this is Shaqib."

Arden looked to Shaqib to translate, but even as he did, the lead guy broke in with, "I learn English a little sometimes when I was a boy. I don't remember too much. My name is pop superstar Michael Jackson."

And with that, the other nine Afghans broke into hearty laughter.

Arden just looked at the Afghan, his cheeks too damned cold to force a smile. "What's your real name?"

"Raja."

"Well, Raja, Shaqib tells me you and your men know where al-Zumar is."

"Yes, we do."

Arden cast a dubious stare. "That's pretty amazing, considering that thousands of American and Pakistani troops are looking for the guy. So how did you come by this information?"

Raja regarded Shaqib and released a string of words, the tone of which suggested that he'd been irritated by the question.

Shaqib shrugged. "He says he'll be happy to talk if they can come down to the Rover and get warm for a little while. He says maybe we can strike a deal. They don't want money. What they really want is toilet paper."

Arden eyed the ten fighters, imagining them piled into the Rover and stealing all of their supplies, including the toilet paper. He turned back toward the crew, saw Matthews waving his arms for them to come over. "Shaqib, tell him it's all right, I guess."

After another exchange with Raja, Shaqib nodded to Arden, and they led the ten Afghans down the slope.

Not missing a beat, Navarro, who was still on the air, said, "Steve, we've just made contact with some locals, and we're going to see what they know about al-Zumar's location."

"All right," said Vasquez. "They're coming back to us in three minutes."

"Who are these guys?" Navarro demanded as Arden

led the tattered refugees into the Rover's headlight.

Arden gave Navarro a capsule summary and finished with, "They want to negotiate. But I don't see any proof that they know where al-Zumar is. They see we're a news crew. They know we're looking for the man. And they're just cashing in however they can."

Shaqib translated quickly for Raja, who shouted angrily, "We take you to the sheikh!"

Navarro marched up to Raja, wearing a crooked grin. "You speak English?"

"Sometimes a little."

"Good. Two questions. Why should we trust you? And what do you want for getting us there?"

Raja huddled against the Rover, either contemplating the questions or not understanding a damned thing. Shaqib began translating, but the Afghan waved him off. "Just let us get warm," Raga finally answered, then opened one of the Rover's rear doors. Seizing the moment, the other fighters charged to the vehicle and practically threw themselves inside. Arden heard one of them ask in broken English, "Where is the CD player?"

Raga started for the driver's door, but Matthews cut him off, opened the door, turned off the engine, and withdrew the keys. "Sorry, boss," Matthews told Raja. "You're not taking our only ride out of here."

Raja threw up his hands, yelling something at his men, then he turned back—

And found himself staring down the barrel of a .45-caliber pistol.

The fact that a weapon had been drawn and aimed at Raja was bad. Very bad.

But the fact that Navarro himself had pulled that pistol made the situation even worse.

Arden lifted his own rifle, stunned over how fast everything had gone to hell. But how? Damn it, his attention had been drawn to the Rover. "Lower that weapon!" he boomed at Navarro.

The "war correspondent" spoke through his teeth: "If you did your job, I wouldn't be standing here."

"But we talked about this," Arden said, as pissed as he was dumfounded.

The facts were clear, though Navarro had quite obviously and quite recklessly chosen to ignore them. War correspondents who carried weapons were violating the Geneva Convention and forfeiting the protection that document provides for journalists in the field. Someone back at the office had even brought up Ernest Hemingway, who had served as a reporter during WWII and had purportedly kept firearms, bazookas, and grenades in his hotel in Paris, arguing with authorities that the weapons were in his room because the military had run out of storage facilities. Arden hated it when that happened.

So what was Navarro's excuse for carrying a weapon? He was an asshole.

With no time to bitch further, Arden worked hard and fast to evaluate the situation. The other nine Afghans were in the Rover, and because the windows had fogged up, Arden wasn't sure if they had actually seen Navarro pull the gun. Vasquez and Hopps were slowly backing away toward the dish a dozen meters off. Matthews, keys in hand, edged back toward the Rover's tailgate. And poor Shaqib stood at Raja's side, reflexively raising his hands, along with the Afghan.

Alternating his gaze between the Rover and Raja's rifle, Arden cried, "If you don't lower that weapon, I swear to God, Navarro, I'll shoot you myself." And with that Arden lifted his M16 and trained it on Mr. Pistol Bearer himself.

"You don't have the balls," the reporter shouted, then glowered at Raja. "And you tell your fucking guys to get out of my truck and get out of here."

Shaqib looked to Raja, uttered a few words.

"You make trap for us, Shaqib!" Raja cried. "You make trap!" Then he shouted something in his native tongue, something that made Shaqib hit the deck, even as one of the Afghans inside the Rover bust out a rear window with the butt of his rifle.

As the safety glass fell, two Afghans inside fired blindly, while, on the other side of the truck, a door opened, and a few more bounded out.

At the sound of that first shot, Navarro had answered with a shot of his own, capping Raja, who'd been diving for Navarro's legs. The Afghan crumpled, his blood splayed across the snow as Navarro dropped himself, using Raja's body for cover.

Swearing, Arden hit the snow, rolled, and, peering beneath the truck, he spotted the legs of the others as they emerged from the other side. He opened up with three shot bursts, striking one man's legs, then another, then a third. As they fell, he finished them off, then got onto his knees, huddled near the Rover's rear tire. Flicking his gaze between the rear door with shattered window and the remaining Afghans, who were starting after Vasquez and Hopps behind the dish, he trembled through the fear and the adrenaline rush.

Someone gasped his name, and Arden recoiled at the sight of Kevin Matthews lying across a drift, gloved hands gripping his chest. Though Matthews's heavy jacket hid the blood, no doubt he'd been shot, shot with an AK at close range.

Purging the image from his mind, Arden burst from behind the Rover, saw the three Afghans he had shot, saw another three running toward the dish and firing wildly. He took aim at them, but gunfire originating from the Rover raked across his path, and he rolled to evade.

By the time he looked up and swatted snow from his eyes, shots echoed. Vasquez screamed. And out there, at the foot of the dish, Paul Hopps collapsed onto his back, his camera falling just behind his head like a grave marker.

Something stung Arden's shoulder, then came the dreaded warm, wet sensation, followed by a bolt of lightning running up and down his arm. Shit. It was all he could do to ignore the wound and concentrate on the Afghan who came forward, dragging Vasquez by the hair. She struggled a moment more as Arden sighted the man gripping her and rat-tat-tat sent the guy staggering back and choking on his own blood.

Free now, Vasquez ran forward, either ignoring or wholly unaware of the two remaining Afghans behind her and the others still in the Rover.

Arden fired at the two behind, but even as one took a round in the shoulder, he got off a round that ripped through Vasquez's chest, knocking her face-forward into the snow. She lifted her head, her gaze finding Arden's. "Fuck, John, it hurts. It really hurts. And I think I'm going to die. I think . . ."

Bang! Another round from the Afghans punched her back, finishing her.

Given his current position on the ground, Arden resigned himself to the inevitable. He had but one regret: that he wouldn't be dying as an active-duty Marine. Well, there was one more regret: that he hadn't shot Navarro when he'd had the chance. The reporter was somewhere behind Arden, probably still hiding behind Raja. Hopefully one of the Afghans would spot Navarro and do the American people a favor.

Viewing the world now through a haze, with people moving as though underwater, Arden watched as one of the Afghans ahead took aim, and Arden did likewise, a heartbeat away from pulling his trigger—

Then he heard Shaqib's voice as something hard, a rifle stock probably, came down on the back of his head.

TEAM DOGMA
EN ROUTE TO EXTRACTION POINT STINGRAY
NORTHWEST FRONTIER PROVINCE
PAKISTAN
0245 HOURS LOCAL TIME

Lance Corporal Bradley Houston wasn't big on snow. Wasn't into skiing. Wasn't a Christmas kind of guy. Didn't care for the entire winter season. You didn't get much snow growing up in San Diego, and while you could go up to the mountains and ski, most of the time Houston opted for a surf or boogie board. The whole snow thing just left him cold.

Really cold.

Of course, the wind and snow didn't seem to bother the other operators, who had turned denying their misery into a science. And they didn't seem to care about those damned dogs getting closer, either. Sergeant Rainey, the God among men, the Chesty Puller of his generation, had a plan. Well, the Sarge's plan had better be a good one. A very, very good one. Or maybe, as Houston suspected, Rainey was just making it up as he went along, leading them from atop a mountain of false bravery and bullshit. Rainey was no Chesty Puller. Informed that his Marines were surrounded during the Chosin Reservoir campaign, the famous Chesty had remarked, "Fine, that will make it easier to kill them." That's the kind of Marine Chesty was, the kind of Marine Rainey would never be. But don't get him wrong. Houston did not hate the man—he hadn't known Rainey long enough for an emotion as strong as that—he just hated that Rainey never took his suggestions seriously. Houston felt that he deserved at least that much respect. After all, he had cruised through the pipeline to become a Force Recon Marine, and Rainey didn't even appreciate Houston's jokes, let alone his accomplishments. It was as though Houston's own father had been cloned into a Marine, and really, wasn't the whole point of joining the Corps to escape from that idiot?

Dad. The word was a joke when applied to one

Mitchell Thomas Houston, Southern California real estate man. "Now, Bradley, what I'm doing here is creating an empire, an empire for you and your sister to share after your mother and I are gone. Don't you realize that you weren't born to live a normal life? We're privileged people, and with privilege comes a lot of responsibility. I guess what I'm trying to say is grow up. Get a life. Get this insane idea of joining the Marines out of your head. The military's a place for low-income people and minorities. It's a lot different than when your grandfather was a Marine, and I don't care how great he's telling you it is, it's not for you. You were born to sell real estate, just like me. Running this business will allow you to see and do things that average people only dream about. It just amazes me that you want to throw that all away to go running around playing Army with some inner-city thugs."

Damn, Houston could still see the man, standing there in the kitchen, his gray hair impeccably groomed, his suit flawless, his fingers weighted down heavily with gold and diamonds. What a poser. "Dad" had no idea that he had sacrificed his children for his career, but maybe Houston's joining the Marines had been a wake-up call. Of course, the man had already threatened to disown him, cut him out of the will. Houston had told him to shove it all up his ass and had taken a taxi to Camp Pendleton. Done deal. Welcome to the United States Marine Corps. Now drop and give me twenty!

Houston had dropped and had given them his twenty with pleasure because joining the Marines was a decision he alone had made. Dad no longer had control. And there was the operative word: control. Houston had seized back his life. Ironically, he had once again given away control to the Marines, but working with a unit was different from working with a dictator. In the field, rank didn't come into play very much, and every member of the team was—in theory—considered an equal. Houston thought that maybe one day he'd get promoted and lead his own Force Recon Team, but first he'd have to survive working with Rainey.

All right, so how to earn the man's respect? Don't bitch. Do the job. Don't screw up.

Well, one out of three was a start, right?

And hey, it wasn't Houston's fault that that farmer dude had blown the team's cover, not that Houston would ever admit to the others that he had been taking a piss at the time—which was why Rainey's whole peeing episode had made him extremely uncomfortable. No, he'd stick to his story: he was working the camera when the guy had sneaked up and snatched his sidearm. Sometimes you just had to go, and he'd been holding it for hours.

In truth, though, it had been his fault, and he had lied about it. He was some Marine, all right. Chesty Puller was rolling over in his grave about now, and grandpa, the former first sergeant, would shit his diaper. Houston sighed heavily, wondered if he'd ever fess up. Maybe after it was all over. Better to tuck away the guilt and stay focused on the trail.

They zigzagged along yet another ridgeline among the thousands of ridgelines that scarred the frontier, and

Houston hadn't realized how high they had ascended. He could no longer see the valley's surface, and the treetops had washed into a blur of gray and white. Sure, the wind had died down, but the snow was still falling, and Houston found it colder and harder to breathe. While he and Vance kept hard on point-man McAllister's heels, Doc and Rainey fell back ten meters or so, with Rainey pulling up the rear and repeatedly pausing to peer through his Nightstars.

"Hey, man, you all right?" Vance called back, lowering the boom mike from his lips. "You're huffing a little."

"Air's getting thin."

"Yeah, and we're walking on thin ice here—literally."

"You got that right. What's up with the Sarge?"

"He's fixin' to do something."

"You know they're going to release those dogs any minute, right?"

"Yup."

"You worried?"

"Nope."

Houston took another few steps, realized he couldn't hold back anymore. After all, he liked Vance, the quiet and amiable fisherman from Florida. Even the guy's slight Southern accent didn't bother him. "Hey, Vance, man. Sorry."

"What?"

"You know, for all this."

"Forget it. Besides, the Sarge is getting off on all this. Don't let him fool you. You did him a favor."

"I can think of better favors."

McAllister's voice broke over the tactical frequency: "Dogma One, this is Dogma Five, over?"

"Five this is One, over," Rainey replied.

"Ridgeline ahead drops pretty fast. It'll slow us down."

"Roger that. Houston, get back here. Doc, move on, over."

Houston picked his way down the ridgeline, passing Doc, who slapped a palm on his shoulder and told him to be careful.

When he reached Rainey, he found the man hunkered down, holding two plastic bags of a brownish-white powder.

"What's up, Sergeant?"

Rainey widened his blue eyes and proffered one of the bags. "Time for a little lesson in the field."

"What is this stuff?"

"Little mixture of cocaine and dried blood."

"Cocaine?"

Dismissing Houston's surprise, Rainey stood and marched off the ridgeline, ascending a dozen meters through a narrow col to a pair of pines jutting up from the next bluff. "Get up here, Corporal."

With the bark of dogs sounding just on the other side of the mountain, Houston put his legs in motion, and, gasping for air, reached the Sergeant, who had already opened his bag and was spreading the mixture around on the snow. "Go up to those trees ahead and dump yours."

"All right. But can I ask how you got cocaine—"

"Houston, when are you going to—"

"My mistake, Sergeant. On my way."

Houston reached the trees and began spreading the powder. He wasn't sure what they were doing. Maybe the scent of cocaine would draw the dogs away. Or maybe, just maybe, the dogs would inhale enough of the mixture to trip out of their minds. Yes, that was Rainey's plan. Clever trick. But would it really work?

Abruptly, Rainey came running right at Houston like a big, green linebacker ready to mow him down. "Come on, Corporal, the goddamned dogs are loose!"

05

For the past ninety minutes, Mohammed al-Zumar had been second-guessing his plan. As Shaykh had suggested, the most obvious place for the Americans to set down a chopper was in the nearest valley, and they had pinpointed a spot about a half kilometer south, southeast of the cave complex, where the ground grew more level, the trees more sparse. The American pilots had no stomachs for obstacles and uneven ground, let alone snowstorms, and they would pick a zone with the widest margin for error. Thus, al-Zumar had sent Fathi's team of twenty men to set up an ambush within the heavily wooded perimeter that stood between that zone and the foothills below the cave complex. Fathi and his team would bury themselves in the snow to evade the chopper's thermal imaging, and then, at the last possible second, they would spring their trap on the pilots and on any ground troops who escaped Malik's team.

The plan had sounded reasonable. They would eliminate the Americans, then immediately push north for their rendezvous in Chitral before the bombing began.

So why was he continually reviewing the plan, questioning every move they were making? He wasn't sure, but that cold feeling had not gone away. Allah, it seemed, was speaking in bare whispers, and al-Zumar could not hear . . .

As he shifted through a long tunnel, ducking his head occasionally and following Shaykh toward the cliff entrance where they had set up their satellite dish to monitor western news broadcasts, his reservations found his voice. "Shaykh, we should call Fathi and bring him back. Then we will head north. Engaging the Americans now will call too much attention to ourselves."

The old man froze, did not look back. He lowered his head a moment, then turned slowly, his flashlight casting him in a surreal glow. "Mohammed, you are your father's son. And to him I said this: the path to martyrdom is forged by men who lead with a firm, uncompromising hand. You have made a decision. Stand by it."

"What if they discover our location before we leave? Making a statement here might ruin everything."

"You said so yourself: the Americans won't leave this valley alive. A small victory here will warm the hearts of these very tired and miserable men. Come now, let's go see how the jihad progresses across the sea."

Sighing in resignation, al-Zumar followed the old man through the tunnel and out onto the cliff, where they shifted tightly along the ice-slick rock at their shoulders, then slipped into a secondary cave entrance, where two of his communications people, their names long since forgotten, huddled before a small, battery-powered television, grinning broadly and shouting Allah was great. Al-Zumar crouched down and widened his gaze on the screen. Wolf News anchor Steve June was muttering something too quickly in English for al-Zumar to fully understand, though he recognized phrases like "terrorist attacks" and "untold numbers dead."

One of the communications people translated quickly and excitedly for al-Zumar, who could barely comprehend the magnitude of what had happened in Denver, Chicago, Los Angeles, and New York. Shaykh grabbed him, kissed both cheeks, then hugged him, whispering, "The infidels have once more felt our wrath, and soon they will leave the holy land and beg for our forgiveness. We will return to Saudi Arabia in triumph!"

"Yes," al-Zumar said. "Our will is unbreakable."

The other communications man switched the channel to Al Jazeera, the most widely watched news station in the Arab world, where the images from those American cities flashed, along with a narrator's voice in Arabic.

Abruptly, a tinny-sounding voice came from al-Zumar's portable radio. He acknowledged the man, one of his lookouts, who had called with significant news: a small reconnaissance team had intercepted an American news crew. The lookout had no other information, save for the fact that they were en route and requested assistance.

"Did you get their GPS coordinates?" al-Zumar asked.

The lookout said he had and relayed them to al-Zumar, who realized after a moment that the group was coming in from the south, southeast—

Heading right into Fathi's ambush.

Al-Zumar frantically switched tactical channels to Fathi's frequency. He called for the lieutenant, then told Shaykh what was happening.

"Fathi probably has his radio turned off to avoid detection," Shaykh said. "In fact, if you recall, you have reprimanded him on more than one occasion for too much talk with his men."

"And now I wish I hadn't."

Stroking his moustache, al-Zumar weighed his options. Sending a man down to alert Fathi could compromise the entire ambush, yet leaving Fathi out there to unknowingly ambush his own people would likewise. The best case scenario had Fathi realizing that the reconnaissance team was friendly before a shot was fired. Could he trust Fathi to identify the intruders before he ordered an attack?

Al-Zumar discussed the matter with Shaykh, who listened attentively then finally said, "After your father died, no one trusted his young son, but I urged the others to give you a chance. Now give Fathi his."

Drawing in a long breath and closing his eyes, al-

Zumar sought Allah's guidance and prayed for relief from that terrible cold still clinging to his soul.

WOLF NEWS CREW
NORTHWEST FRONTIER PROVINCE
PAKISTAN
0310 HOURS LOCAL TIME

John Arden realized with a start that he was inside the Land Rover and that a madman was at the wheel. Then he remembered his shoulder, his head. And shit, there was the pain, the dull, aching pain occasionally punctuated by terrible needles as the truck shimmied and bounced. He blinked hard against his blurry vision. There wasn't much to see anyway, just the Rover's ceiling, alive with shadows.

Where was he again? Yes, in the truck, lying across the backseat. He felt pressure at his wrists and ankles. Tried to move. Couldn't. Someone put a hand on his forehead. He shivered, lifted his head. "Shaqib?"

"Don't talk, Mr. John. You're hurt."

Grimacing, Arden wriggled himself up, seeing now that his hands were bound in front by twine, his legs likewise. The madman at the wheel was one of the Afghans, with a dead or unconscious Navarro sandwiched between him and another guy. Arden glanced back into the cargo compartment, where a third Afghan crouched among the camera equipment and supplies, the muzzle of his rifle a few inches from Arden's head.

Only three left? Not bad. Navarro had taken out Raja, and Arden had brought down those first three, then maybe that second pair. And maybe Navarro had picked off another one. But why was Arden still alive to play math games?

"Shaqib . . ."

"Like I say, don't talk, Mr. John. I check your wound. Not too bad. The bullet went through, and the bleeding has stopped, thanks Allah. I put a bandage, but I am not a doctor. We will get you one." He lifted his gaze to the front seat. "Navarro is alive. They only hit him. They knew better than to damage the prize."

"What do you mean? Do they know who he is? They get Wolf News in Pakistan? Or did you tell them?"

The translator glanced away.

"Shaqib, I'm talking to you!"

The Afghan in the cargo compartment grunted something, and Shaqib retorted harshly, then regarded Arden. "Mr. John—"

"Shaqib, if you don't tell me what's going on here . . ." Arden let the sentence die, realizing that threat-making would just waste time and energy. He softened his tone. "Shaqib, please . . ."

"Mr. John, we're going to see al-Zumar. Really."

"They weren't shitting us?"

"Do you mean the toilet paper?"

"No, I mean they weren't lying. These guys really know where he is?"

"Yes."

"Then your initial contact, that guy whose brother

supposedly works for al-Zumar, he was telling the truth?"

Shaqib shrugged. "I think so. Yes."

Arden narrowed his gaze, dropped his voice to a growl. "So Shaqib, how long have you been working for al-Zumar?"

The glassy-eyed translator frowned. "What do you talk about?"

"You heard me. If these guys really are taking us to see al-Zumar, then you set us up from the beginning."

"Why you think this?"

"I'll tell you why. Just before the first attacks, al-Zumar said he wanted to be interviewed by a western reporter, somebody famous he said, but then, after the attacks, he went into hiding. I think he still wants to give that interview. Probably tape it, smuggle it out for broadcast on Al-Jazeera without giving up his location. So he put out the word. He knows a lot of British and American news crews hire local translators, and I bet he even knew Navarro was coming here. Al-Zumar's probably offering you a nice piece of change to get him the prize."

Shaqib pursed his sun-browned lips, folded his arms over his chest.

"How far off am I?" Arden asked. "Or am I right on the fucking mark?"

The translator sighed heavily. "I do not work for al-Zumar. I only wanted to take you to see him because it would benefit both of us. Mr. John, please believe me. I did not want anyone to be captured or killed. And no one would have been harmed if Navarro had not brought a gun. When he took out that pistol, the Afghans thought it was a trap, a plan by the military to capture al-Zumar, and that he was not a journalist because they know journalists do not carry guns. All we had to do was go with them. And now they no longer trust me, either. I am a prisoner, like you. They say that al-Zumar will deal with all of us."

"Shaqib, you fucking idiot. Do you understand how this works? They take us to al-Zumar, and when he's done with us, maybe he holds us ransom while he tries to get some of his buddies in Cuba released. If that fails, he kills us. He'll probably kill you, too."

"Maybe. But al-Zumar has been known to keep his word. The money will go to my family. That's all that matters. I'm sorry, Mr. John."

"You're sorry? You will never be sorry enough."

"Mr. John, you do know they wanted to kill you. And they would have."

"You talked them out of it?"

"You're the most dangerous one. They are taking a risk by keeping you alive. I told them you were once a Marine and that al-Zumar would want to question you. He could learn something about the military here."

"Wow, thanks for the favor, but letting them kill me back there would've been quicker and less painful. Next time you want to save someone's life, ask first."

"I'm sorry, Mr. John. You are a good man."

"Yeah, a good man in some very bad company."

In the front seat, Navarro stirred, and the Afghan to

his right began slapping him across the cheeks as he shouted things to the others and laughed.

Incensed, Shaqib hollered back, then ripped the man's hand away from Navarro.

"Yeah, don't let them damage the goods," Arden said.

"What the fuck?" Navarro asked, finally coming to. Arden assumed that they had pistol-whipped Navarro, since the reporter groaned at the slightest movement of his head. "Who's back there?"

"It's me. And Shaqib's here, too."

"Well there's a fucking surprise. What did they do? Leave the others back in the snow?"

Shaqib glanced painfully at Arden. "Yes."

"Well, Mr. Arden, now that we've been captured by these fucking terror goons and the rest of the crew is dead, I think an FYI is in order: you'll be getting your pink slip—if you don't get a bullet first."

Arden made a lopsided grin. "I quit the moment you pulled that gun, you asshole."

"At least I know I'm an asshole. You think you're a bodyguard, but what you really are is a washed-up old grunt who's never known how to read a situation. But that's beside the point. What I can't figure out is why they kept you alive. I mean, I would've shot you."

Before Arden could devise a smart-ass answer, the Afghan in the passenger's seat pointed at something in the snow-covered trail ahead and began shouting worriedly.

That the Afghans had managed to get the Rover even farther up the mountain remained a small miracle, but apparently their well of miracles had just run dry.

The driver cut the wheel hard left, and the Rover fishtailed, struck something hard, an outcropping maybe, then tilted nearly forty-five degrees as it began sliding sideways down the mountain, the tires rumbling and kicking up snow, the engine revving ineffectually, the Afghan in the back screaming in Arden's ear. The silhouettes whipping by were, in fact, pine trees, and it was only a matter of time before—

They struck one! Took the hit in the left-quarter panel, just beyond the driver's door, spun around as the windshield splintered like ice, then bang! Another tree connected with the right-quarter panel on the passenger's side, and the side window burst into fragments of safety glass as they swung around once more and kept sliding, the Rover now very much a toboggan with a wailing Afghan at the wheel.

Something hit the driver's-side front tire a millisecond before the rear tire made impact, and suddenly Arden felt his stomach heave as the Rover slammed onto its side, shattering more glass and sending the equipment and supplies in the back rattling and crashing down on the Afghan scrunched up there. In the meantime, Shaqib collided with Arden, while Navarro and the Afghan seated in the passenger's seat shot up onto the ceiling a moment before they fell onto the driver.

Fearing that the Rover's momentum would send them into a roll, Arden tried bracing himself by shoving his boots against the driver's seat while digging his back into his own seat—but the seat wasn't there. He was lying on shattered glass and snow, a pair of heavy Anvil supply cases pecking at his shoulders. The Rover continued sliding another few meters, then, remarkably, it came to a halt, the engine still chugging along, two wheels spinning on the snow.

Shaqib moaned softly, muttered something in his native tongue.

"I got my foot on the driver's throat," Navarro said, his voice tight with exertion. "Shaqib? Reach up. See if you can untie me!"

But the Afghan who lay across Navarro was still conscious and had taken possession of Navarro's pistol back at the old campsite. He pressed the muzzle to Navarro's ear and grunted something.

Navarro swore as the Afghan lifted his voice and jammed the pistol even harder.

Shaqib's voice came low and shivery. "Mr. Navarro, he wants us to get out."

"Is this guy kidding? Ask him if we look like we're in a position to get out?"

As Shaqib and the Afghan exchanged heated words, Arden glanced back into the cargo compartment, where the Afghan was pulling himself up, blood dripping down his face from a deep laceration across his forehead.

Without warning, Arden felt hands fumbling with the twine around his wrists. Slowly, Arden turned his head and regarded the translator, who nodded solemnly.

The Afghan behind them elbowed his way up, past a sheet of cobwebbed glass, then, with his rifle slung over his shoulder, emerged outside, near the rear tire.

Dividing his attention between that man and the guy lying across Navarro with the pistol still jammed in Navarro's ear, Arden figured that once loose, he should devise a plan to eliminate the Afghan outside, leaving Navarro to contend with his pistol-wielding buddy. But guilt and proximity got the better of Arden. The Afghan atop Navarro was right there, the pistol just a lunge away.

And, with his hands coming loose, Arden made his move.

The guy fired—but Arden had already been pulling his hand away, and the shot missed Navarro's head by a hairsbreadth, the ring deafening.

Before the Afghan could get off another shot, Arden wrested the pistol away, flicking the hot muzzle around, taking a firm hold on the weapon a second before he capped the Afghan point-blank, blood and gray matter jetting across the busted windshield.

Though crushed beneath Navarro, the driver emitted muffled cries as the Afghan outside began digging away the shattered windshield with his rifle's muzzle, trying to get a clean view of the Rover's occupants so he could take a shot.

Exploiting that fact, Arden leaned forward and emptied the magazine, glass tumbling away to reveal the Afghan staggering back a moment before he hit the snow and began rolling down the mountainside.

Just sitting there, breathing a moment, heady from the firing and trying to think clearly through his thundering pulse, Arden realized that he should've put a bullet into the driver. He could've shot the guy right through the back of his seat—and as that mistake took hold, a single shot rang out.

Arden jolted. Wondered if he'd been shot. Didn't feel anything.

"Aw, fuck, am I shot?" Navarro screamed. "Am I shot? Am I shot?"

The driver's exact position wasn't clear, nor could Arden tell if that driver had, in fact, taken the shot. He squinted once more outside, saw the other Afghan's body lying in the snow. The shot had come from the driver.

Shaqib immediately pulled himself away from Arden and started back for the cargo compartment and the broken window above.

"Shaqib!" Arden cried, then strained with everything he had to lean forward and begin pulling at the twine binding his ankles. "Shaqib!"

"I don't think I'm shot," Navarro said. "I think this guy shot himself by mistake! Yeah, he did! He did!" Navarro rose from behind the front seat. "I got his weapon."

"Oh really?" Arden asked. "Weapons and assholes don't mix."

Navarro waved the pistol. "Maybe this asshole's going to shoot you."

"Mr. John?"

Arden glanced back to Shaqib, who had hesitated in the cargo compartment. "Jesus Christ, can you just give me a minute?"

Shaqib nodded, glanced over at Navarro, who just lay there, breathing heavily.

"All right, what do you want?" Arden asked.

"We are a long way from the old camp. You can check with the GPS. But I think we are very near to al-Zumar."

"I think he's right," said Navarro. "We didn't come this far for nothing."

"You guys want to go up there, looking for al-Zumar, be my guest."

"First we stash these bodies," said Navarro. "Then mark these coordinates, go up there, see what we can see, and if by morning we can't find al-Zumar, we come back here and I see if I can raise Camp Liberty Bell to send someone up for us."

"Sounds great," Arden said darkly. "Sign me up. Twice."

"You're coming with us," Navarro said.

"I thought I was fired."

"You've just been rehired."

"And I just quit—again."

"He's been shot," Shaqib said. "And he needs a doctor."

"Oh, there's a good reason why I should go up the mountain with you guys. Maybe our terrorist buddies will admit me into their fucking ER." Arden steeled his gaze on Navarro. "You're insane. I don't know what you're trying to prove, but I'm not going anywhere."

Navarro thrust out the pistol. "Oh, yes, you are."

Arden's eyes drew up to slits. "Better scumbags than you have pointed weapons at me. And what do you need me for? Protection?"

"Maybe. Maybe you'll be a witness in case I buy it. Maybe you'll come in handy somewhere down the line.

Maybe you're the only other American I know here."

Arden grinned sarcastically. "You think you can kill al-Zumar, don't you . . ."

"I know I can kill him. But I'm going to interview him first. Rick Navarro kills world's most-wanted man—and Wolf News will have it all on tape. Yeah, that'll play just fine."

"It's all about you, huh? What about the others? Oh, I know, you'll turn them into martyrs—when you're the guy who got them killed in the first place."

"Hey, fuck you, Mr. Arden. That'll haunt me for the rest of my life—the same way it'll haunt you."

"The same way? I don't think so." Repressing a grimace, Arden slowly rose, fought for balance. "I'm going back down the mountain. Shaqib? Let's start pulling out this stuff. I want to set up a pack."

"Mr. John, please. You need a doctor."

Arden's dizziness confirmed that, and he really wasn't sure he could make it down the mountain. He fumbled through his pockets for his cell phone. Gone. The Afghans had taken it. "All right, maybe I'll just stay here. Navarro, get in touch with Liberty Bell. Shaqib? Find one of our GPS units. Maybe we can call in our coordinates."

Navarro's lip quivered, then he searched his pockets for his own cell phone, came up empty. "Even if we can find a phone, the signal will break up in all these mountains."

"Well, we're going to try," Arden snapped. "Search these guys."

Navarro frowned, his eyelid twitching a little. "Just remember who's in charge here, Mr. Arden. That's all."

Arden snorted. "At this point, *Rick,* God's in charge."

Shaqib cocked a brow. "Allah."

K-9 PATROL IN PURSUIT OF MARINES
NORTHWEST FRONTIER PROVINCE
PAKISTAN
0325 HOURS LOCAL TIME

Malik trudged toward the dog teams on the bluff, the sounds of distant gunfire still on his mind. He pressed his portable radio to his cheek, called the operator in the caves to report the firing. The operator had no information to provide. If that mystery weren't enough, there was something wrong with the dogs. They and their trainers had been stalled for a few minutes—minutes they did not have to spare.

Reaching a stand of pines, the portly twenty-eight-year-old with a thick beard drew back his head in confusion. Two of the dogs were rolling in the snow, as though their backs were on fire. The third dog walked shakily, its head swaying drunkenly, its front legs occasionally failing.

"Poison?" Malik asked one of the trainers.

"I don't know. We found something in the snow. A dark powder. I'm sorry. The dogs are no good to us now."

"Then shoot them."

The trainer recoiled in horror. "Do you know how valuable they are? If we kill them, the sheikh will not be happy."

"Are they going to die anyway?"

"I don't know."

Trembling with frustration, Malik cried, "Then just . . . just take them! And get out of my sight!"

"Yes," the trainer said nervously. "I'll get them back to the caves."

Malik shouted at the other men, who were just standing around, two of them smoking cigarettes when the whole bunch was supposed to be pursuing the Americans. The group's actions weren't surprising, though. They had heard about the suicide squad, about how the Americans had butchered their comrades, and they were afraid. Malik saw it in their eyes. At any other time, he would take a moment to rekindle their fires, remind them of how great Allah is, remind them of their places in paradise. But there was no time, and the delay infuriated him.

His voice booming, Malik ordered them off, told them if they did not eliminate the evil Americans, he would shoot them himself.

And all five knew he was serious; they had seen him kill their comrades before—

The same way the sheikh might kill Malik if he failed.

Shuddering, Malik took up his own rifle and charged off into the storm.

"Well, I'll be damned," Cpl. Jimmy Vance said, staring through his M40A3's night-vision scope. "Someone spiked the Puppy Chow." He switched on the tactical radio. "Dogma One, this is Dogma Four, over."

"Go, Four."

"We've thrown the hook, over. Repeat, we've thrown the hook."

"Understood. Report on shots fired?"

Vance, like everyone else, had heard the distant gunfire coming from down the mountain, and while he had scanned the area with his Nightstars and night-vision scope, he hadn't spotted anything. He reported the bad news to Rainey.

And with that, he sprinted up the ridgeline, chasing after the others. He always liked it when Rainey held him back to see if the bad guys got dead the way bad guys should, but at the moment, the show wasn't particularly interesting. The dogs got high. No one got dead. No sign of who was firing below. Big deal. He'd rather get the order to cap those bastards on their tail—because some varmints just need killin'.

However, Vance understood why that order would not come. They had, as he'd heard countless times during training, become trigger pullers, and when that happens things usually turn for the worse. Also, you didn't want to lead the bad guys right back to Point Stingray, where they could take potshots at the chopper. As they neared the extraction point, it was all about stealth and not unlike sight-fishing the beds for bass during the spawn, when you had to sneak up on those lunkers with soft plastics, pitch or flip your bait real gentlelike, then wham! You got the strike and hauled that bad boy out of thick cover and into your boat.

All of which was technical redneck fishing speak for what you did to catch a ten-pound largemouth bass during the spring in Central Florida. And all of that was the most exciting thing Vance could imagine, short of being a sniper on a Force Recon Team. Everybody knew him as the bassman, the fishing nut, the guy who spent night and day talking about fishing, reading about fishing, and dreaming about fishing. What most of his buddies didn't know was that to be good at the sport, you had to be a little obsessive-compulsive. You didn't just throw a worm and hook into the water and wait for a bite. Bass fishing is a science. You have to take into account season; wind velocity and direction; water temperature; water clarity; water pH level; rocks, weed lines, brush piles, and other forms of structure; and the location of the fish, be they chasing bait on the top, suspended, or feeding off the bottom. And those are just a few of the factors.

Catching terrorists or eluding them was often a hell of a lot easier than catching bass; then again, the fish weren't trying to kill you. Vance sighed, aching to be on the water. Driving his sorry ass over a snow-covered slope half a world away from the Kissimmee chain of lakes back home was no longer any fun. And it wasn't like they had a Bass Pro Shop or a Cabela's on every corner in Pakistan. The place was night-and-day different from the solitude of the lake on an early morning, the mist rising above the water, the whir of Vance's baitcasting reel sounding just louder than the hum of his trolling motor.

"Hey, man, you with us?" Doc asked as Vance met up with the group behind the cover of a fallen tree. "You look like you were fishing again."

"Yeah," Vance said shyly as the group moved out, Vance taking the rear.

Doc waited to fall in beside him and asked, "How does your woman handle it?"

"What? My fishing addiction?"

"Yeah. See, my wife wants me addicted to loving her and nothing else. But a man needs playtime." Doc winked. His wife was a civilian surgeon making the big bucks and biding her time until Doc got out. Vance had met her once, and she didn't strike him as the type who would ever give Doc his playtime.

"Well," Vance began awkwardly. "My girl used to handle it just fine. But it wasn't the fishing that got in the way."

Big Doc sobered. "Hey, man, I'm sorry to hear that. This just isn't the life for some people. She Dear-John you or what?"

Vance nodded. "In the old days you got the letter. Something to hang on to, right? I got email, day before we came up here. Can't see her handwriting. Can't smell her. Just cold typing. And they say it happens a lot, that's why you see it so much in movies. Never thought it'd happen to me. I don't know. I still love her. I mean I think about her all the time."

"You're young. You'll get over it. And you'll move on." Doc jogged ahead, which was just as well. No time for chatter. Just think. Just move. Keep low. Remain silent.

They shifted down along another icy ridge, heading toward a heavily wooded valley in the distance. Beyond all those snow-painted pines lay the DLZ. Vance figured they'd reach it in about three hours, though the wind had picked up again, and the snow fell more heavily, rising to over a foot deep in spots, which would definitely slow them down. Unlike Houston, who repeatedly told everyone how much he hated snow, Vance enjoyed it. The snow reminded him of his grandmother on his father's side. Nana lived in Maine with her lesbian lover Aunt Jenna, though everyone considered them "roommates." Vance and his folks would go up there for the holidays and almost always enjoy a white Christmas with "them two old spinsters," as Dad called them. Every year he tried to talk them into moving to Florida, but they always refused. Although there was a town named Christmas about an hour north of Vance's house, there sure wasn't any snow, and those old ladies loved snow. In Florida you were lucky to have seasons at all. Just a blazing hot summer with lots of rain, and a mild winter. Spring and fall were just afterthoughts. At the moment, Vance couldn't help feeling like he was on vacation, hiking through the mountains and getting ready to head back for some of that chicken soup those old ladies would spend half a day cooking. Yes, it was vacation, all right, and that feeling diverted his thoughts from Cindy.

Damn. He had just reminded himself that he was doing a good job forgetting about her—and that reminder had brought it all back! He missed her tracing circles around his Adam's apple, missed her calling him Pooh (a name no Marine should be proud of but one he enjoyed), missed those nights when she had come out to California to see him and they stretched out in bed, just dreaming about what it'd be like to get married and have kids. But she had "some serious issues" with him being gone all the time, and her "life was slipping away while she waited for him", and she knew she was being selfish, but she "wasn't getting any younger" and wanted to meet new people (which to Vance meant she already had). As Rainey had once said, it takes a special kind of man to become a Force Recon Marine, but it takes an even more remarkable woman to marry him. "Amen," McAllister had said, triggering a fit of laughter.

Vance had not replied to Cindy's email, and he wondered how guilty she would feel if he died up here in the mountains. He didn't want to punish her for what she had done or in any way enjoy her misery, but she certainly hadn't made running the op any easier. When on a mission, Vance always prided himself on having a mind as clear as some of the lakes he fished. Getting dumped stained the waters and left him feeling lonely and even regretting the choices he had made.

And damn, he had not wanted to blab about getting DJed, since word might get back to Rainey. Loose lips did, in fact, sink ships, and Vance wanted the Sarge to consider him a premier rifleman, a weapon of destruction full of pride, piss, and vinegar. In fact, he had not made a single mistake thus far. His heart and his aim had held true. Rainey always relied on him to get the job done, and he had always come through.

Vance sighed in disgust. His eyes were tearing up, his damned nose running again. He backhanded away the wetness, muttered a curse, and got a little tighter behind Doc as he shifted back and swept their rear for bad guys, twice seeing Cindy appear from behind a pine to tell him she was sorry. *Stop thinking about her!*

There were, after all, many fish in the sea.

06

CAMP LIBERTY BELL
FIFTH FORCE RECONNAISSANCE COMPANY
THIRD PLATOON HEADQUARTERS
NORTHWEST FRONTIER PROVINCE
PAKISTAN
0345 HOURS LOCAL TIME

While the other members of third platoon huddled around the television in the media tent, watching news of the terror attacks piped in via satellite, Sgt. Kady Forrest remained at her post. She tried to keep herself calm as she waited, God, she waited, for Rainey's team to make contact with Delta Eagle Seven once more. The last call had been nearly two hours ago. Something bad was going to happen. Kady just knew it, but she wouldn't betray her worries to Lieutenant Colonel St. Andrew, who sat at the desk opposite her station, studying a weather report on his laptop.

"Where's the helo now?" he asked suddenly.

Kady checked her notes from the last contact she had had with Capt. Tom Graham. She read off the heading and speed and Graham's estimate that he'd reach Point Stingray at approximately 0645 hours local time. Then, even as new info came in through her earpiece, she added, "The ground order's been lifted. Warthogs are finally in the air and en route to strike target in quadrant D9H, sir. ETA approximately forty-five minutes. Estimate strike accuracy at 97 percent."

"The front's already moving through those coordinates," St. Andrew replied. "But there's another one right behind it. In any event, they'd best be at one hundred."

"I'll tell them that the Marines expect nothing less, sir."

And that woke St. Andrew's meager smile. "You do that."

Of course, Kady would inform those air force jocks in a much more polite manner than St. Andrew would. Kady was still walking on eggshells around the man, and she prayed Major Roxboro would return from his briefing to temper the lieutenant colonel. She spoke softly into her headset, requested 100 percent accuracy from those pilots, who rogered that, though their tone conveyed their annoyance. How they expected to cover their asses with a 3 percent margin of error was beyond Kady. Besides, weren't they after a single target? You either hit it or not.

A familiar voice came over Team Dogma's tactical channel, and Kady put a hand to her headset and froze. "Delta Eagle Seven, this is Dogma One, over?"

"Dogma One, this is Delta Eagle Seven, over."

"Seven be advised we are approximately two-point-five hours from Point Stingray, over?"

"Roger that, Dogma One. Our ETA now zero-six-forty hours, over."

"Zero-six-forty hours, understood. Be advised we may be towing five-to-ten individuals. Will try to lose or terminate, over."

"Roger that. Delta Eagle Seven, out."

Because Rainey communicated with Graham via the 117 Foxtrot backpack radio, every time he keyed his mike, his location and station ID should be transmitted. But leave it to Rainey to get paranoid and disable that function, despite the embedded crypto. He didn't want anyone to know exactly where they were—especially the enemy, and Kady couldn't blame him for that. She just wished she could better track his progress.

A call suddenly came in from one of the company's intelligence chiefs. Since heavy bombing was only hours away, they were recalling all news crews from the area, but they had failed to make contact with one: Rick Navarro and Wolf News. The army had launched a Blackhawk to recon the area, and those pilots had reported no sign of the crew in their last known location. Kady reluctantly swiveled her chair and shared the news with St. Andrew.

"Never a boring day or night, eh, Sergeant? Now we have a civilian news crew running through our bomb zone?"

"I believe so, sir. I have the coordinates of their last known position, which puts them about ten kilometers south of Delta Eagle Seven's track."

"Get me that pilot. Couldn't hurt to have him take a

look for that news crew while he's en route to Stingray."

"Yes, sir."

As Kady keyed in the chopper's frequency, she had a feeling that the "something bad" somehow involved that news crew, and she wanted to call Rainey and tell him that no matter what, he should get his ass out. Pronto.

AL-ZUMAR AMBUSH TEAM
NORTHWEST FRONTIER PROVINCE
PAKISTAN
0345 HOURS LOCAL TIME

Fathi ul-Ansar and two of his best fighters shifted swiftly and stealthily along the perimeter of their ambush zone, heading toward the sound of those shots. He had spent several precious moments contemplating whether or not he should send a team to investigate, but if Malik's report was incorrect and the Marines had somehow bypassed their position, then they could very well be establishing an ambush of their own, perhaps reinforced with more troops. Fathi's imagination had run wild with the idea, and while he should have sent off two scouts to report back, he couldn't help but lead the team himself. The sheikh would not approve of that decision, but knowledge was everything, and at the moment, Fathi knew nothing. He could not bear to wait for scouts.

The trouble was, an American helicopter was on its way, and if they were spotted, the pilot would alert the ground troops or even signal their own ambush. Thousands of soldiers could charge up the mountain, and poor Fathi and his meager band would be cut down like dogs.

They huffed and puffed up the mountainside, finally working their way along a string of hogbacks and down into the foothills, where something off to his right caught Fathi's eye. He picked up his binoculars, and while they weren't equipped with night vision and the snow continued to fall, the silhouette he spied was definitely not a boulder or an outcropping. The lines were too even, the shape rectangular.

"What is it?" one of his men asked.

"I'm not sure. A vehicle, maybe."

"Someone tried to drive up here?" the man said, already beginning to chuckle. "They must be Americans."

"I saw them drive when I was in New York City once," the other man said. "They were terrible. But the cab drivers . . . they were good. They were, however, not Americans."

Fathi's brows narrowed in anger, and he put a finger to his lips. One of the men shrugged. The other brushed snow from his turban and started toward the object.

WOLF NEWS CREW
NORTHWEST FRONTIER PROVINCE
PAKISTAN
0400 HOURS LOCAL TIME

Although Navarro had found his cell phone in the dead driver's pocket, getting a call out of the mountains was about as difficult as getting themselves out, and Navarro's battery had just thirty minutes of charge left. Arden wasn't expecting a miracle—just something to go right for once, damn it. Shaqib had found the portable GPS, but Arden couldn't be certain that the coordinates reported were true, since an error message regarding a weak satellite link flashed on the display. He was no electronics expert, but Arden knew enough to rely more on his instincts than on the technology—something the Corps had taught him well. But he didn't need those well-honed instincts to realize that without a clean line of communication, they could rot for a long time on the mountainside. He huddled just inside the shattered Rover, his boots balanced on the driver's side door, his rifle gripped tightly in one hand and pressed to his chest. At least the Afghans had remembered to pack it, along with the AKs of their dead comrades and the rest of the equipment, including Arden's binoculars, which he used now to keep watch. If al-Zumar's people were up the mountain, then they had certainly heard those shots and would send down scouts, not that Arden alerted Shaqib to that possibility because the wiry man might freak out and abandon his task. The translator stood alone outside, shoveling snow atop the three Afghans. Meanwhile, back in the cargo compartment, Navarro stuffed canteens, food, and clothing into his big rucksack.

"You're making another mistake," Arden said. "If al-Zumar's up there, you won't get anywhere near him without a bullet between your eyes."

Navarro flashed that cocksure expression, the one Arden hated the most. "Still think you're not coming, huh?"

"Don't think. Know. I figure we stay here, fire a flare at any low-flying aircraft. Maybe if they see us, they won't drop a cluster bomb on our heads."

"Not before I interview al-Zumar, at least."

Arden cracked a grin in disbelief. "What makes you believe he's really up there? Who knows who these guys were."

"Our little friend outside is what makes me believe. You said he cut a deal with al-Zumar's people. This has all been arranged, and those guys weren't operating in the middle of nowhere without a camp nearby. We're close. We're very, very close."

"What is it with you, man? You just don't stop, do you?"

At that Navarro stopped packing. "You don't get to be me without busting your ass and making sacrifices. And no, I don't stop. Ever. That's why I'm better than the next guy. That's why I get the stories other people are afraid to touch. As an ex-Marine, you should appreciate that."

"There are no ex-Marines."

"Well, excuse me."

Arden shook his head at the man. "You know, some people might say that attitude is what got your crew killed."

"People like you?"

"We make it out of this, you can bet I'll spill my guts. And in case you haven't checked lately, you're already the guy America loves to hate. I'll just be feeding one beast to another. You know how it works."

"Yeah, I do. I'm not the first correspondent to violate the Geneva Convention, and I won't be last. Now we both know I acted in self-defense. They fired the first shots."

"Because you drew your weapon."

"They were stealing our truck."

"No, they weren't. You pulled the gun and made them think that Shaqib had set them up, you asshole."

"You know what? I'm not going to waste my breath defending my actions."

"Don't. But I want you to listen to me good. If you do anything else to endanger my life, I will not hesitate to shoot you."

"You're kidding, right? This from the guy who threatened to shoot me once before—and hesitated. Yeah, you're some fucking bodyguard."

"Yes, I am. I just need to find somebody worth protecting."

"Uh, Mr. John?" Shaqib called. "We have the company."

"What?" Arden called, rising furtively to look up, past the Rover's hood.

Shaqib stood there, hands raised above his head. A young man, an Arab probably, with a short beard and piercing eyes, jabbed an AK into Shaqib's back, while two others, assumedly Arabs as well, trained their rifles on Arden. The young leader shouted something while Shaqib rattled off sentence after sentence, probably explaining who he was and begging for his life.

Alternating his gaze between Shaqib's shovel and the mound of snow, the young leader motioned for Shaqib to dig, and as the translator did, he kept talking, talking a mile a minute, until he uncovered the first Afghan.

After one glimpse at the body, the other two Arabs launched into tirades and waved their rifles.

Arden figured this was it. His trigger finger felt heavier.

Shaqib said something.

The young leader answered, thought a moment, hollered at the others, who didn't look happy.

Snow crunched near Arden's boots, and there was Navarro now huddled behind the Rover's hood, clutching one of the Afghans' rifles. The guy always had to be a wild card, didn't he?

Arden warned Navarro with his eyes, but the reporter just winked and whispered, "They have to be with al-Zumar."

"Shaqib?" Arden sang darkly. "Talk to me."

"It's not good. I tried to tell them that these other three died in the accident, but they don't believe me. The other two want to shoot us."

"And the leader guy?"

"I'm trying to convince him that we're too valuable to shoot."

"Hope that works because you will die in the crossfire. Trust me on that."

An even more motivated Shaqib, his tone almost musical, worked the young leader, and after a long moment, the guy answered softly, and Shaqib called back, "They want you to get rid of your rifle and come out. No funny business."

No funny business? It had been years since Arden had heard that phrase. He decided to call their bluff—

and Shaqib's—with a little funny business of his own.

"Tell them they can shoot you. We don't care."

"Mr. John? Come on, man. You know I did this for my family. You know I think you're a good man. I won't betray you again."

"You heard me, Shaqib. Tell them they can shoot you."

"You want to test me, Mr. John? Then all right. I will tell them. I will not lie."

Shaqib spoke nervously with the young leader, who muttered something, then hollered, "I am Fathi. You come out, we don't shoot anybody. Come out. Let's make a deal."

Whether Fathi had seen the American game show of the same name Arden couldn't be sure, but he uttered the phrase with the baritone and practiced enthusiasm of a real MC.

"We either get into a gunfight with these guys, or we trust them," Navarro said.

Arden closed his eyes, took mental note of the three men, their positions, their rifles. He visualized himself springing up from behind the Rover to fire three times for three precise kills. He filled his lungs with cold air, opened his eyes—

And saw Navarro rounding the Rover, his hands raised in the air. "We're an American news crew," the correspondent said. "I'm Rick Navarro. I've come to interview Mohammed al-Zumar."

Shaqib translated rapidly as, cursing, Arden rose himself, resigned to the fact that Navarro had once again taken a workable situation and turned it into shit. Maybe if Arden shot the reporter, the bad guys would be thrown off-guard, making them ripe targets. Still, there were three of them.

Fathi's two cronies high-stepped through the snow, edging closer to the Rover, their weapons still pointed at Arden. The taller one motioned at the ground with his rifle, and Arden groaned in resignation then placed his weapon on the Rover's side panel. He came around, one hand raised, the other lifted as high as his chest. Any higher and the jabs of pain would come.

But the tall guy didn't like Arden keeping that hand low, probably fearing Arden would reach for a pistol hidden in his coat pocket, a pistol that wasn't there. The tall thug barked something at Arden, waved his rifle up and down.

"I've been shot, you greasy bastard. My whole shoulder's throbbing. And I can't raise my goddamned arm anymore than this. Shaqib? Tell him!"

Shaqib rattled off something, then said, "Okay. It's okay."

The tall guy bore his banana-colored teeth and held his position.

"So who are these ugly bastards?" Arden asked Shaqib.

"They won't say for sure if they work for al-Zumar. But I think they do."

"Tell them we want to see al-Zumar as soon as possible," Navarro said.

"Yeah, and tell them that if they decide to shoot Mr. Navarro here, I'd be happy to help them out," Arden added.

Navarro gave Arden the evil eye.

"Let's make a deal," Fathi repeated. "You go to the sheikh. It's perfect. No one gets shot. Okay?"

"You'll take us to see al-Zumar?" Navarro asked breathlessly.

"Yeah, it's no problem. He wants the interview. You give it." The young man banged his chest. "And I am hero."

"Just what we need, another terrorist hero," Arden muttered.

Fathi took a few steps back from Shaqib but kept his rifle on the translator. The young Arab squinted in thought a moment, then began a heated discussion with his men. It seemed the taller guy had some issues with what he was hearing, but the shorter one wagged his fat head at whatever Fathi was proposing.

"What're they talking about now?" asked Arden.

"I don't know why, Mr. John. But Fathi says they can't call for help and they have to get back."

"Get back where? To their caves?" Navarro asked.

Shaqib shrugged. "They need to get us to al-Zumar, but they don't know how to do it—because they can't come with us."

"Well, tell them to give us directions," Navarro said. "We'll walk, for God's sake."

"And we'll get shot by one of al-Zumar's lookouts," said Arden. "There's a plan right there."

"Why can't they come with us?" Navarro asked.

"I'm not sure. They're doing something else, but they're trying to watch what they say."

Arden raised his brows at Shaqib. "I don't like this

shit one bit. Something's going on. See if you can figure it out."

The Arabs had lifted their voices, and for a moment,
all three regarded Arden, Navarro, and Shaqib.

"What are they talking about now?" Navarro asked.

"They're fighting over using the radio," Shaqib answered. "Fathi will not call."

"Why not?" Arden asked.

"I don't know." Shaqib lowered his voice, leaned toward Arden. "I did hear something."

"About using the radio?"

"No, Mr. John. You don't understand."

"Well, I'm standing right here," Arden said, his
frustration warming his icy cheeks. "Why don't you
tell me?"

"They did use one word you should know."

"What's that?"

Shaqib took a long, shivery breath. "Ambush."

DELTA EAGLE SEVEN
EN ROUTE TO EXTRACTION POINT STINGRAY
NORTHWEST FRONTIER PROVINCE
PAKISTAN
0415 HOURS LOCAL TIME

Piloting a twenty-year-old UH-1N Huey slick through a
snowstorm in the middle of the night might sound like
treacherous duty, but Capt. Tom Graham, 1st Lt. Martha
Ingram, and their crew of two enlisted men had complete faith in their aircraft and in the skills of all those

who serviced her. The four Marines thundered through the night at 105 knots, skimming along the treetops, with Graham holding tight as the Pratt and Whitney engine whined against the buffeting winds. Stripped of machine guns and rocket pods to keep the bird fast and light, as well as extend its range, the Huey's strength, like a Force Recon Team's, hinged on its ability to remain undetected. The bird could slip in low under enemy radar and land in those areas impossible to reach by conventional ground vehicles. And, as Graham had been told countless times, he was a Force Recon Marine's second-best friend, next to his rifle. Graham was a green angel dropping down through the red smoke. He was a sight for sore eyes.

And saving the day never got old.

The captain checked his instruments, adjusted his boots on the pedals, then course-corrected once more as a particularly nasty gust struck the Huey's portside. "Anything?" he asked Ingram, whose gaze remained on the new thermal imaging system's display.

"Nada. And do they really think we're going to find a lost news crew in this?"

"Stranger things have happened."

"Yeah, like my brother getting to fly Cobras," Graham said.

"Thought that was old news. I never pegged you for the jealous type."

"I'm not. It's just that he loves rubbing my nose in it, keeps telling me how much better his bird is." Graham sighed deeply. "I'll flip him the bird next chance I get."

"And I'll remind him that we operate the most

widely used helicopter in the world and fly missions that are a lot more dangerous than his because we're not sitting atop all that firepower. We're sitting on a big, fat gas tank."

"He won't get it. Never has. Never will. You don't have any kid brothers, do you?"

"Only child."

"You're lucky."

"Oh, come on, Tommy. Penis envy is one thing, but Cobra envy? And you know, Brad getting to fly Cobras doesn't mean he's any better than you. You got ten years on him, ten years that no one can take away. And you got real combat experience. So there it is."

"Thanks, Mom. My Cobra envy is gone, completely gone, I tell you."

"Good. Because Marine Corps chopper pilots do not whine. It just ain't in the job description."

"You know I wouldn't say this to anyone else."

"Which bothers me, Tommy. You're always giving me way too much information. Jack says I know you better than him, and he's my husband, for god's sake."

"Hey, I didn't know that. I'm sorry. I'll keep the venting to a minimum."

"Maybe you need a shrink."

"Or a wife."

"No kidding. If I had a dollar for every complaint I've heard from Jack, I'd be sitting on some beach somewhere, sipping rum out of a coconut shell."

"And where would Jack be?"

She hesitated. "Look, just clear your head. No doubt

that even with all this snow, the zone will be hot. Real hot."

"Won't be the first time Rainey's phoned home from Hell."

"Yeah, and he always says he's buying, but just like the last time, we wound up paying for all the drinks." Her tone grew serious. "When he gets onboard, I'm going to remind him."

Graham read her fear. "Hey, don't worry. He'll make the rendezvous."

TEAM DOGMA
EN ROUTE TO EXTRACTION POINT STINGRAY
NORTHWEST FRONTIER PROVINCE
PAKISTAN
0500 HOURS LOCAL TIME

Special amphibious recon corpsman HM2 Glenroy "Doc" Leblanc hated being stereotyped as "the triple B": the big, bald, black guy. That's just what he was on the outside, but many people had a hard time getting past that. They told him he looked like this Hollywood actor or that one, and that if he ever chose to leave the Corps, he should study acting or even become a technical advisor on military films. Doc had little interest in that. If he ever left the Corps, he knew he'd go work as a paramedic back home in Miami, where he was born, though he had been raised on the island of Martinique until he was twelve. Doc carried with him the lessons and stories taught to him by his grandfather, and he often began a story with "cric, crac," the introductory call used to begin tales. Doc's ancestors had worked in the cane fields of Martinique, and he had seen old photographs of them standing outside their little huts called *ajoupa* and looking so tired, so very, very tired. They had had to face not only the ignorance and poverty of plantation life, but had to learn to preserve who they were on an island where the French culture saturated everything. Knowing their stories made Doc empathize with the locals he and the others encountered in Pakistan and Afghanistan. While he had had a pampered life when compared to those tribal peoples, he knew quite well that had he been born a century earlier, he might be living on a dirt street lined with shacks, and he might be hacking at cane himself.

But you would never know what lay hidden in the big, bald, black guy's head unless you asked. Some took him for an inner-city linebacker who had flunked out of high school because he had a low IQ, had no father figure in his life, and had spent too much time listening to hip hop. They assumed he had wobbled down to his local Navy recruiter and had enlisted because it was either that or life as distribution executive of illegal pharmaceuticals. They didn't know that his grandfather still practiced medicine back on Martinique. They didn't know that his father, mother, and two sisters ran a hugely successful dry-cleaning business in South Beach. They had no idea that Navy corpsmen assigned to Force Reconnaissance companies are a special breed, that they are some of the hardest guys in a group of very hard guys.

Doc's pipeline had run a remarkable seventy-two weeks, not including travel and administrative time. He had attended the seven-week Field Medical Service School at Camp Pendelton, the twelve-week Basic Reconnaissance Course, the three-week Basic Airborne Course, and the eight-week Combatant Diver Course. From there he had shipped off to more specific schools like the Amphibious Reconnaissance Corpsman Diving Medicine Course at Panama City, Florida, and the twenty-four-week Special Operations Combat Medics Course at Fort Bragg. And, finally, Doc had met the vigorous challenges facing him at the famous 18-D course also at Fort Bragg, where he had learned to independently assess and provide medical care for a variety of conditions and injuries. He could even perform minor surgery. If that weren't enough, he had joined third platoon during Phase 2 iteration and had gone through the exact same training as every other member of the team. Despite not having a degree, he liked to joke that given all of his training, he now had a doctorate in destruction.

At the moment, though, he wished he had a degree in sprinting through high snow because he was fast losing his breath while trying to keep up with McAllister, Rainey, and Houston as they cut a path through a series of foothills stretching off toward the forest below. The fact that his Para SAW weighed over fifteen pounds, not including the ANIPEQ-2 infrared laser illuminator and aiming device, probably had something to do with that.

A series of explosions in the distance drove McAllister to signal a halt.

"There go the Warthogs," Rainey said over the tactical frequency. "Better late than never."

"I hope we accomplished something here," said Houston. "I hope we're not running for our lives so we could blow up a couple of huts."

"You can stow that right now," Rainey spat. "Terry? Let's move out."

Doc glanced back to Vance, who had hunkered down to inspect the ridge behind them through his night-vision scope.

"Anything?" Doc asked.

"Not yet. But they're back there. Wait. All right. Got one. And there's another." Vance quickly reported his finding to Rainey, who acknowledged and urged them on.

"How many you think?" Doc asked Vance.

"Two. Twenty. A hundred. Between the snow, this ridge, the foothills, the trees, there's just too much cover. When we get to Stingray, I'm hoping we get a chance to take out some of these guys before we rally on the chopper, otherwise they'll pick us off like we're in a PlayStation Two game."

"No doubt. Let's get out of here."

At least the storm had let up, if only a little. The wind had certainly died, and save for their boots thumping through the snow, the foothills took on the atmosphere of a morgue, everything frozen in time and space, with ancient spirits passing through boulders and trees. McAllister would appreciate that comparison. Houston would just shudder it off. Vance would relate it to an ice-fishing trip in Minnesota. Rainey would say that this is one morgue we need to fill with bodies. They were vastly different people, all right, but when they came together on a mission, they were like parts of a single consciousness working with fluid and deadly precision.

Doc took in a long gulp of the icy air, his breath coming warm and thick as he sidestepped over some meter-high rocks whose brown-and-beige backs shone through the snow. Though his legs were beginning to cramp, he vowed to keep his pace. He wouldn't be the one to ask for a break, especially after just getting one. As a kid when riding his bike uphill, he had always taken his father's advice: keep your head low, don't look up, and keep pedaling. So he fixed his gaze on the footprints ahead, and, squinting through the gloom, he marched on through the pain, his breath keeping time as he told himself that he had to get home for his family. He would be a selfish bastard if he gave up and got himself killed.

To pass the time, he went over practice parameters for gunshot wounds, for broken ankles, for every injury he could imagine that someone on the team might sustain. He mentally sifted through all of his medical supplies, his drug box, and reminded himself that he had taken along as much as he could hack. God forbid he ran out of something in the field. He could not live with the guilt of knowing a fellow Marine had died because Doc hadn't been willing to pack something extra. He boasted that his ruck was heavier than anyone else's, even McAllister's, but when the gauntlet had been dropped, McAllister had refused to let his pack be weighed, and he would never explain why. He had simply bought Doc a round, and that was that.

Well, here I am, Doc thought, having run out of mental check lists. *Stuck in the 'stan, as they say. Predawn. Zero-dark-thirty and feeling fine. Liar. My knees are wobbling. Somebody better call for a halt, or this is one badass black man who is going down.*

Forty steps later, the signal to halt still had not come, but at least they were heading down a fairly steep slope instead of up one, and it felt good to just slide a little, slide a little more—

And shit, Doc slipped, twisted his ankle, then went rolling down the slope, one arm flailing, the other gripping his Para SAW. Never mind the ice in his face and the rocky ground striking his chest and back like a WWF wrestler. Never mind the gear popping loose from his vest and his bush cover flying off. Never mind all of it. He had let the others down, damn it.

07

"Oh, man. Doc? Doc?" McAllister called back.

"Yo, Doc?" Vance hollered.

Even as Rainey turned his head, he reacted, breaking off the path and charging sideways across the slope to reach the corpsman, who made a final roll, landing flat on his back, a veil of snow draping over him.

"I'm good to go," Doc said, reaching up with fingerless gloves to brush off his eyes and cheeks. "No problem. I'm good to go."

Ignoring a sudden and tightening knot in his stomach, Rainey braced himself. "You're the corpsman, man. Talk to me."

"Nothing broken and nothing to talk about."

Rainey seized the man's wrists and hauled him quickly to his feet. "You sure you're good?"

"I'm good."

"Here you go, Doc," Vance said, handing over the Para SAW.

Doc winced. "I didn't bust up old Betty, did I?"

"I don't think so," Vance said.

"All right, no more time for bodysurfing. We need to haul some serious ass," Rainey said.

And that set Vance and Doc in motion. In the meantime, Houston and McAllister, who had remained up the slope, were just dropping to their bellies.

"What do you got, Five?" Rainey demanded over the radio.

"I've finally tagged them. Got six so far. Probably more. Maybe another team just south. And the party kicks into high gear once we reach Stingray."

"Range?"

"About twelve hundred meters."

"Too close for comfort."

"Close enough for killing."

Rainey cleared his throat. "All right, gentlemen. On your horses!" As he sidestepped up the hill, he kept his gaze on Doc. The corpsman was doing his best to hide his new limp, but you couldn't fool an old Recon Marine like Mac Rainey.

Arden, Navarro, and Shaqib shifted wearily toward a quartet of pines whose limbs creaked in the breeze. The Arabs followed closely, and occasionally, Fathi issued directions to a bleary-eyed Shaqib, whom Navarro had recruited to carry the late Paul Hopps's camera. God forbid Mr. Celebrity Reporter should meet the world's most wanted man and not be prepared. Reluctantly, Shaqib had shouldered the camera and had slipped on the heavy gear vest within which Hopps had stored spare batteries and a spaghetti of wires.

Before they had left the Rover, Fathi and the two other Arabs had spent a few minutes tearing through the cargo compartment, pocketing what they could: money, food, candy, and, of course, the greatest commodity of all—toilet paper. Fathi had stuffed three rolls in a small knapsack, along with the magazines from the Afghans' rifles, then he had ordered the shorter Arab to carry those weapons, seven rifles in all, though Arden suspected that Fathi had missed one or two stuffed beneath the big anvil cases. Whether he carried seven rifles or nine, the short guy wasn't thrilled with shouldering all that weaponry, and the weight slowed him considerably. If Arden were to make a move, he would first leap on the short Arab, seize the guy's weapon, shoot him point-blank, and, using the man's body for cover, make Fathi the next target, followed by the tall Arab. Sounded like a plan, but Arden doubted he could pull it off without Navarro and Shaqib. Would they help? No way. They had their own agendas. And Arden had his: stay alive and get the hell out of there.

Tossing a glance to the tall Arab whose gaze seemed distant, Arden shifted up closer to Navarro. "Have you noticed we're just working our way through these foothills?"

"Yeah, so?"

"We're not heading up the mountain."

Navarro shrugged, kept his gaze ahead. "Means nothing."

"Shit. You going to believe me now, or do the bullets have to fly?"

"Maybe al-Zumar's coming down to meet us."

"You idiot. If he hasn't moved out of here already, he's a heartbeat away from taking off. And I bet he knows that ground troops are close. These guys aren't taking us to see al-Zumar. They don't know what to do with us."

"So Shaqib heard the word ambush. So fucking what? I'm not subscribing to your paranoia, Mr. Arden. No, I don't trust these guys, but they're all we got. So let's see where this ride takes us."

Fathi stage-whispered a command, and Shaqib translated the order: "Shut up!"

Arden tossed back a dirty look, then shook his head at Navarro. Damn it, he wasn't paranoid. Al-Zumar's people were setting up an ambush for either Pakistani marines, British commandoes, or U.S. forces. Fathi and the other thugs were clearly involved, and if they were returning to their positions . . .

Then again, they wouldn't be that stupid, would they? They wouldn't drag a valuable American news crew into the middle of an ambush. Arden considered what he'd do, were he Fathi. He wouldn't leave the news crew in the danger zone. He would have them taken out of the crossfire and maybe up to the caves. That was the most logical solution. But Arden wasn't dealing with men of logic.

A birdlike whistle broke the silence. Another whistle came from somewhere ahead, and Fathi answered with a whistle of his own, then called out something.

Slowly, a figure emerged from behind a tree. Fathi double-timed toward the figure, speaking quickly and gesturing to the forest, then up the mountain.

"Shaqib?" Arden called.

The tall Arab swung his rifle on Arden. "Shut up."

"You're a quick study."

"Shut up!"

Arden turned to Shaqib. "Can you hear what they're saying?"

Something flashed in Arden's peripheral vision, and he shifted his head fractionally. An AK's muzzle hung just a few inches from his forehead.

"Fucking shut up!" the tall Arab cried.

"I can't hear them, Mr. John," Shaqib said, his voice quavering. "But it's better we don't talk."

Arden grinned crookedly at the butt-ugly man behind the rifle. "Yeah."

Navarro suddenly walked off toward Fathi, the shorter Arab hollering for him to halt. Arden called the reporter's name, but the idiot ignored the warning and the rifle trained on his back. He waved to Fathi and approached, saying, "Okay, let's make a deal? We made a deal. Now where is the sheikh?"

Whether Fathi understood the question or not didn't seem to matter. He ripped a pistol from the figure's holster and shoved it in Navarro's face.

The courageous war correspondent raised his hands. "Uh, Shaqib? Tell him I'm sorry for insulting him, if that's what I've done. Tell him I want to see al-Zumar."

Sloughing off the camera and letting it fall to the snow, Shaqib offered Navarro's request, then listened attentively as Fathi gave what might be an explanation, Arden couldn't tell. Still, Fathi kept the pistol on Navarro, and Arden had to admit that he enjoyed seeing the reporter squirm.

"What's he saying?" Navarro asked.

"He says you should do what he says and you get to see al-Zumar. If you don't, he shoots you. He says he's willing to accept the sheikh's wrath if you don't follow his orders. He's says he's changing the deal."

"Tell him that's fine with me," Navarro said. "Tell him I've come a long way for this, but I'm not a very patient man."

Shaqib did, and Fathi lowered the pistol but got directly in Navarro's face. The young Arab uttered something, the words steely, forceful.

"He says you are rude," Shaqib translated. "And you look taller on TV."

Before Navarro could respond, Fathi issued orders to the tall Arab, who pointed toward a slope paralleling the forest.

"We're going up there?" Arden asked.

"Up there," the Arab repeated.

Arden sighed exhaustedly and started off as Shaqib made a face and bent down to fetch the camera.

Navarro joined Arden, saying, "These barbaric fuckers notwithstanding, I will get that interview with al-Zumar."

"I know you will," Arden said. "But in the afterlife."

"Meaning you'll have failed as a bodyguard. Again." With a snort, Navarro plodded ahead.

Shaqib caught up with Arden, and they braved the slope for about thirty minutes, reaching a narrow, icy precipice, where the tall Arab ordered them to halt. Fathi and the other Arab had remained behind, and it seemed Mr. Banana Teeth would be their guard. The snow had all but tapered off, the zephyrs falling into a gentle breeze. The Arab stole a moment to fish around in his pockets, producing a pack of cigarettes and a lighter. He offered a cigarette to Arden, who declined, but Shaqib snatched one for himself and, following a few words with the man, announced that Mr. Banana Teeth's name was, in fact, Haroun. They lit up, and Arden hoped that Haroun's addiction might give away their location to whomever was coming.

"Ask him how much farther," Navarro told Shaqib.

After a few words with Haroun, Shaqib said, "We are here."

"What do you mean?"

"We stay here until Fathi comes for us."

Arden scratched his stubbly jaw as it all hit home. "Shit, man. They're setting up the ambush down there, and we got press-box seats."

Shaqib muttered a few words to Haroun, who suddenly ditched his cigarette and jabbed Shaqib with the business end of his rifle.

"What?" Arden asked.

"I don't know. Maybe I say something wrong," Shaqib said. "My Arabic is sometimes not good."

"What were you trying to tell him?" asked Navarro.

"I just asked him the truth about the ambush."

Arden nodded. "I think he got the message." Narrowing his gaze on Haroun, Arden asked, "Who's coming? Americans? Are you setting up an ambush for Americans?"

Haroun said something, then spat in the snow.

Shaqib sighed, pulling his collar tighter about his neck. "He called you an infidel, Mr. John."

"Tell him I'm the infidel who's going to send him to Hell."

"Mr. John, we don't want—"

"Never mind, Shaqib. Don't say anything. All I know is, there are three of us and one of him."

"Forget it," said Navarro. "This is as close as we've ever come. I'm not blowing it now."

Arden lowered his voice to funeral depths. "Then I'll do it alone."

"Shut fucking mouths," said Haroun, a fresh cigarette dangling from his lips. He sat cross-legged on the snow, his AK held close to his camouflage jacket as he put a finger to his lips. "We wait."

Smiling at Haroun, Arden put a finger to his lips and muttered, "I'm going to shoot you in the head. Twice. Okay?"

Haroun mimicked Arden. "Okay."

"Shaqib, come here with that camera," Navarro ordered. "I'm going to make you a cameraman. Something happens down there, maybe we can catch it for the people back home."

WOLF NEWS STUDIO
ATLANTA, GEORGIA
2005 HOURS LOCAL TIME

"In case you've just joined us, we have breaking news from Pakistan. According to military officials at Camp Liberty Bell, our own Rick Navarro and his news crew have been listed as missing. Let's toss it to Tamira Gibbs, who's standing by at Camp Liberty Bell. Tamira?"

Anchor Steve June rolled his pen between his fingers and glanced past camera A to where the monitor showed Tamira Gibbs giving her report outside a long row of olive-drab tents. The bitch, with man arms because she worked out too much, overenunciated her words and spoke in a tone so exaggerated that June found it too much to bear, especially since she didn't know any more than he did and was bullshitting her way through the piece. But June's producer demanded live coverage from Pakistan to create a sense of urgency and to have Gibbs pout sexily as she expressed her false worry over her missing comrade.

And so they fed the beast what it wanted.

About thirty seconds passed, and June was so absent from Gibbs's report that he missed his cue and suddenly snapped to as his producer shouted through his earpiece, "Back to you, Steve! Going to commercial."

"All right, then. Tamira Gibbs reporting from Camp Liberty Bell in Northern Pakistan. We'll return to this breaking news right after these messages."

June let his shoulders slump and reached for his eleventh cup of coffee as Newford, one of the sports analysts, came over to the desk with a clipboard in hand. "Twenty bucks gets you in the pool. It's over a grand already. Nothing to sneeze at. Largest one yet, Steve. You in or what? Come on. I need a decision here."

"I want to know what I'm betting on."

"Whoever comes closest to the day and time they find Navarro's body wins."

June thought a moment. "Whoa, hold on here. You got a problem. What if he makes it out alive?"

"Well, we're not real worried about that. We figure that once those terrorists get to know Rick the way we do, they won't keep him alive for too long. But if for some crazy reason he actually does survive, then we're going with the day and time he's rescued."

"Christ, the man's missing. He could be dead. And you fucking people are taking bets? This is disgusting," June said as he fished a twenty out of his wallet.

"No one's picked Tuesday yet," Newford said.

June handed over the bill. "Okay. Tuesday's good. Eight P.M. Dead or alive."

AL-ZUMAR CAVE COMPLEX
NORTHWEST FRONTIER PROVINCE
PAKISTAN
0615 HOURS LOCAL TIME

Although al-Zumar sensed that Allah was close and was watching every move he made, al-Zumar's prayers seemed to have fallen on deaf ears. Those icy fingers still clawed at his heart, and the premonition of something terrible to come grew stronger, coming on with the ferocity of winter in the Hindu Kush Mountains.

"Are we ready to move?" al-Zumar asked Shaykh as they walked through a cave where they had stored their spare munitions.

The old man stroked his beard. "Yes, but still no word from Fathi or that reconnaissance team with the news crew."

"Once they do ambush the Americans, we will use the diversion to move quickly. I wish to take only ten of my bodyguards, including Fathi."

"Understood. The smaller our party, the smaller our chances of being seen. The others will remain behind to fight until they are martyred." Shaykh threw an arm over al-Zumar's shoulder. "All right, then. We will finish our preparations. However, we will have to travel by foot until we reach the valley."

"We have no mule team?"

Shaykh shook his head.

"So we walk," al-Zumar cried in defiance. "Let the entire American army try to catch us. We will just . . . walk away."

TEAM DOGMA
EXTRACTION POINT STINGRAY
QUADRANT E2C
NORTHWEST FRONTIER PROVINCE
PAKISTAN
0630 HOURS LOCAL TIME

Think. Move. Communicate. Think. Move. Communicate.

Rainey used to consider himself in good shape for his age, but at the moment, his legs felt like flaming rubber and his heart chugged like the misfiring engine of his first car, a 1971 Dodge Dart. He wouldn't even consider his back. After the mission he'd get a job ringing bells in Notre Dame.

But the pain reminded him of the good news: he was still alive, still able to think, move, communicate.

He had wanted to reach the extraction point before daybreak, and he had announced that intention to the team. Sunrise would occur in just a few minutes. And in just a few minutes they would reach the forest perimeter, penetrate a quarter klick to the clearing, and blow the smoke.

One look at his team told him enough. He had pushed

each man to his limit—and then some. The red-faced Houston coughed and gasped for air. Big Doc still tried to hide that limp, but it was there, the sting creeping into his eyes. McAllister's face had gone to cold stone, and whenever he wore that walking-dead expression, you'd best leave him alone. Finally, even young Vance, the always dependable Vance, seemed icy, winded, and preoccupied. Rainey kept reminding himself that these were hard men. They could take it. But it was hard to ignore their faces, hard to ignore the fact that once they reached the perimeter, old Murphy and his laws might take over and turn a fast extraction into an even faster bloodbath.

McAllister called for the next halt. Somewhere out past the clearing came a distinct and welcome thumping. Rainey scrambled up to Houston and seized the radio's mike. "Delta Eagle Seven, this is Dogma One, over."

"Dogma One, this is Delta Eagle Seven, over."

"Seven, we have Point Stingray in sight. Our ETA five minutes, over."

"Roger, One. Our ETA approximately ten minutes, the clearing to our port side, over."

"We'll be off your starboard. Turn forty-five and approach. LZ will be hot, over."

"Roger, One. See you boys on the ground. Delta Eagle Seven, out."

"Sergeant, you ever get a bad feeling about an extraction?" Houston asked, probing the trees through his scope. "'Cause this one's making me sick."

Rainey made a face. "Well, Corporal, I'm sorry the situation and accommodations don't meet your high standards."

"Sergeant, I didn't mean—"

Rainey waved off Houston, then gave McAllister the high sign. Hunched over, his team darted one by one toward the next cluster of pines, the chopper's incessant thumping growing loud, much too loud, and sending chills down Rainey's spine.

WOLF NEWS CREW
NORTHWEST FRONTIER PROVINCE
PAKISTAN
0630 HOURS LOCAL TIME

That's a Huey slick, thought Arden. He would bet his last dollar that Fathi's ambush was meant for United States Marines, probably a Force Recon unit trying to extract.

And there was no way in hell that Arden would permit his brothers to be slaughtered. He hazarded a glance at Haroun, who sat about three meters away, long-faced, his AK still held firmly in both hands, his attention riveted on the chopper zooming in above the treetops. Navarro and Shaqib sat off to the Arab's left, and Shaqib still toyed with the camera, his gaze focused through the eyepiece as he tried to get a clean shot of the chopper.

"You getting it?" Navarro asked for the nth time. "You getting it?"

Plotting ten different ways to kill Haroun, every one of them scaring the hell out of Arden, he opted for the first plan, probably the most dangerous one. He bolted up, ripped the camera away from Shaqib, and, with his shoulder aching, reared back and came at Haroun.

The Arab whirled, releasing a triplet of rounds that cut wide as Arden used the camera like a bat to whack him solidly in the head.

Haroun fell back and squeezed off another salvo before Arden dropped the camera and clenched the man's throat. While Arden had killed men before, he had never stared point-blank into the enemy's eyes, had never known killing as intimately.

"What the hell are you doing?" Navarro cried, sliding an arm beneath Arden's chin then locking it around his neck. "He's our ticket to al-Zumar!"

Screaming something, Shaqib grabbed Haroun's rifle and tried to rip it from the man's hand.

"Let him go!" Navarro wailed. "And Jesus, did you damage the camera?"

Arden squeezed harder, and even if he didn't kill Haroun before Navarro could pull him off, he knew one thing: if there were Marines in the valley below, they had heard the shots. That was enough.

TEAM DOGMA
EXTRACTION POINT STINGRAY
QUADRANT E2C
NORTHWEST FRONTIER PROVINCE
PAKISTAN
0631 HOURS LOCAL TIME

At the sound of gunfire from above, Vance hit the snowy deck, rolled to seek cover behind a pine, then hoisted up his big sniper rifle and searched for the source. Pines dotted the slope, and it was far too steep to reveal every nook and cranny. He saw nothing, heard nothing—

Until multiple rounds splintered the limbs just above him, tore through the snow, dug little paths parallel to his boot prints. And while Hell was still breaking loose, Vance realized with a start that those rounds weren't coming from the bad guys on their tail.

"Got them at about two hundred meters out, over," Doc reported coolly over the tactical frequency. He flinched as two rounds did a Black-and-Decker job on the tree to his left shoulder. Fire superiority might be the best combat medicine, but Doc had a terrible feeling that his skills as a corpsman were going to prove more valuable than his skills as a shooter. Nevertheless, he settled the Para SAW onto its bipod and hoped that at any second Rainey would allow him to unleash the lead dogs of war at a cyclic rate of 750 rounds per minute, a rate that would turn any backsliding Muslim into a devout follower.

Yet even if the automatic weapons fire gave the bad guys pause, Doc had still counted fire originating from at least a half-dozen positions ahead. And the enemy fighters behind them had not even opened up. Rainey would give the order. They needed suppressing fire to cover their run to the clearing, a run that posed even more problems. The ground sloped down only a few degrees, and save for the thinning stands of pines, there wasn't much cover. Maybe Rainey would call off the chopper, drive them to the high ground. Doc didn't know.

"All right, Doc. Finish your mag. But no more," Rainey said. "Drive them right. Meanwhile, the rest of you rally left, up to the clearing. And Houston, you tell that flyboy to get his ass down here. Let's do it!"

08

Captain Tom Graham thought he saw movement between the trees below, but he couldn't be sure. The shadows were still long, the sky an oppressive gray, and between the snowdrifts and the fettered canopy, his eyes could very well have tricked him.

"Where the hell's their smoke?" Ingram asked.

"See if you can spot them," Graham said, his gaze flicking to the thermal-imaging display. "Dogma One, this is Delta Eagle Seven, over."

Dead air.

"Dogma One, this is Delta Eagle Seven, over."

Before Graham could listen for a reply, Ingram cut in. "Whoa, I got maybe ten combatants down there, maybe more." She rapped a knuckle on the display. "Got another handful on the other side of the forest.

Looks like our boys are right in the middle."

"Screw this. We aren't waiting for smoke." Graham banked hard to right, decreasing altitude at an alarming rate and making his final approach for the clearing. He would like to see his brother take the Huey's controls and do the same without suffering a heart attack. What the kid knew about seat-of-the-pants flying would fill the head of a pin.

"Delta Eagle Seven, this is Dogma Three, over."

Now you answer, damn it. "Three, we're coming down on the LZ, over."

"Seven, we are taking heavy enemy fire but are en route, over."

"Dogma Three, we are—"

"Oh, shit!" Ingram cried.

Graham swung his head to port and saw a flash rising from the trees, an agonizingly familiar flash, a flash that had rocket-propelled grenade written all over it.

WOLF NEWS CREW
NORTHWEST FRONTIER PROVINCE
PAKISTAN
0640 HOURS LOCAL TIME

Arden would not release his death grip on Haroun, despite the explosion resounding in the distance.

"Let him go," Navarro hollered, increasing his own chokehold.

Growing lightheaded, Arden ignored the reporter and closed his eyes, intent on finishing off the terrorist scumbag beneath him. Just another few seconds . . .

Haroun gasped, gurgled, and his legs writhed as he tried to pry Arden's hands free. But Arden swore that it would take Allah himself to remove those hands from the Arab's throat.

"Mr. John," Shaqib said. "I have the rifle. You don't have to kill him."

"Don't you get it?" Navarro added. "If you kill him, they might kill us before we get near al-Zumar!"

Arden craned his head against Navarro's grasp, saw that Shaqib did, indeed, have the weapon.

"Let him go," Navarro rasped.

TEAM DOGMA
EXTRACTION POINT STINGRAY
QUADRANT E2C
NORTHWEST FRONTIER PROVINCE
PAKISTAN
0640 HOURS LOCAL TIME

Tanking down air and charging through the snow, Houston nearly stopped as the events before him smacked home. About three hundred meters ahead, up in the clearing, the Huey, its tail rotor blown completely off, listed with a surreal slowness to port.

No, this wasn't happening. Couldn't be. No one could shoot down their bird. They were Marines. United States Marines! They were supermen. Invincible. Heartbreakers, ass-kickers, life-takers. Houston had ignored the old timers, the guys who told him that he wasn't a God, that he was a fragile being, and that the only way he'd keep himself alive was to be smart. Suddenly, those old guys were right. They weren't supermen, and al-Zumar's assholes had blown up their ride!

Twenty feet. Fifteen. Ten. Five. The Huey hit ground on one skid, the other still hanging as the rotors tilted precariously toward the snow and a string of pines.

Reconsidering that career as a real estate man, Houston willed himself on, hearing old Doc's Para SAW rattling and spewing shell casings. Ahead, the Huey's rotors finally burrowed into the snow a moment, whipping up a snow cloud before they snapped off and boomeranged away. The entire flying machine fell in a smoking heap onto its port side, the mist backlit by orange flames licking along the fuselage.

"Oh, shit," he muttered aloud, dropping to his haunches. "Oh, shit . . ."

The cockpit still looked intact. Had to be survivors in there. Had to be. Figuring Rainey would order them to rally on the Huey, Houston broke left, bounded for a tree—

And found himself running directly toward a turbaned gunman raising his rifle.

Bad guy. Instincts now. React! Dive. Elbows hitting. Fire! Fire! Fire!

With arms growing steely, Houston lay on his gut and tried to keep his aim true. He caught the guy in the groin, then the hip, and, fearing that he would be shot as the thug fell, he rolled once, his big ruck and radio jabbing hard as he came around and fired again.

Shivering through the adrenaline rush, Houston stole

a glance up. Got the guy. One dead mother. On to the next. What was that? Someone crunched through the snow behind him. He wanted to whirl, tried, felt incredibly weak.

Hands dug beneath his armpits, and abruptly Houston was on his feet.

"They got the chopper," Vance said, winded, his expression torn.

"I saw it! I saw it! Shit, man. Where's the sergeant?"

"Dunno. Thought you knew. I lost him."

"Come on!"

Reaching into a part of himself he didn't know was there, Houston found new strength. He hustled off with Vance at his shoulder.

"Got five moving in from the east side on the chopper," Rainey reported over the radio. "Can't get to it. All of you rally up the slope directly west of the crash site. I see some boulders up there, over."

Doc acknowledged, then came Houston's turn. He did what he could to keep the tremors out of his voice. The other operators sounded cool, but if they were anything like Houston, they were repeatedly reminding themselves that this wasn't a training exercise, that every move counted, that mistakes would get you killed.

As Houston ran, he couldn't help but sweep his gaze right, where about fifty yards off, a trio of terrorists dodged from one cluster of pines to another.

"Hit the deck!" he told Vance a second before the salvos tore over their heads.

With snow mounded up to his chin, Houston leveled his rifle and took aim. Just like on the range, he told himself. He sighted the first bad guy, watched him drop under Vance's remarkable shooting. Sighted the next guy. Vance dropped him, too, just as the guy leaned out from his tree. Houston found the third shooter, a big man clad in a tattered corduroy jacket, and squeezed off three rounds to drop the man before he could fully lift his rifle.

"Nice," Vance said, then nodded toward a big hunk of the chopper's tail rotor that had been thrown about twenty meters away. "Ready?"

They pushed up on their hands and knees, then stormed for the meager cover. They got about halfway there when the pop-pop of AKs sounded and the rounds began whistling through their wake.

Swearing against the ankle-high snow and the bulk on his back, Houston once more reached into his reserves to get to that tail rotor, and as he lunged for it, something snapped at his ear and blew his bush cover clean off. He dropped to his belly, a meter shy of the wreckage, grabbed the cover, glanced over his shoulder, saw a hole in his ruck, realized a round had penetrated the canvas and had arrowed up, taking his bush cover with it. He pushed a finger through the hole in the bush cover's rim. Just a few inches to the right, and Dad's real estate firm could purchase some farmland.

Ignoring a sudden flurry of incoming, Vance seized him by the back of his vest and hauled him behind the still-smoldering rotor section. "Are you hit? Are you hit?"

"I'm okay," Houston answered.

The fisherman dropped to one knee then squeezed off three more rounds. "Got yourself a fine souvenir there."

Houston slapped the bush cover onto his head. Yup, the boys of third platoon would marvel over the new guy's "lucky" and "holy" cover.

Crinkling his nose at a burning stench mixed with aircraft fuel, Houston sent his gaze skyward. A pillar of black smoke rose above the treetops, marking the crash site. He picked out their rally path directly west. "Point is up there. I think I see the boulders. Ready when you are."

Vance lowered his rifle, caught his breath. His glassy eyes and red nose might be symptomatic of the cold air, but they still made him look as frightened as Houston felt.

"Are we going to make it?" Houston blurted out.

"Shit," Vance said in an exaggerated hillbilly cadence. "There's a twenty-pound lunker back home with my name on him. We ain't dying here. No way. No how. *Vamos.*"

"You're the man, Vance."

The sharpshooter winked. "Yup. The *fisher*-man."

K-9 PATROL
NORTHWEST FRONTIER PROVINCE
PAKISTAN
0640 HOURS LOCAL TIME

Malik, a man who considered himself one of the sheikh's finest lieutenants, a man smarter and wiser than that impetuous Fathi, drove his men into the thick of battle. It was a fine day to be martyred, and he was ready to kiss the virgins' hands in Paradise.

Releasing blood-curdling cries, the group charged into the forest, firing madly, firing at anything that moved. They were prophets teaching a hard lesson to the infidels. And within Malik's men lay the fury of their ancestors, men who had raged over these same mountains and had shed their blood for their families, for their beliefs.

As they advanced toward the perimeter, Malik's stomach churned as they swept past one, two, three, four dead men. He was witnessing the work of experienced killers, the work of American Marines.

Muzzle flashes stole his attention, and he darted left to a tree while triggering rounds in the direction of the incoming. Someone cried out—in Arabic. A man dropped face-forward in the snow.

A realization more icy than anything Mother Nature could throw at him struck Malik so hard that he had to blink to be sure. He and his men had been firing at Fathi's ambush team, the one the sheikh himself had warned him about. His mouth fell open as he wondered just how many of their own people his group had killed.

"What are you doing? You madman!" Fathi cried, rushing out from behind the trees to Malik's left.

"We received no radio contact from you. We didn't know you were here!"

"You lie! The sheikh himself told you. And now in attacking us, your people are letting them get away! They're driving to the high ground!"

Unable to respond, Malik decided that his failure would not reach the sheikh's ears. He trained his rifle on Fathi.

"You want to shoot me like a dog?" Fathi asked. "You go ahead."

Malik did not see the other man off to his right until a terrible boom from that direction sent him crashing to the snow, warm blood pouring from his neck.

Where are the virgins? he thought.

CAMP LIBERTY BELL
FIFTH FORCE RECONNAISSANCE COMPANY
THIRD PLATOON HEADQUARTERS
NORTHWEST FRONTIER PROVINCE
PAKISTAN
0645 HOURS LOCAL TIME

Delta Eagle Seven's Mayday had sent chills knifing through Sgt. Kady Forrest. Rainey and his team were running across a snow-covered valley, pursued by God knew how many of al-Zumar's fighters, and they needed more than anything to extract.

Could it get any worse? For the first time since she had known him, Kady began to seriously believe that this time Rainey wasn't coming back. This time she would sit at her pathetic little station and listen to the news that his body had been recovered, that the man she loved was dead.

Damn it, she wanted to get onboard the next Cobra

gunship and go in there herself. She would make those bastards pay, all right. She wanted to smash something. The animal inside, the one Rainey often awakened in her, had had enough. Time for release.

She bolted up from her chair.

Raised her fist.

And then, as if by a miracle, Rainey's voice broke over the command frequency:

"Beacon Light, this is Dogma One, over."

"Dogma One, this is Beacon Light, standby, over."

Kady swung toward Lieutenant Colonel St. Andrew's desk. "Sir, I have Sergeant Rainey."

St. Andrew practically climbed over his desk to get to her station. "I want an update—now!"

Kady switched on the monitor so that St. Andrew could listen in. Then she held back those emotions threatening to explode. "Dogma One, this is Beacon Light. Report your situation, over."

"Beacon Light, we've been taking enemy fire from at least ten positions. Thus far we are five standing tall, but Delta Eagle Seven is down. Repeat. Delta Eagle Seven is down."

Kady sighed inaudibly. Rainey was okay. He sounded good, but he was an expert liar over the radio. Still, he couldn't hide the gunfire Kady heard in the background. "Roger that, Dogma One. Received their Mayday, over."

"Beacon Light, we believe injured personnel are within that aircraft, but we are cut off from that location, over."

"Dogma One, this is Dogma Leader," St. Andrew

said, having slipped on a headset of his own. "Rally north to new extraction point Sigma. Forwarding coordinates now." The colonel nodded to Kady, who initiated the encrypted uplink to Rainey's GPS.

"Beacon Light, we believe aircraft personnel will be killed or captured if we abandon this position, over."

"Dogma One, you just stated that you are cut off from the aircraft, over."

"Yes, at the present time. Request permission to monitor the situation before rallying on Point Sigma, over."

"Negative, Dogma One. Clear the area immediately. Repeat. Clear the area immediately, over."

He's right, Kady thought. *Don't worry about those pilots, Rainey. Just get your ass out of there!*

"Dogma One, did you receive my last transmission, over?" St. Andrew asked. "Dogma One, do you copy?"

TEAM DOGMA

EXTRACTION POINT STINGRAY

QUADRANT E2C

NORTHWEST FRONTIER PROVINCE

PAKISTAN

0646 HOURS LOCAL TIME

Huddled behind the boulders with Houston and McAllister, while Doc and Vance served lookout duty, Rainey swore exactly three times before keying the mike again. "Beacon Light, are you asking us to abandon those aircraft personnel, over?"

There, Rainey thought. *Let him repeat the order. Let him live with it.*

"Dogma One, you are to rally immediately on new extraction point, Sigma. Helos are en route. Beacon Light, out."

"Asshole," Rainey muttered. "Well, at least I got to hear Kady's voice again."

"And she's sounding awful sexy," McAllister said, fighting off a shiver.

"You watch that, Terry."

"Hey, man. These days I have to live vicariously, if I'm going to live at all."

Houston shrugged. "So what now, Sergeant?"

Rainey was about to answer, when Vance interrupted. "Hey, Sergeant? They're near the chopper."

"Yeah," Rainey groaned. "And we're out of range."

DELTA EAGLE SEVEN
NEARING EXTRACTION POINT STINGRAY
NORTHWEST FRONTIER PROVINCE
PAKISTAN
0646 HOURS LOCAL TIME

Inside the downed Huey, Graham unbuckled himself from the pilot's chair, then swung himself down to Ingram, who hung in her seat, suspended above the Huey's crushed door. Through the bubble that usually lay at her feet but now sat off to Ingram's left, Graham saw two armed fighters rushing forward. He flipped open his holster, withdrew his MEU pistol.

"Lieutenant?"

"Can you get me out?" she asked, then coughed hard. "I can't reach my buckle."

"Yeah, I got it," he said, freeing then guiding her up and out of the seat. He chanced a quick look to the hold, saw the rest of his crew. Or what was left of them. Lopez had bought it in the initial explosion, his back a cushion for shrapnel. Smitty had fallen back, into the burning tail assembly. Graham was about to head back and fetch their tags when heavy thuds sounded from the fuselage above.

"Got your sidearm?" he asked Ingram, now coughing himself.

"Those aren't Rainey's people?"

He shook his head.

She grabbed his hand, looked at him gravely. "If we fire first—"

"I know what you're thinking. Forget it." Graham slipped back, behind Ingram's seat, and took aim at the pilot's side door. The window there was cracked, and when the butt of an AK came down on it, the glass showered easily into the cockpit.

In unison, he and Ingram fired a pair of rounds, more warning shots than anything else since from their vantage point they couldn't see the guy trying to break inside.

They did, however, see the tear gas canister drop squarely into the pit, the aerosol fumes immediately biting at their eyes, noses, and mouths.

Like a man floundering to remain afloat and oblivious of the sharks around him because if he didn't tread water he'd die anyway, Graham grabbed Ingram and drove her up, across the pilot's seat, toward the shattered window and into the hands of the enemy. Tear gas meant they wanted to take them alive. And tear gas meant that they wouldn't be firing their weapons anytime soon.

A hand reached in through the window, took Ingram's wrist, and the man outside hauled her up. Now, unable to see anything, Graham surrendered to the movement around him, a man, perhaps two, now climbing into the cockpit, probably wearing gas masks, their voices in Arabic and muffled. One of them yanked the pistol from his hand, but he didn't care. He needed to get out there. He needed to breathe.

WOLF NEWS CREW
NORTHWEST FRONTIER PROVINCE
PAKISTAN
0647 HOURS LOCAL TIME

Propped up on an elbow, John Arden lay in the snow, rubbing his sore neck. Haroun sat opposite him, doing likewise under the tentative scrutiny of Shaqib, who wielded the AK a little too carelessly, and Arden had to remind the guy twice not to swing the barrel in his direction.

"Sorry, Mr. John, but you know, you did right. It is better to keep him alive."

Navarro, who had just finished searching Haroun for other weapons and had come up empty, turned his attitude on Shaqib. "Tell our buddy he's going to take us to al-Zumar right now."

Shaqib spoke the words, and Haroun's reply came in a brief monotone. "He says he will."

"It's that easy?" Arden asked, already expecting a double-cross.

"I think he wants to be a hero, Mr. John. I think he'll take credit for delivering us to the sheikh—because if Fathi learns of his failure now, then Haroun is a dead man. He wants to take us to the sheikh. He really does."

"I get it. If we get there before Fathi knows what's happening, then maybe al-Zumar won't have the hero killed."

Navarro picked up the camera, carefully scrutinized it, pressing buttons and staring through the eyepiece. Satisfied, he looked up, turned a scowl on Arden. "You're lucky it still works. Now, Shaqib, tell him he'll be a hero. Tell him I'll interview him, too."

As Shaqib translated, Arden rose and peered down into the valley, wishing like hell he had his expensive binoculars, but they were down in the Rover. He feared the worst for whomever was trying to extract. With their chopper gone, they would have to evade the enemy until another arrived, and who knew how long that would take. It seemed those boys weren't any better off than he was, but he would rather take his chances with them than with a sellout, a nut, and a terrorist. He shifted to the edge of the precipice, trying to catch a glimpse of the chopper. The smoke was everywhere, and he couldn't see much beyond.

All right. He had a decision to make. Let Shaqib keep the weapon and follow these idiots to al-Zumar or seize the rifle and take charge. If he did the latter, then he would immediately shoot Haroun. Lose the threat and the extra baggage. But that shot would call the others.

Option number two: He could walk away. He doubted Shaqib would gun him down, and he suspected that the translator would not turn over the rifle to Navarro. Could he make it back to the Rover without being spotted? Not with all those bad guys down there. Maybe he could hide until they took off?

A shout from below startled Arden. He covered his brow, squinted, saw Fathi and another man working their way up the slope. Decision time. Break from the group or stay, and if he remained, he had better get them moving. "Okay, Fathi and another guy are coming up. We're moving fast and we're moving now," he told Navarro and Shaqib, then pointed at Haroun and made the motion. "You. On your feet!"

Haroun stood, looked blackly at Arden, then mumbled something in Arabic.

"Lead the way," Arden said, with Shaqib quickly translating behind him.

"Nice to see you're working with us," said Navarro. "I get that interview with al-Zumar and we live through this, you won't have to work another day in your life."

"Oh, yeah?"

"Yeah. I already have the title for your memoir: Guarding Navarro: One Man's Journey into Hell with the World's Most Courageous Reporter."

TEAM DOGMA
EXTRACTION POINT STINGRAY
QUADRANT E2C
NORTHWEST FRONTIER PROVINCE
PAKISTAN
0648 HOURS LOCAL TIME

Vance's nose was running again, and in the moment it took to pull back from his scope and wipe it, something glimmered in the corner of his eye. He snapped his head right, squinted across the slope. Tall pines. Snow drifts. A tiny, almost indistinguishable flash. Wheeling around, he brought his rifle to bear on that glimmer, focused his attention on the scope, upped the mag setting, and saw three people threading their way toward a ridge, a skinny terrorist holding a rifle, another turbaned guy who appeared unarmed, and, whoa, holy shit, two other men who could be Americans, one of them somewhat familiar and carrying a camera. That familiar guy turned his head.

"Son of a bitch."

Rainey squeezed his way up between the two boulders, placing himself beside Vance. "More surprises?"

"Remember that night we were watching the news, and they were talking about how Rick Navarro was coming out here to cover the war?"

"Yeah, I remember that. I think he is in-country, isn't he?"

Vance titled his head toward the glimmer. "You tell me."

Digging out his pair of Nightstars, Rainey got up on his elbows. "You're kidding me, man."

"No, Sarge. I'm pretty sure. Guy with the camera. Skinny little runt in the back has got them. Don't know what's up with that other guy. Maybe he's an Arab. Don't see any weapons."

Rainey continued staring through his binoculars. "So they tear-gassed Ingram and Graham, and now they got Rick Navarro and maybe some guy from his crew."

Vance breathed a heavy sigh. "Them's the facts."

Doc's voice sounded over the tactical frequency. "Dogma One, this is Dogma Two, over."

"Go, Two."

"All I see now are Graham and Ingram. The rest of the air crew must've bought it in the crash. They're taking them back toward the perimeter. Be advised I count five, maybe six bad guys combing the slope. ETA our location maybe ten, fifteen minutes, over."

Rainey slapped Vance on the shoulder. "Let's go, bro. And Corporal?"

"Yeah, Sarge?"

"I've been meaning to ask. You all right?"

"Yeah, just cold. And we ain't had nothing to eat in a while."

"Nothing else bothering you?"

"Doc told you?"

"Told me what?"

"He didn't tell you?"

"About what?" Rainey's question left no room for escape.

"It's nothing. I got an email. That's all. Come on." Vance slid down off the boulder, kept his head low, and scooted down to where McAllister and Doc were lying beside a pair of waist-high stones.

Vance had blown it all right, really blown it. Rainey did not need to know. Now the truth would come out. And the sergeant might even second-guess a decision involving Vance because the sniper had just been dumped by his girlfriend. Vance didn't need that, didn't deserve it. Okay, so he was depressed. But his feelings had zero effect on his performance. In fact, down in the valley, he thought he had fought with an even sharper vengeance. Just ask Houston.

"Hey, Corporal," Rainey said, pulling Vance around. "I know you're tougher than any bad news."

Vance eyed his boots. "Yeah . . . I got Dear-Johned is all."

"Good for you."

"Sarge?"

"You could be like Terry there. Marry them before you really know. At least this one cut the rope before the knot was tied. You could've had kids, then she drops the bomb. You lucked out."

"I guess so, Sarge."

"Good. All right. Where's the other shit bird?" Rainey swung the boom mike closer to his lips. "Dogma Three, this is Dogma One, over? Dogma Three this is Dogma One, over?"

Houston had situated himself next to a big rock and a pine about twenty meters above the group, and from that vantage point he could dissect most of the valley. A tingling sensation on his neck made him sweep his scope right, where, for a moment, he glimpsed a tiny cave entrance way up the mountain, perhaps a thousand feet above. No, it wasn't a cave entrance. Just a shallow depression. Houston was never that lucky. But then again, the bush cover on his head definitely meant something. For the hell of it, he took another look, saw movement up there, two men, one with a gray beard, the other a black one, then the image blurred and he struggled to refocus.

AL-ZUMAR CAVE COMPLEX
NORTHWEST FRONTIER PROVINCE
PAKISTAN
0650 HOURS LOCAL TIME

Although Shaykh thought it unwise, al-Zumar wanted to see the destruction for himself. He and Shaykh stood just outside the southeast entrance, hands dug deeply into their pockets as the wind turned on them.

Below lay the burning chopper—a testament to his warriors' strength and courage and a rude awakening to the infidels. Fathi's report of two pilots captured, along with Rick Navarro and two members of his news crew, rang freshly in al-Zumar's ears as he inspected the damage. Despite the risks, he would take all of his prisoners to Chitral, use them as shields or bargaining chips as necessary. Shaykh was right; they were too valuable to leave behind. Al-Zumar's fighters who remained behind would finish the Americans. And while the bombing missions would undoubtedly commence, another front was moving in to thwart the infidels.

His plans to escape were unfolding perfectly.

Perhaps too perfectly.

"The air is getting colder, Mohammed, but the victory below has warmed their hearts."

"Then why not mine?"

"Give it time. But now, we must go meet up with our team and our prisoners."

Al-Zumar nodded, turned back for the cave, then hesitated. Oh, yes, the cold had crept even deeper inside, and now he feared it might never leave. Compelled by the sensation, he let his gaze sweep along the foothills and couldn't help feel they were being watched. Shrugging, he waved Shaykh on toward the shimmering stone and darkness beyond.

TEAM DOGMA

EXTRACTION POINT STINGRAY

QUADRANT E2C

NORTHWEST FRONTIER PROVINCE

PAKISTAN

0651 HOURS LOCAL TIME

That has to be a cave entrance, Houston thought. And the discovery gripped him so thoroughly that he did not acknowledge Rainey's tinny voice crackling in the earpiece until the sergeant made his third call.

"Dogma One, this is Dogma Three, over."

"Three, report your situation, over."

"Getting positive identification on a cave entrance, over."

Interesting how Rainey's reply took a moment. Maybe a few things could actually startle the old man, who finally said, "Paint that target, then get down here. We're moving out, over."

"Sergeant, if we got time, I can break out the MP-SIDS, take a couple of pictures?"

"Just do what I said and get down here now."

"Roger, out."

Houston dug into his vest, yanked out his Nightstars, set for laser ranging, good from 20 to 2,000 meters. He ranged out on the target, and using the RS232 interface uplink, he transferred the data to his GPS. At least targeting information could eventually be transferred to Camp Liberty Bell for force fires, but Houston thought an accompanying picture would seal the deal on his discovery and job well done. Rainey might even forgive him for his initial screw-up.

Nah. The Sarge was the grudge-holding type. Memory like an elephant. Smelled like one, too.

With the target painted, Houston crawled away from the tree, then rolled over and began sliding down toward the boulders.

Snow-covered and breathless, he reached the group, with Doc still glancing hard through his Nightstars. "Man, you people are ugly," Houston said, sniffling and trying to lighten the dire atmosphere.

But Rainey's impatient gaze trampled all over the attempt.

"Sorry," Houston said.

The sergeant waved a finger across his throat: the sign for them to kill their tactical radios. "All right, Marines. Our orders are to rally on the new extraction point. Problem is, the bad guys have Graham and Ingram—and get this—they have Rick Navarro and some other news guy. Houston spotted a cave entrance above us, and my money says all our people are being taken up there, either to that entrance or some others we haven't seen."

"Wouldn't it be funny if we were sitting right below al-Zumar himself," McAllister said. "I mean these guys have to be part of his army."

"Stranger things have happened," said Rainey. "But I'm not concerned about that. I'm concerned with the fact that by the time our relief team inserts, our people will be long gone. We have a chance right now to get up to those caves and recover those people."

"Tactical Recovery of Aircraft Personnel," McAllister sang in a mock official tone. "I got point on this TRAP, Sarge. Just say the word."

"Whoa," Doc said, looking away from his binoculars. "Hold on a second. I'm ready to go, too, because I'm watching them carry up our pilots. But let's think about this. Sarge, if we get in those caves, we don't know how many guys are up there and how well armed they are. We don't know if the place is booby-trapped or what. Plus, we'll be breaking orders."

"We just have to get our story straight," Vance said. "We were heading toward the new extraction point, took fire, got driven back into the caves and cut off."

"I'm not ordering any of you to do this," Rainey said.

"But I think we owe it to Graham and Ingram. Much as I harass them, they have come through time and again for us. Leaving them to the wolves just ain't my style."

"Yeah, and if we rescue Rick Navarro, then maybe we get on TV," Houston pointed out while wriggling his brows.

Rainey drew back in surprise. "Corporal, I figured you'd be the first one to complain."

"No way, Sarge. See, I'm thinking it was all meant to be, you know? We had to be here so we can go after them."

The sergeant returned a dubious gaze. "So a higher power directed that farmer to steal your weapon? Your incompetence had nothing to do with it?"

Houston fired up his grin. "Exactly."

"Well, there it is, gentlemen," Rainey said with a chuckle. "Doc, we're not going up unless everyone's 100 percent committed. I know you're thinking about your family. And I hate to dump it all in your lap, but the rest of these operators have made up their minds."

Doc nodded, pursed his lips in thought. "We'll, we ain't Force *Four* Recon. We're Force *Five*."

09

The pain in Arden's shoulder started up again as he, Haroun, Navarro, and Shaqib reached a narrow fissure in the mountain wall. Arden tensed against the knives and tried to focus on the entrance, which, oddly, did not appear guarded.

Haroun shouted in Arabic before drawing any closer. Two turbaned men darted out of the shadows, rifles drawn. So there were guards, after all, and Arden should have spotted them. The grimy-faced men narrowed their bushy brows and spoke curtly in turn, their words punctuated by jabs with their rifles.

After a little song and dance by Haroun, his mouth working furiously, the guards cautiously allowed them inside, both challenging Arden with their eyes. As he passed the thinner one, the guy muttered, "Fuck you, American."

"Oh yeah, he likes me," Arden said in a deadpan.

But Navarro and Shaqib weren't listening. Navarro kept close at Haroun's heels, urging the tall Arab to move faster, and Shaqib was somewhere behind. When Arden glanced back, he saw the translator handing over his rifle to the thinner guard.

"Shaqib?"

The translator rushed up, away from the man, saying, "Sorry, Mr. John. They wouldn't let us go any farther unless I gave it to them."

"Well, we haven't gotten very far," Arden said as another four guards abruptly blocked their path, motioning everyone to put his hands in the air.

"They want to search us," Shaqib explained, then confirmed that fact with the oldest guard, a fat man whose white beard unfurled like a snowy carpet from his chin.

One guard with a long neck patted Arden way too hard on his wounded shoulder. Arden gasped, pretended the act hurt much worse than it did, listened as the man announced something to the group. Maybe the bad guys would deem him injured and not much of a threat. He hoped what they assumed would kill them.

Two minutes and four dirty looks later, the guards finished patting them all down, and satisfied, they fell in behind Arden as Haroun led them onward.

The tunnel, sometimes only a meter wide, other times nearly five, meandered down at a steady thirty degrees, the ceiling pitched and irregular. Then, maybe a thousand meters later, the path suddenly leveled off as they entered an oval-shaped chamber whose ceiling hung five or six meters above. Toothy stalactites jutted down, some of them nearly reaching the floor. A musty stench clung to the damp air, and Arden sniffed and grimaced as the guards' flashlights painted the next path, a gaping seam in the stone wall about ten meters ahead.

"Well, this is interesting," Arden said aloud as he surveyed perhaps one hundred coffin-sized wooden crates, their lids lying haphazardly amid the pile. "They were storing munitions." He kicked something, saw it was an instruction manual for a machine gun, the text in Arabic. Beyond the manual lay a couple dozen shell casings, along with discarded batteries, empty packs of cigarettes, big sacks that presumably held rice, and even a few cans of Coca-Cola. The Arabs didn't recycle.

"Hold on a minute," Navarro said, turning to shove the camera back into Shaqib's hands. "This is good. This is really, really good. Let's get some of this."

"Get some of what?" Arden asked. "It's a garbage dump."

Undaunted, Navarro reminded Shaqib how to operate the camera, then positioned himself in the foreground and folded his arms over his chest. If Arden didn't know better, he would swear that Navarro's gung-ho-get-the-story-at-all-costs attitude was beginning to falter. The man looked drawn, even a little scared, and that eyelid of his continued to twitch.

"Okay, Mr. Navarro."

Arden tossed a look back at the guards, who found the whole scene quite entertaining. They smiled and seemingly poked fun at Navarro as the reporter began:

"Ladies and gentlemen, I'm here now in the first chamber of what appears to be an incredibly complex series of tunnels and caves, within which I believe al-Zumar and his warriors have established their stronghold. I'm hoping to chronicle this journey into the heart of darkness as we descend farther, in search of the world's most wanted man. What you're seeing behind me are abandoned munitions crates, and the sheer number indicates that these thugs are well supplied, well armed, and they definitely mean business." Navarro paused, his expression growing long. "But before I go any further, it is with great regret and sadness that I report some terrible news. My bodyguard and translator are the only crew members left to embark on this journey with me. Just hours ago, my producer, cameraman, and engineer were tragically murdered in a gunfight with Afghan refugees recruited by al-Zumar. I can only pray that their bodies are soon recovered, and my thoughts and prayers remain with the families of those brave Americans who paid the ultimate price to bring you the truth."

Arden had almost forgotten how much he hated listening to Navarro's reports. Almost.

"Standing nearby are four heavily armed guards who are keeping a watchful eye over us." Navarro tipped his head off camera, and Shaqib panned right to capture an image of the four Arabs, who smiled dumbly and even waved at the camera. Arden had assumed that they would want to conceal their identities, but the allure of the American media machine was too powerful, even for them. "Should we do anything to incite these men, I'm sure they would not hesitate to shoot us."

Apparently feeling left out and dumb enough to expose his identity, Haroun shifted right up to Navarro, then faced the camera and smoothed out his jacket. "And standing with me now is Haroun, yet another Warrior of Mohammed." Navarro looked a little flustered that the Arab had picked his own cue, but he didn't miss a beat. "We began our journey with him, and he has promised to take us directly to al-Zumar. Should that happen, I want you to know now that I will speak with the man. I will ask him the hard questions. And if push comes to shove, I will mete out justice the way any good American watching this would. I'm Rick Navarro, reporting for Wolf News." Navarro gestured for Shaqib to switch off the camera.

Haroun shouted something to Shaqib, who said, "He wants to know why you didn't interview him."

"Tell him that happens after he takes us to the sheikh." And then, as though he were in charge, Navarro waved the entire group toward the exit. "I want to get to him, and I want to get to him now because God knows when the bombs are going to drop."

Arden just stood there until one of the Arabs nudged him in the back, the AK's muzzle digging in hard. His emotional seams were beginning to tear. He cursed himself for letting it go this far, but part of him secretly hoped he would actually meet Mohammed al-Zumar. Murderer and madman with a huge price on his head, al-Zumar had become a notorious celebrity, and Arden was, damn it, starstruck and further enticed by the notion that if he met the man and survived, he could, as Navarro had said, make a career out of the experience. Of course if he did that, all of the interviews, the book deals, and the public-speaking engagements might turn him into a bigger whore than Navarro.

The idea was tempting . . . But could he live with himself?

For the sake of his own sanity, he pushed all of that from his thoughts and concentrated on the moment, on staying alive.

With his gaze darting about, he slipped on into the next tunnel, the sadistic guard prodding him again.

EXTRACTION POINT STINGRAY

QUADRANT E2C

NORTHWEST FRONTIER PROVINCE

PAKISTAN

0730 HOURS LOCAL TIME

Taking instructions from Doc, who had watched the pilots being whisked away, McAllister led the team across the slope, then up to the crest, where the snow had blown down to just inches and the hump was a heck of a lot easier on the old fart walking point. Well, McAllister wasn't that old, but high-stepping through snow for most of the night made him feel like an eighty-year-old playboy who had just treated a pair of seventy-nine-year-old twin sisters to his Viagra overdose.

After crossing a half-dozen shallow depressions, then shifting along a hair-raising hogback that robbed McAllister's breath at least twice, he called the halt, dropped to his gut, fished out his Nightstars, and focused on an arch-shaped opening about forty meters above, the hole set directly into the mountain face, its curves suggesting that it had been man-made.

"Okay, Sarge. Got the entry ahead," McAllister said into his boom mike.

"Roger that. Houston, you paint the target. And I want all of you to get your silencers on your pistols and rely on Ka-Bars if you can. We'll drop as many as possible before firing a shot. Once the shit hits the fan, they'll move our prisoners quickly. First shot starts the clock. Terry and Vance, you're up. Houston and Doc next. Sound off when you're ready."

McAllister attached the silencer to his MEU pistol, double-checked his vest and rifle, then withdrew his Ka-Bar, the big blade flashing white with reflected snow. He told Rainey he was good to go, listened as the others rang off.

"All right. God bless us all. Execute!"

With his pulse like a timpani drum in his ears, McAllister lunged off toward the left side of the opening, Vance to the right. Coming up from below the entrance helped conceal their approach, but one curious guard could ruin their advance. None came, and as they reached either side of the cave and stood tightly against the rock, Vance got down on his hands and knees, leaned in for a quick look. His head snapped back, and he faced McAllister, lifting two fingers.

Doing his best to conceal his labored breath, Doc came up behind McAllister, while Houston took Vance's side. Once more, Vance flashed two fingers indicating two guards, and the pistol sign meant they were both armed.

Rainey, who had taken McAllister's side as well, pointed to his mouth, then inside the cave. Simple gambit: draw the two close enough to the outside so that they could be taken quietly. And now Rainey would get to test out the Arabic he had been practicing.

Shuddering as the words broke the silence, McAllister listened as Rainey said something or other to the guards. Maybe he insulted their mothers or their intelligence, who knew, but lo and behold, the first turbaned guy, as gaunt as he was hairy, drifted out. He uttered a few words, unaware that in the next heartbeat he would confront five of the hardest, deadliest men on the planet.

Vance slapped a palm over the man's mouth and slashed his throat.

Houston wrestled the rifle from his grip before he could fire.

And it all happened so quickly that by the time McAllister blinked, he realized that Vance and Houston were already dragging away the body.

In the next instant, the second guard was right there, just around the corner, and he would reach McAllister before he blinked again.

Hardening himself to the reality of the moment, McAllister shoved himself past the corner, grabbed the man's throat.

The guy emitted a strangled cry before McAllister punched the blade into his heart while Doc relieved the Arab of his weapon.

As the guy fell, the blade came free, and McAllister wiped it on the dead man's back, then helped Doc and Rainey drag him away.

Two down.

"What did you say to them?" McAllister asked Rainey.

The sergeant winked at Doc. "I told them we were giving away free copies of *Hustler* magazine. Seriously, I think I said we have an injured man out here and need help. Now don't forget those weapons. And Terry? Throw on some of the bigger guy's clothes. Vance? You play dress up, too."

Vance nodded and shouldered the first guard's AK, while McAllister took the second's, along with a pair of magazines. They could cause a little confusion by using the enemy's weapons and clothes, make them think they were firing on their own people, given the AK's distinctive pop.

"Listen up," Rainey said over the radio. "They ain't rolling out the red carpet and lighting the torches for us, so when you're ready, pop on your NVGs. Don't want anyone getting scared of the dark."

The dark didn't scare McAllister; everything else did.

Well, if I buy it here, it won't be so bad, he thought as

he finished slipping on the terrorist's dusty jacket over his vest, then he removed his AN/PVS-7B night-vision goggles from their carrying case, slid them over his head, then stowed his bush cover in favor of the terrorist's turban. *Don't know if I can go back to infantry. Don't know if I can do that.*

Oh, he could. He was lying to himself, trying to believe that he had a death wish so that the fear winding up his back like pins and needles would be ignored. He might be short when it came to serving with Fifth Force Reconnaissance Company, but he was hoping for a long life afterward.

With the Ka-Bar jutting from his gloved fist, his MEU pistol in the other hand, and his vision enhanced by a six thousand-dollar pair of Star Trek glasses, McAllister clung to the shadows along the wall and walked as silently as he could down the tunnel, seeing nothing but cold rock ahead, the scene glowing a nuclear green. He suddenly fancied himself a tunnel rat of the twenty-first century, experiencing at least in a small way what those guys had gone through back in the Vietnam era. But they had had it worse. Those narrow tunnels had been booby-trapped, subject to cave-ins, and some of them were so narrow that you couldn't turn around once you were inside. You forged on, killed anyone or anything in your path, and slid back out of there at a snail's pace, hoping someone didn't shoot you in the ass. The caves of Pakistan offered far more mobility, but the terrorists would exploit that advantage as well.

"Smell that?" Vance whispered from just a step behind, his turban too large and sliding down, toward his NVGs. "Tear gas. Pilots definitely came down here."

McAllister nodded, moved on. The passage turned left, and suddenly a stone wall confronted him. Dead end?

"What the hell?" Houston muttered, coming forward and looking like a tan insect with a single camera lens protruding from beneath his bush cover.

"I smell the tear gas," Vance repeated. "They had to come this way. They had to."

"They did," Rainey said. "Got footprints over here, and check this out."

Nearly lost in the gloom to their right sat a two-meter-wide opening in the floor where the tunnel had caved into another below. Huge hunks of rock had piled up, forming a makeshift path of stepping stones leading about five meters down to the floor.

McAllister dug his boots into the sandy earth, more to allay his nerves than free any snow or ice that clung to the tread.

"Terry, you fall, you're fired," Rainey said.

"And no unemployment. Sucks for me."

Using the fist with the Ka-Bar to brace himself, McAllister leaned down and slid sideways onto the first bridge of rock. When his boot reached the next jagged outcropping, he heard voices below, the kind of company he did not need while perched precariously on the stone ladder. He crouched down, froze. Heard the shuffle of boots.

Closer. Closer now.

Someone called out in Arabic. McAllister glanced back, looked to Rainey for a hand signal.

WOLF NEWS CREW
AL-ZUMAR CAVE COMPLEX
NORTHWEST FRONTIER PROVINCE
PAKISTAN
0740 HOURS LOCAL TIME

The air inside the tunnel grew suddenly colder, and Arden felt a breeze on his cheeks. He suspected they were nearing an exit, but the path ahead remained dim, lit only by the guards' flashlights until they rounded a corner, the tunnel doubling back and pouring into a wider, foyerlike chamber illuminated by several beat-up kerosene lanterns. About thirty AKs were lined up against one wall, with crates of magazines stacked nearby. Three more fighters who might just be locals sat against the opposite wall, eating spaghetti and meatballs from American-supplied food containers. In fact, three massive crates of food sat behind them, with a couple of boxes of Kraft macaroni and cheese lying on top of one.

"Oh, you have to love this," Arden said under his breath. "We're feeding the bastards. Wonderful."

Shaqib, who had been speaking with one of the guys eating spaghetti, regarded Arden. "He says these crates fell from the air and killed two of his camels, so he joined al-Zumar's army to get back at you Americans for killing his camels. He also says they thought the spaghetti was lambs' brains."

One of the guards barked something into a radio, and for a second, Arden thought he heard the man use the phrase "yabba dabba doo" and did a double take. "Shaqib, ask him what yabba dabba doo means."

"I don't have to. It is the name we give to the crates that fall from the sky. These crates."

"Are you kidding me? Did some American tell you that's what they're called?"

"I don't know. It's just the name."

"It's from an old TV show called *The Flintstones*."

"That's what some soldiers call us."

"What?"

"They call us the Flintstones," the translator said quite seriously.

Arden raised his good hand in surrender. "Ah, this is getting too weird for me."

Navarro, who had been listening impatiently, finally blew and grabbed Haroun by the jacket collar. "Where the fuck is al-Zumar?"

The tall Arab wrenched away Navarro's hand and spoke violently, raising his voice to such heights that the other guards began hushing him—

Even as Mohammed al-Zumar himself, trailed by an old man and two young fighters dressed in tan camouflage shifted into the room.

Without realizing it, Arden found himself taking a step back from the young terrorist, whose penetrating gaze, broad shoulders, and trimmed beard made him seem far more Western than the pictures the American media repeatedly flashed on screen. That he was capable of murder and mayhem on a global scale was hardly evident. In fact, al-Zumar could easily be mistaken for a somewhat bookish MIT grad who lived in Wisconsin, drove a Volvo, and liked sprouts on his burgers. Even the trademark camouflage jacket, the one that made him resemble a young Castro, was gone, in favor of a heavy green parka, black woolen cap, and blue jeans.

The world's most wanted man scanned the room. He nodded as he came upon Shaqib, then hoisted his brows at Navarro and spoke firmly in Arabic.

"He's says you look different in person," Shaqib translated. "And he says you're not worth much as a hostage. He says the Americans already want you dead."

With that, al-Zumar laughed heartily. "A joke," he said with a heavy accent. "I make a joke."

The joke will be on you, Arden thought. *You're going to get a cluster bomb up your ass before the day is over. No more* jihad *for you.*

Navarro mustered the lamest grin Arden had ever seen, then said, "You expressed a desire to be interviewed by a Western reporter. I'm that reporter. Are you willing to give me an interview?"

Shaqib translated, and when he finished, al-Zumar's expression darkened a moment before he seized Navarro by the throat and shouted angrily in the reporter's face.

"Jesus Christ, Shaqib, what the hell did you tell him?"

"I think what you said. My English is not perfect!"

Without warning, Arden found the muzzle of an AK pressed against his chest, and the Arab brandishing it, one of al-Zumar's bodyguards, smiled like a wolfhound.

"Tell him you screwed up the translation," Navarro cried. "Tell him!"

His voice cracking, Shaqib did his best to explain. After a moment's scrutiny, al-Zumar released Navarro, shifted back to the old man, and whispered a few words.

"Yeah, now they're deciding whether to shoot us in the head or the back," Arden moaned.

Al-Zumar faced Navarro once more and spoke calmly in English. "We travel now. I tell you when for the interview." His gaze shifted to Shaqib. "He will come. He is no good translator, but he is only one."

Shaqib issued a few words, indicating Arden's shoulder as he did so. Al-Zumar leveled his gaze on Arden, then suddenly unzipped Arden's jacket and pulled it down to inspect the wound. He turned to one of his guards, fired off an order, and the man hustled off. "Not bad," al-Zumar said. "We have doctor."

Though Arden couldn't bring himself to thank the man since the bastard's people had been responsible for the wound in the first place, he did nod.

"You are news people?" the terrorist asked.

"Just came along for the ride," Arden quipped, though he suspected Shaqib would never capture the irony in his translation.

After listening a moment to Shaqib, al-Zumar said, "So you are bodyguard and United States Marine."

Arden slumped and leered at Shaqib. "For God's sake, don't be volunteering information!"

"Sorry, Mr. John. I don't know what you say, so I tell him who you are. The guards would tell him anyway."

Al-Zumar waved his index finger in front of Arden's face. "We watch you. If there is problem, you die first."

"Buddy, at this point you'd be doing me a favor."

After the echo of Shaqib's translation, al-Zumar frowned. "You are no martyr. Only infidel."

The fanatic in al-Zumar reared itself, and mistaking him for some MIT grad was no longer possible. Arden could sense that the fire in his eyes had been kindled long ago, and along with that fire came the reminder that when al-Zumar was through with them, he would make yet another statement by, perhaps, executing them on video. Arden would play prisoner for now, but the act wouldn't last. It couldn't. He would probably die trying to escape, but that would be a better death than shrinking to his knees and taking one in the back of the head. Marines did not die like that.

A trio of shots popped and echoed, the racket coming from deep within the tunnels.

Al-Zumar hollered orders, and reacting in fear, the guards ushered Arden, Navarro, and Shaqib forward. The world's most wanted man lingered behind, pressed his radio to his ear, and spoke angrily.

"What's he saying?" Arden asked Shaqib.

"Something about two pilots they captured. They're going to meet up with us."

"Anything else?"

The report from two separate rifles, both AKs to be sure, reverberated before the translator could answer.

"Something about the Marines. I don't know."

"There was a team trying to extract. I bet they're coming in to rescue us."

"I hope not," Navarro said. "We don't need any rescuing."

"Not from al-Zumar, anyway. Just from you."

"Shit. They'll ruin it for us—after everything we've been through."

"You're not getting jack out of this guy. He's just fucking with you. Look into his eyes, then tell me he's a guy you want to bargain with while you ignore the fact that he's just fucked with L.A., New York, Chicago, and Denver."

"I'm giving him a voice, and that's something I know he wants. It's the bait."

"Smart. Trust a man who's killed more innocent Americans than anyone in history."

"My trust is not in him. It's in me. I know what I'm capable of. All I need is that interview. After that, you and I are going to make history."

"God, you don't see it. You've already dug our graves."

A glare shone through the tunnel ahead, and soon they flooded out onto a broad, snow-covered cliff, with a trail leading off to the north and down the mountainside. Yet another cave entrance lay below, with another pair of fighters poised on either side of the entrance.

"We go down now," Shaqib said, as one of the guards repeated a command.

With more salvos echoing throughout the caves, they crossed onto the trail, with Arden realizing that only two of al-Zumar's guards escorted them now. Two guys. It would take about ten minutes to reach the next entrance. A better opportunity might not present itself. He had to do something.

TEAM DOGMA
AL-ZUMAR CAVE COMPLEX
NORTHWEST FRONTIER PROVINCE
PAKISTAN
0750 HOURS LOCAL TIME

Where is he? There. No, that's not him. There he is. Just reach out a little more. You don't see me.

Pop! Pop! Pop!

You're gone. No casket. No wake. No burial. Now breathe, Terry, breathe. But where's the next one? Oh, man, where is he?

McAllister hated the way things had gone down, but it wasn't like he had had much choice in the matter. As he had looked to Rainey for a signal, the son of a bitch terrorist scumbag had spotted him—or at least his silhouette, even while crouching down, and apparently McAllister's turban failed to fool anyone. The cross-eyed goon had cut loose a few pot shots that had strayed meters wide of the stone ladder. Still, the thug's poor aim hardly mattered. The alarm was out. All the name-calling in the world wouldn't change that.

In the seconds that had followed, McAllister had used his NVGs and the confiscated AK to take out the guy who had spotted him, along with Dark Jacket Number One and Dark Jacket Number Two as he had affectionately dubbed them before sending their corduroy-clad hides crashing to the floor, their souls scrambling for Allah.

Then another guy, a shadow, had appeared at the foot of the ladder. He had vanished a moment, returned, then, springing from behind a raft of stone, he had swallowed three rounds and had staggered drunkenly toward the wall before shrinking.

But where was the next one?

Hearing McAllister engage the fighters below sent Rainey into command mode:

"Doc, you got our asses. Vance and Houston, get down there and flank them, over."

The two Marines, one of them wearing a turban and dirty jacket that did a lame job of disguising him, dropped onto the stone ladder and hustled recklessly downward. Rainey had to admonish them to be careful as Doc set up the Para SAW a few meters back.

"Once we're clear, I want you down in a hurry," he told the corpsman. "We're pushing forward and pushing fast."

Doc winked. "Don't wait up for me. I'll already be ahead of you."

After a quick slap on the big guy's shoulder, Rainey left Doc and slid onto the ladder himself. He slipped only three times, well, that was a lot, before dropping to one knee and sweeping the tunnel with his NVGs, darkness yielding to the grainy green light. The turbaned Vance kept tight to the wall on his right and advanced slowly, with Houston hanging close to the left wall, his movements sharp and well guarded. Maybe the kid had paid attention during his close-quarters-combat lessons and actually understood the night-attack SOPs.

Rainey certainly knew those procedures well. One of the basic decisions he had had to make before entering the caves involved being hasty versus being deliberate. Trading time for information minimizes surprises on an objective, but when you have no time with which to bargain, then you go in hastily, your jugular exposed.

Two more fighters came rushing forward, their weapons directed at nothing in particular as they opened up. If they were familiar with the concept of lying in wait for your enemy, there was no evidence. And if they had a plan, it involved springing traps in the hopes that they got off a fatal round or at least alerted their comrades before they bought it. Rainey hated martyrs . . .

As did Vance and Houston, who, with sporadic gunfire, added two more souls to the long line leading into Paradise.

But where the hell was McAllister? "Dogma Five, this is Dogma One, over."

McAllister ignored the voice in his ear. He pressed his back against the wall, hidden by a slight bulge in the rock, as a stoop-shouldered fighter of about nineteen started down the tunnel, a flashlight duct-taped to his AK, the beam wiping across the floor.

"Dogma Five, this is Dogma One, over."

As the fighter's light swung his way, McAllister rolled to confront the guy and squeezed the AK's trigger.

Jammed!

He could toss the weapon and reach for his MEU pistol. He could use the Ka-Bar still in his grip to gut the terrorist before the guy pivoted to fire.

Or he could just react without thinking. He grabbed the barrel of the AK, and even with the knife in one hand, he managed to swing the rifle like a baseball bat. As the two locked gazes, the AK's heavy stock came down on the fighter's head, cracking it open like a coconut. The guy crumpled to his back, and before the dust settled, McAllister buried the Ka-Bar in the boy's heart.

"Dogma Five, this is Dogma One. Terry, you there, over?"

"Dogma One, this is Five," McAllister began, panting and surveying his location. "I'm about twenty meters ahead. Tunnel forks up here, over."

"Terry, we just took down another pair. You didn't see them, over?"

"Negative. Just finished off one myself."

"Then be advised, there must be another tunnel between you and us. We'll rally on you, over."

"Roger, out."

Lying on his belly, Doc leaned into all forty-one inches of his Para SAW, one hand on the forward vertical grip, the other firmly fastened around the pistol grip. He fixed his gaze on the tunnel leading outside and waited for Rainey's signal. The faintest rumble met his ears, and though the sound came from miles away, he felt certain the B-52s and Warthogs were inbound, along with the extraction chopper they would never meet and the second Force Recon Team assigned to recovering the pilots. There was going to be a party, all right, and even if the bombs did not drop very close, the vibrations they caused would ruin any cave-dweller's day. The thought of being buried alive under tons of rock in the middle of nowhere made Doc want to call Rainey himself and get things moving.

At least for the moment, there wasn't any . . . wait a minute. Movement ahead, maybe forty meters up. One guy crept forward, polishing the cave wall with his sleeve and jerking his rifle. Nervous kid, no doubt. Another guy with a matted beard followed him. Then two more materialized on the opposite wall, skulking tightly together, not realizing how pathetic their approach looked and that they had already been spotted by an American with a very big gun.

Doc took in a long breath, let it out slowly, calmly, getting in touch with his hand, the rifle, the men advancing. Just four? Yes. He could finish the two on the left and swing right, but his first salvo would send the two survivors onto their bellies, and his rounds could fall long or short. He needed a one-two punch.

"Dogma Two, this is Dogma One, over."

"One, this is Two, over," Doc whispered.

"Okay, Doc. Get down here. We're rallying on

McAllister's position straight ahead. Be advised that there may be a secondary tunnel, though we don't see it, over."

"Be advised I have four bad guys advancing on my position. I'll be down ASAP, over."

"You need assistance?"

"Negative. And trust me. You'll hear me coming, over."

"Roger, out."

Doc already had the fragmentation grenade in his hand. He waited. The targets would be in range any second, but as Murphy dictated—so would he. Although he did not require a hatred of the enemy to do his job, he still thought of his family back home, thought of all those innocent civilians who had been killed by al-Zumar's sleepers in the United States.

Pulling the pin was easy. He lobbed the grenade toward the right side of the tunnel, then aimed his Para SAW at the guys on the left.

Four, three, two—

He opened fire as the grenade flashed white and blasted apart the wall beside the two thugs. With smoke billowing and debris fountaining to cloud his view, Doc knew very well that those men had been torn to bloody ribbons a finger's snap before being buried under the debris. Execution and burial with drive-thru efficiency. You want flowers with that?

Now with only two targets to worry about, Doc bit his lip and put his Para SAW to work, rounds beating a jackhammer's rhythm, the vibration working its way into his arms and chest. Targets terminated? Despite the

NVGs, he couldn't tell. Then again, those fanatics would need a miracle to survive the thunder and chaos he was throwing at them.

Satisfied with his assault, Doc wrenched the automatic weapon up and toward his chest. In one surge he stood and hobbled off toward that hole in the floor, his ankle throbbing again. He refused to acknowledge the injury. He would not give life to the pain. He would conquer it because he was the corpsman—not a patient.

Pieces of the wall to his immediate right chipped off, and for a second the adrenaline rush stole his senses.

Then it dawned on him. One of the bastards back there had received his miracle and was firing.

Or, more likely, a fifth guy had been holding back, out of grenade range and view. The guy had watched his brothers get cut down, though he had not bolted in fear. The dumb bastard had chosen to seek revenge. And worse, he was a crack shot.

Blinking against the bursts of flying rock, the ricocheting rounds unnervingly close, Doc reached the hole and lowered himself to the next perch. He considered using another grenade, thought better of wasting it on a single man.

Instead, he found purchase on the next ledge, set down his hot Para SAW, then situated himself parallel to the stone, his body completely shielded by the rock above. He peered cautiously beyond a sharp-edged lip, his MEU pistol with silencer balanced in his hand, his forearms bracing the weapon. Stones crunched above.

Be careful out there, Daddy. Okay?

Doc forced his older son's voice out of his head,

stared hard through the NVGs, knew his pressure and pulse were way up—

And there he was! Leaning over the edge and getting ready to mount the first step.

Doc had a perfect shot, with the guy's head at the end of his sight. Without a single flinch, Doc put pressure on his index finger. The round whispered out, and the terrorist came tumbling down the ladder, rolled by, and splayed across the floor, his rifle lying at his side.

Only then did Doc realize why he was getting dizzy. He had forgotten to breathe.

Houston covered the tunnel to the left, while Vance had taken the one to the right. Old man McAllister wasn't having a particularly good morning and opted to remain behind Houston to catch his breath.

"Splitting up is a bad idea," Houston muttered.

"Nobody asked you," snapped the old man, who ripped off the turban he'd been wearing and tossed it aside. "Fucking thing smells."

"Don't worry, Sergeant. We all know you're short with Force. We'll get you home to your paddle ceremony somehow."

Houston had attended a few of those. When a member left the company, he received an engraved paddle and a certificate of his service. Everyone got to say a few words about serving with that operator, and while tears were usually kept in check via jokes and teasing, most people felt equal measures of loss and honor for being fortunate to serve with such an individual. For some operators, the paddle ceremony was the highlight of their careers. But Houston sensed that for McAllister, it represented the beginning of the end.

"Hey, you don't look so good," Houston told the old man. "Why don't—"

"You going to talk? Or pay attention to that fucking—"

McAllister was going to say "tunnel," but the multiple report of AKs cut him off. Houston answered in kind, targeting the pair of muzzle flashes even as rounds zipped overhead and caromed off the rock behind him.

"Question!" Houston cried over his own firing. "How we're supposed to find anybody in this maze with these assholes firing shit at us!" The words had barely left his lips when he began to regret them. He was pissing and moaning again instead of sucking it up and living by the team's decision, a decision he had endorsed in the first place—until he had seen what they were getting themselves into.

Yeah, it was best to let his rifle do the talking. The bitching made him feel better, but it hardly changed the situation. Besides, sticking around and making at least a few of these mothers pay for what they had done to the good old U.S. of A. was a job best left to the Marines, and even if his father didn't give two craps about the work he was doing, Houston felt proud to be in Pakistan as a representative of the most powerful armed forces in the world.

He ceased fire. Silence came from the tunnel ahead.

"I got them," he said confidently.

"Or they stopped firing," said McAllister, his scarred lip twitching.

Doc and Rainey came storming up the tunnel and dropped in behind Vance, whose rifle suddenly boomed.

"Still no sign of that mystery tunnel. The hell with it," Rainey said over the radio. "Terry? You and Houston take the left tunnel. The three of us are going right. I'm betting that they wouldn't take our guys out of the south side, with the chopper wreckage down there. So there's definitely another way out, probably on the north side of the mountain. So we push deeper. First team to make it outside gets the GPS coordinates. We'll rally on you, over."

"We're good over here," Houston responded, then raised his brows at McAllister, who nodded gravely.

"Clock's ticking," Rainey announced. "Move out!"

"Just stay right behind," Houston told McAllister. "You watch the rich boy from California clear the path."

Houston knew that's what McAllister had him pegged for, so throwing it back into the guy's face felt good, and Houston needed a little ego booster before ferreting through the dark crevices of the unknown.

A warm sense of satisfaction washed over him as they passed the bodies of two more fighters, the ones he had targeted just moments before. "You were right," he said softly to McAllister. "They did stop firing—'cause I gave them an extraspecial amount of killing."

"Do the words swift and *silent* mean anything to you?" McAllister asked.

"I get the point," he retorted. "Just like they did."

Houston didn't know why, but suddenly McAllister was grabbing his ruck and drawing him back a few steps. The old man shifted around, a finger to his ugly lip as he leaned down and directed that finger toward a trip wire about six inches above the floor and spanning the tunnel's width.

Shuddering, Houston crouched down and took a closer look. "I should have seen it," he whispered.

McAllister nodded in disgust.

Houston imagined his legs blown off by the lens-shaped and unforgiving Claymore mines al-Zumar's people had set nearby. He imagined lying there, shaking like a leaf, blood jetting from his appendages. Then he looked at McAllister. Whoa. The old man had saved his life. Houston already owed Vance a save, and now he owed McAllister. If he got any deeper in debt, he would have to turn into a one-man army to compensate. But maybe returning the favor wasn't necessary. In the Corps saving your buddy's life was as natural as breathing, but Houston still felt the desire to return the favor. If things got any worse, he might get that chance.

"Thanks," he told McAllister, and he really meant it.

"Now I walk point."

No argument from Houston. They stepped gingerly over the trip wire, and McAllister paused, reached into his ruck, and withdrew a yellow piece of paper. He slid the paper under the wire and set a small stone atop it, marking the spot.

"What is that?" Houston asked.

"Just an old receipt from an oil change I've been meaning to get rid of." McAllister regarded the tunnel ahead and pointed on.

Still feeling the shakes of the encounter, Houston kept hard on McAllister's heels, knowing that if fighters ahead suddenly launched a barrage, McAllister would go down first. Ordinarily, he wouldn't ponder that fact. Point men buy it. Way of the battlefield. But the guilt was setting in.

I should have seen that wire. I didn't. I don't deserve to be walking point. My carelessness could get us both killed.

"What was that?" McAllister suddenly asked, whirling, his neck craning as he swept his NVGs across the tunnel.

Houston felt something nudge his boot. He looked down.

Grenade!

First reaction: reach down, pick up the bomb, and throw it. But how long did he have left on the fuse? He might already be dead and contemplating saving his life from, in fact, the afterlife. No, things felt real. He hadn't heard an explosion. He was still very much alive. *Do something!*

Struck by a lightning bolt of action, Houston shifted his boot ahead, then kicked the metal ball with his heel, even as he shouted, "Grenade!"

He and McAllister dashed forward, and the idea that there could be terrorists waiting in the shadows ahead never crossed Houston's mind—

Until the gunfire sent him hard onto his gut . . .

And the grenade exploded with a terrific clap behind them, setting off the trip wire and a triplet of secondary explosions from the Claymores. The pressure created by the explosion tugged at his shoulders, the air getting sucked this way and that.

And if that weren't enough Hell express delivered to their little neighborhood, McAllister, in an effort to eliminate the targets ahead, pumped and fired a 40 mm low-pressure grenade from the M203 grenade launcher attached to his rifle. The old man accomplished that task in the two seconds he had while falling onto his own belly.

With a cave-in rumbling behind them, McAllister's grenade popped loudly, stinging Houston's ears and setting off yet another small collapse ahead. Repressing a cough as the dust swelled over him from the rear, Houston just lay there silently, his gaze fixed on McAllister, who reached out through the cloud and held up a finger to wait.

The hissing died off, and McAllister nudged Houston's shoulder. They clambered to their feet, staggered to the nearest wall.

Though no dust got into their eyes, the NVG's lens got dirty, and Houston wiped it twice as McAllister pushed forward, into the smoke.

"Dogma Five, this is Dogma One, over."

"Don't worry about it, Rainey," McAllister muttered. "Just cleaning house. Pressing on."

"Heard it over here. Just checking. Roger, out."

About twenty paces later, they came upon a grim sight.

"Whoa, road pizza with pepperoni," Houston said,

stepping over a dirty arm here, a mangled leg there. The rest of that fighter lay ahead in a tattered, crimson heap. Houston wasn't one of those guys who viewed death with that weird, almost mystical fascination, and he wasn't one of those guys who got off on all the blood. He just dealt with the violence as best he could, remembered his training, and tried to let what he saw pass over him. Sometimes he imagined that he could store all the horror in a box, one that he would overnight to his father so that the asshole could experience just a small taste of what it was like to be a Marine in a war zone. Dad had no clue, no conception, and certainly no compassion. He was too worried about closing costs and commissions to even consider what Houston's life was like.

"Road pizza with pepperoni, you say?" McAllister asked dryly. "Looks more like anchovies to me."

The old man had made a joke to compensate for the nightmare before them. Pretty lame stuff, but a joke nonetheless. Maybe McAllister actually liked him, though Houston wouldn't bet on that. Not yet, anyway.

Once they had passed the killing zone, counting three casualties in all, they followed the tunnel for another minute until it gradually ascended while veering left. The fact that they met no more resistance did not ease Houston's fears. Either the bad guys were gathering somewhere ahead for a major offensive, or they were gathering to the rear so they could, as Vance might say, bushwhack their asses. Of course, they could all be dead, but wasn't that one of Murphy's Laws of Combat? If you assume the enemy is dead, those "dead" soldiers will kill you.

Flickering light danced along the ceiling about twenty meters up, and Houston slid up his NVGs, blinking hard to adjust his vision. McAllister, his goggles also raised, signaled for them to split up, he taking the right wall, Houston the left. Houston couldn't tell for sure, but there could be a chamber up there, and an exit was close, judging from the drop in temperature and the breeze filtering inside.

Mindful of his step and willing himself into a being of pure air, unseen and unheard, Houston advanced, his rifle feeling solid and comforting in his hands.

A look to McAllister. A nod in return. They drew closer, neared a corner, and, after a pair of hand signals and a count of three, they rounded it.

With a start, Houston drew back, having nearly knocked over a man in a dirty brown tuxedo jacket and black turban. The guy took one look at him, threw his hands in the air, and wailed like a wounded jackal.

Stealth is a byproduct of alertness, Rainey knew, but when stealth doesn't work, an old-fashioned hailstorm of fire would, if it didn't obliterate the enemy, at least make you feel good.

So, signing the words "I feel good" in his head, Rainey rushed forward with Vance, both men firing at the tiny muzzle flashes that seemed miles instead of meters away. Doc trailed behind as rear guard, and that ankle didn't slow him down.

They advanced like men trying to penetrate a perimeter, men who paid no heed to mines or concertina wire, men who would throw themselves forward with so much ammo and force of will that even those they had already killed would sit up and take notice.

Pumped up. That's what they were. War faces on. Mean genes raging. Gazes sweeping for traps.

They were Neanderthals with clubs shooting the magic fire.

And the enemy was on the run! Three guys had just abandoned their positions. While Vance dropped to a knee and *boom!* took out one, Rainey came to within a few steps of another guy, who chanced a look back. Rainey capped him.

The guy dropped. And shit, Rainey tripped over him, stumbled, nearly fell, kept moving.

One guy now. Still running. Fast guy. Had to be young. Didn't need Nikes. Just needed a United States Marine on his ass to win a gold medal.

Salvos echoed from the rear. That was Doc and his Para SAW. Rainey guessed he had only a few seconds more to cut down the kid in front.

Light at the end of the tunnel. An idiom. A fact. There it was, the kid heading straight for it. Rainey could pause, take the shot. Okay. He stopped, jammed up his NVGs, stared through his rifle's scope, got the kid in his crosshairs.

Click.

What was—

Sounding like a belch from hell, Claymore mines ripped themselves apart and swallowed the kid. He had failed to see the trip wire, the one his buddies had probably set, and the explosion knocked Rainey flat onto his back, the rucksack deadening most of the blow. Thank God the mines had been set to blow perpendicular to the tunnel, otherwise Rainey would have received a breakfast bowl of shrapnel thrown in his face.

"Sarge, man, you okay?" Vance said, hustling over.

Rainey thrust out his hand, and the fisherman took it. "They might have been baiting us toward that trip wire. Who knows."

"Yeah," Vance said, hauling him up. "And you know the last thing I ever want to be is the bait."

That raised a grin from Rainey. He hadn't meant to make a joke of nearly being killed. Maybe it was better that he had.

"Got another one back there," Doc said, shifting backward, the Para SAW clutched at his hip. "And they just keep coming."

"Well, we aren't sticking around to kill them all," Rainey said, then he did a quick head tip toward the light about twenty-five meters up.

"Dude, I have no idea what you're saying!" Houston said to the screaming guy in a tuxedo jacket, now flailing his arms.

McAllister slapped a palm on the barrel of Houston's rifle, forced it down, then regarded the screamer. "Easy now. Easy. We're Americans."

Houston frowned. "This guy ain't no Arab."

"Oh, and you can tell?"

"Not by looking at him. But no Arab would surrender."

"Bullshit. Search him," McAllister ordered.

After a thorough pat down, Houston took a step back from the man. Geez, his teeth were bad, and he was as bony as a teenaged girl with an eating disorder. Yet, oddly enough, he smelled like tomato sauce, as though he'd just had himself a plate of spaghetti and meatballs.

With a shrug, McAllister regarded the guy and widened his eyes. "We're Americans. We're looking for the other Americans." McAllister pointed at his eyes. "Did you see them take the other Americans?"

"Americans," the guy repeated. "No shoot! I like America."

"Oh, man. We got some local guy who joined up, then probably switched sides when things got a little too real," McAllister said. "He doesn't understand me. Screw him. The exit has to be up ahead."

"But what do we do with him?"

The local switched his gaze from Houston to McAllister, and then, even before the sergeant could answer, he bolted off, toward the exit.

Houston whipped around, ready to shoot—

"Hold your fire!" McAllister shouted.

"Are you nuts? We can't trust any of these fuckers!"

"I said hold your fire, Lance Corporal. Now come on!"

They rushed past the crates, through the adjoining tunnel, and reached a cliff just outside where multiple boot prints had trampled the snow.

Hanging back just inside the tunnel, Houston observed the prints, pointed them out to McAllister, who gave the signal for them to split up again, and take either side of the exit. When they were ready, they slipped soundlessly out, keeping tight to the wall, and, seeing no one else on the ledge, Houston stole a moment to slip on his Nightstars and follow the serpentine trail dropping away from them. "Got two bad guys, and it looks like our buddy Navarro and the other guy. Plus the third one, the little one. They're heading toward another exit down there."

McAllister, studying the group through his own pair of binoculars, keyed his mike. "Dogma One, this is Dogma Five, over."

"You outside yet, Terry?" Rainey asked.

"Just reached a ledge. Got our news crew out here, heading down to another exit, over."

"I have you in my sights," Rainey said. "We just came outside. We're about thirty meters above you. I see that news crew, over."

"Orders?"

"They're going to reach that next exit in less than a minute. Set up for shots. Vance? You got the goon on the right, Houston you got the goon on the left. I'll take the little guy up front. Execute on my mark, over."

Houston waited his turn, issued his curt and affirmative reply, then leaned against the wall, setting himself up for the shot. Vance and his sniper's rifle would have the best chance of success, but Houston figured he could take his target as well. How the Sarge would ever hit that scrawny guy was beyond him.

"Okay," Rainey said. "Steady now. Steady . . ."

Houston squinted hard through his scope, the crosshairs floating precisely over his terrorist's back.

A click at his ears sent his gaze to the right, where Mr. Local Guy in the brown tuxedo held a pistol to his head. *No,* Houston thought. *This cannot be happening again!*

AL-ZUMAR CAVE COMPLEX
NORTHWEST FRONTIER PROVINCE
PAKISTAN
0805 HOURS LOCAL TIME

Mohammed al-Zumar and Shaykh reached the northernmost tunnel exit, where they, along with the bodyguards, would rendezvous with a few of Fathi's people and with the captured pilots. En route to their position were Navarro, his bodyguard, and the fast-talking interpreter who turned the Arabic language into an abomination. Al-Zumar would eventually kill the man, if only for that.

A weary yet exceedingly agitated Fathi arrived, just after the men carrying the tear-gassed pilots. "My Sheikh. There are, we believe, only five Americans. They're in the tunnels now. We will kill them."

"Very good," al-Zumar said, cocking a brow at the tall Haroun, who stroked his beard pensively. "And your man here has delivered to us the American news crew."

"Not him," Fathi said, turning his searing gaze on

Haroun. "I ordered him to remain with our hostages. He chose to bring them here. And for that—"

"It is no matter," said the wizened Shaykh, who stepped between Fathi and Haroun, hands raised. "They want us to fight among ourselves. They want us to turn our backs on Allah. But we will not. As soon as the American newspeople arrive, we will walk out of here, our heads held high."

With all the warning of an earthquake, a powerful rumble worked its way up, through al-Zumar's ankles. He listened hard, heard the cluster bombs exploding in the distance. "They usually come at night," he told Shaykh.

"They are trying to beat the second storm heading this way, the one that will mask our escape."

Al-Zumar shuddered against the cold, the terrible cold that would not release him, the cold he feared would remain with him until death. "Fathi, leave the pilots here with my bodyguards. Return your men to the caves to finish off those Americans. Have Haroun lead that team."

"Yes, my Sheikh," the boy said, growing long-faced and assuming that he was not traveling with them.

"Then be ready to move out with us," al-Zumar added, brightening the boy's mood. "I want you at my side."

"Where I belong, my Sheikh." With renewed vigor, Fathi jogged off toward the other side of the tunnel, where his men were holding the prisoners.

"My Sheikh," Haroun said nervously. "I thought it wise to take the prisoners here. I feared the Americans might recapture them."

"You made the right decision," al-Zumar said.

"Yes, my Sheikh, but now I fear Fathi. I will go out and fight those Americans, but if I die, the bullet will come from him or from one of the others—not from the enemy."

Al-Zumar placed a hand on the man's shoulder. "Rest easy, Haroun. The bullet will not come from him. It will come from me." Al-Zumar jabbed a pistol into the man's heart.

Haroun's breath came in a shiver. "But my Sheikh, you said I made the right decision."

"You did. You told me the truth."

"Mohammed," Shaykh warned, his crooked index finger slicing the air near al-Zumar's face. "You earn only their fear by killing the insubordinate, not their respect. Haven't we discussed this?"

As always, the old man was right. And al-Zumar did not want to kill Haroun because the tall fighter had disobeyed Fathi's orders. He wanted to kill the man because he thought an act like murder, a powerful and visceral act, might somehow warm him inside. He needed to get warm. Needed to feel confident about their course of action, and drawing blood—proving his power to himself and all those watching—might just do that.

Or not.

He withdrew the pistol, took a step back from Haroun. "Kill those Americans. Kill all of them. And I will find a special place for you in my army—if you learn to obey orders."

Haroun, trembling violently, composed himself, nodded, then took off running.

Shaykh smiled after the man, then he favored al-Zumar with appreciative eyes. "You're gaining wisdom by the hour, Mohammed." He turned and gripped al-Zumar's wrists. "Who knows? Perhaps by the time we reach Chitral, you will no longer need my guidance."

"You never left my father. And you will never leave me. Only a fool would not keep you at his side."

"Yes, you're right," Shaykh said, chuckling over his immodest agreement. "And this is where I belong. It is the *jihad* that drives me on. The *jihad* is too important to abandon. And maybe, just maybe, I have taken a liking to a boy who would lead a revolution."

Al-Zumar nodded. "Shaykh, we go out now from the caves. We go out into the mountains, where we are most vulnerable. It may take yet another day to get there." Another round of explosions sent dust fluttering down from the ceiling. Al-Zumar glanced up and sighed deeply. "Where is that news crew?" He had sent them along the mountain trail in the hopes that they would be safer outside. He started for the exit, intent on finding them himself.

TEAM DOGMA
AL-ZUMAR CAVE COMPLEX
NORTHWEST FRONTIER PROVINCE
PAKISTAN
O8O5 HOURS LOCAL TIME

Turning his head fractionally while lowering his left hand away from his rifle, Houston jerked that hand—

And ripped the pistol away from Mr. Local Guy's grip. "Dumb fuck!" he cried, then withdrew his Ka-Bar and knocked the guy onto his back.

The guy gasped. So did Houston.

I'm going to end your life. And I'm not God. I'm just a guy. Holy shit. This is it.

Yes, Houston still held the guy's pistol, but he had learned that if possible, it's better to kill an enemy with your own weapon, the one you've cleaned and double-checked, the one you trust not to misfire. More than that, Houston needed a quiet stabbing to the lung or heart instead of a loud capping.

He needed his knife.

"Don't kill," the guy pleaded. "Don't kill."

Houston didn't.

McAllister did. Slashed the guy's throat right in front of Houston's bulging eyes. The kill had not been particularly clean or silent, but the old sergeant didn't seem to care. "Okay, kid," he rasped. "You were right. Mercy sucks."

WOLF NEWS CREW
AL-ZUMAR CAVE COMPLEX
NORTHWEST FRONTIER PROVINCE
PAKISTAN
0808 HOURS LOCAL TIME

The explosions coming from within the mountainside should have sent John Arden into action. Al-Zumar's two guards were right behind him, and he should have used the noise as a diversion to drop and take out at least one of them. Why had he listened to his fear and permitted himself to fall deeper into their grasp?

The answer didn't matter. There was still time left. He would make his move. They were almost at the next tunnel, where they would surely encounter more guards. Should he tip off Shaqib? How without alerting Navarro? Forget it. He had to act immediately. No time to think about it. No time to second guess and wonder if—

"Uh, excuse me," he said, suddenly turning around.

The guard to his right failed to lift his AK before Arden latched onto it, driving the muzzle away from his chest.

Shots rang out. Had they come from the guard's weapon or from the guy beside him? No. They sounded distant.

"Holy shit . . ." he gasped, then looked down. His jacket was covered with blood. The guard was falling toward him, a bloody oval spreading across his chest.

And the other guard had been capped! He dropped like a puppet, the strings cut, his forehead a vortex of blood.

Behind Arden, Shaqib cried out. Had he been hit? No, a shot had burrowed a hole in the mountain, just over the little guy's shoulder. Their saviors above had mistaken Shaqib for a bad guy; then again . . .

Arden peered up the mountain, searching for the source of those shots. He knew Marine Corps marksmanship when he saw it. He waved with his good arm, felt something jab him in the back.

"I told you, we don't need any fucking rescue," Navarro said. "Now walk!"

"It's moment-of-truth time, Rick," Arden said. "You shoot or let me go. Either way, the show's over. You want that interview? You get it yourself. Our boys are up there, and I'll get out with them."

"You were hired to do a job!"

"You still think I work for you?"

Navarro's tone softened a little. "Mr. Arden, I need you to come with me."

"Look, man, you want to throw away your life because you think you can interview the world's most wanted man, that's your fucking business. I'm done." Arden whirled, the AK now jamming him in the chest. He reached up, grabbed the muzzle, lifted it to his head. "Pull that trigger. Or let me go."

TEAM DOGMA
AL-ZUMAR CAVE COMPLEX
NORTHWEST FRONTIER PROVINCE
PAKISTAN
0810 HOURS LOCAL TIME

If Vance would have known that the taller guy was going to turn around and confront one of the guards, he would have held his fire for at least a second. Even as he squeezed the trigger, he had realized that the good guy was turning and that he might shift right into the shot.

But thank God he hadn't. Yeah, he got sprayed with blood, but he was okay. Gutsy son of a bitch he was, standing up to armed men. But his timing sucked. And worse, Rainey had missed his shot on the little guy, but now it didn't seem that guy was armed. He just carried a camera. Maybe he was part of the team, some local camera guy, who knew.

Now what? Two, three, four guys out from the cave and on the trail, running toward the hostages. And there was Navarro, jabbing a gun into the taller guy's head. What the hell was that about? The little guy just stood there, and then he began waving on al-Zumar's fighters.

"All right, gentlemen," Rainey began over the radio. "I don't know what the hell we're looking at down there, but Doc and Vance? Lay down a little fire on those guys coming out of the cave. We'll see if we can buy our hostages some time to climb back up the trail. In the meantime, Terry? You and Houston rally on them. I got a hunch our pilots are just inside that cave and we're looking at the rendezvous point. Roger, out."

Wasting no time, Vance set about directing his sniper rifle toward the oncoming bad guys. The M40A3, with its McMillan A4 stock and excellent M118LR ammo, spat rounds, and two more turbans flew like Frisbees as their owners tumbled. Vance would not give Doc a chance to open up before he killed the next pair, air-mailing a slug to one man who took it in the heart, while the other did the third-eye dance, writhing a second as his head snapped like an antenna in a car wash. Four kills, four seconds. Not bad for a country boy who'd rather take aim at some lily pads with a plastic worm. Vance had broken his own record.

Yeah, getting Dear-Johned was really affecting his

skills. He was sharper than ever, and oh, yes, he wanted to live, wanted to go home, wanted to look Cindy in the eyes and have her tell him to his face that she didn't want to be with him, that she wanted to throw it all away, that she didn't think they were worth it.

Two more guys bolted from the cave. And feeling the anger that she had inspired, Vance leveled the bastards—pan, aim, fire; pan, aim, fire—as they strained against the glare to spot him.

He was a jilted lover, a one-man killing machine, and a bass fisherman all rolled into one lanky blond Marine who wasn't taking shit from anyone. Men would die. They would die hard.

He wiped his nose and suddenly felt no pride in his accomplishment. He had not been the cool shooter with the eagle-like eyes, the professional who drifted from target to target with mechanical precision, making exact adjustments for range and wind velocity while keying in on his target and terminating with zero remorse. He had been a Wild West gunfighter, his hands guided by emotions instead of muscles.

"All right, Vance? Doc?" Rainey called. "I don't know what Navarro's doing, but let's get down there."

Taking his cue from the fighters getting picked off behind him, Navarro muttered, "Asshole," whirled away from Arden, cried out to Shaqib, then hauled ass toward the cave.

Arden waved once more to the Marines above, though he couldn't see them. He dropped to his hands and knees and crawled toward the nearest AK, lying a couple meters off.

More fire from somewhere near the cave sent him diving for the rifle. He reached it, rolled, faced the cave entrance, spotted two dark-skinned guys firing up at the mountain wall.

Had they seen him? Thought he was dead? Arden leveled the rifle on them, jammed down the trigger. The gun rattled while making its familiar pop, and his rounds punched one guy to the snow, but the other one ducked back inside the cave.

Time for analysis. Better make it quick. He had given up his location. The next man to emerge from the cave would target him. Several meters back from the entrance stood a hump, a boulder probably, draped in layers of snow. If he could get behind it.

On three. One, two—

Incoming fire ripped over his shoulder as he ran, angled right, around two fallen guards, kept advancing toward the boulder. No sounds other than that big drum pounding in his chest. A few more steps. He decided to return fire. Tried. Shit. The clip was empty. He threw away the rifle, kept heading for the boulder.

A shout in Arabic sent his gaze up. Two guards were on the trail, their weapons trained on him. They could have easily gunned him down. Wait. He recognized one of them: Fathi.

"A good try," the young Arab said in English. "But now you come with us."

Arden broke from his dash into a walk, then slowed, stopped, looked around. There were no Marines charging toward him to save the day.

He took a huge breath, realized how thirsty he was, then resignedly raised his good arm, which ached almost as badly as his feet. *I'm not strong enough,* he thought. *I'm just too scared to die. But isn't one bullet in the heart better than being tortured by these bastards?*

The fear overcame him. He didn't know what death was, didn't want to know. Didn't want to feel it. "Okay. Okay . . ."

TEAM DOGMA
AL-ZUMAR CAVE COMPLEX
NORTHWEST FRONTIER PROVINCE
PAKISTAN
0813 HOURS LOCAL TIME

While poised on the ledge, Doc had had a chance to rest his ankle. Then Rainey gave the order to move out, and the damned thing had started throbbing again. His logical side told him that he had just sprained his ankle and that he ought to take a chance and remove his boot, examine the injury, and, perhaps apply some tape for support. A no-brainer. But his emotional side said suck it up, be a man, and if you get a chance, take a look, otherwise do not acknowledge. Just do your job.

With no trail outside to work with, they had ducked back into the tunnels to ferret out another exit, perhaps the one Houston and McAllister had used. Rainey and Vance were hauling ass, and Doc hated their pace and the fact that they had returned to the rat-and-cheese game of tunnel warfare. His big Para SAW wasn't designed for point-blank confrontations, and he longed for a lighter weapon, one he could lift more quickly. Oh, he would manage. He was just complaining about everything to get his mind off the little stabs of pain that now accompanied the throbbing in his ankle. Then, of course, there was the insanity of the mission.

The mission? What mission? The real one had ended when their cover had been blown back at Point Mongoose. Sure, they were doing the right thing now. And they could justify delaying their extraction to save American lives. But Doc's instincts told him that someone on the team was going to get hurt. Someone on the team might even die. And with his luck, well, his wife and boys didn't need that news—they needed him very much alive and back home.

And, oh, did he miss home. The breezy summers in Miami. Some complained about the humidity, but not Doc. He loved the heat, loved watching his boys splashing in the pool, loved lying there on his chaise longue with a beer in his hand and a ball game on the TV. Maybe he would go to South Beach, visit the folks, pick up a little dry cleaning (nice to have Mom still doing his laundry since she owned the business!), and get some of Mom's home cooking. What a life. He had the house, the cars, the pool, the beautiful wife and kids. It wasn't the American dream. It was the American reality. And it was what he was fighting for. He had to remember that no matter how shitty it got, those kids and his wife, that life they had forged, was worth dealing with the inherent contradiction of being a special amphibious recon corpsman. A private had once asked him, "So which do you like more? Killing people or saving people?"

"I don't like killing anyone," he had said. "But it's part of the job."

They had taught Doc how to deal with the tough questions, the moral and ethical dilemmas all soldiers face and the even more painful ironies associated with being a corpsman. They had taught him how to shut down. But Doc had soon realized that the more people he killed, the harder it became to dissociate himself from the targets, from the people, the faces, the families he had destroyed. He couldn't turn off his emotions without shutting out his own family, and he refused to do that. You had to feel something.

"Doc, come on, man, we got the exit over here," Vance called back.

Huffing and puffing, his boots scuffling across the tunnel's cold, hard floor, Doc stage-whispered, "Coming. Right behind you."

Although the tunnel had turned up in a gradual incline, Doc, along with the others, had not realized that they would wind up near a string of humps just a dozen or so meters from the mountaintop. With his eyes adjusting once more to the snow glare, he pulled himself up across a pile of stones and crawled onto the ledge, where Rainey and Vance lay on their stomachs, using their Nightstars to inspect broad, white waves of trees that, standing so far below, resembled toothpicks occasionally dotted with spots of green and brown. To the east hovered a wall of gray clouds lumbering toward them, a massive front promising massive amounts of snow. And to the west rose great plumes of smoke as the bombing continued, the B-52s leaving white figure eights in the darkening sky.

"Whoa," Doc said, taking in the view a little too quickly and losing his breath. "We're a long way up."

"Took a wrong turn at Albuquerque," Vance said, doing the poorest Bugs Bunny impression Doc had ever heard.

"And you don't want to know our elevation," said Rainey, checking the GPS strapped to his wrist. "But you can tell the air's a little thinner up here."

"So now we go back in, look for another exit," Doc said, his frustration mounting quickly as he turned back.

"Wait a minute," said Vance. "I think I got something."

Doc dropped down beside them, wrenching free his own binoculars, and, following Vance's angle, he scanned the valley below and came to hold on some foothills where, amid the snow drifts, a group of fifteen or so individuals trekked north toward the forest and the mountain beyond. Zooming in, Doc realized that while two of the people wore tattered canvas jackets common among some of the local tribes, their pants were unmistakably Marine Corps issue. Moreover, their hands were bound behind their backs and guards gripped their arms, leading them on. You'd have to be just off the bus to Parris Island—or flying high above in a reconnaissance plane—not to recognize them. "Bingo. Got the pilots," he said.

"And it looks like Navarro, the tall guy, and the short guy are with them," Rainey said. "Jesus, they got out of there fast."

"These guys got secret tunnels all over this place," Vance groaned. "At least now they're out in the open."

"But for how long?" Rainey asked. "And where in hell are they going?" He began pulling up map images on his GPS.

Doc was about to comment on their next course of action, but reverberating gunfire drove his gaze south, to the trail nearly indistinguishable below.

"Dogma Five, this is Dogma One, over," Rainey called into his boom mike.

"One? This is Five," McAllister said. "We can't get near that tunnel. Count six, maybe eight shooters holding there. Can't waste the ammo, over."

"Can you get off that trail and slip down into those foothills?"

"Maybe. Can you throw down a rope?"

Rainey smirked at the wisecrack. "Just go for it. When you're down there, contact me. We've spotted our pilots and Navarro's group heading north, exiting right where those foothills trail off from your position. We'll rendezvous there, over."

"Roger, out."

"Gentlemen," Rainey said, rolling onto his side. "We either go back in, look for another exit and kill anyone who gets in our way, or"—Rainey pointed to a rather steep, hair-raising course snaking down the mountainside—"we try to follow this ridgeline all the way down."

Descending such a grade would ordinarily be done with climbing gear, including mission-specific ropes, carabiners, and the like. Of course, they had been on a picture-taking mission and hadn't packed the ropes, let alone the St. Bernard with the little safety barrel under his chin.

"Doc, you up for it?" Rainey asked.

"I am good to go, Sergeant." Doc rose and eased out to the ridge, noting that it fell off at about a forty-degree incline. He dug one boot in the snow while lowering the other.

"Hey, this one ain't bad," Rainey said, following to the right. "We've done this before. Always one foot and one hand on the ground, moving from rock to rock, tree to tree. Take apart the climb. Is it coming back to you?"

"Actually, Sarge, last night's dinner is about to repeat on me," Vance said, shifting in behind Doc and accidentally kicking snow onto Doc's hand and arm.

"Sorry," the fisherman said.

"It's all right," Doc assured him. "Just don't remind me of food. I'd kill for some bacon, eggs, and flapjacks—"

"With strawberry syrup," Vance added.

"Strawberry?" Doc frowned deeply. "Boy, you got to

have pure Vermont maple syrup, otherwise you are going straight to pancake hell."

"What about you, Sarge?" Vance asked.

Doc shook his head. "You forgetting about him and his protein shakes?"

"Sarge?" Vance called again.

But Rainey's attention lay elsewhere. He had one hand on the ground as he leaned sideways, the other hand balancing the Nightstars over his nose. "They're gaining some serious ground. We have to speed this up. Let's move, Marines!"

Well, well, well, the rookie had taught old McAllister a lesson, and getting stuck with him wasn't getting stuck after all. The kid had even found a respectable course down to the foothills. The trick was to descend without drawing fire. The trick had to involve keeping the guards near the cave busy until they were far enough down so the boulders and occasional pines would shield them.

But damn it, they weren't magicians or master strategists. Sure, McAllister had lots of plans. He planned on taking a shower when he got back. He planned on going bass fishing with Vance. He planned on visiting his favorite titty bar, where he would breathe in cheap perfume wafting up from gravity-defying breasts as he told stories of glory and adventure to women who would, for two hours, pretend to be interested in more than the stack of twenties in his wallet.

But a plan to escape? Shit. You had him there.

"Okay, here's what I'm thinking," the kid said as they pressed themselves into tight little packages inside a meter-deep depression along the trail, their intended course just a few meters back. "We hit 'em with a couple of grenades and run like hell."

"That's all you got?"

"What do you got?"

"Look, man, it sounds stupid."

"If it's stupid, and it works—"

"It ain't stupid," McAllister finished. Damn Murphy and his laws again.

"We won't have much time to climb down to the next foothill. I saw a ledge overlooking this real big drift. Drop's only about five, six meters."

"Oh, only six meters," McAllister said, imagining himself diving headfirst into an empty swimming pool.

"Come on, old man," Houston said, that youthful fire flickering in his eyes. "Live a little dangerously."

McAllister had to smile, given who he was, his experience, and their current situation. He pulled out a grenade, saw that he only had three left in his cache.

Houston had his own firecracker ready. "Don't miss." He pulled the pin, wound up, and pitched, immediately drawing gunfire from the cave.

Ripping his own pin out with his teeth, McAllister sent his bomb skyward, then hauled his weary ass after Houston. Neither he nor the kid flinched as the grenades struck successive blows, boring through heavy rock and silencing the incoming gunfire. McAllister chanced a look back, saw only smoke, returned to the slope—

That suddenly dropped away at an alarming grade, and McAllister's legs slipped out from beneath him. He flapped hard onto his ass and began sliding down toward Houston, his heels cutting across ice beneath a few inches of snow, nothing there to slow him down. He tried balancing his weight with his rifle, then drove the weapon's butt into the ice.

The kid had barely turned back when McAllister hit him, knocked him flat onto his side, and the two of them went rolling down the slope, toward that ledge Houston had mention, a ledge with a sheer drop-off.

And McAllister knew that their momentum was too great.

He hit the ledge first, landing flat on his back, his rifle held high across his chest, the rucksack and vest jingling with all the junk stowed inside. But that jingling was short-lived as suddenly, he no longer felt the snow and ice beneath him.

Just air.

And there was Houston, right beside him, swearing and plummeting down.

Down. Down. For three heartbeats.

Then, with a breath-stealing thud, McAllister sank nearly a full meter into the snowdrift, snow blasting into his face and grating across his cheeks, his legs buried somewhere beneath, his rifle a snow-covered icicle.

"You all right?" Houston asked, having landed on his side, only his left arm, head, and part of his torso visible above the drift.

"Seven meters," McAllister said, brushing off his face. Jesus, he didn't know snow could hurt so much.

"What?"

"The drop. It was seven meters."

Houston glanced up the hill, let his gaze fall back on their position. "You're right."

McAllister let his guard down and winked.

Finally, a grin from the kid.

Then it was back to business. "We got snow jammed up our sleeves, pants, everywhere. Our body heat will melt it. Cold and dry is survivable. Cold and wet is not."

"Hear that." Houston shivered audibly, then began pulling himself out.

Glad that he hadn't broken anything, or at least it felt so, McAllister looked around for some wood to knock on. Since his rifle's stock was covered in snow, he settled for his noggin, beat his fist twice on his temple, then started digging himself free. "We'll head to those trees, then work our way along the back of that next hill, coming in from the east toward those foothills Rainey's talking about."

"Yeah," Houston said. "If we don't freeze first."

12

Captain Tom Graham's eyes were still irritated from the tear gas, despite the water the terrorists had given him and Lieutenant Ingram to flush away the contamination. Still, he saw enough to realize that Rick Navarro, that guy from Wolf News, had been captured with them, along with another guy who seemed part of Navarro's news crew. Thus far the thugs had kept them separated from the newspeople, with Graham and Ingram held tightly near the front of the group and driven quickly on, through the valley, the snow knee-deep in spots. The man up front with the black woolen cap was clearly the leader, and he kept the old man with long beard at his side. If Graham didn't know better, he would swear the guy was Mohammed al-Zumar himself, but many Arab men sported similar beards and had equally dark complexions. Still, there was something about the guy that was very, very familiar. But he couldn't be al-Zumar. The world's most wanted man wouldn't be stupid enough to try walking away from the greatest military machine on the face of the Earth.

"Captain . . ." Ingram's anxious tone was unmistakable. She had never been captured before, and for that matter, neither had Graham.

"Just remember the Articles of the Code of Conduct," he told her. "And you heard that gunfire. Sounds like Rainey's coming after us."

"No, they'll order him out. Send in another team, probably," Ingram said. "But that team will be too late. And even if they're not, how would they ever find us?"

The guard holding Graham's left arm squeezed hard, said something in Arabic.

"Guess they don't like us talking."

"No, no, it's okay," came a voice from behind. A little guy holding a big camera hurried up beside them. "They want you to talk to me."

"You work for Navarro?" Graham asked.

"I did," the wiry guy said. "I am Shaqib. I will translate for you. The sheikh wants you to know that if you do what he says, he won't kill you."

"And he's the sheikh?" Graham said, lifting his chin to the black-capped man up front.

"Yes."

"What's his real name?"

Shaqib stared curiously. "You don't know?"

Graham faced Ingram, whose sore eyes widened. "No way," she said. "No way. I don't . . . I can't . . . believe this."

"I guess when our luck goes bad, it really goes bad," Graham said, staring hard at the man up front. "So that's Mohammed al-Zumar."

"To some, a great man. A prophet."

"To others, a maniac. A murderer," Graham said. "You have no idea how many lives he's ruined."

"I think I do. But he won't kill you. He will try to trade you for some of his people being held by your government. I heard him say this."

"They've had other American prisoners before. And do you know what's happened to every one of them?"

Shaqib lowered his gaze. "I will help you stay alive."

"Why? You don't work for him?"

"I work for my family, not his. I do what I must do. But I don't want to see you die. I am tired of death. I have seen too much."

"All right, you want to help?" Graham asked. "Tell me where we're going."

"North. I don't know for sure. Maybe over the mountains and into Chitral. There is a small airstrip."

"You think he'll try to fly out from there?"

"Maybe. I have heard them mention Tajikistan more than once. The sheikh may have allies coming to get him."

"This guy's on the run," Graham told Ingram. "And I doubt he'll waste any time trying to bargain with us."

"Then why hasn't he killed us?" she asked.

"Maybe, if he has to, he'll use us as a shield—or if

our guys manage to corner him, he'll play the hostage game." Graham regarded Shaqib with a hard stare. "So what now? You tell him everything we've said here?"

"I know you don't trust me. It's no problem. But I will tell him that you will do what he says." The translator lifted a thumb, shook it, then hurried on ahead to catch up with al-Zumar.

"It's like a dream," Ingram said, her voice cracking. "A very bad dream. I mean, what are the odds?"

"Yeah, I know. We've been looking for this guy for months, and we get shot down and bang, here we are, walking into the mountains with him. Maybe it's about fate."

"Or about one of us pissing off God. And I'm sorry, Captain, but this is all your fault." She smiled weakly at him.

"I'll take the blame. You just hang in there. You have to believe we'll be rescued, because there's a lot of power in just believing."

"Okay. But that's hard when your eyes are burning and your ass is freezing."

Graham nodded and trudged on through the snow, the guards driving him hard, the idea of planning an escape growing more remote. They were just two against—what was it? Ten, twelve armed gunmen, including al-Zumar and his Obi-Wan advisor? And even if their hands weren't bound with old twine, and even if the little translator guy did help them, could they really seize weapons and take out enough men before someone got off a fatal round? Negative. The Articles of the Code of Conduct said that if taken prisoner Graham should do everything in his power to try to escape. The articles said nothing about foolhardy acts. A successful escape would involve waiting, watching, and seizing an opportunity when it came.

Of course, Graham still couldn't write off Rainey and his team. The phrase "no one gets left behind" was tattooed on Mac Rainey's heart—right next to the words "I never buy my own drinks."

OUTSIDE AL-ZUMAR CAVE COMPLEX
NORTHWEST FRONTIER PROVINCE
PAKISTAN
0915 HOURS LOCAL TIME

Still shaking from his near-fatal encounter with the sheikh, Haroun charged through the foothills toward the south cave entrance. He would turn his fear into courage, his courage into victory. The Americans were still coming, and he would find them.

Reaching the top of the next foothill, he jolted and dropped to his gut as below, someone shifted from one pine to the next. A fellow fighter? Maybe. He could call out to the man, but if he were wrong . . .

Better to just wait and let the guy advance. Wishing he had a pair of binoculars, Haroun dug himself a little deeper into the snow and continued peering over the crest. No shadows wavered across the hill, and even the limbs seemed, for a moment, utterly motionless. But what was that? A slight crunch of snow? From behind?

From the right? He swung his head this way and that. Still nothing.

He reached for his pack of cigarettes, pulled them out, realized what he was doing and put them away. He took up his AK in both hands and cursed his addiction.

There was something. A limb swaying. A bird? Just the wind. He focused once more on that limb, a broad one extending from the pine like an arm with six gnarled elbows and long talons heaped with snow. Anyone just below? No. Haroun listened as the wind whistled down across the foothills and dark clouds abruptly hid the sun. How long could he remain there when the Americans were probably killing his brothers back in the cave?

He dug his boots into the snow. He had good footing, enough to propel him up and over the hill. He would charge down to the first group of trees, where he would seek cover, wait, then drive on toward the next bluff.

"Kill those Americans. Kill all of them. And I will find a special place for you in my army."

"I will do it, my Sheikh," Haroun muttered aloud, even as the faintest sound of footfalls met his ears.

His head never made it around before a horrible pain broke across his back, accompanied by heavy pressure, as though someone had just punched him in the back.

He rolled onto his side, glanced up through tearing eyes.

A middle-aged man with a scarred lip and a Marine Corps bush cover balanced crookedly on his head sighed, probably in disgust. The soldier, his face covered in smeared camouflage paint, held the bloody blade that had just impaled Haroun's back, and as Haroun lay there, bleeding inside, bleeding to death, he reflexively gripped the man's wrist, wanting to retaliate, wanting to show the Americans that he was a Warrior of Mohammed, that he would fight the *jihad* to his last breath, that they could take his life but that his spirit was Allah's. One day the infidels would pay for their sins. One day . . .

The Marine wrenched free of Haroun's hand as another soldier, a younger man with boyish features, joined the first. He searched Haroun's pockets, took the pack of cigarettes and said, "Bet you would've smoked more if you knew you'd die like this."

But Haroun did not understand the words, and the soldier just dumped the cigarettes onto the snow. The older soldier tipped his head, and, without a word, the two left, their footsteps lost in the wind.

A warm, wet sensation flooded into Haroun's chest, and his limbs began to tingle. He closed his eyes, realized he could no longer breathe. His lungs had filled with blood. *My Sheikh, do you have a special place in Paradise for me?*

TEAM DOGMA
OUTSIDE AL-ZUMAR CAVE COMPLEX
NORTHWEST FRONTIER PROVINCE
PAKISTAN
0918 HOURS LOCAL TIME

Rainey had been taught that it's better to aim for a 70-percent solution rather than devising a perfect plan that is implemented too late. After taking all available information into account, you dreamed up the best plan with the highest chance of success—and well, maybe you didn't have all the particulars worked out, but you had enough to get started. The enemy would certainly inspire your creativity, and at the very least, you'd deliver your 70-percent on time.

A 70-percent solution? Think I've gone for more like 60, Rainey thought as he, Vance, and Doc negotiated their way down the last part of the ridge, their rifles slung, their hearts—at least Rainey's—in their throats.

"Dogma One, this is Dogma Five, over," came McAllister's voice through Rainey's earpiece.

"Five? This is One. You there yet, over?"

"Standing by. GPS coordinates to follow, over."

Rainey hesitated a moment as he flipped the protective cover off the GPS unit on his wrist, activated the device, and plugged in the two sets of three numbers as McAllister read them. "Coordinates received, over. Our ETA approximately ten minutes, over."

"Better haul ass. I've tagged our group, but we're going to lose them soon, over."

"Do not lose them. Repeat. Do not lose them. If that means moving out, you move out. We'll catch up with you, over."

"Roger, out."

While Rainey had paused, Doc and Vance had reached a breach in the ridge and were lowering themselves into it. At about a meter deep, the breach would provide excellent cover as they skirted around to where the path spilled out into the foothills.

And while Rainey had paused, it had begun to snow again. Another front, damn it. Those bonnet boys would be pulling out soon, no doubt. The weather was a blessing and a curse: Rainey and his team would not be blown apart by a cluster bomb with Mohammed al-Zumar's name on it. The storm or an enemy bullet would do the job.

As the snow glare faded even more, and the mountains grew strangely dark for morning, Rainey beat a furtive and wary path down to the gap, keeping one gloved hand on the ice as he hopped down and joined his men.

"Just like a trench," Vance said, hunkered down and shifting along the gap.

"Or a foxhole," Doc said, his breath trailing like car exhaust. "Not that any foxes actually use this thing. They all dropped dead from the cold."

"Hey, Sarge, when is the next helo going to reach the secondary pickup point?" Vance asked.

Rainey checked his watch. "Well, they were already in the air, so I'm guessing a couple of hours, give or take."

"Colonel St. Andrew's going to shit a brick when he finds out we've ignored their calls and we're not there," said Doc. "Problem is, we won't be back at camp to see that." Doc looked over his shoulder, winked at Rainey.

"He's a good guy," Rainey said. "Just trying to do the right thing. We've all worked for bigger assholes than him. And it's not his reaction I'm worried about."

They knew what he had meant, and both men fell silent because neither of them had any idea what it was like to have your girlfriend listening in every time you executed a mission. Doc's wife was no platoon radio operator, and Vance, well, he had just been DJed, but Rainey had heard that the girl was a civilian.

Most guys, Rainey knew, spared their spouses or significant others the details of what they did, opting for more general phrases and euphemisms. Instead of "I stabbed a guy, and his intestines popped like sausages on a grill," they said, "I encountered enemy resistance and neutralized the activity." Of course, there were always a few who got off on sharing the grim and the grisly. But they were the exception. War was a nasty business, and the details just weren't important to Rainey's relationship with Kady. Thus, he used neutral language when describing his field activities, but she knew damned well exactly what he had done.

"You don't actually like killing, do you?" she had once asked him.

"Yeah, I do."

That had sent her springing up from the hotel room bed. "You do?"

He had smirked. "What do you think?"

"I don't know."

"You think I'm some warmonger or something—just because I'm a Marine? I mean you of all people—"

"I've never killed anyone, so I don't know what it feels like. I'm just asking."

"If I like it . . ."

"Yeah. I mean that has to be a feeling of power, right? You *are* playing God. You're ending someone's life. You're making that decision."

"But is it really my decision? Did I order that bad guy to start shooting at me? Did I force that bad guy to swear his allegiance to some psycho asshole who likes to destroy American landmarks and kill innocent people?"

"We're not talking about him. We're talking about you. And I'm asking you, do you like killing?"

"Think about it, Kady. If I have to kill somebody, that means my cover has been blown. That means I'm a trigger-puller and I've already failed my mission. You should go ask those guys in infantry if they like killing, not me."

"So you don't feel anything? Just failure?"

"What is this? A psych evaluation? A third degree or something? Didn't I already take this course?"

She had closed her eyes and had fallen back on her pillow. "I just want to know you. I want to know what it feels like to be you."

Rainey had stretched out his weary arms and legs sore from a ten-mile hump the day before. "Sweetheart, it hurts."

"You don't sound happy."

"Kady, right now, I'm very happy being with you. I just wish we could talk about something else, like what we're going to get for dinner. You know, when I'm out there, I'm just acting and reacting. Guy's right there in front of me, about to pull the trigger, I take him out and move on. No second thoughts. I can't feel bad for that guy, and neither should I be partying over his death. We're both soldiers. Both trained to do the same thing. Hell, if there wasn't a war going on and his politics weren't too radical, I might even buy him a drink. We understand each other. We know what it's like to do a job most people don't want. Pop stars with belly rings are heroes, not us."

"Thank you," she had whispered, then had kissed him on the cheek.

"For what?"

"The truth."

Rainey smiled inwardly as he followed Doc and Vance down to the foothills, the snow falling harder now.

That Kady Forrest was a piece of work, all right, and while Rainey was a hard man, he had fallen hard for her. Very hard. Shit. The ring he had bought her sat back in his footlocker at Liberty Bell. That ring had been sitting there for two weeks, and Rainey realized that when he got back—if he got back—he would end two decades of bachelor bliss. He would slip that ring on her finger and ask her to be his wife.

You dumb ass, he thought. *You could've realized that before you came out here to get shot at and freeze half to death. You die up here, and it'll kill her when she finds that ring in your locker. It'll just kill her.*

But wasn't that human nature? He had to see, really see, what losing her might be like. And now he knew he couldn't let her go. *But I'm still a dumb ass.*

Three rounds ripped into the snow, just above Vance's head, and as he hit the deck, he cried, "Incoming!"

The kid could've spared the announcement. Rainey and Doc knew incoming fire when they saw and heard it, and that fire always got their attention. Crawling on his hands and knees along the trench, Rainey came up behind Doc, who, with his Nightstars in hand, was about to range out on the next hill.

"Forget it," Rainey said, pushing away Doc's binoculars. "We just keep low and keep moving. You got time for a firefight? I sure as hell don't."

"Tell them that," Vance said, a fresh salvo shoveling snow onto his head. "And just down there, where this trench widens, we'll be out in the open until we get to those trees at the base of that next hill."

"Without looking, how many you think, Doc?" Rainey asked.

The corpsman listened intently to the next two salvos. "Three guys, probably four meters apart. I remember seeing that first group of trees to our left. That's where they're holding. I'd bet a dollar on it."

"Wow, a real gambling man. All right. We get down to the bottom. Vance, ready on some smoke. We set up a screen. They take the bait, and we crawl on by."

Rainey had just devised another less than 70-percent solution, but he refused to be anal about the math; he was just trying to see tomorrow.

Vance held up the smoke grenade, signaling he was ready, then turned and broke into a hunched-over sprint down the trench. Doc and Rainey followed suit, the incoming still concentrated on their prior position.

Rainey knew that blowing smoke would help blind the enemy to their escape, but he realized that it might also be seen by a bomber pilot who could radio the coordinates back to Camp Liberty Bell. Lieutenant Colonel St. Andrew might misconstrue the data and assume that Rainey and his team had gone to the wrong coordinates and were blowing smoke for a pickup that would never happen. Then again, smoke wouldn't be used unless they had been in contact with the chopper pilot. No matter what, though, the smoke would definitely raise questions, should it be spotted. But should Rainey worry about that now? No way. He gave Vance the signal and the young sniper popped the pin and tossed the fourteen-ounce grenade shaped like a soda can. The two-second fuse lasted only one second (Murphy's Law again), and thick, green smoke rose into the storm's pregame show of flurries.

Interesting how when presented with an obvious target, most poorly trained or inexperienced soldiers will fire mindlessly at it, not realizing that their fire had been drawn to help the enemy escape. In fact, employing such a gambit told you a lot about the men you were fighting. Rainey had expected to encounter at least some older Afghan guerrillas who had dug in against the Soviets, and those men were at least as committed and as stubborn as his own. But the guys below? They had to be raw recruits, Pakistani tribesmen who had signed on with the Warriors of Mohammed because a few local warlords sympathetic to al-Zumar had ordered them to serve or be shot.

While the popping of AKs grew ever more fierce, Vance and Doc bounded across the hill, reached the smoke wall, then hit the deck and crawled beneath the gauntlet of fire. Rainey stole a moment to peer through his Nightstars. Three muzzle flashes lit before the smoke draped across his field of view. He considered lobbing a grenade, only because the guys were kicking up so much fire that they really pissed him off. Nah, they weren't worth it. He dropped down, followed in Doc's furrow, and joined his men at the trees.

"What do you think?" Rainey asked Vance, who was already reading the path ahead.

The kid lowered his Nightstars. "We can follow this tree line all the way across."

"Good. Doc, how's the ankle?"

The corpsman feigned innocence. "What ankle?"

"Right. You're okay, man. You know that?"

"I am much better than okay. It's you rookie operators who keep me on my toes."

"Whoa, Sergeant. Take a look at this," Vance said, thrusting out his Nightstars.

Rainey accepted the binoculars, peered down the tree line, swept up to the next rise, and found at least a dozen fighters establishing positions between and behind the pines. "Can we get around them?"

"Yeah, but that'll take time."

Doc sighed loudly through his teeth. "Well, we're not taking them on. Like you said, Sarge, we don't have time for a firefight."

"No, we don't," Rainey argued, calculating how long it might take for them to cut across the next foothill and advance from the back side, out of enemy view. He shifted the boom mike closer to his lips. "Dogma Five, this is Dogma One, over."

"One, this is Five, over."

"Terry, where are you now?"

"We're still holding here. Still have the group in sight. Be advised we're moving in five minutes, over."

"Roger that. Be advised we have approximately a dozen bad guys setting up between your position and ours, over."

"Dogma One, I can see at least two of your bad guys from here. Up on the ridge to the east there's another group of five, maybe six, over."

Rainey drew in a deep breath, scanned the ridge in question, spotted the men shifting along the ledge. He glanced away from the Nightstars, considered how far McAllister and Houston were from the other group blocking their path. "All right, Terry, I want you to get up behind the guys blocking us, then direct your fire on those guys on the ridge. Let me know when you're in position. Houston continues tailing our group. Execute on my mark, over."

"Roger that, moving out. Execute on your mark, out."

"What's on your mind, Sarge?" Vance asked.

"Well, we got these guys in front of us, and those guys up on the ridge. McAllister's going to get them firing on each other. See, they've got time for a firefight, so we'll kick-start the party. When hell breaks, so do we. I know you're tired. But we have to haul with everything we've got. We get pinned here, we're finished."

"So we break to the west?" Doc asked. "Get behind that long slope over there?"

"Exactly," Rainey said. "And then we go back to playing catch up."

* * *

"It's up to you, kid," McAllister said, slapping a big hand on Houston's shoulder. "Keep eyes on at all times. If you lose them, this whole thing is shot to shit—not that I want to put any pressure on you. Be good now."

"Hey, thanks, Sergeant. At least you still have a little faith in me."

The old man gave a half-shrug and scampered off between the trees, drawing closer to the guys cutting off Rainey, Vance, and Doc. It took but a moment for the falling snow to consume McAllister, and with that, Houston turned and trotted off himself.

So the whole thing rested on his shoulders. No problem. He now had an even better opportunity to prove himself as a first-class operator. And while the team represented the eyes and ears of the commander, Houston represented the same for Rainey. He was proud to accept the responsibility, and he knew, he just knew that he could do the job, do it well, and walk away feeling very good about himself. It was time to let the real E-3 Lance Cpl. Bradley Houston shine.

At the next tree, he dove for cover, then crawled up a little bunny hill to peer down across the next valley, where he had been observing the pilots and news crew just a handful of seconds before.

They were gone.

He practically tore open his vest to get at his Nightstars, zoomed in, surveyed the entire area, his heart triphammering in his chest. The wind began blowing the snow sideways, and visibility diminished by the

minute. Just trees and valley. No terrorists. No pilots.
No news crew. *Nada.*

Shuddering with panic, Houston rose and scrambled
down the hill, running madly to get closer, to get a visual, to get sight of something that said he hadn't blown
the mission.

Again.

13

CAMP LIBERTY BELL
FIFTH FORCE RECONNAISSANCE COMPANY
THIRD PLATOON HEADQUARTERS
NORTHWEST FRONTIER PROVINCE
PAKISTAN
0920 HOURS LOCAL TIME

The mood inside the command tent had not changed. Most officers and enlisted personnel remained as cold and crisp as the air outside, exhibiting a level of professionalism both expected and demanded of Marines. But Lieutenant Colonel St. Andrew was that live wire, that burst of static electricity that caught you off-guard, and Kady tensed every time new information reached her station:

"Delta Eagle Nine still reports no contact with Team Dogma," she said. "Their ETA to Extraction Point Sigma is approximately two hours, ten minutes."

Lieutenant Colonel St. Andrew, who'd been leaning over Kady's shoulder, growled in her ear, "Get Rainey for me. Now."

"Yes, sir." Kady switched to the correct frequency. "Dogma One, this is Beacon Light, over. Dogma One, this is Beacon Light, over."

"Anything?" St. Andrew asked impatiently.

"Still waiting, sir. Their radio operator's equipment could be damaged, or they could be in the middle of—"

"Don't make any excuses for them, Sergeant. Just make contact—"

"Yes, sir."

"—because the last thing I'm going to be is a pissed-off lieutenant colonel with a rogue in the field."

Kady tensed even more. "Yes, sir. Dogma One, this is Beacon Light, over. Dogma One, this is Beacon light. Report your situation, over."

In all likelihood, Rainey and his guys were making their way toward the extraction point, and knowing Rainey, he would make contact with the helo when the situation proved safe.

But Kady couldn't forget that Rainey was still a Marine, through and through, and the thought of leaving captured personnel behind might've been too much to bear. He might've taken his boys in after those downed pilots, and if he did that and got himself killed, Kady would never forgive herself for falling in love with a man who didn't know when to quit. But deep down, wasn't his determination, his ability to keep going when others would fall, what she admired most about him?

"Sir, still no contact with Team Dogma," she said, ripping herself back to the moment. "But there's a report coming in now from one of the Warthogs. He's spotted smoke in the mountains."

"Let me have the numbers," St. Andrew ordered.

Kady requested the coordinates, read them aloud to St. Andrew, who compared them to something he glimpsed on his computer screen. Something clicked in his eyes, and he hustled out of the tent. Kady had jotted down Rainey's last known position and made a comparison for herself. Yes, Rainey's team could have easily blown that smoke, but if they had, they were too far west of the new extraction point.

Platoon radio operator Sgt. Tonisha Grant, a spirited woman in her late twenties, approached, shaking her head. "Kady, sweetheart, I can't let you have the station anymore. You were off duty twenty minutes ago, and the lieutenant colonel knows that. Time to get some sleep."

"Sleep? What's that?"

"It's what those of us who aren't in love do."

Biting her lip, Kady held back the tears.

"Hey, don't worry. If something happens, I'll send word right away. You know I will."

Kady stood, removed her headset, and a tear finally escaped. "You promise me?"

"I promise. Now get some rest."

Donning her heavy coat and buttoning it all the way to the collar, Kady uttered a weak thank you and a goodbye to her friend, saluted the lieutenant colonel, then left the tent.

Outside, the snow was already up to her ankles, the gravelly path between tents all but gone. Shivering, she headed absently toward her billet, her mind's eye con-

juring up pictures of Rainey in the mountains, running
for his life.

Shaking off the image, she broke into a jog and
nearly knocked over two Pfc.s who were too cold to
care. Yes, she would try to get some sleep. Maybe an
hour's worth. Then she would request permission from
Major Roxboro to remain in the command tent as an
observer. He was a good man, an understanding man.
He would grant her that request. Colonel St. Andrew
would probably glare as though she were part of his
problem. He had no right to be upset with Rainey—not
when he didn't know all the facts. Rainey was not being
a rogue; he was just being Rainey: a man who would
give his life to defend the stars and stripes, to defend
what most Americans take for granted. And that meant
he would endanger himself, but he would not make a
decision that wasn't in the best interests of the Corps
and the nation. Of that much, Kady felt certain.

TEAM DOGMA
0.3 KILOMETERS NORTH OF AL-ZUMAR CAVE COMPLEX
NORTHWEST FRONTIER PROVINCE
PAKISTAN
0925 HOURS LOCAL TIME

When Houston wasn't serving as one of the team's
scouts, he was, of course, the radio operator, monitoring both the tactical and command frequencies for traf-
fic pertaining to Team Dogma and its mission. When a

call from Beacon Light came in, he was supposed to perform a simple and obvious task: key the mike and answer it! But Houston had ignored the most recent call from Beacon Light because Rainey had ordered him to observe command frequency silence, an order that Houston had no trouble obeying. Better to let the operators in the field work things out without the armchair lieutenant colonels stepping in to say things like, "Well, you boys had better clean up your act, speed up your pace, and bring us back some terrorist heads for the media." Well, they wouldn't say it like that, but their meaning would be painfully clear. Yes, it was far better to keep the brass at bay, get the job done, then let them know what happened after the dust settled.

And thank God for Rainey's order, because at the moment the last thing Houston needed was a chat with headquarters when he had lost visual contact with the pilots, the news crew, and the terrorists.

He reached the next pine tree and paused there, breathing hard like a dog, like a fool who had botched the mission. His lips were beginning to chap, his heart beginning to fail from beating so goddamned hard. *Where the hell are you people? You were right there! Right there!*

Still screaming in his head, Houston strained to see through the trees, the descending clouds, and the snow coming down like big, fat corn flakes spray-painted white for some high school theatre production. What he need to see was that damned group. He literally shook with the desire.

After a beat of static that jolted Houston, Rainey's order came over the tactical frequency: "Good to go? All right, Terry, Fire!"

McAllister let loose with his M4 on the bad guys working the ridge. The shots sounded distant, and Houston realized just how far he'd come from the cave exits. The bad guys answered in kind, multiple reports followed by a jumble of echoes as, hopefully, the bad guys began targeting each other and, hopefully, McAllister summarily got his ass out of there before the group in the trees got wise.

But where would Houston establish the rendezvous point? He didn't have the group in sight. The ploy to get the sergeant, Doc, and Vance to their side of the foothills was already underway. What was he supposed to do? Call and tell them to forget about it?

Screw that. All those people didn't just vanish via green-screen special effects. They were on the ground. Somewhere. Funny, it was all about finding the right piece of real estate. It was all about their location, their location, their location. Houston guessed that his old man hadn't realized how selling real estate and running a Force Recon operation could be compared or how they could collide. And Houston estimated he had about five minutes to locate that vital piece of real estate containing their hostages before Rainey would call for his location. That's right. Five stinking minutes. *Come on. You have to be here. Come on!*

Houston narrowed his gaze so tightly that it hurt, but the Nightstars told no lies, told no tales.

* * *

Maybe the cold was getting under his skin, Vance wasn't sure, but he just didn't feel right as he broke left, leading Doc and Rainey toward the back side of the foothills as the thugs ahead continued trading fire with their buddies on the ridge. The adrenaline was pumping, sure. And he was leaning forward, leading with his rifle, and plowing hard through the snow, the muscles in his hips aching. It was supposed to be one of those moments when you're swept up in the intensity, when you don't think, just act; one of those moments when, if you're asked to describe it later, you have a hard time remembering anything because you were just part of the fog of war, the blur, and sometimes even a mindless cog in the killing machine.

But Vance would remember very clearly what it was like to run across the slopes, breaking away from the fighters ahead, not because his senses were highly engaged, but because he was suddenly pretending he was Cindy, now a Marine, now doing his job while he waited for her back home. How would she react? Okay, she would be scared out of her mind. But so would he if he had to teach first graders all about the world. He would tell them that his girlfriend was overseas fighting a controversial war from which she might never return. Damn, that didn't sound very good. You could stick all the little paper flags you wanted on it, but the fact remained that Vance had been gone for months. He could be gone for as long as a year . . . or even forever. No amount of patriotic feelings and fervor could take away the loneliness or the fear.

So maybe she's right, he thought, as he slid down several meters, making a haphazard descent toward a knot of boulders whose backs were piled high with snow. *Maybe I'm not being fair?*

Doc's Para SAW drummed thunder behind Vance, and he whirled, having not seen the two fighters just off his right shoulder.

Rainey held a confiscated AK on one guy and triggered a round that punched the man's neck, while Doc's slugs tore into the chests of both men, who tumbled back onto the bloody snow.

Vance thought of apologizing, but he knew the sergeant wouldn't have it. He returned to the path, picking up the pace, his mind clearing to that empty state of action and reaction. Getting Dear-Johned had finally caught up with him. He had been so preoccupied that he hadn't sensed that attack. The look on Rainey's face said that he didn't suspect anything. Really, the whole thing had happened so quickly that no one would blame Vance for reacting a second late.

Still, Vance had not seen the look on Doc's face, so when the man neared him and said curtly, "Stay alert," Vance returned a quick, "I will."

And for once Cpl. Jimmy Vance, a man who made his living by imitating a ghost, did not appreciate someone seeing right through him.

McAllister stood, his back to a pine tree, his weapon held upright, the barrel just inches from his cheeks. He breathed very quietly through his nose. He did not move a muscle. Thought better of even blinking.

They were just behind him. Their commander had heard McAllister's shots and had ordered them back to investigate. By the time McAllister had thought of running, time had run out.

Two men. Ugly bastards. Even uglier than him. An accomplishment. Give them an ugly award. Pin medals on their asses. Do not get close enough to smell them.

No, McAllister had no intention of that. He listened to their footfalls, visualized exactly where they were, considered popping the pin on one of his metal funballs, but the job could be accomplished more efficiently with a solid pivot and an even more solid grip on his weapon.

Just another few seconds. Why wasn't his whole life flashing before his eyes? For that matter, why wasn't his death? Blame it on the cold. Maybe the antifreeze in his brain had gone bad. No, his entire being was focused on the sounds coming in, the slightest creak of limbs, the snow coming down almost silently, save for the breeze, the continued crunch of those footfalls, closer, just another step. Life itself was wrapped up in those sounds.

Full automatic-weapons fire cut through the still forest as McAllister reached the end of his pivot. The two fighters staggered backward, clutching their abdomens, and before they hit the ground McAllister was already withdrawing in a full sprint.

Why couldn't he lighten his pack? The damned thing tugged so hard on his shoulders that as he reached the thickest of four pines and stole around the tree for cover, he swore he would collapse. He just had to have all that stuff, didn't he? A security blanket. A liability. *Well, now you pay the price, old man.*

But, hey, he had removed that old receipt, right? His pack was at least an ounce lighter . . .

Off again. Boots thumping into the snow, his shoulders fighting against the pack. "Dogma One, this is Dogma Five, over."

"Got you, Terry. We've reached the back side of these foothills and are on the move, over."

"Roger that."

"We'll rally on Houston. Dogma Three, this is Dogma One, over."

As McAllister ran, he waited to hear the kid's voice, but Rainey had to repeat the call—and still no Houston. Geez, had the kid been shot? *No. Please, no.* McAllister felt responsible for Houston, and man, he didn't want to be the last team member to have seen the kid alive. Houston was a know-it-all on the outside, but McAllister had already seen just how vulnerable he could be. Houston was trying real hard to be accepted, probably too hard. You had to appreciate that.

"Dogma Three, this is Dogma One, over."

Answer him, damn it!

Houston's eyes were beginning to tear—and not from the cold. How could the hostages have disappeared so quickly? He couldn't believe it. And now Rainey was calling for his location so the team could rally on him, then resume following the group. He took a final look through the Nightstars, saw how the valley spread out like a white carpet impaled by trees that now resembled gravestones, one of them his own.

But what was that? A drop-off? He hadn't seen that earlier. Off to the left. Yes, there it was, a gully running parallel to the tree line and all but concealed from view unless you caught it from the right angle. A snowdrift made it appear as though one side of the gully connected with the other, but it didn't. It didn't!

"Dogma Three, this is Dogma One. Report your situation, over."

"Standby," Houston said, then took a deep breath, held it, and shot off, darting from tree to tree, heading deeper into the valley and sweeping to his left, toward where the ground banked then funneled into the gully.

"Dogma Three, this is Dogma One, standing by for ten seconds, over."

That's all I need. With the rhythm of his pulse clashing with the clatter of his boots, Houston hopped down, into the gully, slipped, and went sledding on his ass some three meters to the bottom, digging up rocks and dirt and ice that came tumbling after him. He cursed, raised the Nightstars—

And believed in miracles. He had found the hostages. They trekked about a quarter kilometer ahead, the sides of the gully rising nearly a meter above their heads. Man, those terrorists were smart bastards, knew the real estate inside and out, and had planned their escape almost perfectly. Almost.

"Dogma Three, this is Dogma One. *Report your situation. Now!*"

"Dogma One, this is Dogma Three. I'm in a gully that runs along the tree line," Houston began, even as he activated his GPS and sighed as the satellite signal came through. He rattled off the coordinates, then added, "Have the package in sight. Can remain at this location for approximately three to five minutes, over."

"Roger that. We'll be there before then, out."

With a trembling hand, Houston continued gripping the binoculars, keeping the hostages in sight. He had never been as scared in his life, even when staring down the barrel of an enemy soldier's rifle. He told himself it was all right now, he had found the hostages, he hadn't let the team down, and there was no way in hell that he would move from his position. He pulled a black woolen face mask from his pack, tugged it over his head, only his eyes showing, his breath now hidden, his red and sore nose growing a little warmer. Another look through the Nightstars showed the hostages still humping away, though the two guards in the back were repeatedly hesitating to check their rear.

A pair of stones tumbled down behind Houston, and one struck him in the shoulder. He dropped the Nightstars and brought his rifle around.

But it was just McAllister, who had never signaled his approach over the radio or otherwise. The old man skidded his way down into the gully, then leaned forward, palms on his hips as he struggled for breath.

"Good way to get yourself shot," Houston said.

McAllister smirked. "What's the bad way?"

"Dogma Three, this is Dogma One. We're right on top of you," Rainey said.

"See, at least they signaled," Houston pointed out.

"Cut me some slack, kid. All right?"

"Hey, I didn't mean—"

"What happened? Why the standby? You lose them?"

Vance, Doc, and then Rainey did the awkward butt slide and dropped in behind them, saving Houston from a reply. In the distance, cries in Arabic echoed off, and the gunfire died into the faint hiss of falling snow.

"Well, our magic didn't last long," Rainey said, inspecting the gully with his binoculars. "But there they are. And whoever's leading them is doing a damned good job."

"Yeah, and at least they're dressed for the weather," Vance said, his teeth chattering. "Unlike us. What happened to this being a little eight-hour photo opportunity?"

"Can't hack the cold?" Rainey asked. "Jesus, Corporal, you're starting to sound like Houston over here, who by the way has sense enough to don his face mask. The rest of you get them on. It ain't getting any warmer."

"I got some of those portable hand warmers if you want them," McAllister told Vance. "I know I packed them somewhere."

"No, it's all right," the sharpshooter said, his tone growing steady for Rainey's benefit. "I can hack the cold."

After Rainey pulled on his own face mask, he said, "Marines, are we good to go?"

They formed a circle and banged fists in a little morale booster. Sans the usual grunt of "ooh-rah!" they shifted off, one by one, McAllister on point, Vance just behind, then Houston, Doc, and Rainey.

When time permitted, Houston decided that he would answer McAllister's question regarding the standby, but he would avoid one of his characteristic wiseass replies and instead offer the truth. The more time he spent with the team, the more he admired them and the more guilt-stricken he became about lying. He would confess his screw-ups, do everything he could to better himself, and, in doing so, he would become a true Marine, as hard and loyal as they were. Fitting in wasn't about getting in touch with them; it was about getting in touch with what he really wanted.

WOLF NEWS CREW
EN ROUTE TO CHITRAL
NORTHWEST FRONTIER PROVINCE
PAKISTAN
0935 HOURS LOCAL TIME

Surrendering to al-Zumar's men had sent John Arden into a depression that he feared he could not beat. During his military career, he had not dealt with many failures, and even when he had failed, he had often been rewarded. Arden's CO had said that he liked to reward failure because people who never fail are not pushing the envelope.

Well, Arden had pushed the envelope on this one, all right. He had let himself be swept away into Rick Navarro's macho war fantasy, and the reward for his participation would be death. What else could he do except continue walking through the gully, continue trying to stay warm, and continue feeling sorry for himself?

Well, he could make a break for it. Get shot in the back. Bleed to death in the snow. Damn, if he could just get close to those pilots. If they had a chance to talk, even if only for a few minutes, perhaps they could formulate a plan that would allow at least one of them to get away and deliver al-Zumar's location to the brass. But they had been carefully separated, and al-Zumar was using Shaqib as the translator/go-between. Getting close to the pilots would only earn Arden that bullet in the back. Unfortunately, al-Zumar's men, including the hotshot Fathi, weren't too bothered by Navarro tossing a word or two Arden's way:

"You all right?"

Arden glanced sidelong and leered at Navarro.

"That good, huh?"

"Fuck you."

"Just hang tough, okay? I need you."

"Nobody gives a shit about what you need."

"Hey, man, the American public needs me. They need the two of us right now."

"What they need is al-Zumar's head on a pole."

"Thought you were going to say mine."

"I'm hoping that when this is over, you'll be in so

many pieces that they'll need a team of forensic guys to identify you."

"That's nice. Really nice. But you're forgetting our plan. We're going to interview al-Zumar, then take him out. And it's all going to be recorded in living color."

"Fuck, man. Look around. We're hostages humping across the mountains in a snowstorm. You think this is a TV show? You won't get your interview, let alone take him out. What you'll get is shoved to your knees. Yeah, they'll videotape it as they slash your throat. You want to talk living color? You'll get to watch the blood spill out of your neck until you're dead."

"Mr. Arden, you're so naïve. You have no idea of the political ramifications of something like that. Al-Zumar needs me as much as I need him. We're his voice right now, his connection to the Western world."

"You're dreaming, man. He doesn't need you. What's to stop him from making his own tape, smuggling it off to Al-Jazeera, and letting them act as his connection to the West?"

"Tapes like that lack authenticity, and it's hard to tell when they were made. I've recently been on the air live. People know I'm here. I know he wants his people all around the world to know he's still alive. An interview with me will prove that."

"So he makes his own tape and holds up a fucking newspaper with the date showing. He still doesn't need you."

"Yes, he does. Because you know what? I think he's feeling a little sorry for himself, kind of like you. I think he wants to sit down with a representative of the American media and make his case."

"Oh, I think the people in Los Angeles, Denver, Chicago, and New York will tell you that he's already made his case. No, the only reason he needs us is as shields or bargaining chips. That's it. There won't be any interview. But I'm betting there will be an execution: *ours*."

"Okay, maybe too much talking," Fathi said, shouldering his way between Arden and Navarro. "You hush now."

Arden must have given the young terrorist a dirty look, though he had only meant to acknowledge the man. Fathi answered with a rifle stock to the back of Arden's head—not hard enough to knock him down and out, but enough to make him see stars and hustle to get away.

Wiping snow from his eyes and realizing with a start that he could no longer see al-Zumar and the old man anymore, Arden wondered how much longer their captors would lead them through the blinding snowstorm. He knew all too well what extreme cold could do to the body: chilblains would form, causing swelling and itchiness, then frostbite would set in, followed by hypothermia as their core temperatures dropped. They would grow tired, grow even more reluctant to move on, and begin squinting hard, very hard. Arden had trained in mountainous terrain and had witnessed one of his buddies fall prey to the cold. The guy had become irrational, thought he was back home and had to shovel his driveway free of snow. He had broken away from Arden's squad and had begun digging mind-lessly with his hands. Two corpsman had hauled him away as Arden and his buddies had shivered, looked on, and had considered their own fates—or at least Arden had.

Shouts in Arabic from ahead sent the guards on either side of them hunkering down, and one guard grabbed Arden's wrist and drove him toward the snow.

Shaqib, who had been shuffling a few meters in front of Arden, tugged down the dirty scarf covering his face and said, "They're bringing a rope."

"Yeah, to hang us with," Arden muttered.

But in actuality the rope would keep the group together, and with thugs in front and behind him, Arden watched as Fathi shoved the rope under Arden's bound arm, then passed it through Navarro's, daisy-chaining them together. Somewhere ahead, past a dense curtain of snow, the pilots had probably been linked up as well. They were one big, bound, happy family now, headed straight toward an icy morgue.

Another shout: the signal to move on. For a few seconds, Arden imagined himself standing there in defiance. If he refused to go on, no one else could. But once again, he surrendered both to them and his depression. *This isn't me,* he told himself. *I don't give up. Ever. I have to stay with this, bide my time, and make a move when the probability for success is at its highest. I am not going to feel sorry for myself anymore. I am going to remember who I am. I am going to show them there is no human being on the planet more stubborn, more tenacious than a United States Marine.*

"Dogma One, this is Dogma Five, over."

Rainey had worked on and off with McAllister for the past five years, and he had become an expert in reading the subtleties in the man's tone, even when McAllister spoke over the radio. "What do you got?" he asked tersely while sweeping their rear and shuffling on to keep up with Doc, who, if he had any ankle pain, was still biting his lip and standing tall.

"We don't hustle up, we're going to lose them, over."

"And if we get too close . . ."

"Yeah, I know," McAllister groaned. "We lose them, we're screwed. They spot us, we're screwed."

True, their radio chatter hardly lived up to Marine Corps standards, but as far as Rainey was concerned, phrases like "kill that motherfucker" and "we're screwed" were technical terms—especially on the battlefield.

So how could they kill those motherfuckers and avoid being screwed? They needed to get ahead of the group, project the terrorists' course, and establish an ambush. Simple idea. Difficult to plan during a raging storm.

"Just don't lose them," Rainey said. "We'll keep up, out."

There had to be a way to tilt the playing field to the

enemy's disadvantage. As it was, the terrorists had the storm working for them, and they more than likely knew their course and what lay ahead, given their expert decision to follow along the gully for nearly the past hour. No way in hell would Rainey underestimate them. During his time in Pakistan, he had already seen some of al-Zumar's more underequipped recruits pop out of caves with no shoes, bleeding feet, and single magazines to their names. What they lacked in gear they made up for with courage. They were formidable foes and already had ice in their blood. Cunning and surprise would beat them. A war of attrition would not.

Which was where the ambush came into play. But how to set one up when they were trailing behind, about to lose the group, and could no longer get a decent GPS signal to examine the terrain? And never mind the extreme cold and the thought that his men could succumb to the weather. Suddenly falling back to the secondary pickup point wasn't looking so bad after all. Rainey wouldn't have to fib his way out of a court-martial, and chances were good that all of his people would make it out.

Second thoughts sucked. He had vowed that he wouldn't question his decision to go after the pilots and news crew. Everyone had agreed, even the more reluctant Doc. All for one, one for all. But the farther they traveled into the mountains, the higher the risk became. They had only taken along a half-dozen Meals Ready to Eat each. After that, they'd be melting snow and divvying up the last bags of trail mix.

"Dogma One, this is Dogma Three, over." It was

McAllister again, and he sounded even more bleak.

"Go, Three."

"Be advised I have lost visual contact, over."

Rainey swore to himself. "Still have their tracks, over?"

"Affirmative. But they're getting covered up real quick. I can see maybe ten, fifteen meters in front of me. After that, it's all snow."

"All right. Try to reestablish contact, and do not stop moving, over."

"Roger that," said McAllister, and if he had any breath left, his voice failed to reveal it. In fact, he sounded a couple of beats shy of a heart attack. "Dogma One, out."

Staring hard through the storm, Rainey spotted the group's footprints, though as McAllister had indicated, they were mostly filled in with fresh snow. Worse, the gully was beginning to widen to nearly two-dozen meters, giving the group more room to shift its course.

But how much longer could those people withstand the weather? Sure, the fighters would deal with it, but they had to take their hostages into account. Graham and Ingram had been tear-gassed, and they hadn't been dressed for the cold. Even if the terrorists had given them clothes, how long could they, along with Navarro and his counterpart, last in the storm? If the bad guys were smart, and it seemed they were, then they were already considering a shelter, probably another cave, where they would recoup for a while before heading back out.

And that recuperation period was all Rainey and his

men needed to lay their trap. But could Rainey really count on them stopping? Maybe he had to. He felt certain that their escape plan had not accounted for the storm, since the front had moved in so quickly. But then again, rumors had it that al-Zumar had access to advanced communications equipment, that he might be monitoring Western news channels in addition to the local broadcasts. Bottom line: he could have known of the approaching front hours in advance and could have tipped off his men.

"Dogma One, this is Dogma Four, over," Vance called.

"Four, this is One."

"Uh, you'd better get up here. McAllister is down."

14

The second Doc heard that Sergeant McAllister was down, he charged past Vance, reached McAllister, dropped to his knees, and wriggled off his pack.

"Think he hit his head," Vance said.

Doc opened a flap, dug into one of his medical pouches, and produced a penlight.

McAllister lay on his side, trying to squelch his panting, and as Doc directed the light into the sergeant's eyes, he said, "Look at me, Terry. Look at me."

"How am I supposed to look at you with that damned light in my eyes?"

The sergeant's response told Doc a lot as he ran through a mental checklist of signs and symptoms associated with head injuries. McAllister's pupils were equal and reactive to light—a very good thing, and a quick removal of McAllister's face mask and examination of the sergeant's ears revealed no fluid that might indicate a fracture. "You know where you are?" Doc asked.

"I just tripped. Help me up. There's no time. I'm good to go."

"Whoa," Doc said, his index and middle fingers placed firmly on McAllister's neck to get a carotid pulse. "You need a little breather here."

"How is he, Doc?" Rainey asked.

"No signs of any serious head injury, but his pulse is way up. The man's winded, and I'm betting his core temp has dropped. I could check, but he'll have to drop his drawers."

"Drop my drawers?" McAllister asked incredulously. "Doc, they have to look a whole lot prettier than you for me to do that . . ."

Rainey squatted down, locked gazes with McAllister. "Terry, I'm serious. Are you good?"

"Remember what you told me the first day we met?"

Rainey shrugged.

"You said you only want three things from your men: their hearts, their minds, and their souls. They can do whatever the fuck they want with the rest."

Rainey cocked a brow. "Yeah, I did say that."

McAllister exhaled loudly and pushed himself up. "So why are you asking me if I'm good to go? Besides, you know that before we left I put on my Lightweight Cold Weather Underwear Set, and I'm all toasty. Never mind what Doc says."

At least McAllister's sense of humor had not gone to ice, and Doc noted that Rainey, along with the others, definitely appreciated that. So did he, but the fact remained that the sergeant wouldn't last much longer without some warmth and rest.

But they couldn't rest—not without losing the hostages, and there was little doubt that Rainey would order them on. Though the sergeant wore his face mask, his eyes conveyed that fact very clearly.

"I'm ready," McAllister said, wincing over the weight of his pack. "Just a little off balance."

"See that overhanging rock," Rainey said, pointing to the stone a few meters ahead. "Get him over there, Doc. The three of us will break. Houston? Vance? Regain visual contact with our hostages. Do you read me?"

"Yes, Sergeant," Vance snapped.

"We'll find them, Sergeant," Houston added.

And, looking more phantomlike as snow collected on their utilities, Vance and Houston trotted off down the gully. Watching their terse movements—seemingly unaffected by the cold—Doc suddenly felt envious of their youth.

"C'mon, this ain't right," McAllister said. "I took a little spill. I'm ready."

"Terry, we ain't getting any younger—or skinnier. I don't feel like carrying your big ass out of here."

"Nobody's going to do that. Nobody."

"If I have to, I will," Doc said, thrusting out his chest a little. He had carried injured men off the battlefield before, taking on both the man and the heavy pack. Marines who had watched Doc had called the feat nothing short of remarkable, but Doc liked to think it was simply one of those adrenaline-induced moments when you didn't think about the weight of the guy. You only thought of saving a life, and as a corpsman, that was just part of your job.

"Doc and his ankle are going to carrying you out? I don't think so," Rainey said. "Discussion is over."

McAllister glanced away, taking a long, hard look down the trail. Then his gaze lifted to the gray sky and the falling snow.

"Just a little breather," Doc assured the man. "That's all. Okay?"

After issuing a loud sigh, McAllister said, "All right, then. The patient is ready to be moved."

Doc rose and helped McAllister to his feet. Though the sergeant tried to conceal his dizziness from Doc, his misstep toward the alcove and sudden shift of weight to the left betrayed him. The man was struggling, and Doc grew more concerned as he led him toward the little overhang. They, along with Rainey, sat beneath the stone, exploiting the meager shelter by tucking themselves tightly against the earth at their shoulders.

Though the break was meant for McAllister, Doc was thankful for the moment to take some weight off his foot. His ankle still ached. A lot. He didn't want to look, knew the swelling was now significant, and at this point if he removed his boot, he'd be done for. He dug out some ibuprofen from his pack, downed eight hundred milligrams—a "medic dose." You'd need a prescription to get that much from an ER.

"Dogma Four, this is Dogma One, over," Rainey said softly into his boom mike. "Sound off for radio check."

"Dogma One, this is Dogma Four. Read you loud and clear, over," Vance said.

Houston jumped in, did his own check, and satisfied, Rainey told them to report their progress every five minutes or as necessary.

"So how're we supposed to catch up with them?" McAllister asked Rainey. "Ain't seen any checkered mules around here for hours."

"You think I've failed to consider that?" Rainey asked.

"Yup."

Well, Doc wouldn't talk to the sergeant like that, but Rainey was used to his assistant's challenging remarks and second-guessing; in fact, McAllister had once told Doc that Rainey encouraged other opinions and sometimes even demanded to be questioned, that is, up until the time to carry out a final and legitimate decision. Doc wasn't the type to test that out, though, especially being "the outsider" on the team, the Navy corpsman and not officially a Marine. Sure, they treated him like any other operator, but Doc always thought it best not to push his luck. He would voice his complaints, but he would never go as far as McAllister routinely did. Just wasn't him.

Rainey had removed his fingerless gloves in favor of a black leather pair with full fingers, and he was just finishing up with the gloves when he decided to take on McAllister's remark: "We won't have to play catch-up,

Terry. These guys can't stay out in this weather for much longer. Dead hostages are no good to them. They'll find shelter and hunker down."

"Just like us," Doc said. "I mean this whole place . . . no human being deserves to be here. Desert of sand, desert of snow, that's all it is."

"You haven't seen enough," Rainey said. "I could show you parts of this country that're really beautiful. Too bad our bad guys booked the trip. They obviously don't know jack about fun-filled family vacations."

Doc reflected on his last vacation with his wife and the boys. They had gone to Cozumel, an island off the coast of southeast Mexico. There, they had gone snorkeling above sunken ships and airplanes, and the boys had learned to ride all kinds of watercraft. But the trip became even more memorable because Doc had actually saved a four-year-old girl's life. She had wandered too deeply into the water, had not donned her "water wings," and had been swept out into the surf before her mother had known what was happening. Doc had just been coming out of the water when he had heard the mother screaming, and thankfully he knew enough Spanish to get the details from her. He and his boys had searched the water—

Until a tiny head bobbed up just a few meters from Doc's hip. He grabbed the limp girl, drove himself like a machine toward the shoreline, and began immediate chest compressions and breaths. CPR on a child is different, but Doc's training had prepared him for such events. To his own amazement, he was able to revive the girl as lifeguards arrived to take over. He explained to them that he was a Navy corpsman, and they had told the girl's mother that she was lucky, very, very lucky that Doc had been there. It had been a matter of right time, right place. But Doc wondered if maybe fate had something to do with it, too. Maybe that little girl would become someone influential, someone who would touch many more lives. Maybe saving her was meant to be. Doc's grandfather would surely agree. The old man would turn the tale into something miraculous and mystical, and probably say that Doc had, at that moment, been guided by spirits not skills. *Cric! Crac!* Let the stories begin!

"What are you thinking about, Doc?" Rainey asked, his gaze softening a little.

"Nothing. Just trying to keep warm. Problem is, there's too much of me to keep warm."

"Hey, either of you guys ever fart while having sex?" McAllister asked as he struggled to rip open one of his Meals Ready to Eat.

Doc leaned over and frowned at McAllister, though he had forgotten that his face mask hid the expression. "Excuse me?"

"It's a simple question. You ever fart while having sex?"

Rainey rolled his eyes at Doc, then said to McAllister, "Everyone at one time or another has farted while having sex—or before sex, which I have to say really kills the mood."

"Not true," Doc said abruptly. "I have never once

farted before, during, or after sex. That's really disgusting and I'd rather not have this conversation, whether you monkeys think it's funny or not."

"I don't ask to be funny," McAllister said. "Just looking for advice with the ladies."

"You want to know why you keep getting dumped?" Rainey asked. "Sorry, buddy. It's just your looks and your personality that are the problem."

"Yeah, if you pick up some new ones, then you can fart all you want while having sex, and she won't care none," Doc said, smiling so broadly that the face mask's wool got in his teeth. "She'll be in love with you because you'll be that sensitive man she's been looking for all her life."

Toilet humor. It was so juvenile, so ridiculous, that they couldn't help but laugh at themselves—for laughing. And yes, McAllister had brought up the farting to be funny because he knew they needed more than just a physical break. Doc winked at the man as McAllister gobbled down a granola bar, alternating it with a piece of bacon from his MRE.

Vance's voice crackled over the tactical frequency: "Dogma One, this is Dogma Four. We have reestablished visual contact, over."

"Roger that, Dogma Four, over."

"The gully crosses into a few hills, and we think there's a cave on the opposite mountain wall. We got a shadow, but we can't see much, over."

"You hear that?" Rainey said, covering his boom mike. "Possible cave. And that's where our hostages are going. Dogma Four, continue your eyes-on. Let me know if our package enters the cave, over."

"Roger that, out."

WOLF NEWS CREW
SOMEWHERE NORTH OF AL-ZUMAR CAVE COMPLEX
NORTHWEST FRONTIER PROVINCE
PAKISTAN
1048 HOURS LOCAL TIME

John Arden groaned in disgust as he shambled on through the snow, his legs feeling like sticks of ice, his arms crooked and seemingly frozen in place. The scarf kept the wind off his nose, but it repeatedly blew up, allowing the air to chill his chin and neck. He had asked Fathi to tuck the scarf into his collar, but the guy had just laughed and had pretended not to understand. Fathi wouldn't even brush the snow from Arden's shoulders.

Fathi had just spat on Arden's chest and had shoved him on.

"How are you doing, Mr. John," Shaqib said, drifting back along the rope, still carrying the camera, his hands unbound.

"I'm wonderful," Arden answered in a monotone. "How are you? Having a good day, I hope?"

Shaqib, though clearly not the world's most adept translator, recognized the sarcasm and softened his expression. "Don't worry, Mr. John. We're going to stop soon. There is a cave just ahead. They will give us something to eat and drink, and we will get warm before we set out again."

"Set out for where?" Arden asked.

"I still believe we are going to Chitral."

"And what happens to us there?"

"I don't know. But remember what I told you, Mr. John. I will do what I can. Just don't turn your back on me."

"Oh, don't worry. I won't."

Shaqib smiled. He didn't get the message. He was going for the one-hand-washes-the-other thing when Arden was trying to tell him that he would never again trust him. Communication, or the lack thereof, had to be a casualty of war, maybe the second after truth. Still, as much as Arden now despised Shaqib, he understood that the man had seized an opportunity in a land where opportunities were as rare as fresh drinking water. Arden might have done likewise, and Shaqib had known the dangers associated with finding al-Zumar. He had risked his life to help his family. It was just too bad that Arden and the others had become the translator's means to an end.

"What's going on?" Navarro asked, hustling to catch up with Arden.

"They're getting out the shovels so we can dig our graves. Problem is, the ground's frozen. And maybe they're not giving us shovels at all. Maybe you're going to ruin your manicure and dig a hole with your bare hands."

"Thought I saw a cave up there," Navarro said, his

voice quavering, his choice to ignore Arden's barb just as well.

"Shaqib says we're stopping soon."

"Thank God. I can't feel my ears anymore."

"But your mouth still works . . ."

Navarro snorted. "When's the last time something positive came out of your mouth?"

"The day before I took this job. After meeting you, it's been downhill ever since."

"C'mon, Arden. Okay, you're a pessimist, but you're also a war junkie. Just like me. You're not happy unless you're in the shit and complaining about it. We're really not so different. You do it with a gun, I do it with a camera and a voice-over. We both need to be here. We wouldn't have it any other way. We're making history right now. How do you want to be remembered?"

The guy was so full of shit it was laughable, but it hurt too much to grin, so Arden just moved on, and Navarro was smart enough not to demand an answer. Besides, any more conversation would light Fathi's fuse.

Within five minutes the mouth of a very large cave grew from the snowy gloom. Arden picked up the pace, wanting to run inside to shield himself from the godforsaken wind. He came up hard on Shaqib, who nodded soberly and worked his legs more briskly. Together, they entered the cave, whose ceiling hung some three meters above them, its depth lost somewhere in the darkness over a dozen meters ahead. Two of al-Zumar's men switched on flashlights, and they scuffled onward, the shadows long and dancing above the group.

Arden glanced to his left, saw a slot machine, a Las

Vegas-style slot machine standing upright in the tunnel, its face dark but showing two grapes and a lemon. Now what in the hell was a slot machine doing in a cave in the middle of no man's land in Pakistan? Maybe al-Zumar had had the thing shipped in to entertain the men? Maybe he had attached it to a gas-powered generator? No doubt al-Zumar was a gambling man, pulling levers and taking chances.

Moving on, Arden concentrated on the path, taking in every corner of the tunnel as they turned right and walked on for at least another ten minutes, the tunnel dropping in a lazy grade and narrowing to just a meter before widening again into a gallery about twenty meters wide, though its ceiling rose just two meters.

Feeling a bit claustrophobic but much warmer, Arden crossed to one clay-colored wall, where Fathi pulled the rope from between Arden's bound arms and gestured that they have a seat on a row of empty shipping crates.

Meanwhile, al-Zumar gave orders to several of his bodyguards, two of whom jogged off toward a secondary tunnel. Yet another pair returned to the tunnel the group had taken, probably sent back to the mouth of the cave, where they would stand watch. No matter how you sliced it, if Arden was able to escape from this gallery, he would still have to face at least two more fighters. But with al-Zumar and the other bodyguards right there, nearly within arm's reach, trying to escape seemed well-nigh impossible. Instead, Arden decided to get near the chopper pilots while al-Zumar was huddling up with his men and all gazes were locked on him.

Glancing furtively at the group, Arden crossed directly to the pilots, their wrists also bound behind their backs, their faces covered by scarves. "Hey, my name's John Arden," he muttered softly. "I'm with Navarro's news crew. Or at least I was." He took a seat on one of the crates, and the pilots quickly joined him.

"That's Rick Navarro over there?" the female pilot asked, her gaze straying to the correspondent, who managed to sweet-talk Shaqib into removing his scarf and was in the process of demanding some food and something warm to drink.

"What the hell were you people doing out here?" the male pilot asked. "Didn't you get the call?"

"Guess we missed that one. Wouldn't have mattered anyway. Navarro's hellbent on getting an interview with al-Zumar."

"His story of a lifetime's going to be the story of his death. And by the way, I'm Captain Tom Graham, United States Marine Corps. This is First Lieutenant Martha Ingram."

"I'd shake your hand, but . . ." Arden glanced over his shoulder at his bound wrists. "You know, I was an E-5 with the First Battalion, First Marines in Kuwait. Semper Fi."

"I was still in college back then," Ingram said. "But at least we got another Marine with us."

"Seems like we're headed to Chitral," said Graham. "He's probably got some allies waiting to smuggle him out."

"Well, I say we pass on the city tour," Arden said. "Got any ideas?"

"Looks like he's got ten men, plus the old man. I'm not sure about the skinny little guy, Shaqib."

Arden cocked a brow. "Don't trust him. And if we come up with a plan to get out of this, don't worry about Navarro."

"What're you talking about?" Ingram asked.

Arden stared hard into the young woman's eyes. "He wants that interview so badly that he'll screw us over to get it. I would not put that past him."

"Arden, you're a Marine," Graham said. "You know no one gets left behind."

"No *Marines* get left behind. I mean you want to know why I'm here? We ran into some Afghan refugees working for al-Zumar."

"Oh, no," Ingram groaned.

"Oh yeah. But there wouldn't have been a problem. Our translator was just trying to help us find al-Zumar. He hooked us up with some Afghan refugees, but the deal went south when Navarro pulled a gun."

"Doesn't surprise me," Graham said. "Guy's reputation precedes him. So what are you? His producer?"

"Would you believe his bodyguard?"

"You can't see it right now because of this scarf, but I am smiling," Graham said. "And yeah, you should've kept your day job with the Corps."

Arden sighed. "Tell me about it."

"Look at them over there," Ingram said. "Like wolves making their plan. At any moment, one of them is going to come over here and break us up."

"So what's your game plan?" Arden asked, the desperation flooding into his voice.

"We were supposed to pick up a recon team before we got shot down," Graham said. "I know the team leader, and I'm betting that he and his men come in after us."

"Maybe they will. But if they don't?" Arden asked. "Then what?"

"Look at these guys," Graham said. "Trigger-happy motherfuckers, one and all. We force a contest, we lose."

"Not necessarily. I say we come up with something that involves using Navarro as the bait. That asshole wanted me to put my life on the line for him. Now comes payback."

"He won't go along with that," Ingram said. "I wouldn't."

"You would if you didn't know you were being set up."

"Yeah, and how will that go over if we get out?" Graham asked. "You know that asshole will get on the air and tear the Corps to shreds. No. We're going to sit tight for a while."

"Maybe they won't let us sit tight," Arden said. "Maybe they'll torture us."

"If that happens, I'll be the first one on them," said Graham. "But I don't think that'll happen."

"Uh, excuse me, but that man right there would have absolutely no problem slicing off our heads and holding them up to the camera."

"Look, at this point maybe he'll try to trade us, use us as a shield. With that in mind, he'll keep us alive until the last minute," Graham said. "He'd be stupid not to."

"So we take advantage of that," said Arden.

A shadow passed over them. Arden craned his head, his gaze falling directly upon Mohammed al-Zumar, who had approached silently and now loomed before them. He had removed his cap to reveal bushy black hair, and his green parka was unzipped to expose an expensive woolen sweater. Again, you could easily mistake him for some guy on a ski trip, but those eyes, those penetrating, maniacal eyes sent a chill down Arden's spine.

"Maybe you think to run away," said al-Zumar in a mock jovial tone. "But where would you go? Would you walk home to America?" The man hunkered down and actually smiled.

Arden looked to Graham. Would the captain respond to that? It seemed not. In the meantime, Ingram just sat there, her eyes glassing up.

"No, you stay," said al-Zumar. "But I know you are soldiers. You do what you do. For now, we have food. Warm tea." He called in Arabic to one of his men, who began unfastening the straps on a heavy pack.

"I didn't know your English was so good," said Graham.

Al-Zumar frowned.

"His English is not that good," Arden said.

"It is good enough," the terrorist snapped as he tugged down Arden's scarf. "Remember, we watch you." He reached over and pulled down Graham's scarf, followed by Ingram's. "There. You look good. You will look good on video."

"We won't be making any tapes for you," said Graham.

"You want to be a TV star, no?" asked al-Zumar. "All Americans want to be TV star." He faced Ingram, who flinched. "What about you? TV star? Hmmm?"

The woman just looked at him, her chest rising and falling, her breath growing more ragged. "Sounds like you're the one who wants to be a TV star. Maybe you'll get your wish."

15

"You cold?" Houston asked Vance as they lay on the edge of a hogback, flat on their bellies, with Vance inspecting the cave through his binoculars. "I said, you cold?"

"Uh-huh."

Houston swore under his breath. "The older guys get to take a break. What do we get?"

"Uh-huh."

"You listening?"

"Uh-huh."

"Come on, man!"

"Shuddup," Vance ordered, his gaze never straying from his binoculars. "Looks like they've posted only two guards at the entrance. Think about it. They wouldn't have gone in there if they didn't have another way out. They've thrown only two guys up front. Probably have another team posted at their back door. If we find that exit, we can seal them inside, radio for help, then just sit on them till St. Andrew sends reinforcements, along with our medals. Y'all game or what?"

Houston huffed. "Yeah, okay. Better check with the big dog first."

Vance swung up his boom mike. "Dogma One, this is Dogma Four, over."

"This is One," Rainey answered. "Report?"

"Be advised we are approximately a quarter klick north of your position. Our package has entered a cave. Two bad guys posted just inside, over."

"Good. Stay put. We'll rally on you, over."

"Negative," Vance said.

"Come again?"

"Dogma One, we think there might be an exit on the other side of this mountain. Maybe we can seal them inside. Request permission to have a look, over."

"Dogma Four, standby, over."

Houston switched off his tactical radio. "He wants to talk it over with his golfing buddies."

Vance put a finger to his lips. The wind blew. The snow kept falling. Houston cursed once more.

"Dogma Four, permission granted to find that exit," Rainey said. "We'll rally on your current position and maintain visual contact with the first entrance, over."

"Roger that. We'll holler if we find something, out." Vance slid back on his hands and knees, the hogback concealing them from the guards in the cave. "Hey, we can hump along these hills, cross over that entrance, up where that next slope levels out a little, then we can circle around."

Houston gave a solid tug on his lucky bush cover, pulled his face mask a little higher over his nose. "All right, let's go hunting."

They jogged back down the hill, hit a ravine, started down it, heads low to keep the snow out of their eyes.

Hills. Pine trees. Snow. Initially serene, the landscape had become a miserably cold hurdle, and Houston decided that if he never saw another snowflake again, he would be a happy man. Even the color—all that white—sapped away at his mood.

Five, maybe six minutes later, they reached the last of the foothills and began their ascent of the mountain itself, beating a path between the sagging shrubs and bowing pines that would take them about forty meters above the cave opening. Neither of them had considered it at the time, but Houston wondered if the terrorists had, perhaps, another entrance or exit near their current position, and if so, he and Vance might stumble upon it, blowing their cover and sending the thugs holding the hostages into a major and immediate flight.

He just had to keep his eyes open, his ears trained on every snap of twig. That wasn't too hard. He had already developed a Marine's instincts, though admittedly his were not as well honed as Vance's.

When they were directly over the cave, two things happened at once:

Houston put his boot down and sank into the snow up to his waist—

And automatic-weapons fire boomed and echoed across the valley.

"Shit, that's coming from the gully," Vance said. "Dogma One, this is Dogma Four. How about a sitrep, over?"

The gunfire continued, with carbines and the Para SAW adding their voices to the AKs. Rainey was obviously busy.

Vance, whose gaze had lifted to scan the valley, had not seen Houston fall.

"Hey, Vance?"

"Buddy, we have to get on the other side of this mountain. If we can hear it, they can hear it. And they're going to move."

"Yeah, I know."

"So come on!"

Vance had still not looked down.

Houston stood there, rocking himself back and forth, trying to free his boots from the snow as the fisherman started away. "Hey, Vance?"

Houston finally had his partner's slack-jawed attention. "Shit, man. What happened? What're you doing down there?"

Houston shoved out his hand. "Uh, asking for a little help?"

"Yeah, yeah." Vance started toward him.

"But watch out don't get—"

"Too close?" Vance finished as he plummeted up to his waist. "Aw, shit. Last thing we need."

"Just try crawling," said Houston, now frantically trying to free himself. "I think I got one boot out."

"Man, listen to that fire. Three, maybe four bad guys out there with Rainey and the guys," Vance said nervously. "We have to get the hell out of here." He shoved himself forward, making a sizable dent in the snow whose top layers had already frozen into big plates that Houston was already cracking and shoving aside.

"Okay, I got it," Vance said, clambering his way out of the hole even as Houston finally freed himself.

With a knot forming in the bottom of his stomach, Houston kept closely behind Vance as they pushed on across the mountainside, the slope growing steeper, nearly forty-five degrees and threatening to send them tumbling like Olympic skiers, guns and gear airborne—along with themselves.

"All right! Fall back!" Rainey ordered Doc and McAllister as he swung around and charged down the gully.

A round sliced jarringly close to Rainey's ear, and though he ducked out of reflex, the movement would never have saved him the way the wind just had. He feared the enemy would compensate and their aim would become true, deadly true.

Earlier, Rainey had had a hunch that the guys back near the caves would come after them, despite the weather. But why hadn't they arrived sooner? Maybe they didn't know where their comrades were taking the hostages. They had simply tracked Rainey's team into the gully. Sure, the team could have done a better job of concealing their departure, but stealth had been sacrificed in the name of speed. And sure, the team could easily waste precious time trying to pinpoint the locations of the incoming fire, easily waste more ordnance on those men, easily fall into the trap of a firefight, but they had evaded that trap before and knew exactly what they had to do: answer the incoming with enough suppression fire so that they could make their break. Getting out of the gully and to that mountain before the terrorists and hostages fled was priority number one.

"Where are you, Doc?" Rainey asked over the radio.

"Not too far behind. I can just barely see you and McAllister."

"Sergeant, this shit is too thick for me," McAllister said, from just a few steps behind Rainey, rounds driving through the snow and pinging off the rock and earth at their shoulders.

"Then you'd better move and stop wasting time asking me if you can become the phantom blooper."

"You're a mind reader," McAllister said.

"If we had the time, I'd let you go to town with your grenade launcher, I really would."

"Damn straight," McAllister said, breathing hard. "But lead us not into temptation . . ."

Rainey grinned inwardly. "And deliver us from evil."

The path came at Rainey as though he were watching it on a theatre screen, the snow rolling beneath his feet, the flakes blowing through the gloomy sky, the gully trailing away as he led them down into the foothills.

Warning sign: reality was beginning to bend, his peripheral vision beginning to narrow.

Rainey squinted, squinted again. He had been subjecting his body to extreme cold and a hellish mountain hump through some of the most rugged terrain he had ever encountered—yet he felt giddy, almost delirious over the idea that he was taking the biggest risk of his life, let alone his military career. It was all or nothing. He was proud of himself for pushing the envelope— what Marines do, what they should always do—yet in doing so his body was screaming for a cease-fire. He had read stories of other operators who had miscalculated the risks of a mission and had bought it because they had not recognized their physical limitations. One of his instructors had said that a man pushed to the outer edge of what is physically possible will often manufacture reality as he would like to see it rather than what it is. Thoughts of hallucinating under the stress troubled Rainey. A lot. Just a few months prior, during a dark-side training operation, he had not eaten or slept for three days as a self-initiated test of endurance. He had spent the final hour of the op blabbering to Kady about their plans for the future. Of course, Kady had not gone into the mountains with him. Doc, McAllister, Vance, and Matt Thomas, the guy Houston had replaced, had all listened attentively as Rainey had expressed his intimate secrets. Later on, McAllister had said that at first listening to Rainey was really funny, but the more he had gone on, the more they had realized how deeply he was hallucinating. And that had scared them. If Rainey took himself to that place again, he might not return in time to be useful to the team. Going there would put them all at risk. Yes, giving McAllister that break had been the right thing to do, even if it had given their pursuers time to catch up with them. And yes, it was easy to think of the others and ignore his own well-being. Too easy, in fact. If he was going to be an effective team leader, he needed a body that wasn't waging war against the mind controlling it. Obvious? Hell, yes. Easy to forget? Hell, yes.

And really, how was he supposed to do anything about it when running through the snow was the only way to stay alive? He had to deal, but old Terry just behind wasn't faring very well. Neither was Doc with his sore ankle. Factor in the cold, the high chances of getting frostbite, and Rainey thought, *I'm running all of us into heart attacks.*

At least for the moment, the mountains had grown quiet as their pursuers regrouped and assumedly climbed down into the gully. Rainey figured there were four, maybe five back there. He doubted there were any more than that, but Murphy might have his way with them.

Rubbing his eyes twice and blinking off the snow and blurriness, Rainey finally picked up two sets of boot prints, fresh snow nearly filling them. "Okay, got Vance and Houston's track," he told the others.

No response.

"Gentlemen, are you with me?"

"Yeah," Doc said, his voice cracking over the radio. "I'm . . . I'm . . . I'm . . . with you."

"Me, too," McAllister said, sounding equally frozen.

An urgent-sounding Vance broke into the channel. "Dogma One, this is Dogma Four, over."

"Go, Four," Rainey answered, wincing in anticipation of the bad news.

* * *

Vance and Houston had taken cover behind a pair of shrubs, watching as about a hundred meters below them, the terrorists, along with the two pilots and newspeople, rushed out of a gaping, ice-covered fissure that more closely resembled a giant crack in the ground than a cave exit. The satisfaction of knowing that he was right about the bad guys' back-door escape plan comforted Vance about as much as a 3/0 offset worm hook stuck in his arm. If Rainey, Doc, and McAllister had just moved out a little sooner, then the team could have sealed the hostages inside the cave.

However, that was assuming there were no other exits. Vance almost wished the plan wouldn't have worked so he wouldn't feel so bad over their failure. But really, they hadn't failed yet. As in bass-fishing tournaments, the game ain't over till the last lunker's been weighed in, and Vance knew that he and his teammates had yet to bring all of their weapons and training to the table. Rainey liked to call them "hard" men, which sometimes got a laugh from the rookies whose minds were in the gutter. But hard men like themselves did not give up. Nothing was over. Not yet. But Vance had made it sound that way when he had called Rainey. And now he got to play messenger, which positively sucked:

"Dogma One, be advised we are on the north side of the mountain and observing our package leaving this location via a secondary exit."

"Good job."

Vance was taken aback. He figured Rainey would be pissed and, at the very least, take it out on him. But he didn't.

"Maintain contact," the sergeant went on. "Do not lose sight of them. We'll try rallying on you, but advance if necessary."

"Roger that. Be advised the drifts on the mountain above the primary entrance are a meter or two deep. Avoid if possible, over."

"Roger, out."

Houston focused his attention through his Nightstars. "Think that little rest did them good."

"What do you got?" Vance asked, pressing his own binoculars to his eyes.

"They're hauling a lot more ass than they did before. We're going out again soon. You think the Sarge and those guys will ever catch up with us?"

"Yeah, eventually," Vance said, lowering his binoculars and trying to get a signal on his GPS. Miraculously, he did, their elevation probably helping. "Yup. No doubt those guys are headed for Chitral. Got the map right here."

The little LED screen showed the coordinates: Chitral, Pakistan 35° 53' 15"N 71° 48' 01"E.

"How long will it take?" Houston asked.

"Well, if they stop and the storm lets up a little, they can probably get down into the valley in ten, maybe twelve hours."

"If we can't get ahead of them, we'll never set up a decent ambush."

"Looks like we'll have to follow them into town. I think we got a better chance there than out in the open."

"You're kidding me."

"No, really. Once they get there, maybe the leader's going to divide up his people, maybe send some after transport, some after food, while the rest guard him and the hostages."

"Plus we got more cover there," Houston said, beginning to buy into the idea.

"I don't know want Rainey has planned, but if I were him, I'd just keep them in my sights until we reach town, then we move in fast. I think if we try hitting them beforehand, they'll cap those hostages in a heartbeat. Yeah, I know they probably want to bargain with them or something, but once they know we're close, those pilots and newspeople will just be baggage, and they'll shoot them just to prove what bastards they really are."

"You're probably right. But you know they could have another way station out there. We might get another crack at sealing them off."

"I doubt it. That fire said way too much. They know we're out here. They won't make the same mistake twice. If there's another cave, they'll send in one or two guys to get supplies while they keep moving."

"Damn, you're giving these guys a lot of credit. I mean, you've seen how poorly trained some of them are. What was it, like two weeks ago that we saw that dumb-ass guy trying to fire his AK without a magazine and wondering why nothing was coming out?"

"That guy was a local hire, not an Arab. Those guys down there are the best of the best. I don't know, I could be wrong, but I think al-Zumar is close, very close."

"I wish," Houston said with a snort. "Shit, man. Me and you hunting down the world's most wanted man? That'd be pretty damn cool. And what better people than Force Recon Marines to do the job?"

"Yeah, we're good, Corporal. But he's good, too. Just remember that."

WOLF NEWS CREW
SOMEWHERE NORTH OF AL-ZUMAR CAVE COMPLEX
NORTHWEST FRONTIER PROVINCE
PAKISTAN
1130 HOURS LOCAL TIME

Arden's pulse raced over the thought that the Recon Marines were near. They might even be planning an attack as he and the others were shoved onward into the valley, hands still bound, no rope to link them together. Maybe at any moment they were going to be saved.

Or they were going to die.

As Arden had been rushed out of the cave, he and the pilot Graham had exchanged a few words regarding the gunfire they had heard outside. Graham took it as proof positive that the boys he was supposed to pick up were in pursuit. Ingram didn't care who was responsible for the gunfire; she was thankful that the shots had distracted al-Zumar, who had been in the middle of a screaming diatribe in response to her insult.

At first reluctant to believe that Marines were still after them, Arden finally gave in when he heard the distant but discernable rat-tat-tat of a Squad Automatic Weapon. Sure, terrorists could have stolen such a weapon or could have taken it from the death clutches of a fallen Marine, but the fact that the SAW seemingly answered the AK fire argued in favor of a Marine presence.

And, well, it just felt better to believe that his brothers, his Marine Corps brothers whom God created on the Eighth Day, were out there trying to save his ass. He could not have felt more proud of those men, and it didn't matter if they were successful or not. The fact that they were trying meant everything, and their efforts had washed Arden clean of his depression.

Mr. John Arden was ready to get it on.

He glanced back at Fathi, smirked, nodded confidently.

"What?" the man asked, rushing up to Arden and shoving him in the shoulder. "What?"

"Four words, buddy: the Marines are coming."

Fathi glanced erratically to the foothills around them. "Where? Where are your Marines?"

"They're coming for you. And when they do . . ." Arden shivered violently for dramatic effect.

While Fathi's comprehension of Arden's meaning was unsure, the words did elicit another blow to Arden's shoulders.

"The Marines are coming," Arden repeated, now

summoning his best spooky voice. If he couldn't physically take on the enemy, then he would screw with
their minds. It was high time he fought back any way he
could.

"Shut up," Fathi cried. "And move! Move! Move!"

Arden caught Rick Navarro's attention and winked
at the man, who just furrowed his icy brow and
stomped on. "What's the matter, Rick? Things not going your way?"

A rifle stock came down across Arden's back so
heavily that he fell immediately to his knees, the pain
sudden and shooting up and down his back and into his
arms and legs. He doubted Fathi had broken his back,
since he still felt everything, but the blow was going to
leave one nasty bruise.

Fathi crossed in front of Arden. "Maybe you were a
soldier, but you don't know what soldiers are. We do.
This place is nothing to us. Easy. For you . . . no. This is
hard. Very hard. There is no Happy Meal here. Get up!"

With teary eyes, Arden threw one leg out and pried
himself to his feet.

"You are shit," Fathi said. "Infidel shit." He pushed
Arden forward, drove him hard so they could catch up
with Navarro and Shaqib, who had already moved on.

"How long till we get to Chitral?" Arden asked Fathi,
not expecting an answer.

"Only the sheikh knows."

"So we are going to Chitral . . ."

"We go to Chitral," Fathi said with a chuckle.
"Where else would we go?"

Arden steeled his expression. "McDonald's."

CAMP LIBERTY BELL

FIFTH FORCE RECONNAISSANCE COMPANY

THIRD PLATOON HEADQUARTERS

NORTHWEST FRONTIER PROVINCE

PAKISTAN

1140 HOURS LOCAL TIME

I can hack it. And if the news is bad, then I'll go on, because that's what we do. That's all we can do.

For Sgt. Kady Forrest the news could not have been worse.

Fact number one: Delta Eagle Nine had reached Point Sigma and had hovered there for approximately ten minutes with no sign of smoke and absolutely no contact from Rainey or any other member of Team Dogma. Lieutenant Colonel St. Andrew had hollered to the high heavens, swearing not once but three times that he would have Rainey court-martialed.

Fact number two: The Huey, along with its Cobra escort, had been recalled to base, but just moments ago, contact with the Cobra and its crew had been lost. If the chopper had crashed in the snowstorm, then, in a tragically ironic set of circumstances, two brothers would have gone down on the same day. Captain Tom Graham had flown Delta Eagle Seven, and his brother, Capt. Brad Graham, had piloted Delta Eagle Nine's Cobra escort.

Fact number three: the second Force Recon Team, along with members of the Army's 10th Mountain Division, were going to attempt a very dangerous High Altitude High Opening drop over the quadrant where that Warthog pilot had spotted smoke, yet pilots of their C-130 had reported a hydraulics malfunction. The transport might have to return to base without a single guy every reaching the drop zone.

Unable to bear anymore, Kady had returned to her billet, where she sat on her bunk and wondered what life would be like without Rainey. God, she needed something to preoccupy her, something to make her forget him. She got up, donned her heavy parka, and went outside, where two privates wielded snow blowers to clear the path. She walked away from the row of heavy tents, out across two more pathways and up a slope where she and Rainey had often sat, chatted, and looked out across the entire camp.

She plopped down on a big stone near the slope's crest and shivered as she glanced up, the snow dappling her cheeks. She wished the sky promised something more than just gray.

Rainey, I know about the ring. I saw you looking at it one day, but you didn't see me. I know you're going to ask me. And I know I'm going to say yes. But you have to come back to do that, damn it. You have to come back. I'm a liar. I can't hack it. I can't go on. I need you.

16

Although Sgt. Terry McAllister would rather not have terrorists taking pot shots at his ragged ass, he did recognize that said terrorists kept said ass motivated. Highly motivated.

As he jogged on, he tried to forget about the pains in places he didn't know existed, pains that came in the form of imaginary pins, broken glass, burning cigarettes, and right hooks. He strained to keep up with Rainey, his bones rattling as though he were dragging them in a pillow case.

Adversity makes you strong, right? Pain lets you know you're still alive, right?

They had already reached Vance and Houston's last location and were presently struggling to catch up with them, even as those two operators tailed the hostages. A valley with rambling hills and a decent spattering of pine trees lay before them, and beneath those trees the snow had been well trampled. He humped on, his breath hot against the face mask, his legs growing even more wobbly.

During the weeks prior, McAllister had been talking a lot about death, more than he usually did, because as many Marines believed, if you were going to buy it in-country, you would die at the very beginning of your tour or at the very end. That superstition often proved true during tours of duty, but McAllister also applied it to his service with Force Recon, which, he reminded himself for the nth time, was nearing its end. For that reason his paranoia had grown from a pesky mosquito bite to a full-on hive, swollen, itchy, keeping him up at nights.

And at the moment, the pine trees seemed to gather, seemed to raise their limbs and brandish rifles—

"You want the good news or the bad news?" Rainey called back.

McAllister shuddered. *Focus, man! Focus.* "How 'bout no news?"

"Not a choice. So when we reach those guys, I think it's time we check in with St. Andrew. Barring any major problems—like a snowstorm and RPG fire—our helo must've reached Point Sigma nearly an hour ago."

McAllister smiled tightly. "I'm looking forward to your explanation."

"Still thinking of one."

A muffled thud came from the rear. He whirled back,

saw Doc on his hands and knees, eyes narrowed in pain. "Whoa, hold up!" he told Rainey.

"It's all right," Doc said.

"Can you get up?" McAllister seized the corpsman's hand.

Doc got shakily to his feet and glanced to Rainey, who leaned forward, catching his own breath.

"You guys think I've made a big mistake, don't you?" Rainey said. "I'm endangering your lives—maybe for nothing."

"Nobody's said that," McAllister snapped. "Those pilots and newspeople up there got jack without us. So we go."

Rainey nodded. "What about you, Doc? I know you didn't want to do this. We upped the pressure, played the team card when we should've folded."

"My decision," the big corpsman said, then burst to his feet and stomped past Rainey. "And don't flatter yourselves by thinking you can intimidate me. I'm the biggest badass here, and I got the biggest gun."

McAllister grinned and tried to imagine what it might be like to leave a wife and kids back home in the States. Scary. Just plain scary. What would it be like for your kids to grow up without you? Would they really remember you? Would they take what little time you'd had together and cherish it, learn from it, carry it with them for the rest of their lives? You had to hope so. Better yet, you had to stay alive. "You're a hard man, Doc," McAllister called out. "A very hard man!"

"The hardest," he answered as he drove on, into the blowing snow.

"I'm worried about him," Rainey said softly as they broke into their jog, throwing wary glances over their shoulders.

McAllister faked a wounded look, though Rainey couldn't see it. "What about me? I don't rate anything?"

"C'mon, wiseass."

"Hey, I'm worried about *you*," McAllister said. "Sounds like you're guilt-tripping over this. Don't."

"I usually don't."

"So don't. This is what we signed on for."

"Yeah, I know," Rainey answered. "And as Murphy would have it, the pen was full of ink."

Fifteen minutes later, Rainey breathed a heavy sigh as he, Doc, and McAllister reached Houston and Vance. The two Marines had been slowly picking their way along the hills to the east of the valley, keeping the hostages in sight while keeping themselves in the high ground and out of range. Give the young guns a medal, and when they bragged, give them a wet towel whipping to keep them modest.

"They're right down there, Sarge, still moving at a pretty good clip," Houston said, handing over his Nightstars and pointing in the group's direction.

After a five-second inspection of the package, Rainey returned the corporal's binoculars and said, "Contact Beacon Light."

As a surprised Houston unclipped the 117 Foxtrot's mike from his backpack, Vance, who had been monitoring the hostages himself from behind two pines, scrambled back, saying, "Sarge, are we clear on what happened back there?"

"Crystal."

Vance winked. "Thank you, Sergeant."

"Beacon Light, this is Dogma Three, over. Beacon Light, this is Dogma Three, over." Static. "We're nearly out of range," Houston told Rainey as he controlled the radio's parameters with the removable keypad. "And this weather ain't helping."

"I was going to use the weather as one reason why we haven't contacted them sooner. And now we can't reach them to lie. Does anyone else appreciate that irony?"

Houston spoke in a goofy voice. "Duh, I do, Sarge."

Before Rainey could censor the kid, a voice broke over the radio: "Dogma Three, this is Beacon Light. Report your situation, over."

That voice belonged to one of Kady's friends, a radio operator whose name escaped Rainey. He snatched the mike, and at the risk of being detected by the enemy, told Houston to activate the radio's GPS interface to digitally transmit their location to Camp Liberty Bell. He owed St. Andrew at least that much. "Beacon Light, this is Dogma One. Sending GPS coordinates now. We are all accounted for and are north of Point Stingray, en route to Chitral, over."

McAllister whistled, mimicking a falling bomb, then he growled the explosion.

"Dogma One, you were supposed to rally on Point Sigma, over," came St. Andrew's terse voice.

"Beacon Light, we were cut off, under heavy fire, and driven north, over." Rainey glanced at Doc, then Vance, Houston, and McAllister, their eyes betraying their uneasiness over the "bending" of the truth.

"Dogma One, why have you failed to make sitreps, over?"

"Beacon Light, we have been on the move since our last transmission. Also, we suffered a temporary communications malfunction but have since repaired the problem, over."

"Oh, God, that was lame," McAllister muttered. "As lame as it gets."

"Yeah, I could've given you something more technical-sounding," Houston said.

"Dogma One, reading your coordinates now. Why have you been heading north, toward Chitral, over?"

"Beacon Light, we have been evading enemy fire while monitoring the transport of our two pilots as well as two, possibly three civilian newspeople, one of whom we believe is Rick Navarro. They are being moved by a small force of approximately one dozen individuals, over."

"Hey, we can't wait much longer," Vance said, pulling his Nightstars from his widening eyes. "They're almost out of sight."

Rainey impatiently widened his own gaze at Houston's backpack, anticipating the lieutenant colonel to respond or keel over.

"Dogma One, at this time we cannot get a helo to your location. Remain at these coordinates and await further instructions, over."

Rainey shook his head. "Beacon Light, we are monitoring the hostages and are being pursued by hostiles. Unable to maintain our position. Heading north toward Chitral, over."

All right, Colonel, what're you going to do? Write off American lives? We're already out here. You can't extract us. Why not let us do our jobs and continue being your eyes and ears, damn it? And when it comes time to extract, Chitral has even got an airstrip. We both know that.

"Dogma One, maintain surveillance of hostages but do not attempt rescue. I want sitreps every hour on the hour. Will send an extraction team ASAP, over."

"Son of a bitch, he went for it," McAllister said.

"Roger that," Rainey said, grinning. "Dogma One, out."

"He knows everything you just handed him is a crock," McAllister said. "He knows we went after the hostages."

"Of course he does," Rainey said. "But he didn't order us to go after them, and now he's off the hook in case anything goes wrong."

"But then you'll be the fall guy," Houston said.

"And one day, when you're a team leader, you'll be the same," Rainey reminded the lance corporal.

"You should be a general instead of a sergeant," Vance said. "You know the politics, all right."

"I know this: St. Andrew and the rest of them have way too much pressure on their backs. Any of us gets killed, it's national news, and everyone and his mother wants a detailed explanation of why the system broke down and some grunt got shot or run over by a Jeep or stepped on a land mine."

"It's war," Houston said. "Thought that was reason enough."

"You thought wrong. Now you got point."

The kid nodded, stowed the mike and keypad. "I will lead, you will follow."

McAllister shifted up behind Rainey and muttered in his ear, "You good with him up there?"

"Yeah, because the next assault might be coming from the rear."

"I don't know. I think maybe those guys turned back," McAllister said. "We ain't heard from them in a while."

"I know," Rainey said. "And if we do, that's going to send our hostages into overdrive, same way it did before. Plus they'll know someone is still on their tail. We can't afford another shot."

"Well, thank God we're here. Force Recon, the guys who slip in and slip out, right?"

Rainey shrugged and probably read the wistfulness in McAllister's eyes. "You're going to miss this shit, aren't you . . ."

McAllister considered and breathed a heavy sigh.

AL-ZUMAR PARTY
APPROXIMATELY TEN HOURS SOUTH OF CHITRAL
NORTHWEST FRONTIER PROVINCE
PAKISTAN
1305 HOURS LOCAL TIME

Mohammed al-Zumar's contacts in Chitral had still not replied to his radio calls. He feared those contacts had either not arrived or were never going to arrive. The wise Shaykh had repeatedly assured him that all would go as planned, that by the next morning they would be deep inside Tajikistan and surrounded by protectors. Al-Zumar wanted to believe that, but the farther they had walked across the valley, the stronger his premonitions of doom had become. He continually grappled with them, assuring himself that he had literally grown colder, that his environment depressed him and not some evil spirit wrapping its long, icy talons around his heart.

At one point during the walk, he had imagined a meeting with his father, who reminded him that the Americans died because their government was corrupt. "They died because they are misguided infidels who worship their brand-name sneakers and their DVD players and their sport utility vehicles. No, they were not innocent. They were soulless, their lives without meaning. And they gave those lives so that our message might be heard by the entire world. Don't you see? Their lives finally meant something."

Yes, Father, I do.

"The next cave should be over that hill," Shaykh said, his snowy beard hidden behind his scarf, his wizened eyes bloodshot and growing narrow. "We need to stop."

"No, we need to take advantage of this storm," al-Zumar corrected. "We'll grab the supplies Fathi's team hid there, but we will not stop. We will walk for ten more hours because the Americans might still be trailing us."

"You do not trust your men?"

"I trust them. But I trust myself more."

"I understand, Mohammed. Perhaps when we reach the cave, you will leave me there. I'm sorry. I don't know if I can go on."

"If I have to carry you on my back, you are going on."

"I've never been this cold in my life."

"Nor have I. Trust me when I say that. But we can do this—together." Al-Zumar draped an arm over the old man's shoulder. "Don't worry. When we reach the station, we will have time to get warm inside the trucks."

"Those trucks will arrive," the old man insisted.

"I believe you."

Al-Zumar paused as they reached the edge of a clearing. About thirty meters ahead stood the rocky entrance to the next cave. Some months prior, food and water had been stored there as part of a master escape plan. Before launching his first attacks on the United States, al-Zumar had hidden many such caches in caves all over Pakistan and Afghanistan; if the Americans ever learned of how well prepared he actually was, they would sit up in their overpriced office chairs in awe. He wasn't some deranged Middle Eastern man with his finger on a trigger; he was a highly educated tactician, a man whose forward thinking kept literally hundreds of people alive in some of the harshest regions on the planet, but the infidels would never see it that way.

"I wish we could stop," Shaykh said. "But you are right. I will seek strength from Allah."

Al-Zumar paused, turned back to his men, shouted for Fathi and one other to hurry ahead and bring out the packs. The two came jogging up the line, and, shivering and snow-covered, they hurried to obey the command. Al-Zumar waved on the others, sizing them up as they passed him. When Rick Navarro caught his gaze, al-Zumar said in English, "Mr. Navarro, our walk is big, no?"

"You mean long," the reporter said.

"Yes, long. Maybe ten hour more."

"Ten hours? You have to be fucking kidding me. We won't last ten hours."

"It's okay. Ten hours is okay."

Navarro shivered and trudged away.

The reporter's bodyguard, the man called Arden, shifted by and sang a song al-Zumar did not recognize: "From the Halls of Montezuma, to the shores of Tripoli . . ."

"You make music to feel warm?" al-Zumar asked.

"The Marines are coming," the ex-military man answered. "And this is their song."

"Sounds like Michael Jackson," al-Zumar said. All Western music sounded like Michael Jackson.

"It ain't," said Arden. "And it'll be a song you never forget."

The cold was obviously getting to that man, and al-Zumar dismissed him with a wave. He stared into the eyes of his bodyguards, his best men, saw how the cold had extinguished their fire. Maybe they should stop in the cave, rest a while, take a chance.

No. He cried out for them to pick up the pace, told them that Allah was great, that Allah would keep them warm—

Though he remained bitterly and inconsolably cold.

17

Vance could barely keep the Nightstars steady as he scrutinized the grainy green image of the hostages and terrorists being fed to him by the binoculars. Man, oh, man, he was freezing his ass off, felt constipated, and had just one meal left to his name, a meal that was anything but a T-bone with baked potato and baby carrots.

Still, life wasn't all bad. After nearly eight uneventful hours of tailing the bad guys, the team had spread out along a cliff overlooking a narrow valley that broadened into the main part of Chitral. With the snowstorm gone, illuminated windows shone across the landscape in loose clusters hardly as dense as even small towns in the United States. No surprise there, since the population was only about twenty thousand. According to Doc, who had a read a few things about places in the Northwest Frontier Province, the Kunar or Chitral River lay just north of the settlement, and Vance couldn't help but wonder how the trout fishing was. Wouldn't be any lunker bass in that river, but he was betting some nice trout were just waiting for a fly to come floating over their heads.

Fishing was, according to Doc, a big deal in Chitral, as was polo, and while Vance couldn't make out the polo fields very clearly, even with his Nightstars, he had picked out the grandstands and a nearby parking lot, along with another group of structures, some with satellite dishes mounted on their roofs. A TV station maybe? Who knew. Doc had said there was a hospital down there, a library, an old historical fort, and a pretty fancy mosque with a dome and "minarets which are like balconies from where the *muezzin* calls the people to prayer five times a day." Doc knew his shit, liked to know where he was going. God bless him for being a human GPS and travel guide.

"Just how cold is it?" Houston asked over the radio. "Because this . . . this . . . is . . . insane!"

"It's actually getting warmer," Rainey said. "Just stay on task."

"I am, Sarge. But did you know there's a tendency for Marines to become constipated during cold-weather operations? Isn't that right, Vance?"

In a moment of weakness, Vance had confided in Houston, and now he regretted telling the idiot that the plumbing was backed up. "I wouldn't know."

"Gentlemen, that's just a military myth," Rainey

said. "Cold don't bother me. Drop my pants and take care of business. Now cut the chatter."

Below, the terrorists and hostages were just meeting up with two trucks, twenty-year-old Jeeps parked outside a little gas station or "petrol stop" as the locals called it, with two pumps and a single, ramshackle building with Arabic or whatever written on one side. The station lay alone on the very outskirts of Chitral, like a 7-Eleven perched atop Mount Everest. The drivers of the two Jeeps got out, exchanged a few words with the terrorists, then they went running off into the hills.

"Got two fleeing the trucks," Houston said.

"Confirm two," added McAllister. "Vance?"

"Yeah, there's two," Vance responded, zooming in to get a better image of the building. "They're unarmed. And hey, there could be a third vehicle inside the station."

"Damn it, this is happening too fast," said Rainey.

"Where you think they're headed?" Houston asked. "The airstrip or the mountain road?"

"If we don't boogie, we'll never know," Rainey said. "Saddle up!"

Vance made sure he had all his gear and that his ruck and vest were tight. He squeezed his sniper's rifle, the A3 feeling just right in his hands, then he dropped in behind the sergeant, who had silently chosen himself to take point.

Rainey drove them at an insane pace down a slope whose incline Vance estimated at fifty degrees. A crusty layer of ice had formed on the snow and helped slow their sliding, though occasionally Vance hit a patch of ice, and in fear his legs locked up. By the time he reached level ground, he was wind-worn, breathless, and covered up to his abdomen in snow.

Rainey gave them all of two seconds to catch their breaths before issuing his hand signals, although the two trucks were already kicking up dirt and snow as they sped away from the station.

Vance drove right with the others, following in a straight line, coming up behind the building and yanking on his night-vision goggles. As they squatted down behind the building, Vance glanced right, where a tall sign rose improbably from the boulders and snow:

AGA KHAN RURAL SUPPORT PROGRAMME
CHITRAL
AGRICULTURE ACTIVITY

A long list in both English and Arabic detailed the program's activities, which included seed and plant production, and Vance thought he saw something about fruit trees. He was about to turn away from the sign when rounds suddenly punched Swiss cheese holes in the dark letters and white background.

Vance froze, his weapon ready, his gaze burning through the NVGs. That was AK fire. That was close.

The wind hummed.

He waited for the next shot, anticipating it so badly that he thought he heard it. Didn't.

"Nobody move," Rainey said over the radio.

From his vantage point at the corner of the building,

Vance followed the line of fire toward the front. Two men lay before the pumps. Judging from their dress, they had been locals, maybe the guys operating the station. One of them flinched; the other lay supine and motionless.

A man shouted something in Arabic. Another man answered, and Vance recognized one word: sheikh. An engine roared to life, and tires dug into the snow.

"Go, Vance," Rainey ordered.

Reacting in the nanosecond following Rainey's order, Vance slid alongside the building, came around the front, watched as yet a third old Jeep squealed out of the station's single garage and plowed away, following the road down toward Chitral.

"They left a couple guys behind to clean up," Rainey said, drawing closer.

"I think so, Sarge," Vance replied. "Killed these local guys. Didn't want any witnesses."

"But they got allies here."

"No doubt."

"Hey, Sergeant, this guy's still alive," Houston said.

Doc was already on his knees beside a poor guy wearing tattered jeans and several old sweaters. Clumps of snow clung to the guy's long beard, and his eyelids flickered.

"Aw, he's bleeding out pretty bad," Doc said, rolling the man to inspect the gunshot wounds. He went back to his pack, yanked out a 4×4 bandage.

"Don't waste it, Doc," Rainey said. "Don't waste anything. Hate to sound too cruel, but we might need your supplies for us, and I think he's already gone."

Vance crouched down next to Doc, stared solemnly at the dying guy. Man, it wasn't pretty, and it certainly served as a reminder that he would not like to die out here, in the cold, with strangers watching. That had to suck. But maybe the guy, in his last moments, could help them. Maybe that would make him feel good—well, not good, but maybe helping would lift his spirits a little before he passed on. "Hey, man," Vance said to the guy. "Who's the sheikh?"

"You think he understands you?" Doc asked.

"He knows the word sheikh," Houston said. "You know those guys driving around in expensive cars, taking trips to Las Vegas and spending weeks at a time in the whorehouses."

"He's trying to say something," Doc said, putting his ear to the man's mouth.

"Quiet," Rainey said.

The man's lips moved slowly, though Vance couldn't hear anything. Then, his head titled to one side, and his tongue slipped from his mouth.

"He's dead," Doc pronounced.

"He say anything?" Rainey asked.

Doc shook his head. "But I remember reading that al-Zumar's people call him the Sheikh."

"So I heard them talking about the boss man," said Vance.

"Maybe he's here," Houston said. "I'm telling you, we've been following him all this time."

Rainey rolled his eyes. "All right, let's get these guys inside. Terry? Get up on the roof and watch our package."

* * *

McAllister slipped and nearly broke his ass as he fell off a natural gas tank he had been using to scale the wall to the station's roof. He swore, got back on his feet, and completed the climb, his left butt cheek smarting like a son of a bitch.

It only took twenty seconds for him to reestablish visual contact with the first two Jeeps, whose drivers had kept their running and headlights off, though they could not escape night vision or thermal technology. The Jeeps followed a road leading toward the polo fields and the conglomeration of small buildings that made up the bazaar. From there the road forked, and they would take one of two bridges over the river.

Rainey's voice sounded in his ear. "Got them, Terry?"

"Yup. They got a huge lead on us, and they're moving fast toward the river. We'll need wheels to stay in the game."

"See a couple of cars outside those buildings with the dishes up top," Rainey said.

"Yeah, I see them. I hear they're offering, zero down, zero percent financing, and no payments—ever."

"We'll get the keys without firing a shot."

"Works in theory."

"It works when you don't want an international incident. It works when you don't want to put the lieutenant colonel's ass on the line, let alone the president's."

"Since when are you worried about them?"

Rainey chuckled to himself. "Where is the package now?"

"Almost at the polo fields."

Inside one of the Jeeps, John Arden sat between Rick Navarro and al-Zumar's friend, the old man, who nervously stroked his beard. The fact that grandpa Obi-Wan had not showered (in weeks maybe?) was not lost on Arden, who found himself breathing only through his mouth. Could life be any better?

At least the damned heater in the piece of crap truck worked. Fathi, who had taken the wheel from some local guy, appeared especially nervous, since al-Zumar himself sat in the passenger's seat. Three of al-Zumar's bodyguards had shoved themselves into the small compartment behind the rear seat, with two pointing their rifles at Arden and Navarro, the third guarding the Jeep's rear.

"Can we stop and get something to eat?" Navarro asked, his voice thin, his bravado worn to a nub.

Al-Zumar impatiently waved off the question as he keyed the mike of a military radio seated on the floor between his legs. The world's most wanted man was no happy camper. He shouted, waited for a reply, shouted again, then turned and blasted the old man with a string of words that drew an even more fiery reply. Where the hell was Shaqib when Arden needed him? The translator had gone in the other Jeep, along with the pilots.

"What's wrong?" Navarro asked.

"Like they're going to tell you?" Arden said.

"Shut up!" Fathi cried. "Shut up."

Suddenly, all three Arabs spoke over each other, and for a moment, Arden thought they would actually draw weapons to end the argument. Al-Zumar breathed a last, guttural word, and then, an awkward silence followed, the Jeep's grumbling engine filling the void until a voice came over the radio. Al-Zumar answered solemnly, then returned the mike and mumbled something to Fathi, who nodded.

"Food," Navarro said, opening his mouth to make the gesture of chewing. "We need food. And water."

Not to mention medical attention. Arden's shoulder still ached terribly, though the wound had not bled any more. He figured there had to be a hospital or some medical facility somewhere in town, though he wondered if he could trust those doctors.

Why was he worrying about that? No way in hell was he getting near a medical facility. They were simply hostages, and when they were no longer useful, they would be shot and dumped over the side. He leaned toward Navarro. "They didn't lock your door."

"Get over it, Mr. Arden."

"What? Knowing that I'm going to die so you can get your fucking interview? Sorry, I can't do that."

"You're not going to die. Shaqib is with us. He'll help. Trust me."

Fathi pulled to a screeching halt before a row of dilapidated buildings, a daytime bazaar perhaps, Arden wasn't sure, but most of the "shops" didn't have doors, only canvas curtains tied shut with twine. Candlelight came from the windows of two buildings at the end of a dark alley, and al-Zumar pointed at them and uttered something to the old man, who responded affirmatively.

"He's stupid if he stops here," Arden whispered. "Even if those Marines aren't tailing us anymore, they probably reported our last heading. Something's gone wrong with his plan." Arden faced forward, found a .45-caliber pistol pointed at his head, with Fathi's glowing eyes haloing the gun's sight. "Okay," Arden began sarcastically, "I'll shut up."

Al-Zumar spat orders to the men in back, who hopped out and opened the side doors. Navarro got dragged out first, then Arden. They were shoved into the alley, where they met up with Graham, Ingram, and the camera-wielding Shaqib.

"Something's wrong," Graham said, straying closer to Arden.

"I know it. We shouldn't be stopping."

The pilot looked pale and definitely worse for wear. "Fuck, I don't like this."

"What part of it can we like?"

"Just watch me, okay?" Graham asked. "You'll know when the time comes."

"Okay." Arden sighed. "And hey, if I had to be captured with somebody, I'm glad it's you. That's all I can say. At least a few of us will stand up to these bastards."

"Hey, man, I ain't looking for medals or scholarship funds in my name. Just want to go home."

"Don't we all." Arden tossed a look over his shoulder at Navarro. "Well, not all of us."

The reporter was speaking rapidly with Shaqib, saying something about permission to shoot now.

"Shaqib!" Arden called, but he gained Fathi's attention instead.

The young Arab hustled up behind Arden and said, "I know if he wants it done, he will tell me to kill you. And this I will enjoy. Now shut up!"

TEAM DOGMA

OUTSIDE PAKISTAN TV CORPORATION

CHITRAL

PAKISTAN

2120 HOURS LOCAL TIME

Rainey gave the hand signal to halt, and the team paused behind the first of three buildings they had been inspecting. He took a deep breath and gestured for Houston and Vance to take either side of the main entrance door, while he and Doc took the rear door. McAllister slipped off to scale the iron latticework of a radio tower so he could once more get eyes-on the package.

"Dogma One, this is Beacon Light, over? Dogma One, this is Beacon Light, over?"

Shit, Kady. Not now. "Everybody standby," Rainey said, rushing up behind Houston. He lowered the radio's volume and took the mike. "Beacon Light, this is Dogma One, over."

Kady's voice came through loud and clear, and he detected a strong sense of relief in her tone. He hadn't spoken to her in eight, ten, maybe twelve hours, he wasn't sure, but he had assumed she had been standing by and monitoring his transmissions until she was back on duty. "Dogma One, report your situation, over."

"Beacon Light, we are presently on the move, attempting to keep the package in sight. Heading into Chitral District. Will update when we can, over."

"Dogma One, we'll be standing by. The torch is burning, out."

The torch is burning. That was one of Kady's more obvious code phrases. Translation? I love you.

"Okay," Rainey began, forcing himself back to the moment. "Houston? Vance? Go now."

Though Rainey could not see his men, he heard Vance kick in the main door, whose frame was constructed of wood and whose deadbolt would hardly stop a determined Marine. After peeking in the windows, Rainey had estimated that six, maybe ten people were inside the facility, and as Houston and Vance employed the few Arabic words they knew, shouting for people to freeze, two men in dress shirts and slacks bolted through the rear door, coming face to face with Rainey and Doc.

One clean-shaven man gaped in surprise, revealing a gold tooth before he smiled and spoke in perfect English. "Your eyes. You're not Arabs. Are you Americans?"

"Bingo," Rainey said.

The man whirled. "Two Arabs inside! Please, help us!"

"Inside, yes!" the other guy said with a heavy accent. "Go inside! They take the hostage!"

Rainey exchanged a confused look with Doc, then he

realized that the guys had mistaken Vance and Houston for Arab terrorists and seemed okay with the presence of Americans. Better yet, they could communicate with at least one of them. "No, no, they're with us," Rainey told the men. "The guys inside are Americans."

Brandishing his Para SAW, Doc forced the guys back into the building. They entered a remarkably high-tech television broadcast facility. Monitors and other NASA-like equipment with glowing dials and little flashing lights lined the walls. The gold-toothed man led them past those control stations and down a main corridor flanked by computer terminals. Ahead, Vance and Houston had corralled three more men and two women into a cubicle, where they held the group at gunpoint.

"Why are you here?" Mr. Gold Tooth asked.

"That's classified," Rainey said. "All we need is a vehicle. There's a pickup truck out there."

"You're in luck. It's mine."

"We're just borrowing it. Anything happens, the United States government will buy you a brand-new one."

"You bet your ass they will—because I'm a U.S. citizen. My name is Abdells Kobriti, Doctor of Communications, Central Ohio University. I'm here on a research grant."

Rainey grinned at the odds of bumping into an American so very far from home. "I thought I'd run out of luck. Guess I didn't. But I am out of time. Keys?"

"Hey, Sergeant, quick, come look at this," Doc called, his attention having been stolen by a nearby television monitor.

Rainey rushed over, saw pictures of Dodger Stadium, where a massive hole had been blown in the bleachers. Then he saw a smoking bridge missing a huge part of its midsection, with New York skyscrapers towering in the background. He gasped even more when he saw a skeletal heap of a building rising up through the black smoke. A caption in multiple languages identified the ruins as the federal building in Denver.

"You don't know?" Kobriti said. "Al-Zumar's sleepers struck again."

"We've been away," Rainey said. "When did this happen?"

"Early this morning our time. We've all been here since it happened. It's just terribly shocking."

"Those bastards," Doc muttered.

"We have to get them, Sarge," Houston hollered. "Any guy who works for al-Zumar is a dead man!"

"Shut up!" Rainey blinked hard, tried to separate his anger from his mission. Tried. He faced Kobriti. "Keys?"

The man fished out a ring with a half-dozen keys, handed them to Rainey. "Repaying violence with violence is not always the answer."

Before Rainey could respond, McAllister's voice came through his earpiece: "Dogma One, this is Dogma Five, over."

Turning away from Kobriti, Rainey lifted his boom mike. "Go, Five."

"Be advised our package has stopped, over."

"Say again?"

"Repeat our package has stopped. Maybe we've caught a break, over."

"Location?"

"Main road, about a half klick ahead, outside some old buildings. Looks like the bazaar, maybe, over."

"Roger that. Get down. We'll meet you outside."

"On my way, out."

"All right, people," Rainey called to the others. "We're out of here." He nodded to Kobriti. "Thank you."

The man raised his thumb and said gravely, "God bless America."

18

John Arden sat on a creaky old traveling trunk and sipped on a cup of bitter coffee that Shaqib held to his lips. He could barely keep his eyes open. The warmer air lulled him to sleep, almost made him forget that he might very well be living the last hour of his life.

He and the rest of the hostages had been ushered into a twenty-by-twenty storage room cluttered from floor to ceiling with piles of embroidered coats, stacks of round, multicolored hats, long rows of rolled up carpets standing on end, and packages of special hand-made wool material called *Mohikan* that Shaqib said was famous for its good quality. Arden's nose was beginning to itch from all that fabric, and his cheeks still stung from the windburns, but he was glad to come down from the mountains.

At the moment, two of al-Zumar's men stood at the door, while two more offered coffee to Graham and Ingram. Navarro, who had already finished a cup of tea, spoke quietly to Fathi, who said something about food coming soon.

"How is the shoulder, Mr. John?" Shaqib asked, lowering the coffee cup. "We can change the bandage."

"It's all right."

"So, you hate me now."

Arden glanced away. "I'm too tired to feel anything."

"I'm sorry."

"Don't even say it. You want to tell me something? Tell me why we've stopped. Do you know?"

The translator lowered his voice. "I think so. Another team was coming to meet with him at the border, but an avalanche came down on the road. Now he has to fly. He did not want to do that. He is mad. Very mad."

"So they're sending a chopper here?"

"Maybe here, maybe the airport. I don't know."

"You have to find out."

"It does not matter."

"What do you mean?"

After glancing furtively right and left, the translator set down the coffee cup. "I keep a small knife in my shoe. I will give it to you."

"Jesus, now you tell me?"

"I was hoping, maybe, that he would let us go." Shaqib reached discreetly into his boot, produced the pocketknife and passed it smoothly into Arden's hands.

"What changed your mind?" Arden asked, beginning

to work the knife with his thumb and forefinger, sawing slowly but steadily at the twine.

"I heard them say they cannot take us to Tajikistan."

"So our ride ends here."

The door burst open, and in stepped al-Zumar himself, a kebob to his lips. He tore off a huge piece of sweet-smelling meat, then said with his mouth full, "We take a break. We eat."

Shouting something to the guards, the old man wove his way past al-Zumar. He carried a tray of more kebobs, and before he could set them down, the guards surrounded him, took up meat for themselves and sticks for Ingram, Graham, and Navarro.

"You want one?" Shaqib asked.

"Yeah."

While Shaqib went off, Arden finished cutting the twine binding his hands, folded up the knife, then used his middle finger to hold the strands in place so that it would appear that he was still tied. Now what? He assessed distances, positions of guards, positions of weapons, and calculated how many guys were still outside and where they might be posted. Yes, he was free, but the opportunity still wasn't there. A lunge might get him a weapon, might buy him a second to get off a shot, but he would buy it before he could free anyone else. If Graham and Ingram were free, then the three of them could simultaneously launch an attack. But how could he pass them the knife?

"Can you untie me so I can eat like a civilized human being?" Navarro asked al-Zumar. "My arms are killing me. Untie me, let me eat, and while we're here, let's do the interview. I mean, even if I ran away, where would I go? We're still in the middle of the damned mountains here."

Shaqib began translating, but al-Zumar silenced him with a stern look and said something to Fathi, who returned a quick answer, shook his head, then leaned down, hoisted his pant leg, and pulled a knife from a calf sheath. He crossed to Navarro, spun the man around, and cut him free.

"Careful," Fathi warned Navarro, waving his knife a hairsbreadth away from Navarro's nose. "Careful."

Navarro's eyelid twitched. "Yes, I understand."

Well, isn't that great, Arden thought. *The guy who won't help me is free.*

As Fathi shifted back, Navarro went to take his kebob from the nearest guard, but that act sent the guard retreating a step, his weapon whipping up, the safety off. Navarro pointed at the kebob, made a silly munching face. The guard gave him a dirty look and tossed the kebob at Navarro's feet.

Al-Zumar raised his voice at the guard, then slapped him across the cheek. The guard retreated like a beaten dog as al-Zumar crossed to a table where the tray of kebobs sat, then picked up a fresh one. He brought it to Navarro, saying, "He is . . . young."

Navarro accepted the kebob. "And so are you. Thanks."

Shaqib held up another kebob to Arden's lips, and he took a bite, didn't care whether it was cat, monkey, dog, goat, or beef. Whatever it was, it tasted damned good. He took another bite, chewed savagely. And as he ate, he glanced to Graham and Ingram, imagined himself seated next to them and passing Graham the blade.

Okay, so Navarro was free, but Arden couldn't expect his help. Then again, all Navarro wanted was that interview, after which he had said he would try to kill al-Zumar himself. Maybe that was it—let Navarro get the interview, then tell him—

Wait a minute. "Hey, Rick," he called softly.

Wisely, Navarro did not look back. "Yeah?"

"Tell him you want to get some video of us here before the interview. Tell him you want to put me, Graham, and Ingram on camera. Tell him some bullshit about showing the world he has power or that he saved our lives in the mountains or something. You figure it out. See what he says."

"What you talking there?" al-Zumar asked.

Navarro lifted his head. "Before the interview, I'd like to take some video of the pilots, myself, and him. I need to document our present, and you can make a statement about these hostages. You can show the world that you've treated us well."

Shaqib went to work, and surprisingly, al-Zumar allowed the translator to finish.

"Okay?" Navarro asked.

Al-Zumar narrowed his brows, turned back to the old man, and exchanged a few words, his gaze shifting between Navarro and the pilots. Then he broke away from the old guy and faced Navarro. "No."

"Come on. If we don't make it back, this is all our families are going to have. If you think about it, we're inside this little room. There are probably thousands

just like it all over Pakistan and Afghanistan. We don't
have to say where we are, just that we're alive and with
you. Give us that much."

As Shaqib translated, al-Zumar's gaze fell to the
camera lying beside Arden's trunk, then he scrutinized
Navarro, perhaps believing that he could spot a lie in
the man's eyes.

But the world's most wanted man had no idea that he
was confronting the world's greatest bullshit artist.

TEAM DOGMA
CHITRAL BAZAAR
NORTHWEST FRONTIER PROVINCE
PAKISTAN
2140 HOURS LOCAL TIME

McAllister drove the pickup truck because—get this—
he was the only member of Team Dogma who could
drive stick. Unbelievable. Unimaginable. What kind of
fathers and mothers would deny their boys the opportunity to drive stick? Did they really believe that junior
would drive the family's station wagon forever? These
fellows had become Marines! Driving stick should be
in their blood! To be fair, Rainey had said that he had
driven stick years ago but was too rusty. Houston,
Vance, and Doc were sissies, plain and simple.

It was up to old Terry McAllister to save the free
world.

He had nothing better to do.

Instead of taking the left fork toward the bazaar,

McAllister took them straight, heading with the lights off down a narrow road freshly plowed of snow. Rainey suggested that they veer off the road and cut toward a small field behind the row of buildings. McAllister rolled the wheel, and the ride suddenly got rough, very rough.

When they were about five or six hundred meters away from the buildings, McAllister hit a rut, and the pickup's rear tires lost traction. The truck swerved, the tires dug deeper into the snow, spun freely, and McAllister took his boot off the pedal. "Ride's over. We're stuck."

"Maybe we can't drive stick," Houston said from his seat in the flatbed. "But at least we can drive."

McAllister reached over and forced Houston's head back through the cab's open rear window. "Corporal, you talk way too much."

"And now it's my turn," Rainey said from the passenger's seat. "Everybody move out! Vance? You're point."

Reflexively, McAllister shut off the engine and pocketed the keys. As he trotted off, he wondered why he had kept the keys. Then he wondered why he was wondering that. Lack of sleep did not do a body good.

A cold mountain night. McAllister knew them well, and save for Rainey, he assumed he was the only one who could appreciate the stillness, the scent of wood burning in fireplaces, and the distant bark of a dog. He might as well be back in Colorado. Only the landscape and buildings looked different. The *feel* of the place was right, and despite his exhaustion, old man McAllister felt up for whatever they'd throw at him. He sensed his environment was no longer a foe but a home away from home, a place where the body could get in touch with the spirit, a place where instincts told you everything. Mystical crap? Maybe. But maybes should not be ignored.

"There's an alley a little ways up," he told Rainey over the tactical frequency as they slipped noiselessly through shadows clinging to the buildings.

"I see it," Vance said, scanning with his NVGs.

Doc and Houston swept the area with their weapons, their eyes bugged out, their faces masked by black wool. There was poetry in their movements, an unmistakable rhythm born of training and tradition. They were badasses wired to panic, all right, and even though Doc's limp had returned, it felt damned good to be in his and Vance's company.

Abruptly, Vance threw up his hand, slammed himself against the building to his left. He uttered one word into his boom mike: "Down."

They crouched against a patchwork of aluminum sheets rattling in a slight breeze. Rainey was right behind Vance, Doc and Houston next, while McAllister dropped back about two meters behind them, his heart already poking at his throat.

A lone, bearded man rounded the corner. He wore a heavy woolen jacket, a small round cap, and he took deep drags on a long pipe, the tobacco sweet and strong as it wafted McAllister's way. The man shuffled on, then, without warning, he suddenly stopped, glanced in the team's direction, squinted.

"Just hold, Vance," Rainey said over the radio. "Just hold."

The man shrugged, then moved on, singing softly to himself as he puffed on his pipe.

McAllister didn't have Rainey's patience or conscience. He might very well have ordered Vance to take out that guy, who was more than likely an innocent civilian.

But you never knew.

Once the pipe-smoking man was well out of sight and earshot, Rainey gave the signal, and they stole onward, into the alley, slipping up behind piles of empty cardboard boxes printed with the English words PRODUCT OF CHINA, along with several plastic trash cans. *Everything's made in China*, McAllister thought. *Everything except United States Marines.*

After a quick once-over of the alley, McAllister noted that the two Jeeps were not parked at the end of the alley. Where had they gone? He stared hard into the shadows, and the answer soon materialized.

"Their vehicles are gone," Vance reported.

"Not gone," McAllister said. "Just moved. Take another look."

After a few seconds, Vance said, "Damn, sorry I missed that."

McAllister had spied all three Jeeps parked beneath sheets of tarpaulin that dropped down from the walls. At first glance, the camouflaged vehicles seemed part of the structure, since some of the walls were covered by canvas instead of aluminum, tin, or stone.

"Marines, we still need confirmation that our package is here. We're not authorized to engage in a building-to-building search, and that would just blow our cover anyway. No doubt they'll have a few armed guys posted outside. We find them, and we've found the package. Two teams. Doc and McAllister. You sweep left. The rest of us sweep right. Good to go?"

After lifting his thumb, McAllister shifted back to Doc, gave the corpsman a signal to fall back so they could work their way toward the next alley. Big Doc had been pulling his weight on a busted-up ankle for too long, and McAllister wasn't feeling particularly top-notch. Time to get this operation boxed and wrapped for Christmas.

C'mon, where are you, you bastards? McAllister thought as he jogged along the next shop's perimeter, reached the corner, then peered down the alley as Doc checked their rear.

No, it can't be this easy . . .

But there they were: two thugs smoking cigarettes and one-handing AK-47s. They stood outside a narrow, wooden door, and McAllister even recognized one of their jackets. He leaned back, pointed at Doc, then at his own eyes for Doc to have a look. The corpsman did, pulled back, nodded, then turned his eyes skyward and blessed himself.

"Dogma One, this Dogma Five, over."

"Go, Five."

"We're in the next alley. Be advised we have two bad guys posted outside the door of another shop or warehouse. Confirm that one of them was definitely part of our group, over."

"Maintain position. We'll rally on you, out."

WOLF NEWS CREW
CHITRAL BAZAAR
NORTHWEST FRONTIER PROVINCE
PAKISTAN
2150 HOURS LOCAL TIME

Despite protests from the old man, Mohammed al-Zumar allowed Navarro to shoot some video. Arden had his excuse to shift in close to Graham and Ingram so all three would be in the shot. As he did, he passed the knife into Graham's hands, and the man acknowledged the blade with a slight nod.

"Ladies and gentlemen, this is Rick Navarro reporting to you from somewhere in northern Pakistan. In truth, I do have a good idea of where we are, but if I were to disclose our exact location, I'm afraid the Warriors of Mohammed would terminate my life. In fact, my life has been in danger since early this morning, when most of my crew was attacked and killed by Afghan refugees and the rest of us were taken hostage. I'm here now in a storeroom of sorts, along with my bodyguard, Mr. John Arden, and two Marine Corps pilots, Captain Tom Graham and First Lieutenant Martha Ingram, whose Huey helicopter was shot down in the mountains." Navarro pointed for Shaqib to turn the camera toward Arden, Ingram, and Graham. Arden felt like one of the Three Stooges starring in Navarro's ill-conceived and anything-but-funny report.

In the meantime, al-Zumar waved his hand for his guards to get out of the shot. He was smart enough to realize that their identities should not be compromised. He should have taught that lesson to his troops early on, but there was something about the presence of a camera, especially one accompanied by an American newsman, that turned Third-World terrorists into goofy tourists trying to get their unshaven and crusty-faced mugs on camera.

Graham and Ingram stared grimly, and though he wasn't positive, Arden sensed that Graham had already cut himself free and had handed the knife to Ingram.

"As you can see, we're physically and mentally exhausted, having just trekked several kilometers, maybe more, through the mountains to arrive at this place and in the company of the world's most wanted man: Mohammed al-Zumar." Navarro stepped out of the shot so that Shaqib could pan the camera to al-Zumar.

"Ladies and gentlemen, I am the only Western reporter to ever get this close to Mr. al-Zumar. He has agreed to an interview with the help of my translator, Shaqib, who is also serving as my cameraman." Navarro motioned al-Zumar over to a table and chairs, where they sat across from each other, the empty tray of kebobs between them, the light from the camera making both men squint.

Navarro cleared his throat, and his reporter's bravado awakened. "Mr. Al-Zumar, some are calling you the most evil man on the planet. How do you respond?"

Shaqib tensed, glanced at Navarro, then slowly translated.

TEAM DOGMA
CHITRAL BAZAAR
NORTHWEST FRONTIER PROVINCE
PAKISTAN
2151 HOURS LOCAL TIME

Lying on his belly near the alley's end, Rainey lowered his Nightstars and glanced back to McAllister. "So the old dog comes through."

"Mama told me to eat my carrots. I listened."

Allowing himself a momentary grin, Rainey shifted back and regarded Houston. "Paint this target, Corporal, then get back. I want Beacon Light on the horn."

"Aye-aye, Sergeant," Houston said, then he slipped up past Rainey and used the binoculars' laser range finder to get the required coordinates on the warehouse.

"Hey, Sarge, you ain't calling in an air strike, are you?" Doc whispered. "Not after all this."

"Just letting them know where the package is," Rainey said, his tone growing more cynical. "It's up to them. We're not supposed to effect a rescue, just observe."

"If we go in, good guys could die," Vance said. "If we don't go in, good guys could die."

Rainey thought a moment, looked to Vance. "Get around the other side of this place. I want all the exits covered. Maybe bad guys will come out, and then bad guys will die."

"Aye-aye, Sarge," Vance said, then scurried off to circle around the adjoining buildings and come at the warehouse from the east side.

"You've been my man up top," Rainey told McAllister, his gaze lifting to the warehouse's roof. "But I have a feeling that'll be too noisy."

"Glad you feel that way," McAllister said, lifting his face mask and looking somewhat relieved. "You ain't waiting for St. Andrew's blessing, are you? 'Cause that ain't coming."

"Yeah, I know," Rainey groaned.

"Sergeant," Houston said, crawling up beside them and catching his breath. "Target is painted. I have Beacon Light."

Rainey took the mike. "Beacon Light, this is Dogma One. Be advised we are in Chitral, have followed the package to the city bazaar. Believe the package is inside a warehouse at transmitted coordinates, over."

"Dogma One, this is Beacon Light," came Kady's shaky voice. "Have received coordinates. You are ordered to remain in position and monitor package. Extraction helo and second Recon Team finally en route to your position. Estimated ETA: two hours, thirty minutes, over."

"Beacon Light, remaining in position and monitoring package, out." Rainey handed over the mike, lifted his chin to McAllister. "Guess we'll have to come up with some story about being forced to move in—"

"And it'd better be a good one, because you already know you're the fall guy. Me? I'm on the way out. I don't care. But you have to ask yourself: is it worth the risk?"

Rainey had become an adept navigator of the bureau-
cratic minefields associated with action and inaction. He
had already played his hand right with St. Andrew and
had used the complications of the battlefield to his advantage. But at the moment, he would need an outright
lie in order to justify sending his men into the warehouse
to terminate the enemy and rescue the hostages. St. Andrew knew damned well that the team couldn't sit on
their hands for nearly three hours, and he knew damned
well that the presence of more men wouldn't necessarily
mean that a rescue attempt had better odds of success. In
fact, if the helo came in too close, all bets would be off.

Find the essence.

That was a Marine Corps principle. No matter how
complex the situation, you must perceive it in simple
terms. Hostages were inside a warehouse. They could
be moved. Soon. Rainey's team was outnumbered and
growing dangerously low on ammo, but their greatest
strength—the element of surprise—remained intact.
They should exploit that strength now, before it was
too late.

Essence found.

"Dogma One, this is Dogma Four, over."

"Go, Four."

"Looks like one more door here," Vance said. "And
just one bad guy, over."

Two doors. Three bad guys. That might leave seven,
maybe eight bad guys inside, guarding three, possibly
four hostages. Rainey swore under his breath, wishing
at least one more bad guy had joined his buddy to guard

the back door, but shit, if he wanted easy he would've joined the air force.

He stole a few seconds to play out the scenario in his head, imagining his every move and the moves of his men. Damn it. The numbers were shit. The blood would flow. And the chances were high that Marines were going to get hurt. Badly.

You have to ask yourself is the risk worth it?

The risk. Wasn't that part of the job? Why were Marines called America's 911 force?

Because they were first in, last out, and took the risks that no one else dared take. When American lives were on the line, you didn't call the fucking Ghostbusters; you called the United States Marines.

Rainey took in a long breath. Time for a less-bad choice in an imperfect world. "Dogma Four, take out your bad guy on my mark, over."

"Dogma Four, waiting to execute, over."

Rainey fished into his vest for his MEU pistol with silencer. "Terry, me and you are getting in close. Doc? Houston? You guys hang back until I signal."

As Doc crawled back with Houston, and McAllister fished out his own pistol, Rainey spoke softly into his boom mike: "All right, Vance? Good to go?"

"Good to go."

"Terry?"

"Good to go."

Rainey gritted his teeth. "Execute!"

19

Arden had listened to Mohammed al-Zumar respond to the accusation that he was the most evil man on the planet, not to mention the world's most wanted man. Unexpectedly, al-Zumar conceded the point that many could not get past that label. He agreed that the sheer number of deaths were impossible to ignore. He admitted that previous statements made by him suggested that he did not regret the deaths and was even looking forward to "punishing the infidels for their atrocities against Muslims everywhere."

"But I am not evil," he had said, and at the moment, he pointed verbal fingers at others: "The United States and Israel are murderers," Shaqib translated slowly, taking his time to make sure he got the English words right. "None of the killing in the United States would have happened if America was not supporting Israel. You are supporting a regime that murders innocent civilians, that keeps innocent civilians imprisoned in their own homes, that takes what it wants by force without consideration of others. Why does this happen? Because there are more Jews in New York City than in all of Israel, and they persuade your president to endorse murder. Also, the United States poisons the Holy Land with military troops and supports a regime that we do not recognize. I do not know why infidels believe they must force themselves and their ideas on other people. You are already outnumbered. Islam is the fastest-growing religion in the world. And me and my brothers will stop you."

It was all Arden could do to contain himself. He wanted to get up and clip al-Zumar, then clip Navarro for giving the terrorist a platform. But Arden sat there, biding his time, trying to ignore the look of smug satisfaction on Navarro's face as he got the interview of a lifetime.

"Mr. al-Zumar, you know that the president of the United States has declared war on terrorism and on all nations who harbor terrorists. Do you believe there is anywhere you can go where you'll be safe?"

While Shaqib translated, Arden glanced first at Graham, then at Ingram, whose slight curve of the brow told Arden enough. They were all free, all ready to make their move.

Al-Zumar listened closely to Shaqib, replied quickly, and then the translator grew even more nervous as he issued al-Zumar's statement: "You Americans and Israelis are terrorists. You should declare war on yourselves. Me? I will always be safe because wherever I go, Allah is with me. Allah is great. Allah is great!"

TEAM DOGMA
CHITRAL BAZAAR
NORTHWEST FRONTIER PROVINCE
PAKISTAN
2151 HOURS LOCAL TIME

In the interests of remaining undetected, Vance had left his heavy ruck beside two old bicycles and had drawn up within two meters of his prey. You never parted with your equipment, but the freedom Vance felt had to be worth the risk. The bass fisherman lay concealed behind a stack of wooden pallets and plastic crates, observing the bad guy he was about to fillet. With his big Ka-Bar in hand, Vance heard Rainey's order, tossed the rock he had picked up, and the idiot guard fell for the world's oldest trick. He came down from the concrete stoop, started toward the sound—

And never saw the blade-wielding ghoul behind him.

Vance reached around, delivered a mortal wound to the heart, then held on tight until the guard slumped. After silently laying his victim on the ground, Vance jogged back for his gear. "Dogma One, this is Dogma Four. The back door is clear, over."

"Standby," Rainey answered.

* * *

On the other side of the warehouse, Rainey and McAllister exchanged a look, then popped up from behind the crumbling remains of a stone staircase like targets in a carnival shooting gallery, only they weren't the targets—they were the shooters.

Two .45-caliber rounds whispered through the air, and in the next heartbeat, both bad guys dropped, one shot in the head, the other the heart.

"You went for the head?" Rainey asked McAllister, wondering why his buddy had risked the harder shot.

"Guess I still got it," McAllister said.

"In spades, you old mother. All right, Dogma Team? Goggles on. Inside! Inside!"

During Phase 3 MEU (SOC) training, Houston, like the rest of the team, had taken the TRUE (Training in Urban Environments) course and had been thrust into simulated cityscapes where he cleared buildings, designated targets, found and secured hostages, and killed bad guys—all with sniper fire coming at him from every direction. Some guys speculated that the simulated town was much more difficult than the real thing would ever be. That was the Corps for you, train as you fight, or train even harder than you fight. You'd rather face a terrorist thug with an AK than a highly motivated Marine instructor with a hard-on for failing you.

Nevertheless, Houston did not feel any easier about following Rainey, McAllister, and Doc into a dark building, his pulse bounding, his mouth gone to cotton. The unknown would kill him before a bullet did.

"Clear!" Vance shouted from the other side of the warehouse.

No lights? That was curious. Houston's NVGs allowed him to glance down rows of agricultural equipment, including tractors, plows, and metal racks buckling under the weight of irrigation pipes.

"Clear!" McAllister shouted from the right side of the room.

"Clear!" cried Doc from the left.

Houston rushed down the center aisle, his trigger finger about as itchy as it got. Had to be somebody inside. Trapdoor in the floor? Ceiling exit? His gaze ran along the floorboards, then up the wall, across the rafters. He whirled. Nothing. "Clear!"

"Did they bolt?" hollered Vance.

Rainey hustled up behind Houston, whirled and lowered his rifle. "Son of a bitch!"

"What is it, Sergeant?" Houston asked. "Did they know we were coming? Did they hear us and move the hostages?"

The rest of the team rallied around them as Rainey answered, "They're not here. They never were. Guards outside were just decoys, and they had radios, right?"

"I didn't check," Vance said.

Rainey swore again. "You don't have to. Now they've lost contact with them, and they're going to bolt with our package."

"So we get their radios, answer for them," Vance said.

"Works in the movies, but not here, kid."

"Hey, at least we got three of them," Doc said. "And they can't be far, can they?"

The sergeant's eyes looked glassy. No, he wasn't going to cry, but Houston knew utter frustration when he saw it. Would he have made the same mistake? Probably. These guys were easy to underestimate, but the sergeant wouldn't make that mistake again. Better to play them like an equal force as smart and cunning as they were. Question every move. Assume nothing. Make your back-up plan your main one just to keep them guessing.

"Police up those bodies outside," Rainey ordered. "If our bad guys are going to move, they might head back for those trucks. We'll start there. Go now!"

WOLF NEWS CREW
CHITRAL BAZAAR
NORTHWEST FRONTIER PROVINCE
PAKISTAN
2155 HOURS LOCAL TIME

"Shaqib," Arden whispered, even as Navarro asked his next question of Mohammed al-Zumar.

The translator finally turned his head.

Arden nodded.

And the dark-skinned man's face appeared three shades lighter. He widened his eyes, returned the nod. He was in.

Without uttering a single word, Arden and Graham had already devised their attack plan, and with a glance

Graham's way, Arden told the captain that Shaqib would help.

But could Arden really trust the guy? The same guy who had sold him out? Had Shaqib been lying all along?

Well, if he had, Arden promised himself that his first bullet would take out al-Zumar, his second would finish Shaqib, and his third would find Fathi.

Suddenly, the old man bustled into the room and waved off the camera. He whispered something in al-Zumar's ear, and the man's gaze narrowed in anger.

"Now!" Graham screamed.

In unison, Arden, Ingram, and Graham sprang from the their trunks.

One of the guards shouted.

Al-Zumar shoved the old man aside, then gaped—

As Arden took three giant strides, coming hard at Fathi, who had been guarding the door.

The young Arab brought his weapon up—right into Arden's grip. He fired a round, but Arden was already wresting the weapon away, his wounded shoulder freshly ablaze, his mouth twisted in a horrible grimace.

Behind him, screams and several more rounds erupted, though Arden could hardly pay attention. He tore the rifle from Fathi's grasp, brought it around, even as the Arab reached for a pistol at his side.

Bang. Point-blank to the heart. Wearing a glazed look, Fathi dropped, his hands falling away from the rifle. Sans any glib or vengeful thoughts, Arden swung around, saw the door coming right into his face, raised the rifle, found himself tumbling onto his ass as the hard wood made contact with his elbows.

Two more shots rang out, the booms echoing so loudly that Arden thought he would go deaf. He sat up, saw Graham ripping the pocketknife across one guard's neck, saw Ingram getting dragged out of the room by al-Zumar, who had the young lieutenant in a headlock and shielded himself with her body—even as she kicked, screamed, and tried to bite him. Of course al-Zumar had gone for Ingram as a shield, figuring a female represented an easier hostage. But she stomped on his foot and even tried flipping him, though he was just too heavy. Still, she was putting up one hell of a fight.

As Arden got to his feet, Shaqib rushed over, grabbed Fathi's blade, and stabbed another guard just as the man cleared the doorframe.

Above all of that, Rick Navarro hollered cries of "No!" as he cowered in a corner, the camera held tightly at his chest.

Arden leveled his rifle on al-Zumar, wanted to take the shot, trembled, couldn't find an opening, locked gazes with the man as he and Ingram stumbled outside.

More gunfire. Arden turned. Shaqib lay on the floor, his left hip bleeding profusely as he flinched, groaned, and pressed a palm on the wound.

Another round. From where? There, the guard Graham had been struggling with. The terrorist had turned, his neck a bloody mess. Now he faced Graham, about to fire, when Arden sent a slug punching into the guy's chest.

As Graham scrambled for the weapon, Navarro took up the camera, hit a button, and began shooting.

"Turn that fucking thing off," Arden cried as a triplet of gunfire blasted into the room from somewhere outside.

He trained the AK on Navarro. *Take the shot. No one will ever know. You blew it before; don't blow it again. The fucker deserves to die. Do the world a favor.*

"Mr. John, help me, please," Shaqib moaned.

Arden blinked hard, crawled over to the translator, then frantically set down the AK, unbuckled his belt, and slung it around Shaqib's hip. "Pull on this. Keep applying the pressure."

"No more translating for me," Shaqib said, his voice cracking. "I go back to being an artist, like when I was young. Or maybe you and I go to Palm Beach and take care of the dogs."

"Yeah, Palm Beach. Warm. Very warm." Arden pulled the belt tighter.

"Oh, it hurts so bad."

"I know, man. I know. And hey, I've seen gunshot wounds before. You're going to live. Don't worry."

Blood spurted from the translator's wound. The bullet could have struck an artery, not that Arden would tell Shaqib that. The guy needed to maintain hope.

"Thank you, Mr. John."

The words had barely left Shaqib's lips when automatic fire ripped past the open door and drew a perforated line across the back wall, driving Navarro to his belly and sending Arden toward the left wall, dragging Shaqib with him.

"We have to get outside!" Graham cried from the other side of the room, splintering wood raining down on him. "But my clip's almost out."

Arden checked his own clip. Low. Shit. Time to calculate. Shaqib was down and out. Fathi and one other guard had bought it. Asshole Navarro still had a pulse. Ingram was being dragged off to who knew where with al-Zumar and the rest of his bodyguards.

So Graham wanted to "get outside." And do what? Waste what little ammo they had left? They were still outnumbered. They couldn't save Ingram without help.

But they were Marines. They couldn't leave her. And if they remained in the room, trading fire with the bad guys outside, they'd eventually run out of ammo and buy it anyway.

So maybe "getting out there" was exactly what they needed to do. Arden tried to remember the alley, the doorway, what was outside, anything that might provide suitable cover.

And as he did, a faint, almost imperceptible thumping sounded in the distance.

TEAM DOGMA
CHITRAL BAZAAR
NORTHWEST FRONTIER PROVINCE
PAKISTAN
2158 HOURS LOCAL TIME

By the time Rainey and the rest of the team made it into the alley and concealed themselves behind the camouflaged Jeeps, three locals, shopkeepers Rainey presumed, were crouching along the opposite wall and staring at a door hanging half open, a door Rainey and his men had passed during their first recon of the alley.

Muffled gunfire sounded from inside the building, then two turbaned men, their backs to Rainey, shifted outside, turned, and sprinted down the street.

"Vance? Houston?" Rainey called. "They're yours. Doc? Terry?" Rainey gave the hand signals indicating that his assistant and the corpsman would follow him inside.

McAllister slapped a palm on Rainey's shoulder, pointed his thumb skyward. "Our helo?"

Rainey took a deep, frosty breath. "Too early. It's theirs." He tipped his head, and they darted along the wall, prowling their way up to the open door. Doc took one side, McAllister the other, as Rainey ticked off three fingers.

McAllister pivoted and advanced toward dim light filtering through another door at the end of a short hall. Doc fell in directly behind him, and Rainey divided his attention between the path ahead and their rear.

The floorboards creaked, and Rainey swore inwardly over the betrayal.

Doc grimaced. McAllister moved more gingerly, and after another step, putting him just a meter from the door, McAllister looked to Rainey, who gave a terse nod.

McAllister kicked in the door.

"Don't shoot me! Please!"

The voice had come from a lean, dark-skinned man, a man Rainey recognized as the same guy who had carried the camera for Navarro's team. He lay on the floor, blood pooling beneath his leg. Another guy, an Arab whom Rainey also recognized, lay not far from the doorway, lined up beside a thug whose blood trail extended into the hallway, as though he'd been killed outside and dragged in. Across the room, near a stack of carpets, lay one more, a terrorist as familiar as he was dead.

"Take it easy, partner," Rainey said. "We're going to get you out of here. Doc?"

As the corpsman dropped down to help the wounded guy, something rattled in the far corner of the room, and Rainey swung his rifle toward a small table turned on its side.

"I'm an American," came an oddly familiar voice. "Don't shoot, man! Don't shoot!"

Hands appeared, followed by the man who belonged to those hands: Mr. Rick Navarro, celebrity war correspondent.

"Thank God," Navarro cried, looking leaner, uglier, but still famous to Rainey. "Shit, you have no idea how happy I am to see you guys."

"Where are the others?"

"He took Lieutenant Ingram, so they ran off after them," Navarro said, turning around to fetch his camera.

"Who took Ingram?"

"Who do you think? You guys followed us all the way down here, right?"

Rainey nodded.

"And you still haven't figured out who you've been following?"

"Are you kidding me?" Rainey asked. "You're talking about al-Zumar?"

"I was in the middle of a fucking interview with him when my bodyguard and Graham decided to make a break."

"Sarge, that chopper's getting awfully close," Doc said, glancing up then riffling through his medical pouches.

"Navarro, you stay here with this guy," Rainey said, pointing to the wounded man. "Doc, we have to go."

"Just give me another minute."

"We don't have it. Tell Navarro what to do. Meet you outside."

Rainey and McAllister jogged through the hall and moved warily into the alley. With their shoulders pressed tightly against a rusty wall, they waited as Doc hurried to fall in behind them.

"Murphy again, eh, Rainey?" McAllister asked.

"In what way?"

"Here we are again, a minute late and a dollar short."

"That bird's not on the ground yet."

"No, but it will be."

Rainey was no expert at identifying choppers, but whatever was coming to pick up al-Zumar and his clan sounded big, very big, as it drummed in from the northeast.

Doc arrived, and on Rainey's signal, they dashed forward, the alley branching off into a dirt road with ramshackle huts on either side. In the far distance lay an open field, and beyond it, the silhouette of something big, maybe the ancient fort Doc had mentioned. Where would that chopper land? The field? An open space behind the fort? Maybe Vance and Houston had an idea.

"Dogma One, to Dogma Four, over."

"One to Four. Still . . . in pursuit, over," Vance gasped.

"Where are you now?"

"Just reaching a fence near a big field. Looks like the fort's straight ahead, over."

"We're rallying on you," Rainey said. "Dogma One, out."

Before spiriting off into the shadows, Rainey stole a glance over his shoulder. Was that Rick Navarro rushing off into the alley with the camera tucked under his arm?

As Houston sewed up the gap between himself and the two guys they were chasing, something about their appearance bothered him. Yes, they wore turbans. Yes, they were carrying AKs. But the pants on one weren't right. They just—

"Hey, stop!" Houston shouted to the bad guys. "We're United States Marines!"

Vance raced alongside Houston, slammed his shoulder with the barrel of his rifle. "Jesus H. Christ, what're you doing?"

"Those guys were hostages."

"Bullshit."

"Seriously. Hey, you! Stop!"

The two men turned and hunkered down. "Who are you?"

"United States Marines."

"Hold your fire," one man said as he rose and came jogging toward them, ripping off his turban. "Hold your fire. We're Americans! My name's John Arden. I'm an American! I'm an American!"

Houston lifted his facemask. "Lance Corporal Bradley Houston. You guys were hostages, right?"

"Yeah."

"Where's the rest of the group? What's going on?"

"Lance Corporal, I'm Captain Tom Graham," the other man said, arriving out of breath. "What's going on is my copilot is still with al-Zumar, and he's trying to get out. But we don't have time to bullshit. I think they got a Hind coming for them, and that chopper's heading out behind the fort, over near the river. Let's move!"

Graham took off, and Arden chased after, shouting, "You coming, Marines? Come on."

Houston looked to Vance. "Holy shit! Did he say al-Zumar?"

"That's what I heard."

"Oh, man, I was right all along. This is the mission of a lifetime!"

"Y'all want to be famous, huh? Well, we ain't going anywhere till I contact the Sarge."

20

Mohammed al-Zumar had to be careful not to squeeze the young lieutenant's neck too tightly. She was a fragile bird whose wings had been clipped. However, moments prior, she had been an eagle, kicking and screaming until Shaykh had handed al-Zumar a knife that he pressed against her ribs. He would keep the knife—and her—close, even as he stepped aboard the helicopter. If she failed to shield him from an American bullet, she would at least make his final moments pleasant ones. She smelled simply wonderful, despite having been dragged across the mountains.

Al-Zumar should have known that once they had reached Chitral, his escape plan would fall apart. He should have listened to the cold, the terrible, terrible cold inside. First the avalanche, then the loss of contact with his guards, only to be followed by an attack by the hostages themselves, all confirmed his dark premonitions. He had barely escaped the storage room with his life, and he owed that success to the precautions he had taken: first, setting up decoy guards outside another warehouse, and second, keeping a fourth Jeep hidden away from the three he had stashed in the alley. Now, as he, Shaykh, and four of his bodyguards rumbled down a plowed but icy road leading to the fort, Mohammed al-Zumar wondered what obstacle the cold would bring next.

The helicopter pilot called over the radio again. He said he would touch down in about five minutes. Al-Zumar assured the pilot that he and the rest would be there. The pilot said he had been instructed to wait no more than a few minutes for them. Apparently, several aircraft, presumably American helicopters or jets, were en route. Al-Zumar tensed, finished the call, shouted for the bodyguard, Youssef, to drive faster. He wished young Fathi were at the wheel. Young Fathi. Killed by an infidel, no less. He was a good boy, a martyr. And for just a moment, al-Zumar's eyes welled with tears before he blinked them off and whispered in the lieutenant's ear, "Children?"

"What?" she asked, her voice hoarse and coming in a near whisper.

"Children?"

"Do I have any children? No."

"Why not say yes? Maybe I take pity on you."

"You won't."

"To you, I am a monster."

"No. Something worse."

"Then it is good you have no children."

With that, he felt her tremble, but his attention turned to the road, as the Jeep hit a patch of ice. They spun wildly, and Shaykh screamed at Youssef.

"Turn us around!" al-Zumar cried a second before they slammed into a snowbank and came to a jarring halt. "Turn us around!"

Youssef hit the accelerator, and the tire spun. "I think we are stuck," he said, shivering.

Al-Zumar shook himself—in fury. "Get out and see what the problem is!"

TEAM DOGMA
CHITRAL BAZAAR
NORTHWEST FRONTIER PROVINCE
PAKISTAN
2211 HOURS LOCAL TIME

A Japanese-manufactured sedan older than Vance veered onto the dirt road along the fence. To the uninitiated, the car was being driven by an alien, but that was just McAllister wearing his night-vision goggles. Rainey sat in the passenger's seat, with Doc behind him. "Get in!" the sergeant hollered.

Vance and Houston shoved themselves into the torn-up back seat, and McAllister put the pedal to the metal.

"Graham and a guy named Arden should be just up the road," Vance said.

"I see them," said McAllister.

When Vance had called Rainey to report that two of the hostages had freed themselves, the sergeant had replied with more good news: he, Doc, and McAllister were in the process of commandeering yet another ride. And who said Murphy didn't know when to mind his own business? He had taken his laws and had gone home for the evening. Or so it seemed.

"Captain," Vance called through the open window.

"Pop the trunk," Rainey told McAllister.

"Get in the back," Vance told the pilot, who waved Arden around to the back of the sedan. They climbed into the back compartment, and, keeping the trunk door open, Arden shouted that they were ready.

Well, we're one hell of a ragtag bunch, Vance thought. *Five exhausted Marines, one pilot, and one civilian bodyguard all piled into this jalopy. Oh, yeah, we're badasses all right.*

Houston stuck his head out the window, called back to Arden. "So what's he wearing?"

"Who?"

"Al-Zumar! What's he wearing?"

"Jeans. Green parka. Black cap."

"Then he was the leader across the mountains."

"Yeah. But he could've changed."

"Yeah, okay." Houston ducked back inside the sedan. "You hear that, Sarge?"

"I heard," Rainey said evenly, barely a third as excited as Houston was.

"Sergeant, if I have the shot on him, will you let me take it?" Vance asked.

"And if I do, will you give me the blessing?" Houston added.

"So you guys want to kill Mohammed al-Zumar?"

"It's not like we want to," Houston said. "We have to do it for everyone back home."

"Yeah," Vance agreed. "For all those kids who lost their parents, you know?"

"Listen up, Marines. The media has blown this way out of proportion. This man is a terrorist. He has taken a United States Marine prisoner. We're going to get her back. That's what this is about. If you start thinking about all the folks back home and about getting revenge, you'll cloud up."

"That's right, Sergeant," Vance said. "But I'll tell you what, it ain't easy."

"No, it's not. But that's why we're all members of this very exclusive gun club. We are always hard. We are always professional."

Vance glanced over at Houston, who shrugged, then he made a pistol with his fingers and pretended to take the shot.

AL-ZUMAR PARTY
CHITRAL BAZAAR
NORTHWEST FRONTIER PROVINCE
PAKISTAN
2212 HOURS LOCAL TIME

After just thirty seconds of trying, Youssef freed the Jeep, and al-Zumar decided he would not kill the man just yet. They roared off, reached the fort of Chitral built centuries ago, and as Youssef took them past the eroding stone walls, an eerie sensation consumed al-Zumar, sent a chill up his neck, back down his spine. Was it the cold again? Were the spirits of invaders still lingering behind those ancient stone walls and parapets? Were they trying to tell him something? A warning? He tossed a look over his shoulder. A dark plain stretched off to several small buildings he knew from his last visit were part of Chitral's college. He searched the road behind for dirt or snowy mist created by a vehicle's tires.

"Do not worry, Mohammed," Shaykh said. "I never thought I would make it this far, but I have. And we are almost there. Look ahead. There is the Shahi Mosque."

Squinting through the dirty windshield, al-Zumar spotted the mosque's great minarets towering up into the night sky. And then, there it was, the Soviet-made Hind, a magnificent war machine zeroing in on the field between the fort and the mosque. With a hunched back, camouflage markings, and inclined wings supporting heavy guns and rockets, the helicopter inspired fear in even those Americans who piloted the Apache and the Cobra. Al-Zumar had watched video tapes of the helicopter in action against the Afghans, knew very well its lethal potential, but its presence did nothing to allay his fear. Or the cold.

The transfer had to go quickly. Youssef would drive the Jeep as close as he dared to the helicopter, once it was on the ground. Al-Zumar's bodyguards would disperse and cover him as he, the American lieutenant, and Shaykh climbed aboard first. Only then would he let the rest of them board. He communicated that in terse, emotionless sentences to his people, but only Youssef answered, "Yes, my Sheikh." Al-Zumar shouted again at the other bodyguards, and they finally replied. Morale among them was low, no doubt. They had seen too many of their brothers martyred in the last few days. Still, al-Zumar had no reason to believe that their loyalty would wane.

After a quick turn to the right, Youssef flashed the Jeep's headlights twice, signaling the chopper pilot that they had reached the field. Al-Zumar leaned past the canopy, saw the Hind bank right and roar around for its final approach.

TEAM DOGMA (PLUS TWO)
CHITRAL BAZAAR
NORTHWEST FRONTIER PROVINCE
PAKISTAN
2214 HOURS LOCAL TIME

"That's them," Rainey said, having witnessed the twin flashes of light about a quarter kilometer ahead and now using his Nightstars to confirm the target.

"We get a little closer, let me take out a tire," Vance said. "Slow them down."

"And tip them off," Rainey amended.

"If that's the only signal they're giving that bird, then we might be in luck," said McAllister. "There may be some serious distance between them and the chopper."

Rainey lifted his chin at McAllister, then eyed the car's gauges. "Stupid question. We got enough gas?"

"First thing I checked. What we could use is more ammo. I have about a clip and a half left—including my lucky mag, three grenades, and three forties for my two-oh-three. Still got all seven for my pistol."

"How 'bout you, Doc?" Rainey asked.

"I've already dipped pretty far into my second mag," the corpsman answered. "We can give them some hell, but not for long."

"Houston?"

"I'm up two mags. Six for my pistol."

"I hope you make them count, Lance Corporal."

Houston raised his face mask, winked. "You don't have to hope."

"Sergeant, I have almost a full mag, but that's it," Vance said.

"Sounds like me," Rainey said with a sigh. "And I'm assuming those guys don't have full clips back there. It might come down to pistols and knives."

"I wish it was only a fistfight," McAllister said, jerking the wheel as they hit a rut in the icy road. "That's fighting. That's war."

"Do me a favor?" Rainey asked McAllister. "Hang onto your grenades for as long as you can. A bay door opens, you know what to do."

McAllister nodded. "And so do you."

"Hey, I'm not sure, but I think they've—"

Houston never finished his sentence. McAllister had

hit a sheet of ice and now drove them straight into a
fence pole that snapped under the sedan, the top piece
sliding across the hood to shatter the windshield. He
jammed on the brakes, began turning the sedan, even
as they slid down a shallow embankment, struck
something, a big rock maybe, that stopped them dead
in the snow.

Amid the swearing from his men, Rainey hollered,
"Sound off!"

They did and were decidedly alive.

After pulling himself from the car, Rainey crossed to
the back, saw Arden rubbing his shoulder, Graham rubbing his knees. "Good to go?"

"Good to go," Graham said.

Arden echoed in an unconvincing tone, Rainey
shifted forward, waving the whole team on as he broke
into a jog.

All right, so they had ditched the car a little too
soon. He had envisioned driving right up behind the
Jeep and using it and the car for cover. Well, you
couldn't have it all.

With navigation lights switched off, the big chopper
hovered at about five hundred meters from the ground
and began its shadowy descent. Damn, it was one hell
of a gunship, with a barrel machinegun and twin barrel
cannons. Still, the chopper was old, and being Soviet-
made there was no guarantee that its weapons were
fully operational. If they did function, they were only as
good as the pilots operating them. So what breed of flyboy would allow himself to be bought by al-Zumar? No
Top Gun or rocket scientist to be sure.

And suddenly Rainey felt a tad less intimidated by the chopper. Of course, his thoughts were mere speculation, and Murphy might very well be an Arab.

Keeping behind the snow banks running parallel to the road, he led the team toward the field, and they reached the perimeter just as the chopper settled down on its heavy gear.

Completely out of breath, Rainey called for a halt, his tactician's mind screaming through the input from his eyes and ears. To their left lay a mosque, their right an old fort. Out past the field, the river flowed like black oil. How far to the chopper? Three hundred meters? Where was the Jeep? He swung his head, spotted it coming around a corner, breaking off from a winding road beside the fort.

Okay. He sent Vance and Houston across the road. "And Dogma Four, permission granted to take out their tires on my mark, over."

"On your mark, out."

Now where to put Doc? Three small tents had been pitched near the perimeter of the mosque's grounds. Rainey wasn't sure what purpose they served, but they would conceal Doc for the moment. He sent the corpsman pounding off.

"What about us?" Graham asked.

"You're not pulling rank on me, Captain, are you?"

"Not now. But I will later—when it comes time to buy the beer."

Rainey grinned. "Okay. You guys crawl straight up. The second that bay door opens, you suppress the guys inside until your clips are out, then fall back here."

The two men nodded, started off, but Rainey grabbed the bodyguard's arm. "Do me a favor, buddy. You're a civilian. You should be unarmed and holding back here. Don't get yourself killed."

"I won't. Not without your permission, anyway. Good luck."

McAllister cleared his throat. "I know what you're thinking, Rainey. I cover while you go in. Why don't you let me do this for a change?"

But Rainey wasn't listening to his assistant. He stared keenly through his Nightstars, switching between the helicopter and the Jeep. Then he panned over to Arden and Graham, saw they were within range. He swung the Nightstars around to the tents, knew Doc was lying behind them, leaning into his Para SAW, ready to deliver some bad medicine to bad men.

Rainey took in a long breath, pushed the boom mike close to his lips, watched the Jeep begin to slow.

"Dogma One to Four, ready to execute, over."

"Standing by," Vance said.

Propped up on his elbows atop a meter-tall snowdrift, Vance sighted the Jeep's left rear tire through his scope. In most cases he could compensate for the wind's direction and velocity, but the powerful rotor wash created by the chopper was another story. His crosshairs floated over the wheel, but the image fluctuated greatly as micro fragments of ice whipped across, fragments carried by an artificial gale that would affect his round.

"All right, Four, execute!" Rainey ordered.

Vance fired—

But he realized even as he shifted aim for the next wheel that he had missed. "Son of a bitch!" *No, you won't miss this time,* he ordered himself. Target sighted, locked. Breathe easy. And fire!

John Arden squinted at the Jeep, saw that at least one of its tires had been blown out. As that fact registered, two men leaped out of the vehicle, hit the deck, and the muzzle flashes shone like fireflies as the bad guys sought a target.

But Arden suspected that Houston and Vance were already on the move. Hopefully, they weren't heading toward himself and Graham. The last thing they needed was incoming as they waited for one of the chopper's doors to open.

Tingling with the urge to fire, Arden lay there with Graham, concentrating on his aim. He had no scope. It was damned hard to see with all that rotor wash. But his fire was meant to buy time and not meant to be surgically accurate. As his pulse raced, the moment hit him full on. He was serving his country, really serving his country. Again. He was back in the Marines! And he felt like he had never left! *Semper Fi!*

Captain Tom Graham wished he had been more naïve when it came to military aircraft, particularly when it came to Russian gunships like the Mi-24 Hind. He blamed his education on his brother Brad, who studied foreign helicopters the way fundamentalist Christians study the Holy Bible. And while Graham couldn't remember the exact statistics regarding the Hind's defenses and armament, he knew his brother could rattle them off, tell you how small-arms fire could never penetrate the twin cockpits' titanium shells, tell you about the ammo type, the rate of fire, and even the most probable armaments on various versions of the Hind like the D, E, and F. At the moment, though, all Graham tried to remember was the elevation/traverse of the Hind's barrel machine gun. Could the pilot swing that weapon around on them and begin rattling off over four thousand rounds per minute? Did they lie within the weapon's field of fire? No doubt he and Arden were within range.

"Hey, man, when we open fire, I'm going to keep one eye on that barrel machine gun," he told the bodyguard. "It starts moving, and we're out of here, empty or not."

"I hear you," Arden said. "Now if those bastards would just open the damn door."

"Hold tight. I think they're about to."

Doc did not like his position behind the tents, not because they failed to provide suitable cover but because the tents were being used to store big sacks of grain or animal feed or something that smelled like dung mixed in sour milk. He nearly gagged as he watched one of the chopper's bay doors yawn open.

"Dogma Two, this is Dogma One," Rainey said. "Open fire!"

Turning up a white-knuckled grip on the SAW, Doc sighted the bay door and squeezed the trigger a second before Arden and Graham, somewhere in the field across from him, began their own suppression, triplets of fire rattling up from the snow.

Someone inside the chopper managed to pull the door closed, but Doc saw one, two, three men jump down from the back side of the aircraft, utilizing a bay door on that side and the rest of the helicopter for cover. The three guys, all wearing dark face masks like the team, hit the snow, and at least two of them sent three-shot bursts razoring Doc's way and punching holes in the tents to his right. Doc answered with the booming of his big SAW, a booming so near and so loud that he did not hear the whining of the chopper's machine gun as it swiveled toward him. He caught a flash before a highway of incoming worked its way up an embankment and directly toward him. He released the Para SAW and rolled—

A half-second before the heavy fire struck his weapon with metallic clangs then moved on a moment before dying. Doc knew that pilot was lining up for another go at him, but now all he could do was yank out his MEU pistol and scramble to examine his weapon. "Dogma One, this is Dogma two, over!"

"Go ahead, Two," Rainey said.

"Be advised the SAW is down."

The weapon was now a hunk of smoking junk, the sight, feed cover, and scope smashed beyond belief, the trigger a mangled mess.

"All right, fall back to our first position, over."

"Falling back." Doc was about to get up on his hands and knees, then bolt off, but the next incredible wave of machine-gun fire spewed across the snow and came within a half meter of his arm as he rolled from its path. "Jesus Christ, One, I'm taking heavy fire from that barrel gun! I repeat! Heavy fire!"

Collecting a flurry of information, assessing it, then calculating the next move—all within seconds—was what the Corps expected of its Force Recon team leaders. Rainey's ability to do that was why they paid him a lot of respect, if not the big bucks.

But as the situation unfolded, Rainey began to second-guess himself—the very last thing you wanted to do during combat. Applying suppression fire to the chopper's bay door nearest them had only driven the bad guys to the back of the chopper. Fresh men, at least three, were now on the ground, and there could be another half dozen waiting inside. Still, that ploy would make it harder for al-Zumar and his hostage to get to the chopper. They'd have to cross around the back, wasting precious seconds during which Rainey or one of his men could get off the fatal shot.

Zooming in with his Nightstars, Rainey thought he spotted al-Zumar and Ingram, still seated in the Jeep's back seat but leaning far to the passenger's side. Definitely two people, though the wash robbed a distinct picture.

In the meantime, McAllister lay beside Rainey, exchanging fire with the guys near the Jeep. He capped one, wounded a second, but one more remained, the bad guy's weapon like a lone thundercloud erupting against the chopper's turbines.

And then, the scene fell even more silent as the chopper's big machine gun died and the guys on the ground held their fire.

"What're they doing now?" McAllister asked, dumbfounded.

Rainey raised his Nightstars. No movement near the chopper. He shifted to the Jeep, saw it rolling slowly forward, limping along on three good tires.

"All right, old man, this is it," Rainey said. "And you will cover for me."

"Hell, with Doc's SAW down, and Arden and Graham out of ammo, you won't get halfway to that Jeep."

Rainey activated his tactical radio. "Dogma Four, this is One. I need you and Three to take out those guys below the chopper. I need that now, over."

"We're on it, Sarge. Roger, out."

"Okay, Terry, this is where I ask if you want to live forever, but we both know you don't."

McAllister grinned weakly. "I'm scared shitless of dying."

"You? Funeral man? I don't believe it."

"Believe it. But I'm more scared of letting you down. I won't." McAllister banged a fist on Rainey's shoulder.

And with that, they broke from cover and charged across the field.

21

I'm going to take a round, Rainey thought, the premonition so strong that it sent chills needling up his spine.

Houston and Vance fired at the men beneath the chopper, and, as though answering their fire, the last bad guy near the Jeep took a wild shot at Rainey.

"Run wider!" Rainey shouted to McAllister, as from the corner of his eye he saw the chopper's barrel machine gun pivot toward them. "Get out of its path!"

Excruciating pain suddenly gripped Rainey's left bicep, and the rest of his arm felt warm and wet. Son of a bitch, that wild shot had been anything but. His arm began to throb, but he kept on, his mind screaming against the pain.

Like some mechanized dragon spewing fire, the chopper's canopy lit up as the barrel gun rotated and sent a wave of death in McAllister's wake. They were, Rainey estimated, just a few degrees beyond the gun's firing angle—

But still within range of the men below the chopper. A round pummeled the snow and earth just a meter ahead of Rainey, while another struck less than a meter to his left. *Ignore the fire. You're Robert Duvall in* Apocalypse Now, *and nothing can touch you.*

Did the assurance work? How could it? He'd already been shot! "Dogma Three? Dogma Four? Terminate those targets! Now!" Rainey's body had become a rigid sack of muscles and adrenaline, one hand like a vice around his carbine, the other tingling but still functional.

Fifty meters to the Jeep now, the vehicle still rolling slowly toward the chopper.

Forty meters. A shot rang out, the flash originating near the Jeep's right quarter panel.

Thirty-five meters. There was the guy, right there, having miscalculated the Jeep's roll as he scrambled to get back behind it. Rainey barely took aim, triggered a burst, and all three rounds hit their mark.

Thirty meters. Whomever was at the Jeep's wheel panicked and stepped on the gas. The Jeep spun out, and the remaining back tire lost traction.

"All right, break!" Rainey ordered McAllister, and his assistant jogged off, heading straight for the chopper.

Twenty meters. Close enough to see the young bastard behind the wheel. Three rounds punched him into a bloody pulp.

But more gunfire answered from just above the Jeep's hood, and as Rainey flung himself onto his belly, he caught a glimpse of a man with a white beard, the old guy who had kept close to al-Zumar during the trek across the mountains. Only Mohammed al-Zumar and Ingram were left in that Jeep.

Having fallen back to a shallow depression, Houston had the last guy locked in his sights, and he was determined to show Vance that he could neutralize the target as efficiently as the fisherman had neutralized the other two guys. But before Houston could get off his round, the bad guy got off his:

Bang!

Vance gasped.

Houston turned his head, saw Vance gripping his forearm, blood already seeping between his fingers. "Vance!"

The sharpshooter grimaced as another round burrowed into the snow between them. "Shoot the fucking guy."

With his breath gone, Houston returned to his rifle, sighted the bad guy, flinched as another round cut close to them, then . . . he blinked and pulled the trigger. The guy dropped. But had he been shot?

Fuck it. No time to think. "This is Dogma Three. Dogma Four has been hit. Corpsman up!"

The call from Houston sounded in Rainey's earpiece as he crawled on his hands and knees toward the Jeep, the pain in that left bicep almost unbearable now. He knew at any moment the Jeep's occupants—assumedly al-Zumar, Ingram, and the old man—would make their run for the chopper. Rainey thought of lobbing a grenade or sending one via his launcher to silence the old man, but Ingram was probably too close. Sure, he could consider her an acceptable loss, given the nature of his target, but she and Graham had plucked him out of Hell too many times to write her off. Time to return the favor. Forget the grenade.

Unfortunately, Rainey wasn't the only one considering grenades. A dark orb arced across the night sky, and before it hit the ground, Rainey was already on his feet, running straight for the Jeep.

Two more objects split the air, cylinders Rainey recognized as smoke grenades. Despite the rotor wash, that smoke could provide al-Zumar with enough cover to make his run—but that smoke would also conceal Rainey.

Ten meters to the Jeep.

Five.

There was the old man, whirling to bring his rifle on Rainey. Too late.

Rainey rushed up to him, firing as he did so, not realizing that al-Zumar and Ingram were already on the move. The old guy dropped, and Rainey turned his head—

To see al-Zumar and Ingram dematerialize into the smoke.

McAllister's grenade launcher would not do much damage to the heavily armored chopper, so he opted for an old-fashioned hand grenade, the metal ball feeling pretty good in his grip as he stormed into the wash. The idea was to skulk under the chopper and lob Mr. Hand Grenade into the open bay door on the other side. The path looked clear. The three guys below had been taken out by Houston and Vance.

Or so he had thought. One guy lying just a half-dozen meters ahead burst up on his elbows, shedding snow, his rifle coming to bear.

That's when the whole scene turned slo-mo surreal, and McAllister waited for his whole life to fast forward from womb to tomb, images flashing repeatedly.

But only the bad guy's muzzle sparked, even as McAllister pulled the pin on his grenade and let it fly.

The grenade left McAllister's hand—

Just as three rounds tore into his right leg, the first striking his knee, the second his calf, the third his thigh. The leg gave out, and a pain so intense that he couldn't breathe shook through him. His fatigues had been ripped with holes, and bright red blood squirted from them.

Then his grenade exploded, kicking him backward and heaving a fountain of dirt, ice, and flesh.

"I'm not going to lose my arm, am I?" Vance asked nervously as Doc cut away the fisherman's sleeve.

"You're not worried about shooting, are you?" Doc said. "You're worried about fishing."

"You know it."

"Well, I'm not making any promises. Looks like a clean exit. Could've been worse."

Houston, who had been listening to the conversation while staring through his rifle's scope, saw McAllister get shot by the bad guy that Houston was supposed to neutralize. Now if any more bad guys came out of the chopper, old McAllister would just be lying there, bleeding, alone.

"McAllister's down. I'm going after him," he told Vance and Doc.

If they voiced any complaint or warning, Houston never heard them. With his legs working like pistons, he sprinted across the field, expecting fire but hearing none. He wasn't sure if Rainey or the bad guys had blown all that smoke, but he didn't give a shit. He yanked a grenade from his vest, pulled the pin, threw it at the chopper's machine gun, didn't wait or watch for the explosion. He just kept on.

The machine gun rattled, the stream of fire sweeping across the field and toward him. His grenade went off with a brilliant flash just as he reached McAllister and gaped at the man's leg, now a piece of bloody meat wrapped in tattered utilities.

"Don't worry, Sergeant. I'll get you back to Doc, and he'll patch you up good."

"Fuck me, kid. Here . . ." McAllister, his eyes creased in pain, shoved a grenade into Houston's hand. "Get under this bird. Get that bay door open, and let 'em eat this."

Houston took the grenade, though he had two more of his own. He tried to make a decision, his senses overloaded by the thundering turbines, the wash, the look in McAllister's eyes, the rattling machine gun, and the pungent scent of smoke. People were bleeding. People were dying.

And in the next second, all he heard was his breathing and the thumping of his heart.

"Houston, go!" McAllister yelled.

He tore off like an Olympic runner, didn't feel his heavy ruck anymore. Didn't feel the rifle or even the grenade in his hand. He felt only his legs working, the snow crunching under his boots, the desire to duck under the chopper—

And as he did, two figures emerged from the smoke. Houston neared them, looked into the man's eyes, cold eyes, a snake's eyes. And that face. That beard. There he was:

Mohammed al-Zumar.

The world's most wanted man had one arm wrapped around Lieutenant Ingram's neck, one hand holding a knife to her heart.

Ingram tried to say something, couldn't.

Houston dropped the grenade, was about to lift his rifle, when al-Zumar lunged at him, knocked him onto his back, the carbine falling away.

Houston only felt al-Zumar's blade. He had not seen it coming.

With his eyes tearing, Rainey forged his way through the smoke, coming up near the chopper's tail, where for a moment the air cleared. And it all hit him at once:

The bay door was open, and two armed terrorists were about to leap down.

Houston was lying on the ground, clutching his abdomen, his rifle now in the hands of Lieutenant Ingram, who'd been abandoned by al-Zumar.

And the devil himself was being helped into the chopper by a third terrorist proffering his hand.

The first shot came from one of the bad guys still in the bay, and Ingram staggered backward, dropping the rifle, one hand going for her right shoulder.

The next two shots came from Rainey, who capped one bad guy, settled for a neck shot on the second, then he followed with a chest shot to the man reaching for al-Zumar.

Even as that guy screamed and Rainey started running toward the bay, he pumped off a grenade, and *bloop!* the round flew into the open bay. The half-muffled explosion sent al-Zumar running forward, away from the chopper as two men, flames rising from both of their shoulders, staggered toward the opening.

While the grenade had wreaked havoc in the bay, the pilot and copilot lay well forward and had been shielded from the blast. Still, they weren't taking any more chances. Turbines spun up and wailed as the big gunship began to lift off.

Al-Zumar kept running, looked back, saw the fleeing bird, waved, tried to get the pilots' attention as—

Rainey lifted his carbine, squinted into the scope, lined up al-Zumar's head in his crosshairs.

It would all end in a heartbeat. Rainey was God. And he would pass sentence on the world's most wanted and, arguably, most evil man.

"Take him, Sergeant," Houston gasped. "Take him!"

That's right, take him. Be the guy who kills this fucker. Be the guy!

But Rainey didn't subscribe to the media frenzy. He

couldn't hack off al-Zumar's head and put it on a pike to fuel public hatred and provide "closure" for the families. There was no such thing as closure, and interrogating al-Zumar might prove valuable, since there would always be another al-Zumar.

Sergeant Mac Rainey made a tactical decision: be a professional and take the motherfucker alive.

He lowered his rifle, began running after al-Zumar as the big chopper's powerful wash nearly knocked him to his knees. He took his MEU pistol in hand, kept running, running with everything he had, his arm almost completely numb, his sleeve soaked.

The dizziness crept over him, and his legs wobbled like hacksaw blades trying to cut through stainless steel. He took aim at al-Zumar, thought maybe he could shoot the bastard in the leg, thought nothing more as he hit the ground, the snow turning black and wrapping him in darkness.

Seeing that al-Zumar, armed only with a knife, was running alone across the field and that Sergeant Rainey had just fallen, John Arden figured it was time to make his move. He shouted for Graham to join him, but the captain was already bolting down the field for Ingram.

So maybe Arden would get his chance to kill al-Zumar after all. But the asshole had a knife, and all Arden had was a wounded shoulder and a terrible case of dehydration.

But he ran anyway. He needed to do something, be a part of it in some way, support these guys, men who would forever be his brothers.

* * *

Doc was a busy man. Vance had been shot in the arm. McAllister was down. Houston was down. Now Rainey was down. Time for triage. Assess injuries. Treat the most critical man first.

With a burst of adrenaline, Doc left Vance behind and charged down the field. He stumbled across a rock, woke new pain in his ankle. He cursed, began limping, wouldn't stop for anything.

Meanwhile, the chopper was clearing the field, and a lone figure sprinted away, pursued by another figure who might be John Arden.

"I can shoot lefty, Doc," Vance said over the radio. "That Arden guy has no weapon. Let me do it. It's your decision."

"That other guy is al-Zumar?"

"Yeah! Yeah! Come on, give me the order."

Doc reached Houston. One look at all the blood covering the lance corporal's chest was all the argument Doc needed. "Okay, Vance. Execute. Now!"

Vance lined up for the shot. He tracked al-Zumar's movements perfectly, the crosshairs floating directly over the dark figure.

But some shit would happen, right? The gun would jam. The wind would change direction. Arden would get in the way. And al-Zumar would throw the hook or break the line or shake himself free and vanish into the depths of the night. Vance would go down in history as the man who had had the shot—

And had missed.

Jesus, the pressure was just too much to bear. He squinted, blinked, lost al-Zumar for a second, tried to line up once more for the shot.

Rick Navarro glanced up as the giant Russian chopper thundered off toward the mountains. He had just reached the field, decided to turn on the camera again, shoot what he could and provide more of his own voice-over narration:

"I'm not sure, ladies and gentlemen, but Mohammed al-Zumar could be aboard that helicopter. The shooting has stopped, though, and I see at least two people running. I'm going down into the field to see if I can locate any of the Marines."

As John Arden caught up with Mohammed al-Zumar and poured everything he had into a lunge for the man, a shot rang out.

Had one of the Marines capped the bad guy? Arden couldn't be sure as his shoulders made contact with the back of al-Zumar's legs, and the man went down.

Mohammed al-Zumar had heard the shot, had felt John Arden tackle him, but other than that, he felt no pain. He had not been shot, and as he rolled, trying to get away from Arden, he caught a quick glimpse of Graham, AK in hand, rushing toward them, along with one of the American Marines, who carried a sniper's rifle and advanced from the east.

He brought the knife down, across Arden's arm, sliced open the man's sleeve, then booted Arden in the chest and crawled free. Al-Zumar sprang to his feet, jogged a few more steps, saw both Graham and that other American drawing closer. He hesitated, glanced ahead, toward the Shahi Mosque.

"There's nowhere to go," Arden shouted, clutching his arm.

Graham and the other American had clean shots, but they did not fire. They had decided to take al-Zumar alive.

That could not happen. He had sworn to himself and his men that he would resist capture to the very end. He had even obtained a *fatwa* authorizing his suicide in case of capture. Yes, suicide is expressly forbidden in Islam, but the *jihad* could not be compromised.

"Hold your position," Graham cried.

"Another step and we will fire," shouted the other American.

Al-Zumar faced them, his arms in the air, one hand gripping the knife as tightly as he could.

The smoke was clearing, and the night sky shone brilliantly with stars. The Americans shouted something to him again, but he simply took in a long, cold breath, and in that second, he wept for Shaykh, for Fathi, for all the men who had given their lives for the cause. He even wept for himself, for he was about to join them, to join his father on that boat sailing toward paradise.

And suddenly, as the cold blade penetrated his heart, Mohammed al-Zumar felt warm . . . very, very warm . . .

"Aw, shit," Vance said, leaning over al-Zumar, whose legs still flinched.

"He thought we'd take him prisoner," Graham said. "Maybe Rainey would have, but not me. I would've killed him myself."

"Me, too," Vance said, hanging his head low.

"Take a number and stand in line," Arden groaned, blood seeping between his fingers.

Vance sat down in the snow, ripped off his face mask, rubbed his sore eyes. Thank God it was over.

"Vance? Graham?" Doc called. "I could use a hand!"

No, it wasn't over, and Vance's pulse bounded once more. His teammates were down and bleeding. He had to help Doc stabilize them until their extraction helo arrived.

As he and Graham were about to leave al-Zumar, a man shooting video with a big camera, a man Vance quickly recognized as Rick Navarro, came rushing toward al-Zumar's body.

"Hey, Vance?" John Arden called. "You got a lighter?"

Vance nodded and reached into one of his vest's pockets. "Smoke 'em if you got 'em, huh?"

"No, just toss me that lighter. Come on."

John Arden caught the lighter and turned, just as Navarro the Asshole, opportunist to the end, arrived on scene, the camera balanced on his shoulder.

"And here is!" Navarro cried. "Mohammed al-Zumar, the world's most wanted man. Mohammed al-Zumar, mass murderer and perhaps the most evil human being who has ever lived. Ladies and gentlemen, there was no camera around when Hitler died, no videotape of Genghis Khan's demise. But I'm here, Rick Navarro of

Wolf News, to bring you a story of great hubris, fanaticism, and murder; a story that spans the globe; a story whose epilogue is only now being written; a story that has changed our world forever."

"And I'm here, John Arden, to shut your hole!" Arden used his good hand to rip the camera off Navarro's shoulder. As Navarro screamed, Arden jogged a few steps back, dropped to his knees, and tugged open the tape compartment. He extracted the tape and smashed it across his knee, cracking it open. With the tape exposed, he worked the lighter.

"You idiot," Navarro said. "That camera was designed by one of our tech guys. You think you're destroying the only copy? That's just a backup system. Everything's been recorded digitally."

"I know," Arden said, dropping the blazing tape to the ground. He reached into his pocket to produce the camera's memory chip, which he promptly snapped in half. "I had Shaqib take this out a while ago. And now, Navarro, you got what you deserve: nothing."

22

CAMP LIBERTY BELL
FIFTH FORCE RECONNAISSANCE COMPANY
FIELD HOSPITAL
NORTHWEST FRONTIER PROVINCE
PAKISTAN
0700 HOURS LOCAL TIME

Despite having not worn his lucky bush cover (he had tucked it into his ruck), Lance Cpl. Bradley Houston still managed to survive the stabbing he had received from the world's most wanted man. The blade had not penetrated any vital organs, and Doc had managed to replace Houston's fluids to raise his blood pressure until Houston could receive blood. He lay in his bed, with Rainey in the bed to his right, McAllister in the one to his left. Both men had been shot but they, too, would recover, although McAllister might lose his leg. Doc was snoring his ass off in the gurney opposite Houston's, and Vance was sitting up and just staring off into space.

"You all right?" he asked the fisherman.

"Just thinking about the one that got away."

"What're you talking about?"

Vance shrugged. "Nothing."

"Hey, man. Don't you wish we'd get a chance to go on the air and tell our stories? It's the least Navarro could do for us helping to save his ass."

"Dream on. Everything's classified, right? But hell, if by some miracle we're allowed, you can do all the talking."

"Belay that order," Rainey said, his eyes still closed, his voice just north of a whisper. "Nobody's talking to nobody."

Houston smiled. "I think that's bad grammar, Sarge."

"Shut your pie hole. Last thing we need is you up there, telling them how you saved the world from terrorism."

"Not me. Us."

"Shit, we got one guy to off himself," McAllister chipped in. "Maybe his little warriors will be disorganized for a while, but some other idiot will come around and lead them, and more people are going to die. This ain't the information age. It's the age of terror."

"Now you're back to your old self," Rainey said. "Prophet of doom."

"Hey, guys," said John Arden as he came down the aisle between beds. "Now that you're up, I thought I'd come over and say thanks."

Rainey and McAllister nodded. Houston did likewise, though his curiosity got the best of him. "So how'd you ever wind up working for a total asshole like Navarro?"

Arden took a long breath and closed his eyes.

"Blame it on the money. And my temporary insanity. I never wanted leave the Corps, but my back had other plans."

Houston understood that well. He knew of many Marines who had been forced to retire because of injuries (McAllister's name would probably be added to that list)—and retiring usually hurt more than their bodies. Better to change the subject. "Ingram get out of surgery yet?"

"Just now. Graham's with her. She'll be all right. He's not doing too well, though. His brother's Cobra went down. They still haven't found him."

"Bad day for that family," Houston said.

"Yeah."

"How 'bout that little guy, the translator? They evaced us before I heard anything. He make it?"

Arden shook his head. "Fucking Navarro could've stayed with him, could've helped him keep the pressure on that wound. The little guy bled out." Arden's gaze went distant. "You know, he was the one who led us to the Afghans. He was hired by al-Zumar to find an American news crew. But he wasn't loyal to that bastard. He was just trying to make some money for his family. There's just nothing for these people here. Nothing. So they resort to anything. Now I don't blame him. But he's dead. And forgiveness means jack."

McAllister leaned over to Rainey. "Who you calling the prophet of doom?"

"Well, just wanted to say thanks again. And Semper Fi. You're the bravest. And the best."

"No, we're the few. The proud," Houston corrected.

Arden winked. "Wiseass."

Once the bodyguard had left, Houston threw his head back on the pillow, winced over the catheter poking his arm. The damned thing itched like crazy. He forced his thoughts away, found himself focusing on his father, wished he could tell the man what had happened. How would his father react? Would he be impressed? Would he want to brag?

Or would he dismiss the entire event as nothing more than a lucky break?

Houston smiled to himself. He had made his own life and had proven to himself that he was worthy to be on a Force Recon Team. He didn't need Dad's approval, didn't need Dad's respect. Yes, he ached because he didn't have those things, but the approval and respect of his teammates suddenly meant a whole lot more. And, of course, they needed to trust him. So only one thing remained:

"Sergeant?"

"Lance Corporal, I'm too tired to talk."

"About that farmer that got hold of my weapon."

"The farmer who sneaked up on you?"

"Yeah, well at the time I wasn't exactly taking pictures. I was taking something else."

After leaving the field hospital, John Arden found Navarro wolfing down eggs and toast in the mess tent. Mr. Celebrity was caught up in a heated discussion with correspondent Tamira Gibbs over what would've happened to al-Zumar had he been captured alive.

"Good, you're here, Mr. Arden. Have a seat and settle an argument for us."

"Actually, I plan on starting one," Arden said, coming around the table and seizing Navarro by the collar. "You're fucking scum, man. And I've decided that I'm okay with the charges."

"What charges?" Navarro asked, trying to pull Arden's hand away.

"The assault charges you're going to file against me."

"For what?"

Arden cocked his brow. "This . . ." He released Navarro and used his good arm, his good fist.

And Mr. Rick Navarro would be reporting from Pakistan with an eye as swollen as his ego.

Three days after the mission, Cpl. Jimmy Vance received an email from the now notorious Cindy:

Jimmy, I've been thinking about what I did to you, and though it's really hard and I can't say I'm happy spending all these nights without you, maybe I'm just being selfish. I've been thinking that maybe we can work things out.

The email went on with more blabbering about her girlfriend's baby and something about her maybe getting a new car and when was he coming home? She couldn't wait to see him again. They needed to talk.

Corporal Jimmy Vance X-ed out of his email program. Cindy's message would go unanswered. He would let this one get away. It was time to move on to more productive waters.

* * *

Sergeant Terry McAllister had told the others that he "might" lose his leg, but he knew that in the days to come, the leg would come off. The doctors had confirmed that. He would receive his medical discharge, attend his paddle party, and fade away like any other good soldier. He had given them a lot of good years, and as he lay there in that field hospital bed, an acceptance of his fate began to take hold. He was going out with a bang, all right. Other operators would donate both legs for a chance to do what he had done. McAllister had no right to piss and moan. He had been fortunate enough to serve with incredible people who had been charged with some incredible missions. He would accept his discharge like a man.

But he knew that when the moment came to say goodbye to his fellow Recon Marines—the men he had lived with, the men he had nearly died with—taking it dry-eyed wouldn't be easy. However, if he shed a single tear, Rainey would never let him live it down, not because they needed to prove how macho they were, but because if McAllister wet a cheek, old Rainey would be reaching for the tissues himself. And, of course, Rainey would blame it all on him.

"You're far away," Rainey said, sitting upright in bed and lowering his magazine.

McAllister grinned. "No, I'm a lot closer than you think."

As strange as it sounded, special amphibious recon corpsman HM2 Doc Leblanc felt guilty because he had not been more seriously injured during the mission. A hairline fracture to the ankle did not hold up to gunshot wounds and a stabbing. He knew he was being ridiculous, but he felt as though he should have pushed the envelope harder. The counterargument, of course, was that the team needed a frosty medic at all times, and his being there had made the difference, especially in Houston's case. Sure, all of them had been trained in the basic skills of how to deal with combat trauma, but Doc knew the field and street techniques you wouldn't find in the books or during the training sessions—and he had learned them through experience. Oh, he was just being insecure, reminding himself that he was and would always be a Navy corpsman, not a Marine. Still, Rainey had once told him that a hard heart is more important than the color of your uniform. And Doc, for the most part, felt confident that his heart was as hard as any operator's. He should not feel guilty. He should feel thankful. Blessed. His boys had not lost their father. His wife had not lost her husband. And maybe, despite McAllister's grim assessment, the world was now a safer place. Doc promised himself that when he had a chance, he would go back to Martinique, sit down with his grandfather, shout, "Cric, crac!" and then, as they sipped tea and ate breadfruit, he would begin a highly classified tale, sharing it with wide eyes and in whispers.

For Sgt. Mac Rainey, the week following his return from Chitral passed as though it were a typical R&R, days blurring into each other and losing clarity until someone reminded you that it was time to saddle up.

He learned during the debriefing that he was being officially reprimanded for the team's failure to communicate regularly with Beacon Light. The reprimand was
your basic military slap on the wrist, and Lieutenant
Colonel St. Andrew himself had recommend the action.
The man was, Rainey suspected, feeling pretty good.
After all, one of his Force Recon Team's had brought
down the world's most wanted man. St. Andrew's statements to the press were nothing short of jovial, though
he could only say that "members of Fifth Force Recon,
third platoon" were responsible for hunting down al-
Zumar, and he was proud to add that every operator involved was alive and, uh, almost well.

By the third day, Rainey, his arm in a sling, his bicep
bandaged, had returned to his billet and had found the
engagement ring in his footlocker. He would keep it on
his person and wait for the right moment—

Which, oh, God, was upon him as he and Kady stood
on the slope overlooking Camp Liberty Bell.

"Your face is pinking up," Kady said after a long moment of silence.

"It's probably just the cold."

"I don't know. It seems pretty mild today. In fact, I
think it's a really good day."

He reached into his pocket. "Me, too."